Gideon's Wall

Gideon's Wall

GREG KURZAWA

A RIPTIDE PRESS Book

Published by
RIPTIDE PRESS
www.riptidebooks.com

For more information, contact Riptide Press.

ISBN 0-9723456-0-4
LCCN 2003091377

Printed in the United States of America

Cover art by Charles Keegan
Cover design by Jule Sutton

For Michael C. Kurzawa
1972 - 1998

Gideon's Wall

Book One
The Archaist

"From that place which borders life and death there will come a demon bearing seeds of corruption. And the demon will sow its seed, undoing all things which have been done. The river and the mountain will become as sand, and the desert will drink blood. In the dread hour of bloom there will be no living thing which does not weep."

—from *The Mouth of the Prophet*

One

One hundred and thirty eight years ago I was appointed as an archaist of the Loraean Isles. In the century and a half since my
induction, the greater portion of my years have been spent as a
sojourner in foreign lands. I have explored the farthest regions of
Entebay, where the warring clans have so long cultivated their an-
cestral hatred for one another that few bother to even speculate on
its origins. I have walked among the deepest chambers of the
Memnon tombs in Karnak, where it is said the archpriest Akhen-
aten was eternally laid to rest after the wind god Sekhmet-Ra replaced his heart with red clay from the River Anubis. In the jungles
of Mbelaka I have watched the sun rise over the Roaring Falls, beyond which it is rumored the last Ndoki temple lies guarded by the

horned demon Madzou, who devours the souls of irreverent trespassers. I have seen a host of wonders: hidden places of forgotten times, most of them so heavy with age they seem relics of another world.

The Guild has been flinging archaists across the continents for the past seven centuries. There are many of us abroad, and some have gone farther than I. The object of our tireless searching is no secret. We toil in order to sweep back the curtain of the unknown, to lay bare mysteries, to discover and to learn, to get wisdom and understanding. But most of all, we seek to find our place in history. To find this place—and of more pressing importance, to understand it—we must also understand the world in which we live, and how it came to be as it is. We must know those who came before us, those who shaped it, and, if we are able, those who created it. If we do not find the answers in our lifetime, we must leave behind as much as we can for the seekers who come after us. Such has always been our aim.

Which brings me to the barren shore of Shallai.

Once a vast and noble empire, Shallai exists now only as a word on a map. Gone are her people. Ruined are her cities. And if her interior is but half as desolate as her coast, then it seems certain that all of Shallai has been swallowed up by a vast and lifeless desert. Such is the condition of things, and the great mystery of her demise has yet to be explained.

Empires do not die quickly. They are not like men, whose fragile lives can be snuffed out by one thrust of the sword. Be they conquered by outside forces, or made brittle and frail by corruption within, the decline of an empire comes like a slow weight from the heavens.

In Shallai we have found the exception.

When death came for her, it came quickly. Diplomatic communications ceased. Trade halted. Entire fleets of Loraean, Shadrakan and Vaagan merchant ships bound for ports along Shallai's coast returned to their homes without ever having docked. Their captains and their crews swore that the cities of Shallai were gone, the land blighted. Those that threw anchor in her harbors and ventured ashore in search of answers were met with an endless wasteland. Some of the braver crews claimed to have struck inland as far as a hundred leagues. No life was found.

Rumors abounded, fear took root, and all of Shallai was proclaimed cursed. For the past decade her ruins have lain buried beneath a wasteland of heat and sand as though she never existed.

On the day our ship anchored in the bay where the port of Valtyr used to thrive, I walked up to the bluffs where the municipal palace once overlooked the sea. There I stood at the seam binding two disparate worlds. To my right spread the ocean, a deceptive, rolling wasteland of fathom stacked upon fathom. To my left, the carcass of Shallai.

Once bright with life and civilization, this parched land is now sundered and dying of thirst. It stretches flat and broad to the horizon, an arid plain of despair beneath a sun that sits its throne like an angry god. There is wind here; it is hot and constant. It scours the land, prying at the splits in the ground and moaning with the voices of the dead. And yet a mere ten years ago, if I were to stand in the places through which I have walked these past days, I would have found myself in a land of prosperity. I might have strode beneath Sarsicca's gates of silver and bronze, through throngs of people crowding the markets by the wharf. The streets would have been packed end to end with traders and merchants, all baying stridently to attract the interest of passersby. There would have been boats tied at the docks of the port at Valtyr, their masts a forest of headless trees where gulls wheeled and wove between them in thick, bumping clouds. There would have been ships anchored in the bay, great vessels of trade and of war. Farther west, in the city of Tassandra, I would have stood at the steps of the monumental temple of the Arrad Brotherhood.

Now, none of it exists.

Atop the bluffs are the ruins of the palace—if they can rightfully be called ruins. They are thin almost to the point of nonexistence. The remains of marble pillars jut from the ground like the bones of broken fingers, and they crumble at a touch. There is little else to be found, only the rare indication that a vast civilization once prospered in this place; here a crumbling wall, there a pile of bricks. While wandering a lonely slope of beach I discovered the broken arm of a bronze statue, half buried in the hard ground.

Shallai has scarcely left a footprint for us to follow.

I have crossed an ocean to come here, but my journey is yet in its infancy. I stand at the cusp of a formidable expedition, and I cannot say to what far reaches my journey will take me, or what might be waiting there for me. I can only say that I have come to discover a past that has remained hidden for too long.

I have come to exhume an empire.

Two

The maps in my possession are ancient and withered things. Stained yellow with time, they unroll only with much complaining, and what faded words can be found on them are barely legible. Most would discard them as frustratingly worthless, but to me, they are treasures. Illustrated upon the oldest, but most accurate of them, is Shallai as it existed nearly a century and a half ago. We set our course toward Jericho, the greatest city of the empire.

For many days we have dug ourselves deep into Shallai, our caravan dragging itself across the shattered wasteland like a dying beast. The wooden wheels of the wagons in the train bump over deep cracks, and the loaded carts creak and groan as they cut a straight and narrow path through the desert. Every day we discover paltry hints of the old empire. In the empty places where tremendous cities once stood we find scattered stones and leaning walls attached to nothing. Employing the stars as my guides, I trace our progress diligently.

Until the day we found Jericho I had begun to believe that Shallai had been rubbed from the face of the world, her existence wholly reduced to the pages of my decaying charts.

• • •

Is it too impulsive a presumption to conclude that Jericho defies explanation? As greatly as I am tormented by the thought of any piece of history being forever lost, I am forced to admit that in Jericho we may have stumbled across a mystery knotted so tightly that no amount of prying will ever unfasten it. It may be that any attempt on my part to fabricate theories would simply cloud the truth from an eye more discerning than mine. And so I will describe what I have seen without binding to it a concocted theory of my own imagining.

We first saw Jericho while still a great distance off, and at first sight we did not know what we were approaching, for the wall and the gates of the city were beyond the limits of our vision. What we could see was a crooked black spire rising from the horizon, a dark smudge against the cerulean sky. Only when we saw the city spread about its base did we realize the immensity of the black fortress, and only then did I understand that we looked upon the Keep of Shallai, and the city which we had found in the middle of this wasteland was none other than mighty Jericho.

In all of Shallai there had never been a city so great as Jericho, and it was the Keep which made it so. It was the axis around which the empire revolved. As though jealously guarding a terrible secret, its gates were kept barred and its single, thrusting tower secured. Lurking within the dark walls, the Fist of Shallai presided over his empire. He orchestrated the conquering of lands, the defense of his empire, and the crushing of his enemies. Seldom was his face seen, but his judgments were enacted swiftly by the indomitable seraphim, who went out from the black keep to enforce the edicts of their lord with unrelenting strength.

How Jericho has escaped the fate which laid waste to the rest of the empire I am unable to tell. The city, with the solitary keep at its core, stand in defiance of the wasteland which has closed in around them. The walls encircling the city are intact in most places, as are the buildings and the streets. The city lacks only citizens.

Although miraculously left undestroyed by the cataclysmic force which has effectively buried the rest of the empire, Jericho has nevertheless suffered a mild death at the hands of neglect. Without the lifeblood of its inhabitants, the unnatural sands of this desert have crowded in to claim the once thriving city, suffocating it one sluggish inch at a time. From below, probing roots drill through its foundations, peeling it apart with a terrible slowness while pale sand swells upwards through widening gaps. Brambles and thickets fill the streets, and vines flourish, creeping over all they can reach. They smother entire buildings as they climb walls, spill from windows, and wrap themselves lovingly around pillars and statues.

Our foray through the dead city filled us with trepidation. The silence was oppressive, and it was the general state of stagnating chaos which proved so unnerving. Buildings and houses had been violently gutted, their insides ripped out and left to spoil in heaps under the sun. There were places in which entire sections of the city had been burned to their foundations, where mounds of rubble and sagging structures were all that remained. It was as though a war had raged within the city walls. All of Jericho groaned beneath the heavy hand of deterioration, and all around us could be heard the weary creaking of imminent collapse.

Beyond the strewn wreckage there is prominent evidence of plague. I cannot name what disease ravaged Jericho, but it inflicted its own set of scars upon the city, and the vestiges of these wounds are disturbing in a deeper sense than the signs of chaos and warfare.

Lining every street are buildings and homes boarded from the outside, like the faces of men with their eyes and mouths sewn shut. Their doors had been splashed with garish red dye, now faded—a warning to all that plague had been bottled up within. I have seen such things before, and I know that such places were makeshift sepulchers in which entire families had been locked away to suffer and die alone with their disease. I was not able to pass a single of these homes without picturing the unfortunate souls within, trapped in a darkness broken only by the thinnest fingers of light squeezing between the slats.

We passed a sunken pit three hundred paces across and five deep. The ground within the pit was bursting with flora. I can only assume it was there that the bodies of Jericho's dead were unceremoniously dumped, a mass grave filled in by wind and rain over the years. The small jungle growing there thrived on soil enriched by the decomposition of the dead, and the pit seemed a staging point from which all of the city would eventually be conquered.

In other parts of the city, bodies had been laid side by side in the streets. The sheets and canvases once covering them had long ago been dragged away by the wind, leaving the vacant framework of their bodies exposed. Scraps of clothing shredded by the elements clung to what remained of bones bleached white by the sun. In some remote alleys the dead slumped in forlorn, broken piles.

We stayed in Jericho for five days, and even after seeing the destruction, after spending long hours amid the rubble, hunting the streets and the houses and temples for clues, I was unable to determine what force had torn this land apart, or why Jericho had been spared the same fate, only to perish from the inside out while the empire crumbled around it. My hope of finding answers was beginning to wane when my search turned finally to the Keep of Shallai. My exploring led inside the walls of that monstrous and frightening citadel, and hope was renewed.

• • •

If history can be likened to a tapestry, then it is painted on a faithless canvas. All of mankind walks beside this great white sheet as it unfurls, each intent on scribbling down his own small part. While still new, the inks and oils are fresh, and the colors vivid. But they begin to fade the very moment brush takes its leave of canvas. Colors once shockingly bright begin to fade. In time, the canvas goes colorless, its magnificent art all but vanished.

Occasionally there are scenes which do not disappear so promptly—perhaps because they were put down in a sturdier ink, but more often than not because they were drawn in blood. The blood stains while the other colors wash out, leaving incomplete images; not entirely comprehensible, but not entirely gone.

I have spent most of my life peering at the mostly blank tapestry left in mankind's wake. I know that I can never presume to re-repaint this work of art; too much is missing. But I am sometimes able to put a piece of color back into the canvas, or redraw the outline of events long past.

One such outline, gained after years of painstaking study, is the fact that the Keep of Shallai was not built by the empire.

There exist at least two other fortresses identical to the Keep of Shallai in every way: one deep in the lands of the Gaalb, and the other in the icelands to the north. Neither is claimed by any people, kingdom or empire. Within the last fifty years, at least three ar-chaists have been dispatched to these remote places, and all have returned bearing witness of the keeps. Both structures were crafted from the same black stone. No one has yet discovered from what ore it was derived, or where it can be mined.

Even without the mystery of its origins shrouding it, the Keep of Shallai has ever been a foreboding structure.

From the moment we entered its dim halls we felt watched, wading through a rich, undisturbed quiet in which we were tres-passers. The smell of ancient things was heavy, and every room had the feel of a place abandoned to time. Long hours we spent wandering the lonely corridors, discovering treasures of history: letters left unread, trinkets in drawers, and faded paintings hanging crooked from rusted nails. I felt almost guilty brushing through the dusty remains of lives in my search of some relic to shed light on our adopted mystery. I am a thief invading something that should never have been disturbed. I imagined the ghosts of this place crowding around me with the whispers and rustles the dead make to frighten the living. They peered over my shoulders, furious but unable to protest as I sifted through the leftovers of their lives.

After some exploration I found myself standing at one end of a massive corridor. Twenty men could have walked abreast with room to spare, and the ceiling arched dizzyingly high above my head. The tiles of the floor were black, fit so perfectly together that their seams were impossible to detect, and they reflected neither image, nor light. I felt suspended over a dark and bottomless pit, and despite the solidity of the stones beneath my feet, the prospect of dropping into the terrible void at any moment sparked in me an irrational fear. I walked with cautious steps, fighting vertigo.

At the far end of the hall were two iron doors made for giants. They were deeply engraved with images of armored warriors waging war with grotesque creatures of the wildest fantasy. They seemed to move in the light of my lantern, a trick of the fire. Beyond these mute guardians waited the greatest chamber in all the Keep.

My first impression was that I had stepped through a doorway into the inner cavern of a mountain. A slow wind, rich with the musty odor of age and silence was released, and it flowed over me. Supporting pillars shot up from floor to ceiling in five long rows leading to a raised dais. At the top of the platform, imposing in its stout command of the chamber, sat what could only be the throne of Shallai.

It seems a glorious thing to me, that an icon of such power should outlive those who fashioned it. Even after the empire upon which it was founded has turned to dust, this symbol of sovereignty still endures.

As I approached from between the ranks of pillars I held my lantern high, and shadows capered wildly among the columns. I stopped at the foot of the raised dais, in the very spot where those who had once ruled the empire could affix all their attention upon a single man. It was a place where few but the most privileged or severely condemned had ever stood.

How many men, I wondered, had been where I stood? How many had come in triumph and honor, to be exalted, and how many had been dragged to it in shackles and chains to receive judgment from an emperor?

I ascended the dais, an act which once would have earned me death. But with only ghosts to object, I freely climbed the steps until I stood directly before the ruling seat. Turning to face the wide expanse of the chamber, I saw it as only the lords of Shallai had ever seen it, and imagined the throngs of soldiers, seraphim, and noble patricians that had once filled the room. I surveyed the imaginary host with a critical and commanding eye, then sat upon the throne to record all that I had seen.

• • •

My nights have always been like little deaths, but sleeping in the bowels of the Keep, with its black and empty rooms stacked above us like the waters of a dark ocean, inflicted on me a listless slumber.

I dreamed that I stood in the midst of a desert, a great emptiness of cracked land and still heat. Briefly I was without identity, a life without name or face. I looked to my open hands, as though I would discover the story of a life written in the lines of my palms and the dirt beneath my nails. They were hands I recognized, although younger by decades. I touched my face, and my skin seemed unmolested by age. Wishing to see myself, I turned round, but there was nothing to offer a reflection.

The ground beneath my feet was split for want of water, and a colorless sprawl of gray clouds roiled above even though no wind breathed to fuel their restless churning. It was a lonely place, and I walked toward an empty horizon, fearing that I was doomed to walk an eternity, yet never leave the place in which I was standing.

As I walked, friends and strangers came to walk with me. Some of them I recognized, while others wore masks of faces I did not know, pretending to be someone I did. It seemed I walked forever until, far in the distance, I saw a figure garbed in a ragged cloak that had been torn and ripped by the hardships of his travels. The figure was walking away from me, and no matter how loudly I called, he did not turn to meet me. I ran after him, but never gained ground.

When finally I stopped, dragged to a halt by fatigue and frustration, I glanced about and found myself surrounded on all sides by graves. The weather-beaten stones jutted up unevenly from the parched ground. They were cracked with time, as though they had lain beneath this boiling sky forever.

Looking closer, I saw that the stones nearest me were unmarked, and I knew that not a single one of all the hundreds had been inscribed with a name. These were graves in which lay dead men whose names were not known. In every direction the grave markers filled the ground, scattered as though this were an ancient battlefield, and these unmarked stones had sprouted up in the very spots where the nameless warriors had been struck down. As I knelt to caress with my fingers the deep cracks of a stone, a dark shadow descended, and I looked up to find the figure in the ragged cloak standing over me. His face was covered by a deep hood, and his features were hidden in shadow.

"Will you tell them?"

Peering upwards, I squinted to see whose face was hidden in the darkness. "Tell who?" I asked.

"Tell them who died here."

"But the graves are unmarked. None have names."

"They have not been written yet."

"Then how will I know them?" I asked. "And who shall I tell?"

"Look to Gideon's Wall."

When he had spoken these words, the figure in the cloak backed away from me, his face still buried in shadow. Again, I looked around me, for no longer were we alone. Positioned faithfully beside each stone stood a man clad in battle attire. There must have been a thousand or more. In their hands they held broken weapons and cracked shields, and their faces were weary and despairing. On their breasts they bore the insignia of Shallai. All looked to me through the mournful eyes with which the dead watch the living.

I knew that I should be afraid, but I felt nothing. I was aware only of a terrible cold, and I felt myself shivering somewhere else, somewhere away from this desert beneath a boiling gray sky.

"Look to Gideon's Wall," the figure said again.

And there the dream ends.

• • •

The chamber which houses the archives of the empire is secluded on a high level of the Keep, where the air is hot and stale. Rushes and sawdust had been scattered on the floor to capture whatever moisture might creep into the room. There is a high window, but the lone beam of sunlight must fight through a great depth of dusty air, and casts only a dim pool upon the gilded rushes. The chamber itself is of significant size, yet scarcely large enough to contain the monstrous collection of tomes which had been packed and stacked and piled inside over the years. Leaning towers of parchment bound in rough twine reach for the ceiling. Recorded on all of these are the numbers describing in granular detail the expenses, profits and financial affairs of an empire. Shelves of scrolls overflow with more of the same. The sheer volume of economic statistics crammed within the archives is stunning. There is a great deal to be learned from such seemingly uninteresting and tedious facts, for the tracks left by the wealth of a nation will eventually lead to that which it holds dear.

I could have easily endured a lifetime in that place and not read half of the words contained therein, all of them wrapped up in scrolls and pressed between the pages of matching books. The archives are the memory of Shallai, and I knew that if Gideon's Wall was to be found, I would find it there.

I began with the maps.

I uncovered a pile of charts on a wide table toward the back of the chamber. They had been drawn on thick paper and loosely rolled within one another. They did not want to stay spread, so I positioned heavy books to suppress their curling corners.

For hours I pored over them by the light of my oil lantern, studying one after another. Each map was different, and all portrayed Shallai in varying proportions. On the largest of them I traced the thin black lines of Shallai's interior until I had located Jericho. My gaze wound around it in a broadening circle, bumping over every marked city, village, and province. My eyes rushed over places that, at any another time, would have drawn me as a magnet attracts metal shavings; the Drowsing Hills, the plains of Thall-Drabn and the Crypts of Edin. I continued south, leaping and racing over leagues of space, across sweeping plains and lakes and rivers until the map draped over the edge of the table and onto the floor. And still there was more.

I slid the map up and delved into territories the other maps had left uncharted. There were plateaus and deep gorges, and cities perched at the edges of deep woods. Farther south came a range of mountains, as though the continent had thrown up a great wall to mark the end of the world. The word *Mukkaris* had been scribbled along the range in letters as artfully jagged as the mountains they described.

Nowhere had I seen Gideon's Wall.

I have perceived a simple truth in my life; that discoveries and disasters of great import are often brought about by the simplest of accidents. While rubbing the exhaustion out of my eyes I took my elbows off the table to lean back, and the map, which had been held in place by my arms and was now weighted by the heavy lands of the north, began to slide off the back of the table. The undrawn lands beyond the Mukkaris were dragged up until I slapped my hand on the map to keep it from spilling to the floor.

My hand had come to rest on a vast emptiness. But then I spied fragments of writing visible between my splayed fingers. Securing the map with my free hand, I rolled my palm up to peek beneath.

Written in the center of the void, almost lost in the space south of the mountains, were the words *The Sands*. My eyes crawled north, crossing the wasteland back to the Mukkaris. Looking closer, I found a vertical line cutting arrow-straight through the range. It was marked *The Way*, and beside it, written very small and somewhat smudged, as though added by a strange hand, were two words screaming up at me from the past.

I had found Gideon's Wall.

Three

During the crossing of the wasteland I dreamt seven times of Gideon's Wall. I have begun to believe this recurring vision of mine is something more than a dream, that there is hidden meaning within. Many is the culture whose gods and devils communicate through the medium of dreams. But the meaning of mine—if one exists—eludes interpretation.

In this waking sleep of mine I stand alone in a narrow valley flanked by sheer cliffs of red and gray stone. The sun is heavy on my back, for I have been standing there a great while. Around my legs, long grass leans first north, and then south, pulled back and forth by an indecisive wind. Behind me the valley opens into a dry and spacious steppe of long brown grass and scattered, lonely trees with twisting branches and smooth, white bark.

I look at my own hands only to find that they are unfamiliar, younger than I know them to be, and immediately I sense that something is not as it should be. It is a hidden thing, this perversion, an undercurrent coiling slowly beneath all that I see. But it is difficult to define which aspect of the world around me has been wrenched out of proportion, or how it came to be that way.

I begin to walk through the valley, giving no thought to where I have come from, where I am, or where I am going. While it is yet a long way off I see a great structure rising up to bar my way. It seems to be something constructed by men; a fortress perhaps, or a dam built to hold back the tides of a sea.

It is not long before I have come to stand outside the outer gates of the fortress. Within, a great wall looms to impossible heights, spanning the entire breadth of the valley, from one cliff wall to the next, so that nothing beyond can be seen. It is a structure obviously intended for the purpose of war, but I see no soldiers atop the battlements, and there are no guards at the gate.

I sit upon the long grass outside, waiting for the inhabitants to discover me there, and welcome me in. But no one comes.

The gates have been opened wide, and so I enter without invitation, passing through the darkened tunnel of the gatehouse and into the barren grounds of the fortress. The wall rises up before me in all its terrible mass and prodigious glory. It fills the valley, placed there to forever separate the world on this side from the world on the other. I shade my eyes against the sun and lean back to peer up at the lofty heights.

At the east end of the wall is a tower built into the face of the cliffs. It is half again as high as the wall itself, and surely commands a stunning and far-reaching view. There are black windows set in the tower, and I feel eyes watching me from them. Upon a pole high atop the wall hangs the black and red standard of Shallai. It snaps tightly in the wind, and I can hear it faintly cracking even from where I stand. The scene is beautiful in its austerity, tainted only by the feeling that nothing is as it seems.

An inexplicable dread creeps over me as I stand in the desolate yard. I want to call out, but I can plainly see by the way the dark windows of the tower gaze down on me with drained and apathetic stares, and from the loneliness spilling from the barracks, that no human lives within this fortress. And yet I know that I am not alone. Whatever presence it is that shares this place with me lurks unseen.

I cross the vacated yard to the wall, dwarfed and humbled by its immensity. I place both hands flat against the stones. They are cold despite their exposure to the baking sun. For a long while I stand with my palms pressed flat, feeling for a ponderous heartbeat. But if there is one, it is too deep and slow to be felt. There is a wind, as is customary for all places that are ancient and abandoned, and it moves listlessly from place to place in search of life. I listen to the distant howling as it rushes over the top of the wall and through the vacant chambers of the tower. I look toward the barracks, deserted but for the voices of the wind and gyrating devils of dust.

At last, I come to realize that the presence I feel so distinctly is not with me on this side of the wall. It is on the other, just opposite me, perhaps with its hands also pressed against the stones, listening for the sound of my movement—my breathing—just as I listen for it. It is a beast, some hideous aberration lacking name and face. Aghast, I recoil from the wall when I suddenly realize that—as abruptly as I have become aware of it—it has been made aware of me.

Although I cannot see through the wall, I know that it has fallen into a foul rage brimming with malevolence. It is contorted with an irrational and inexplicable hatred. It prowls and paces, seeking a weakness in the wall through which it can reach me. But the wall is unbroken, offering no passage. Stultified, the beast begins to swell until I feel the pressure of its rage building like floodwaters against a dam. I hear faint screams, voices all around me filled with terror, yet so quiet I can scarcely detect them above the wind. The beast surges against the wall, pounding the barrier with its great deformed fists. It is intent on being contained no longer.

And then the wall begins to crack.

I back away as fractures shiver up the stone face. The rifts pull apart, yawning wide. Instead of a beast, torrents of golden sand spill forth. The wall is a dam, and it is holding back an ocean of sand. Although I cannot see him, I hear the beast howling. Its monstrous baying rises with the wind, which now screams over the battlements and slings biting sand across the fortress grounds. As I watch, the wall melts away into mounds of sand, and I am left standing alone and unprotected in the face of unspeakable terror.

Heat roars over me, and I raise an arm to shield my eyes.

The collapse of the wall has revealed an ancient and endless desert. The sky is black, crowded with clouds of boiling pitch. Lightning laces the sky, lashing angrily at the ground in thin, frenzied whips. And there, rising up out of the wasteland is a towering wall of sand. It seems the desert has pulled together all of its essence and cast it into this one vengeful incarnation. Backing it is all the savage might of the storm, and it lifts its great fist into the turbulent sky. The wall of sand hangs poised, a force of destruction leaning forward threateningly, eager to destroy all that cowers before it.

Quaking with fear as though I have been dropped before a wrathful god, I crumble to my knees and hide my face. And then whatever force holds the wall suspended is suddenly retracted, and the sand comes crashing inexorably down.

I awake the moment before I am crushed, a cry on my lips.

• • •

The valley known as the Way is not so different in life as it appeared in my dream. The pattern of mountains was familiar, and I recognized the tilt of the land and the press of cliffs on either side. There is no grass, only sand. Where there is no sand, there is cracked dirt. The sky is pale blue, a dusty dome overhead. The sun is belligerent. That place, along with the rest of the empire,

29

had been laid bare, rasped to the bone by some intensely destructive and unforgiving force.

I felt distinctly that I had walked the valley before, and I even caught myself searching, perhaps foolishly, for my own footprints in the sand. Although I felt no fear, I was plainly haunted by the memory of a beast pounding its rage on stones. I stopped our caravan in the place where I had stood cowering before a towering wall of sand.

"The tower was there," I said, pointing to the eastern cliffs.

The team's eyes followed my gesture. They saw nothing. My hand moved slowly westward, painting across the valley the great wall from my dream. "And there lies Gideon's Wall."

The next day we began to dig.

• • •

I have been an archaist for a great many years, and I have found that history lurks everywhere beneath our feet. Some of it hides just beneath the surface, while the vast, untapped bulk of it lies entombed under layers of rock, soil and sediment, only to be found by the most diligent of seekers.

Gideon's Wall lies just under the surface. One can hardly overturn a rock within this valley without revealing the unburied corpse of a soldier or slave of the empire.

We found a human skull the first day, before even beginning to dig. Partially encased in a slab of hardened sand, its rounded dome had been bleached white by the sun and scoured clean by the blowing sands. I crouched nearby to study it with a patient, exacting eye, half-expecting it to look up and greet me. It was perfectly intact, with half its square chin sunk in the ground and one eye completely buried. With its other, it stared south in silent vigil. I shared its view for some time, following its gaze into the desert over which it kept a lonely watch.

"What have you seen?" I asked it softly, wondering what things had crossed its unblinking gaze. Understandably, it would not break its long endured silence to entertain me with answers.

• • •

A successful excavation requires but three traits: patience, persistence, and a stringent attention to detail. To think that the buried shards of a broken history can be summoned up out of the ground, pieced together, and wholly—or even partially—interpreted in a single day is folly. Oftentimes, we as mankind have enough difficulty grasping what happened to our own selves just yesterday, let alone events which transpired decades past. Patience, persistence, detail; over and over again, until the pieces are all laid out in order and the canvas painted. The process is simple. It is the execution which consumes time and nags at ones tolerance.

The excavation site, be it on the slopes of a mountain, the depths of a swamp, or the cracked landscape of a desert, is divided into a symmetrical grid of squares. Each square is assigned a unique number, and charted with diligent care. Digging commences with the strictest of caution. Dirt, sand and rubble are deposited in baskets labeled in correspondence with the grid square with which they are associated. The contents of the baskets are sifted through with such granularity that nothing larger than a splinter of steel escapes. Any artifacts found are labeled, recorded and stored. In this way it is possible to know precisely where each item, be it a bone fragment or a plate of armor, was found. As more is uncovered, a picture begins to take shape.

Excavation is tedious work, but to blunder forward without discretion would be to overlook, or perhaps even destroy, the precious details which can often mean the difference between understanding, and the evolution of incorrect conclusions.

Before five full days of our excavation had passed we revealed the outline of the tower's foundation, and nearly a hundred paces of the wall. The tower lies in precisely the location it did in my dreams. Its shape is identical, and the gray stones are familiar to my touch.

I am assured now that my visions contain meaning.

We continued to turn the sands gently and efficiently, peeling back layers of dirt and sand to find the ruins hidden by the desert. With each passing day we reveal more of the mighty wall, and my excitement at every uncovered stone escalates. My preemptive imagination, perhaps too eager, covers the bones of these ruins with flesh. It fills in the gaps, and builds for me a fortress over a pile of rubble.

And the desert offers up more than ruins. After fourteen days we had exhumed the remains of greater than fifty men. All are soldiers, judging by the weaponry and battle attire. Many are incomplete, missing limbs and heads, others are torn asunder, and we find only scattered pieces. The bones or skulls of others are crushed, their deaths clearly brought on by grievous injuries. We leave the skeletons half encased in hardened sand, locked into the precise positions in which they fell. We dig around them, seeking something greater, though we know not what.

The unburied bodies and the ceaseless emptiness of the desert have begun to afflict the composure of the men. They have their superstitions, and the solitude of this place has become unsettling for them. I spy them often making hurried signs to ward off evil spirits, and they go about their work with downcast eyes.

Perhaps they have cause for fear.

I have always believed that places possess memories. People see, and after a time forget, trading one memory for another. Or they die, and everything is lost all at once. But a place never forgets. If the exposure of emotion is powerful enough, an event may be forever captured. As visitors, we can sometimes briefly sense the events seared into the memory of a place. Homes become saturated with the lives of those who lived in them, while battlefields and citadels are haunted with the memories of fighting long after the land itself has smoothed over scars of war. In empty dungeons we are touched by the agony and hopelessness left behind by a tormented soul. On the field of battle, if the wind blows just right, we can almost hear the clash of steel.

This place remembers only sadness and pain. Memories that are not mine invade my sleep, saturate my dreams. My nights are fraught with an endless parade of faces, disconnected events and disjointed moments. There is pain and suffering, and I awake as exhausted as if I had not slept at all. The others suffer similarly. It was not until several days past that the lingering presence of the dead made itself known by means other than dreams and voices in the dark.

While sifting through an expanse of newly uncovered ruins, I lifted my eyes to find an unfamiliar man standing hardly ten paces from where I knelt in the shallow excavation ditch. He was watching me with solemn eyes. Startled, I did not move, only stared back at him. I was struck by those eyes, which seemed to describe the deepest, most ageless sorrow with which a man can be haunted. His mouth began to move, and the grave expression on his face showed me that he was trying to explain a thing of dire importance, but I heard nothing. His words were lost somewhere in the unfathomable distance between he and I.

"Speak again," I told him. "I am listening."

Suri, he said with great effort, his eyes and his voice pleading. A whisper, barely there, carried to my ears on an ancient wind. *Have you seen Suri?*

My heart ached in telling him that I knew no Suri.

He faded then, smeared across my vision as though he were made of nothing more substantial than a mirage.

When I spoke of the event privately to the overseer of my team, he hushed me quickly, seemingly distressed at the thought of being overheard. He would only allow me to speak after we had gone into my tent and sealed the canvas flaps behind us. He told me urgently that I must not speak of the dead where they might hear, for to do so was to attract their unwanted attentions. I asked him what else he believed of ghosts and spirits, and he told me, albeit reluctantly and in a low whisper as though he and I were fellow conspirators, of an incident he'd experienced as a young man.

His family had once lived in the northern quarter of a city somewhere beyond the western steppes of the Paynam. It was during the first of the Shadrakan invasions, and the city—being a port along a major river—was laid to siege. He himself was not born until after the city was razed, but growing up he heard many stories of what it had been like from those who had lived through it. His father spoke often of his older sister. She had been five years old when they barricaded the city, and was crushed beneath a collapsing wall. He returned once to the place, long after the siege had ended. Guided by a map of his father's, he traced his way through the overgrown streets of the destroyed city until he found the abandoned house where his family had lived.

"Do you know what I saw there?" he asked, but did not grant me sufficient opportunity to answer. "I saw a child," he said. "I looked up and saw her watching me from a window across the street. She was small, and she looked very sick. Her hair was white. She put her hand on the window, like this—" He put up his hand, fingers splayed, palm out, as though against a glass pane.

"I never told my father that I went back," he said to me. "But sometimes I think about it, and I wonder if I really saw what I thought I saw. I never knew my sister when she was alive, so I don't know what she looked like. But it might have been her in that window, don't you think? Maybe she didn't even know she was dead, and was just waiting there for someone to come back for her, waiting all those years at that window. When I think too much or too often about these things I am unable to sleep."

I asked him if he thought there were a great many ghosts in the ruins of Gideon's Wall.

"I know there are," he answered confidently. "I know they are around us, in the air and in the ground; these things I know. What I do not know—what I have never known—is what they want."

"What would you want, if it were you who had died in this place?"

The overseer mused but a moment before answering. "To be remembered," he decided. "Only to be remembered."

• • •

On the sixteenth day, we uncovered the beast.

It happened early in the evening, when the air is still and hot. I had been recording the past days' events on loose sheaves of parchment at the small table in my tent when I heard a commotion, a loud din of raised voices, near the east end of the site, where the wall stretched across the valley. The men had been digging there all afternoon. Rushing from the tent, I made straight for the site, where a tight knot of men were shouting back and forth between them. They fell to dissatisfied grumbling as I approached, but not before I heard one of them vehemently declare, "It is finished! No more."

"What is finished?" I asked of him. When he refused to answer, staring at the ground with adamant eyes, I addressed my inquiry to all. "What is finished?"

"Saisha will dig no more," another supplied, and the first glared at him, seething in betrayal.

"I dig no more," the one called Saisha affirmed brazenly.

"Why not?" I asked.

Still fitful with anger, the man began to rapidly pour forth an incriminating flow of words in his own tongue while gesturing vaguely at the ditch in which he had been toiling.

I held out my hand to slow the tide of words. "Calmly," I implored him. "Slowly." I have always found it difficult to communicate until fears and superstitions have been at least somewhat allayed.

Another of them stepped closer to me. "He says—"

"I know what he said."

They forget. Every day they forget I speak their language as well—in some cases better—than they. I gave my attention back to Saisha. In his rapid speech from a moment before I had picked out the word *catahein*. "You say you found the *catahein*?" I asked him. "You found the demon?"

He glared at me stubbornly, reluctantly.

"Show me."

It lay but a short distance from the tower, embedded three paces below the packed dirt. In life, the creature must have stood a full head taller than a man, but its spine is curved oddly, and continues past the pelvis to form a tail of extraordinary length. The head is elongated and flat, and the jaws are massive, reminding me of armored beasts I have seen captured from the murky swamps of the Greezen. Such beasts watch from the muddy waters with the patience of a devil, and when they attack, they come swiftly rushing out of the sludge to seize their prey and drag him kicking and screaming beneath the oily waters. But the beast we have found here bears only a fleeting resemblance to the Greezen creature, and I am completely unable to classify it. It is but one more mystery in a land that abounds with them.

I do not know yet what happened here. There are few plausible explanations for the death of an empire: plague, pestilence, demons and war. There is a reason for everything. Every question has an answer, every puzzle a solution. Each piece simply need be found and placed accordingly. Perhaps the ghosts that haunt this valley and these ruins will share freely with me their fantastic tales.

If not, I will dig them up myself.

Four

I concentrate the largest part of our efforts on the eastern side of the valley, at the base of the cliffs. This is where the tower once stood; it was the gut of the wall—the heart from which I hope to pry loose the secrets of this place.

On the third day of digging, three ells beneath the surface, we find the vault.

Shovels clang against the submerged iron surface, and men fall to their knees, sweeping away sand and debris. They dig around it, their eagerness reflected in the rapid swinging of their tools. They pitch and clear bucket after bucket of loose sand, until the majority of the vault's bulk is laid bare. It lies crooked at the bottom of a wide pit, a massive block of iron half sunk in the ground. It is smooth and ominous, a squat black thing staring up from its grave. The men clamber on it, proud that after so few days of digging we are already making discoveries.

The vault refuses to be lifted free; it is far too heavy, even with winches and levers, and so I decide that it should be opened in the pit. It is, of course, sealed.

But I come prepared for such things.

I retrieve my case and set it by the rim of the pit. It is jacketed in the thick, dark leather of a ridgekin, a protection against elements and thieves. Within are my corrosives, acids and poisons.

It does not take long to make what I need. The solvent I concoct is no more than a mouthful, but it will eat through as much as a full pace of solid iron. As I work, the hulking vault glowers at me, suspicious, wondering what I am about.

I pass the leather-wrapped vial to my overseer, who takes it as gingerly as he can in his big hands. He is careful not to slosh or spill even a drop. He holds the vial away from him as he descends into the pit, making his way as though it were a viper he held in his hands. He passes the vial up to the man atop the vault, who accepts it as cautiously as had the overseer, then looks to me for direction.

I nod; he pours.

Steam hisses angrily from the locking mechanism, the seals, and the hinges. Metal bubbles and boils and slides across the tilted edge of the vault like melting fat. It drips in the sand. It digs holes in the ground.

The men are afraid, their previous exuberance dampened now that the lock has sloughed away and the secrets within the vault are that much nearer to being seen. Their fear is justified. Those of them who have traveled with the archaists before now know very well that sometimes things pulled up from the ground have teeth. Again, they look to me for direction, and I indicate that they should proceed.

In a hushed, anticipating silence, the vault is opened.

Soil. Black earth. I can see into the vault from the edge of the pit, and it is plain. The vault is filled to bursting with rich black loam. We have found a treasure of dirt.

The young man atop the open vault crouches down and puts his hands in it. He pulls out two fistfuls, and holds them up for me to see. Clotted bits of moist soil cling to tiny roots that hang from his fists. He is grinning.

"Worms," he calls to me. "There are worms."

I go to see for myself. Atop the open vault I look down at fat slugs and nightcrawlers mindlessly churning the dark soil. I push my own hands into the wet contents of the vault. It is the kind of dirt farmers pray to their gods for.

Three men can fit in the vault at once, and so I set them to work and back away. We know nothing, and so the men go with caution. Buckets are filled and lifted out, carried aside, emptied, and brought back again. Others sift through the growing pile, looking for relics amid the crawling worms. They dig and dig until only their arms can be seen taking empty buckets down, then handing them filled again to those above. They hit bottom, and there is a quiet moment. I am almost ready to call for them when they emerge, hands muddy, faces painted with confusion.

"Nothing," one of them tells me in wonder. "Except this." And I am handed a stiff pouch, something that might once have been secured to a saddlebag.

"This is not 'nothing'," I say.

He shrugs. It is not what he expected, or wanted, and so it is nothing.

Within the pouch there is more soil, luxuriously black and heavy. I dump it upon the ground at my feet, and we look upon all the vaulted treasure of Gideon's Wall.

Cosseted in the pile of soil there is an orb the size of a fist, smooth and perfect. Too heavy to be crystal or quartz, it is neither marble, nor metal. It is solid, or at least it seems so, and the surface is cloudy. As I gaze at it, I feel I am staring into a pool of shade. The air around us does not seem so hot, the sun not so close.

Setting the orb back in its pouch, I spread the small pile of dirt with my hand. And there is one more treasure to be found. It is a fetish of some kind, a graven figurine no larger than the distance between the tips of my fingers and the top of my palm. Carved of some dark, heavy wood, it is a crude likeness of something vaguely man-like. The details of the body are rough and uneven, whittled with a knife too large for such a small piece, without care for beauty or perspective. Altogether it is an ugly thing. I brush away the clinging dirt. Winding and curling all about the brutish little body are etched delicate runes. If they are words of a language, I cannot decipher them. What they can possibly mean, if anything, I am unable to tell.

The figurine fits comfortably in the palm of my hand. I am surprised to find that it is warm, as though it had been laying not in a lightless grave for the past decade, but basking in the sun.

• • •

I have not tried to sleep this night. The figurine will not allow it.

It began the whispering after the camp had fallen into the hushed stillness of night. It is a disquieting sound, a dry rustling that is distant and small. In my tent I am alone with it, and I believe it is aware of this. I feel it is watching me. There on my traveling chest the little fetish stands, immobile but far from silent.

Whispering.

For a long time I do nothing. Some part of me is afraid, however unreasonable. It is only a statue, only a tiny little idol. Only a piece of carved wood. It can do nothing. But I remember the warmth of it, the heat of skin—of life. And what if it were alive? I have seen stranger things. Even so I wish morning would come. If it were light, the statue's incessant whispering would not seem so eerily threatening as it is in this bouncing candlelight.

The shadows play, and the whispering goes on.

I consider, and reconsider. And then I take the thing from where it stands, and the whispering is clearer, though still faint, an endless stream of something I am just barely able to make out. In my hand I feel its warmth. It seems to *breathe*. I take a candle, and I sit at my desk. I bring the statue to my ear.

And I listen to it whispering … whispering …

Book Two
The Ambassador

"I do what I'm told. I stay alive. Let men who are greater than me make decisions."

—Del

One

Del stood in a small room before three of Jericho's chancellors. He hadn't been given the chance to make himself presentable before being brought to them, and he was weary and disheveled. His boots were heavy with swamp mud.

The chancellors were stiff old men, stern and brittle as dead trees. They barely breathed, and only the one in the middle had glanced up when Del had been escorted in. A slight expression of distaste had crinkled his nose, prompting Del to glance himself over. He saw nothing that had not been there before: dirty uniform and dirty hands, a used soldier. He was nothing special to anyone, nothing out of the ordinary.

The chancellors had come from Jericho to find him.

Nothing was said for a long while. The chancellors occupied themselves with the huge volume of papers spread across the table. They seemed very busy to Del, and he wondered if they had forgotten about him. He was very patient. Moving only his head and neck, he let his attention explore the small room, searching for something of interest. The place was bare of furnishings and character, and the plaster on the walls had begun to crack from lack of care. From one small window he could see the perpetually misty rim of the Bayabaar swamps, where the remainder of his corps was entrenched.

The Bayabaar swamps bordered the lands of the Mugh-shin. A dark world choked with fog and black mud, the swamps were a place of tangled vines and knotted boles. Always in the distance could be heard the bellowing of saurian creatures blundering through the mists. It was believed that Mugh-shin spies were trickling into Shallai from the swamps. Charged with the capture of such spies, Del's corps had been dispatched into the heart of the sodden wetlands. For eight months they had endured the foul, brackish waters and stifling heat, acting as sentries of Shallai's borders. In that time, seven men had been lost to enormous snakes, four to alligators, and two had simply vanished.

Thirteen casualties. No Mugh-shin spies.

"You are Del," one of the chancellors finally stated, although he did not look up. Del's attention snapped back, eyes on the three. The old man seemed to have at last found a sheet that contained the information he sought. Not thinking it was a question, Del said nothing. Hardly a moment later the chancellor pointed a pair of sharp eyes at him, slightly annoyed. "Can't you speak?"

"Of course," Del answered calmly.

"Your name is Del?"

"It is."

The chancellor nodded in satisfaction. "Currently you are under the command of Marek Ja. You have proven yourself a fine soldier in many diverse situations, and come with the highest recommendations of every commander you've ever served under."

If that was a question as well, Del didn't know how to answer it, so he maintained his silence while the chancellor went back to perusing his papers. The other chancellors, still occupied with their own shufflings, hadn't so much as acknowledged his presence. He took the time to watch them for a bit, close-set eyes and bald heads bobbing over stacks of parchment. After some time, the middle chancellor lifted a single sheet of paper off the table and took a great interest in whatever was written on it. "You have served Shallai for nearly twenty years." he noted with some concern.

Del never expected to have lived so long. He had not kept track of the years himself, and hearing the number spoken to him was something of a shock, not only because the number was unexpectedly high, but because he hadn't thought anyone cared enough to add them up. He had always though he was anonymous in Shallai's ranks. He wondered what else they knew about him.

"Twenty years," he said quietly to himself. Nearly half his life had been devoted to letting the blood of the empire's enemies.

"Twenty years," the chancellor affirmed. "Is this accurate?"

"I don't know," Del admitted.

The chancellor lifted his paper, tilted it slightly. "It is written here."

Del nodded his acceptance without verifying the proof.

"Men such as yourself are rare."

It sounded like a compliment to Del, but the old man fixed on him such a severe expression that it seemed more of an accusation. Del didn't know how to respond. Should he say, yes? Thank you? What was the protocol for compliments from fussy chancellors? Before he could decide, the old man spared him, and directed his attention back to the table. Turning a sheaf of parchment, he read the things written there while Del was left to wonder what was happening. "You have been offered a command position on five separate occasions. This, too, is accurate?"

"Yes."

The chancellor paused, obviously suspicious. "But you have never accepted?"

"I have no desire for a command."

"Why not?"

"A soldier's life is simpler."

"Then you prefer taking orders to giving them?"

Del had never looked at it in that light before, but when boiled down it seemed to make sense, and so he nodded. The chancellor echoed the movement. "Tell me," he said, setting aside the papers and looking at Del as though he were suddenly prepared to listen. "What do you know of the Bedu?"

The question was something of a surprise to Del. What did the Bedu have to do with him? He knew only what everyone else knew, and he recalled it all in a quick flood. His brow furrowed as he tried to sort the bits of information into meaningful sentences. "They live in the deserts beyond the Way. They were at war with Shallai some decades ago, and Gideon's Wall was built as a defense. I remember something about a prophet, but . . ." Del shrugged. It was unimportant.

The chancellor leaned forward then, and for the first time really *looked* at Del. "Do you enjoy the life you lead?"

Because Del failed to see how his feelings about life could possibly affect anything, he boldly answered, "I do."

"You have given much of your life in dedicated service to Shallai. If offered the opportunity to lead a different sort of life, and yet still serve the empire, would you take it?"

Del opened his mouth to answer, but shut it when he realized he didn't know what would come out. What other kinds of life were there? The chancellor was watching his reaction closely, keeping his silence in wait of an answer that never came. Finally, he dipped a quill in a tiny pot of ink and began to scribble something on the parchment in front of him. Feeling as though he had failed a test, all Del could do was watch the quill scratching across the parchment. He would have paid in blood to see what was being put to paper. While still scribing, the chancellor flicked his eyes at Del. "Dismissed," he said.

● ● ●

Early the next morning, Del was summoned once more to stand before the three chancellors from Jericho. This time, there were no papers to distract them, and he became the focal point of their scrutiny. He was informed without ceremony, yet in a tightly official manner, that he had been selected as the new ambassador to the Bedu nation. He was given a heavy ring bearing the seal of an ambassador, and papers were put in his hand identifying him as a privileged dignitary of the great empire of Shallai. The chancellors explained to him in short sentences that he would surely learn a great deal among the Bedu, but that Shallai was not interested in any sentiments he might develop concerning them. Shallai was concerned only with the faithful service of his eyes and ears, nothing more.

At his first opportunity to speak, Del tried to explain that perhaps a mistake had been made.

They assured him there had not.

It didn't seem to matter to anyone that he had neither the knowledge, nor the experience, required for competency as an ambassador. All he knew was how to be a soldier; how to take orders and kill men.

This seemed to suit the chancellors just fine.

The next day, Del was packed off to Gideon's Wall.

Like all well-trained soldiers, Del was accustomed to calculating odds and understanding situations, especially those that directly affected his continued existence. And so on that fateful morning when he was told he was to be the new ambassador to the Bedu in the wastelands beyond Gideon's Wall and escorted out of the Bayabaar swamps, he knew instinctively that he was never coming back. Hardly the type of soldier to waste time pitying himself, Del went without complaint. He understood that it was his duty to go where he was told to go, and do what he was told to do. He had long ago ceased searching for logic in the decisions of his superiors, finding it best to follow orders without question. If those in charge of orchestrating the vast mechanics of Shallai's armies thought it best that he be removed from the activities at which he excelled—namely the slaying of the enemy—and taken to the desert to act like a diplomat, it was not his place to argue. And whether or not there were sensible reasons concealed beneath such an absurd decree was irrelevant. He had been chosen to do something, and he would do it.

In the space of one afternoon he left the soldier's life behind and became an ambassador, chosen by men he did not know, for reasons no one was bothering to explain to him. Given the circumstances, it was easy for Del to accept the fact that his being chosen was nothing more than blind chance; dice cast by a stranger.

● ● ●

The Way was the only known route through the Mukkaris. It bored straight through the jagged cliffs and bottomless ravines of those impassable mountains to the wastelands beyond. Gideon's Wall had been built at the southern end of the valley, at the point where Shallai ended and the deserts began. It seemed as effective a blockade as the mountains themselves. Del's first impression of the wall was that an enormous dam had been built to hold back a river of godlike proportions. Spanning the entire breadth of the Way, Gideon's Wall was high enough to make him feel a tiny speck beneath it. There was a keep at the eastern end, dressed with all the fortifications of a citadel built for war. What lie on the other side he could scarcely imagine.

He climbed to the battlements that first day to meet the desert. The incredible expanse of land sprawling southward like a dead ocean afforded an extraordinary view. To the east and west, the serrated peaks of the Mukkaris punctured the heavens, so high and sharp that it seemed the sky should bleed. They loomed tall and dark above Gideon's Wall, folding their collective shadow down over the lonely citadel. The wind was angry on the battlements. It roared and growled with hot frustration, clutching at his hair and clothes, first pulling one way, then pushing another, as though unable to decide whether to drag him into the desert, blow him back into the Way, or tear him apart where he stood. Placing both hands on the stone battlements, Del stared full into the hot, rushing wind. Somewhere deep in that wasteland lived the Bedu, and soon he was to join them.

He was given a room high in the tower, a cold and cramped chamber with bare stone walls and hardly enough room to pace. There were no windows, and the stones, thirsty for heat, sucked away the warmth. Alone in the tower, his only company were two or three fuzzy spiders the size of fat hazelnuts. He tried to make himself comfortable, but the cot was too small, and the room too oppressive. After nearly five days of such boredom, Del was finally taken to Ian Manzig, the deacon of Gideon's Wall.

Two

By his own estimation, Deacon Manzig was wasted talent. For seven-going-on-a-hundred years he had presided over the corps of soldiers stationed at the wall, preparing for a Bedu invasion that seemed unlikely to happen in his lifetime, or in all eternity. Proof abounded. In all the days accumulated in the span of seven years, exactly none of them had been spent waging war with the Bedu. According to the deacon, this lack of activity was both unfortunate, and depressing. Had he dug deeper into history he might have learned that not in all the years since the construction of Gideon's Wall had a single Bedu so much as petulantly thrown a rock in its direction. Truthfully, the deacon doubted they ever would.

Deacon Manzig had come to the conclusion long ago, and still firmly believed, that the Bedu weren't coming. This firm belief made every aspect of Gideon's Wall seem a wasted effort, and he nothing more than the court jester upon whom Shallai had dumped the burden of maintaining such an abundance of uselessness. And because he excelled so wondrously in defending Shallai from nothing, Shallai was very pleased with him, and kept him at the wall year after year.

The deacon had determined during the years past that there was no possible way to fail at the task with which he had been charged. The deacon couldn't *give* the wall to the Bedu. They didn't want it. And if the enemy so dreaded by Shallai never so much as showed their faces to him, how could the wall be lost to them? A half-wit and his donkey could hold the wall from an enemy that never attacked. Knowing this, but having always assumed he was highly esteemed by his superiors, he was understandably bewildered as to why Shallai would keep such an exemplary soldier as himself wasting away at the far reaches of the empire. Nevertheless, each season—and there were only two in the wastelands: summer and winter—despite his doing less than the season before, he was a success, and his defense of Shallai was applauded by whichever chancellor still happened to be keeping track of him from Jericho.

The lack of challenge to be found in his position, coupled with the stultifying frustration it spawned, drove the deacon to fatness by way of sheer boredom. After seven years at the wall, he had acquired the look of a man once mighty, but who overly enjoyed the luxuries afforded him by a life-style of indolence and inactivity. Although his arms and legs were still thick, not all of his girth could be fairly attributed to muscle. His belly had begun to sag out like a sack of cream, and his chin had lost the chiseled and rugged aspect he'd once been prized for. Day by day, month after month, a little bit more of the hardness in him leaked away.

For this, the deacon hated the Bedu. They claimed no direct responsibility for the size of his expanding gut, but this was an inconsequential fact, and did nothing to mitigate his hatred. They were blatantly wasting his time, pretending to be insidious warmongers, when in reality they were nothing but scattered packs of grungy, flea-bitten sand-dogs. They were a mock threat. Many a sleepless night the deacon had fervently wished the Bedu would either attack and be done with it, or vanish forever into oblivion. The likelihood of either event occurring was exceedingly slim, but such things didn't curb the deacon's appetite for dreaming.

In alignment with his fantasies, the deacon's most deeply seated desire was for Shallai to one day consult him on a recommended course of action concerning the Bedu. In this recurring daydream he became a larger, more handsome version of himself. Decked in full battle armor, he is brought before the Fist of Shallai in Jericho. He is flanked by noble seraphim who know him by name, and pay respect. With earnest passion he builds his case against the Bedu, explaining that to initiate an aggressive campaign to annihilate them completely is by far the most beneficial solution. In the end the Fist has little choice but to abide by his profound wisdom, and gives him an army with which to kill every last Bedu.

The deacon had already determined that destroying the Bedu would truly be easy, for if the number of nomad sightings at the wall were any indication of the total sum of their population, he suspected the Bedu infestation was relatively small, and that they were hardly capable of scraping together enough warriors to fight a single battle, much less defend against invasion.

And so the deacon waited in a state of half-expectancy. But the summons never came, and it seemed Shallai was doing very well without the benefit of his wisdom to guide her.

Instead, they sent ambassadors.

The ambassadors eventually became bright spots in the deacon's otherwise dreary life, although it had not always been so. In the beginning, the deacon had despised them with his whole being. He despised them because of who they were and because of what they had been sent to accomplish, which was in complete opposition to his own bloody fantasies. Their aim was to create peace with the Bedu; Deacon Manzig wanted genocide. But because they had been sent directly from Jericho, they represented the desires of Shallai. It was hard not to feel betrayed.

To the deacon's great satisfaction, the ambassadors were invariably pathetic, milk-fed sops. None of them lasted long among the Bedu, and they always returned to the wall within several months—some of them sooner—looking excessively skittish and distressed. They wore a wild look in their eyes, like plump little fish in a poolful of sharks. They started at every sound, and generally seemed as though their nerves had been stretched quaveringly taut. Apparently, life among the Bedu was significantly more unpleasant than what chubby diplomats from Jericho were accustomed to. But it seemed Shallai had an endless supply of weak-kneed ambassadors, and one after another it sent them marching into the wastelands, happily burdened with the duty of forging a lasting peace with the Bedu. After a long succession of failures, the deacon still despised them, but also had discovered amusement in the whole process. He took great pleasure in turning them over, fresh and new, to the Bedu escorts that came to retrieve them, knowing that the same escorts would return them like used whores in just a few months time.

The deacon was always first to welcome them home.

"Come," he would invite cheerily. "Tell us what enchanting things you have learned among the Bedu. Share with us your experience."

Seldom did they appreciate his attention, and for some reason never wanted to speak to him—or even look at him. It was as though they were ashamed of themselves. Those with no shame spoke freely, never failing to curse the murderous Bedu and their barbaric ways, nor to mention how every minute they had feared for their lives. But for the most part, they didn't want to share their experiences with the deacon or anyone else, and if anything at all could be goaded out of them, it came out in incoherent mumbles.

"Was the heat disagreeable?" the deacon would inquire in a voice ripe with sincerest concern. "Were the sand-dogs unkind to you?"

Mumble.

"What? Were the women not to your liking?"

After several days of recuperation at the wall, the deacon would pack the used ambassadors back to Jericho, where they were never heard from again. The routine had become vastly entertaining.

Until Del.

Normally, it was the deacon's custom to keep all new ambassadors waiting for an audience at least two days, but he had been feeling surly and dyspeptic of late. He conveniently used this as justification for putting the ambassador off, something that made him feel a little better all in itself. Five days passed before his mood brightened, at which time he sent for Del, ready to frighten and intimidate, as was his routine with all new ambassadors.

But Del was completely different from what the deacon had come to expect of Shallai's ambassadors. He was not a cowering lump of jelly like the others. He was neither overconfident, nor whimpering. He was calm and watchful and at ease. He would not be intimidated. Above all, he seemed capable.

The deacon disliked him immediately.

When the new ambassador was presented to him in his chambers, the deacon dropped his bulk into a chair, and swung his boots onto the table. There were no seats other than his own, as the deacon had never cared for guests to be comfortable in his presence. Comfort was not a privilege to be given out lightly at the wall. He had not bothered to shave for several days, and he scratched at his stubbly chin while sizing Del up with a critical eye.

"You don't look like an ambassador," were the first words out of the deacon's mouth.

"What do ambassadors look like?" Del answered readily.

"Overweight. Bald." The deacon picked a piece of dirt from beneath his fingernail. "Where are you from?"

"Gendrei province," Del lied. It was an easy lie because it was one he'd told a thousand times, one that had been with him since he'd first set foot on Shallai's soil.

"I don't know where that is. What did you do in Gendrei?"

"I grew up."

The deacon's eyes narrowed. "And what else."

"Nothing. When I was done growing up, I left."

"Then what did you do in all the years between growing up in Gendrei and today?"

"I'm a soldier."

The deacon stared at Del. Had a mistake been made? His eyes threw off to the side for a moment, sifting through his memory for something slippery, perhaps something he had heard and then forgotten. When he looked back to Del, there was suspicion in his eyes. "How many years?"

"How many years, what?"

"Have you served," the deacon said with some annoyance. "How many years have you served?"

"I'm not sure."

"Guess."

"Twenty."

The deacon nodded slowly. His mind was churning, molding the unknowns into something he could grasp, something that made sense. "Why did they send you?" he asked bluntly.

"To serve as ambassador to—"

"No," the deacon snapped with severe annoyance. Rising to his feet, he started around the table toward Del. "Why you? Why soldier?"

Del had no answer.

The deacon came to stand directly at his side, glaring a though digging through his head for answers he wanted, b being offered.

"How long will you last?" he asked.

Del squinted. "I don't underst—"

"How long will you stay with the Bedu?" t' in a tone slow and succinct, as though it w hadn't understood instead of the questio dors before you didn't last long."

Del had already heard the stories

57

that had preceded him. None had stayed with the Bedu for very much longer than a few weeks, and it might have been for this reason that Shallai had finally opted to send a man used to blood and fire instead of a cultured wordsmith. They were tired of presenting the Bedu with soft fools in the stead of real men. This, of course, was Del's own opinion, but already it had been made clear to him that Shallai wanted him to stay among the Bedu until they decided to bring him home—or the Bedu returned his corpse draped over the back of a mule. He was the last ambassador they wanted to send.

"One of them came back within a week," the deacon was explaining. "Tail tucked and all weeping about the horrible Bedu and their horrible ways." He seized a piece of fruit from a wooden bowl on the table and half-devoured it with one huge bite. "But then again, they weren't soldiers."

"I'll stay as long as—"

"I say it's a waste of time," the deacon interrupted. He chewed and spoke all at once, bits of juice running down his chin. "It's always been a waste of time. If they think it's going to be different now, sending a soldier, they're wrong. Soldier or not, you won't last. If it was up to me, we would have marched an army into those deserts and wiped out the Bedu a decade ago. Then we could all go home—get out of this cursed place."

"A wise plan," Del said somberly.

The deacon stopped chewing. He routed all of his concentration into a flat stare at Del. It was clear he wasn't able to decide whether Del was truly agreeing with him, or mocking him in some subtle fashion. He nodded hesitantly, and his jaw resumed its slow grinding. "The Bedu are dangerous," he stated, if only to reinforce his opinions. "Every last one of them."

"Of course," Del said.

Still staring, the deacon tossed his half-eaten fruit aside and took another from the bowl. He was agitated, and eating was something of a comfort. After sinking his teeth into the crisp meat he leaned back to his end of the table. "I've sent for your Bedu escort. Sometimes they come in a few days, sometimes it takes weeks. He'll teach you what he can of the Bedu tongue then take you to Aba Ajraan, which I have been told is the capital city of their people. What are your questions?"

"No questions, Deacon."

Ian Manzig nodded, then flapped his hand. "Dismissed."

• • •

During his extended stay at Gideon's Wall, Del learned all he could of the history behind the impassable fortress. It was a difficult undertaking, as most of the soldiers he questioned knew no more than he, and the deacon would not be bothered with him. It was only after a helpful steward, upon becoming aware of Del's unending curiosity and presenting him with three books, that Del finally learned something of the wall's history. A book was a rare and very often valuable thing, and a useful book even more precious. The steward, understanding their value, but not their content, had been keeping the books locked safely away, fearing that some uncouth soldier would burn them for fuel on a chilly night. Unable to read them for himself, he turned them over to Del, hoping the ambassador would find what he sought in their pages.

The first of the three was a thick anthology of tales concerning the origin of all things. Del read slowly, but it seemed even to his poor understanding that it had been written both carelessly and hastily, scrawled across the thick pages in an uneven and wandering hand. After reading the whole of the first tale, some of the second, and flipping idly through the rest, he laid it aside. The second was not bound at all, but tied together with rough twine. Many of its pages were torn in half or mangled, and several were missing entirely. It might have been useful had it been written in a language he could read.

Only the third was of interest to Del. It had been written by a person who did not identify himself, but judging from his deep knowledge of the wall, Del assumed had been present during its construction. Contained between its crudely bound covers was a detailed account of what occurred during each day's labor. This in itself lacked excitement; it was the brief afterward, in which the author, almost as an afterthought, related a vague story of the origins of the wall.

Nearly six decades old, the fortress had been built following a Bedu invasion. Until that time, Shallai had been blissfully unaware of the existence of the Bedu, believing that the desert beyond the Way was void of life. Shallai had been wrong, for within those bleak and barren deserts lived a nation of savages. The leader of the greatest clan journeyed into the deepest deserts far beyond Bedu borders, and was there stricken with a terrible madness. In his madness he raised a horde of warriors, and they took up their weapons against Shallai. Up through the Way they came, intent on bringing destruction. The Fist and his legion of seriph gathered up their own armies and marched to meet the horde in the Way. Both forces were mighty, and when they clashed the ensuing battle consumed lives like tinder in a blaze. In the end, the forces of Shallai prevailed, and the Bedu armies were routed back into the desert from which they had risen.

Now, in that distant age, the Fist of Shallai was a warrior-king called Gideon, out of the province of Kaine. With the immediate threat of the Bedu eradicated, Gideon looked to the future. He proclaimed that a great barrier should be built in the Way, a mighty wall to seal the Bedu in their wastelands forever. He envisioned a fortress thicker and stronger than anything man had ever made. And so the greatest of the architects were summoned to Jericho, and upon their shoulders was placed the burden of designing Gideon's great wall. They labored day and night for the better part of ten months, and finally stood before the throne to present their plans to Gideon. On that very day the order was given for construction to begin.

And up went the wall between two nations.

The history was a short one, some seven pages tucked at the back of the book as though irrelevant and unnecessary. Del read those pages over and over again, studying them until he scarcely needed the words on the page to tell the story of the mad Bedu leader and his senseless war. He knew there was more to the tale than what was told; no war was ever fought in seven pages. But he was powerless to coax a more descriptive past out of the book. He could not force the space between the lines to fill up with words that had not been written, nor tell a tale that had not been told.

• • •

Some weeks after Del's arrival, a Bedu nomad emerged from the deserts of the south. Standing at the base of the wall, his shouts for attention were nearly lost in the emptiness, and he called up to the abandoned battlements for a full hour before being heard. When finally noticed, a small group of soldiers gathered to jeer. "Look," they said. "The little sand-dog has returned." Cupping hands around grins they called down to him, "Go home, sand-dog. There are no scraps for you here."

From his balcony on the tower Del heard the laughter, and his curiosity lured him to investigate. Some of the soldiers spotted him coming across the battlements, and nudges were passed along until the laughter died. All were facing him by the time he joined the group, not one grin left alive among them. Del looked over the edge of the wall, down to the small figure sitting patiently in the shade of a boulder.

"Who is he?" Del asked.

"Ambassador, Sir," one of the soldiers said. "We were about to send word below to allow him entrance."

Del turned a blank look on the soldier. He was not yet used to his new title, nor to being called 'Sir' by men who were his peers. The soldiers must have misinterpreted his flat stare, for a barely perceptible ripple of nervousness passed among them.

"It is Sumir Attalah, Ambassador," another soldier answered.

Del shifted his gaze, but still said nothing.

"Your Bedu escort, Sir."

Up until that day, Del had never seen a Bedu. Having listened to the soldiers talk of bloodthirsty savages and murderous warriors, his mind had painted a picture for him, and he half-expected the Bedu to appear as tusked demons. He soon found this image to be far from accurate.

Sumir Attalah was an extremely energetic and highly likable man of the Bayt Kathir tribe, which at that time meant nothing to Del. His skin had been burnished dark brown by the sun, and his hair and eyes were blacker than coal. Covering his chin was a sparse growth of dark hair, and a constant grin shone from his face, brilliant white teeth agleam. The tribesman wore a long, square-collared shirt of rough wool that hung straight to his shins. The sleeves were short, and covered only half his wrists. Both cuffs, as well as the hem, were tattered and ripped as though chewed by mice. Cinched around his waist was a simple belt, loosely tied, and about his head was wound a cloth, the ends tucked in at his forehead. Sumir never wore anything on his feet. His soles were hard as leather, and the heat of the sand and the sharpness of the rocks never seemed to bother him.

It was Sumir's duty to cure the new ambassador of his ignorance in all matters concerning the Bedu before taking him into the deserts to the great city of Aba Ajraan.

"You do not look like the other ambassadors," were Sumir's first words to Del. He spoke brokenly, but seemed to have an excellent command of Shallan.

"I know," Del said.

"The others were fat," Sumir continued, unprompted. "And bald."

"I know."

"Are you a great man in your empire?" Sumir wanted to know.

"What do you mean?"

"Are you very much important?"

"I'm a soldier."

Sumir did not understand the word.

"A warrior," Del clarified. "I fight and kill for the empire."

"What do you kill for your empire?"

"Other men. Other warriors from other empires."

Sumir was thoughtful a moment. Eventually, he shook his head mournfully, as though these were things of terrible sadness. "The other ambassadors before you, they were men of great power and honor."

"Is that what they told you?"

"Yes. They said they were mighty men. Very important."

"Did you believe it?"

"No."

"I don't believe it either," Del said.

Sumir smiled then, huge and bright. "I think we will like you more than them," he said.

During the following weeks the two men spent a great deal of time together. Del, who had never been able to sleep past dawn, would wake before the sun and cross the training grounds, still covered with frost from the night, to the place Sumir had pitched his tiny tent behind the soldiers' barracks. Del would crouch at the corner of the barracks, where the wind could not find him, and wait patiently in the cold while inside the soldiers slept in the warmth of their blankets. Most days Sumir would emerge shortly after dawn, dark hair sprouting at irregular angles. The Bedu would cast a bright grin toward Del, then go about his morning ritual while Del watched from a respectful distance.

Upon the frozen ground Sumir would spread a small rug, then kneel to face the rising sun. With frigid water poured into a small calabash, he washed his arms up to the elbow, then with sopping fingers cleaned the sand from his ears, eyes, and nostrils. He would spend five minutes or more chanting quietly, bowing occasionally to touch his forehead to the ground. It was the same every morning, and again at sunset. These were the only times Del ever saw the Bedu tribesman without a grin plastered across his face. When he was finished, the smile would spring back to life, and he would aim it at Del and say, *"Salim shalaid,* Ambassador."

"Salim shalaid," Del would answer. "Did you sleep well?"

"As well as any man who is far from home and family."

Del could only nod. Having no home or family of his own, he wondered if the people who did have them slept any better than he.

One day after watching Sumir's ritual, Del asked to what god he prayed.

Smiling, the little nomad pointed past the rising sun. "In the morning, it is to Ak-Anekhan, the bringer of the sun." He swung his arm across the sky. "In the evening it is to Ko-Khetanakan, the bringer of the moon. Greater than both is the Father."

"Who is the Father?"

"The god of the gods," Sumir said expansively.

"There is a legend in Shallai about that one," Del said.

Sumir stopped smiling.

"The legend tells of a dark prophet with nine sons, and a temple where they burned sacrifices of children." He hesitated when he saw the expression on Sumir's face. He'd not intended to cause remorse, and he felt both ashamed and unkind for speaking so bluntly. Relating violent and bloody stories about ones gods was a poor way of showing respect. He stopped speaking, and looked at the ground. "Shallai's legends don't speak well of your gods," he finished softly, and said no more.

After an uncomfortable silence, Sumir leaned forward to look in Del's eyes. "Do you believe those legends?"

"No," Del answered honestly. He'd never believed the legend of the Prophet held any truth at all. How could he believe in them when he didn't even believe in the Bedu gods? Nor in the host of Shallai's for that matter.

"That is good," Sumir said, and he tried to smile again.

"What is the Father's name?" Del asked.

Sumir regarded him for a long moment, then simply shook his head. "Let us talk of other things today, Ambassador."

They never again spoke of gods or prophets.

• • •

For two long months Sumir Attalah stuffed the new ambassador's head with Bedu beliefs, customs, and history, as well as the Bedu language, a harsh and—in Del's opinion—overly complex dialect. There was nothing simple about the Bedu tongue, and Del's prime complaint was the overabundance of words, followed closely by the presence of far too many subtleties.

"It is a language of beauty," Sumir had told him at a point when the ambassador's frustration with the new language had begun to wear him down.

"There are too many words for the same thing," Del said.

"Not the same thing," Sumir said in a tone meant to soothe. "There are many different ways to see something. Why should there not be a word for each? Imagine you wish to tell your lover she is beautiful. In your barbaric tongue you merely blunder and trip over your words. But among my people you will be able to tell in a thousand ways, all of them unique." He had then smiled broadly, as though basking in the glow of his own imagined lover. "If she is a woman of striking beauty but nothing more, you will tell her she is *ahalailen*. If you yearn to hold her, and walk with her beneath the moon, then she becomes *detze w'haran*. And if you adore her with a great, bursting passion you may wish to call her *maye desse*."

Looking up, the little man saw the ambassador glowering at him.

"There's no need for that," Del said. "From now on I want you to teach me just one word for one thing. If it is a kettle, it's a kettle. If it's a dog, it's a dog. I don't care if it's a toothless dog, or a dead dog. It is still a dog." He held up a mean finger. "One thing. One word."

Sumir had regarded him mournfully. "But you don't understand."

"I don't have time to understand."

"You will miss the beauty."

"I'll find the beauty later."

Despite the inherent complexity of the language, by the time their last day together came, not a word other than the Bedu tongue was spoken between them. And even though Del had been adamant in taking the simplest route to fluency, Sumir has still managed to sneak in a broader base of words than was truly needed in any practical situation, for which Del was quietly grateful.

The day they took their leave of Gideon's Wall, Sumir gave him a robe of the type worn by Bedu men. Del shed his own soft leathers in exchange for the long cotton shirt, and around his waist tied a soft russet sash, also a gift from Sumir. Reluctantly, he gave up his boots, and was afraid that he would be expected to cross the deserts barefoot, like Sumir, until the tribesman provided him with a pair of sandals, little more than leather soles held together with thin straps. To complete the outfit, he was given a long length of soft cloth, which Sumir helped him to wind about his head. "To keep the sun from making your brains soft," Sumir told him, after which he stepped back to grin happily at the new Del. "As though you were born Bedu," he said.

Between Gideon's Wall and the territory of the Ajraan lay three days of gravel plains and emptiness. They set out across the wilderness leading a pair of tired pack mules and enough food and water to get them as far as Ajraan territory. Del always had to smile when he thought of those two sad mules. The poor creatures had seemed hopeless and drained even before beginning the journey.

"There is a well at the very edge of Ajraan territory. We will find an escort there, and they will take you the rest of the way to Aba Ajraan."

"Will you show me your map to the well?"

Sumir shook his head. "No map."

"You don't have a map?"

"No."

"If you don't have a map, how will we find the well?"

Sumir had looked at him strangely. "I know where it is."

Del began to object, but stopped himself. What was the use? If the Bedu didn't see the value of maps, he wasn't going to convince them now. What would the maps contain anyway, pictures of sand? Del changed his line of questioning.

"When we get to the well, how will we find an escort?"

"The desert is full of Bedu."

"And what if none of them wants to go to Aba Ajraan?"

Sumir sighed and shook his head. "You worry too much. What man would not want the honor of bringing our ambassador safely to his new home?"

Despite his own better judgement, Del trusted.

At some point during the first day of their trip, he thought of all the others who had set out just as he was now, and he began the game of figuring his own chances of survival among the Bedu. After hours of casual deliberation, he finally settled on a time-frame of approximately three months—four if his luck proved fit. He had traveled much as a soldier, and he understood how easy it was for an outsider, alone and friendless in a city of strangers, to take one wrong step and find himself dead.

At dusk of the third day they reached the well, which, to Del's disappointment, was nothing more than a shallow puddle of murky water surrounded by thorn bushes. The dry brush seemed like a pack of greedy old men huddled together to protect the last of their precious water.

Sumir struck a fire, then nearly smothered it with handfuls of soaked grass. The wet reeds sent up a pillar of gray smoke into the windless sky.

Less than two hours later they were joined by a band of rugged Bedu warriors. Sumir spotted them on the horizon early in the afternoon, and roused Del from napping to watch them come. The Bedu warriors had been camped some distance away, and had come after seeing the pillar of smoke. They were a hard and silent group, mounted on beasts the likes of which Del had never seen. The faces of the animals were long, almost childlike in their innocence, and their thin legs and knobby knees often wobbled, so it seemed they would break. Twisting their long necks in impossible directions, the animals were constantly foraging for green bites from nearby bushes. Their strangest feature by far were the humps upon their backs. Just behind their curly withers were rounded hills topped with shaggy tufts of fur.

"The camels were made for the desert," Sumir said to him while Del marveled at the beasts up close. "For two weeks they can travel without water, as long as there is good grazing." He patted the animal on its long neck, and fondly rubbed the muscle of its leg. "These are much more suited for desert travel than those creatures," and he indicated Del's pair of sad donkeys, which were trying to hide from the sun under a leafless bush.

The tribesmen were clothed much the same as Sumir, with long shirts, and cloths wrapped about their faces and heads. They had brought fresh water to drink, as well as bread and figs to eat, and they shared everything they had. After releasing their camels to graze among the sparse bushes of the well, they crouched down to trade news with Sumir, and listened as he explained to them that Del was the new ambassador, and that he needed an escort to Aba Ajraan. The nomads agreed readily, as though nothing else in all the desert vied for their attention. Del sat with them the while, attentive to the subtle difference in accents and speech patterns. No one spoke to him, and he never said a word.

Early the next day, Sumir bid him farewell and good luck, then turned westward toward the lands of the Bayt Kathir, leaving Del alone with the Ajraan tribesmen.

Only after Sumir was gone did Del become acutely aware of how poorly he fit among the Ajraan. One of the tribesmen presented a camel for him to ride, and led her to Del when it was time for them to leave. "This is Ubajjal," the Bedu said to him. "She is a fine animal. She will carry you to Aba Ajraan." Using a short white stick crooked at one end, the warrior tapped Ubajjal's neck, coaxing her to her knees. He demonstrated how to use her neck as a step to the saddle.

"Now you," the warrior told him, handing him the camel stick. Del pulled himself easily enough into the high seat, but no sooner was he settled, reigns in one hand, camel stick in the other, than the Bedu clicked his tongue and Ubajjal surged to her feet—at which point Del promptly toppled off. The camel gave him a sour look when she was forced to kneel once more, and they began again. The second time Del was prepared for the jolting tilt and rise, and he managed to keep himself mounted.

For two days they traveled south, every step distancing Del from all that was familiar. The gravel plains rose into dry hills plagued with boulders, and gullies carved by flash floods cut across the dirt like scars. Only occasionally did they cross a wide tract of sand, the fingers of the desert exploring new territories. Standing at the edge of a salt flat one morning, Del marveled at how much the land appeared a frozen tundra, something he might have seen far to the north. Only when the sun rose and the temperature soared did the illusion disintegrate. Del decided that aside from the flats and the sand, the whole terrain seemed one vast, disorganized pile of rocks.

Everything changed when they neared the Ashkelon.

Originating in the stony mountains far to the west, the waters of the Ashkelon carved a track of life through four of the seven Bedu territories, and colored a wide belt of green through the otherwise drab expanse of sand and heat. Through the flatlands of the Dahm it curled, then down into the low, rocky hills and red cliffs of the Ajraan and the Nadalii, and finally through the towering dunes blanketing the territory of the Saar. Beyond Saar territories the Ashkelon curved south to disappear into the Sands, the deep and unexplored desert interior.

They followed the Ashkelon upstream, and all along the way began to see the signature of civilization. Across the wide and shallow river he spotted a long-haired boy tending sheep. The boy was barefoot, clad only in a cloth skirt wrapped around his waist. He balanced on one foot and his staff, watching the line of camels and riders pass while his flock crowded the stony bank to drink from the river. They passed sprawling encampments where Bedu herdsmen and their extended families tended flocks and cultivated olive groves and orchards. The tents they lived in were huge and elaborate, and the villages vibrant with activity. There was not a single encampment they passed where women did not call out, and groups of men did not rush forth to greet them, insisting they come to be guests in their tents; to eat, drink, and rest before traveling on.

"We cannot come," Del's escorts would say. "We have the new ambassador from Shallai with us, and we are taking him to Aba Ajraan."

"Let him come too!"

But his escorts were firm, and always refused. Instead, they accepted handfuls of dates and bowls of fresh water, which they drank while riding, then handed back to the children who trotted happily alongside their camels, eager for a glance, or a pat on the head. Nearly two days passed this way, until at last they came to the city of Aba Ajraan.

Forever the undisputed hub of the Bedu nation, Aba Ajraan filled a wide and fertile basin created by a bend of the Ashkelon. It was a city of whitewashed mud-brick houses, of flat roofs and wide streets. Temples were plentiful, and fronted by pillars of polished marble and towering statues three times the size of a man. From what he knew of the Bedu religion, these giant sculptures, carved in sharp angles and odd proportions, were either likenesses of their stern gods or the solitary prophet of the Father. As he rode beneath them, the faces of chiseled stone glowered down on him as though they alone knew him as an impostor. Passing through their shadows infected him with chills.

Leaving the temple district, they passed though a bazaar, a maze of tents and stalls crowded with men, animals, and merchants. There was a great deal of shouting and laughter, and all around them were the noises of bartering and money changing hands. There were scents and music, the quick and flighty sound of flutes dancing around the beat of a snare. The Ajraan tribesmen led their camels slowly through the throng. Del was unsuccessful in ignoring the blatant stares he attracted.

At the very center of the city, rising above the sprawl surrounding it, stood a vast and towering structure of alabaster stones and pillars thrusting up like the trunks of great trees. The tribesmen explained to him that this was the ancient palace, abandoned after the execution of the final sultan to rule the Bedu. Gazing up at the palace grounds, Del marveled at the architecture. Dominated by curves and arches, with balconies and halls left open to the air, and terraces overflowing with flowering vines, the palace of the Bedu seemed a place of wonder.

That same day Del was presented to the kalif of the Ajraan.

The kalif was a hard man, stern and solid as a battle-worn bull. A descendant of the Prophet's eldest son, Ajraan, Ibn Khan was the figurehead of his people, the icon of the Bedu nation. Covering the left side of his thick neck, from jaw to collarbone, was the stain of an intricate tattoo. Long years had faded the markings, and Del did not learn until much later that the tattoo was the brand of the ken'dari, the warrior elite of the Bedu. Although the kalif's dark hair and clipped beard were shocked with the white of encroaching old age, he still looked like the sort of man Del would not wish to cross on a battlefield. Standing a full head taller than Del, who was by no account small, the kalif of Ajraan looked down on him without any kind of fondness.

"He's not fat like the others," the kalif Ibn Khan commented to the men who had escorted Del in. He spoke as though Del weren't present. "This one might last more than ten days."

"*Salim shalaid*, Kalif," Del said with a polite bow. "And I thank you for the compliment."

Astonishment registered in Ibn Khan's eyes for a brief second, but then his brows furrowed to conceal it. He looked to Del's escorts, then back to Del. He cocked his head to one side. "You speak the Bedu tongue. The others never learned more than a few words, barely enough to ask for more food."

"I'm not like the others," Del said plainly.

The kalif placed Del under closer examination, noting the stance, the posture, and the muscles clearly visible even beneath his shirt.

"No, you are not," he said. "You don't look like an ambassador."

"Neither fat, nor bald," Del said.

The kalif's eyes thinned. He left with nothing more said.

According to Del, it was not a good start.

Three months, he thought as he watched the kalif of Ajraan departing. *They'll be sending my corpse home in three months.*

• • •

When the three months Del had allotted himself to live came and went, and still he was not dead, he began to understand how badly the Bedu had been misjudged, and how skewed were the impressions pushed on him by others. Not only that, but he thought he understood why Shallai had finally opted to send a soldier as ambassador instead of yet another pampered old codger. The over-indulgent dignitaries sent before him most likely never had real reason to fear for their lives, except maybe in the twitching of their paranoid imaginations. They had returned home because they could not stomach the food of a culture other than their own, drink the bitter water of the desert, or stand the sweltering days and frigid nights for one minute more. In short, they had been unable, or simply unwilling, to adapt. Del on the other hand, after serving nearly twenty years as a soldier in Shallai's army, had become an old hand at the art of adaptation.

He could scarcely believe that five years had passed since that hot morning he and Sumir walked into the desert and left Gideon's Wall behind. On nights when sleep eluded him, he tried to remember the days of his first month among the Bedu. He had forgotten more of that time than he liked, but some impressions had been permanently fixed in his mind, and they stayed with him still—such as the stubborn insistence of the Bedu on displaying kindness and respect. He had expected hatred and bitterness, the kind of insidious treachery a prisoner might direct toward his jailer. But for his first month in Aba Ajraan he had not been able to walk the city without being invited inside a dozen homes along the way.

They gave him food and *jaffela*, the sweet red wine customarily offered only to honored guests, and asked him to tell stories of Shallai. It seemed they cared little or nothing for Gideon's Wall, or what stood beyond it. The deserts were not their prison, but their home.

They were patient with his incomplete mastery of their language, and when he left they stood in the doorways and called out, *Ak-Anekhan be with you!* It was six months before the merchants in any of the markets would accept his money. "Take!" they would say, regardless of what he was buying. "A humble gift from my family to the ambassador."

He vividly recalled one instance in which a Bedu nomad had caught him admiring one of his camels. "Take!" the nomad had insisted, and only after fifteen minutes of arguing did Del manage to convince him that, although it was an exceedingly fine camel, in the end it would be much happier with its present owner. The nomad finally conceded, and instead of the camel, offered him an expensive cloth belt woven from rich silk, which Del accepted and wore immediately. He had rushed away from the encounter before the nomad decided it would be good to offer him a daughter.

Five years he had spent among the Bedu, and still he wondered if his understanding would ever stretch to fully accommodate them.

Three

Twice a year, once in the fall and again in the spring, Del journeyed to Gideon's Wall for the purpose of making a report to Deacon Manzig. He had never enjoyed his visits with the deacon, as Ian Manzig was habitually rude, never bothering to soften his contempt for the 'sand-dogs'. From their very first meeting, the deacon had made it all too clear that he had lost more sleep over the care and feeding of the lice in the soldiers' barracks than he ever would for the state of affairs among the Bedu. His loathing knew no bounds.

The first time Del returned to the wall, Ian Manzig had already managed to entirely forget who he was. Only after being reminded by his aide, a sickly looking soldier with heavy bags under his eyes and a mop of greasy hair, did the dim light of recognition flicker in the deacon's eyes. He took a long moment to eye Del's foreign clothing, and his contemptuous sneer traveled the ambassador head to toe.

"You've become one of them," the deacon had said abruptly, as though it were cause for great shame. "You look like a sand-dog now. I barely recognized you." Without meaning to, Del looked down at himself. His feet, covered only by sandals, were dirty and haggard from his journey up through the desert. He was dry, hot, and thirsty, and his long shirt was torn in several places from thorns and rocks. It was true that from a distance he could have easily been mistaken for a Bedu nomad, at least by someone who wasn't Bedu, and it was also true that he had not bothered to smooth his rugged appearance on the deacon's behalf. He looked back at the deacon, but made no apologies for himself.

"I've come to make a report," he said.

"Has it been six months already?" With a burdened sigh, he fell into his chair and propped his feet on the table, aiming the soles of his dingy boots at Del.

From the pack he had brought with him, Del produced a handful of bound sheaves. Stepping forward, he dropped the report on the table at the deacon's feet. Ian Manzig looked at it strangely, then leaned forward slightly, as though he had missed something important.

"What's this?" he asked.

"My report," Del said. A pause. "I assume you read?"

The deacon looked up sharply. Although there had been no disrespect in Del's tone, Ian felt that the ambassador's question was an insult only thinly disguised. In defense, he gave Del a hard stare. "Yes," he said shortly. "I'm able." As Del stood by calmly, he leafed the pages with his thick thumb, clearly frustrated at the idea of actually putting forth the effort to read the report in its entirety. He seemed exhausted just being near so many words. After carefully arranging the papers in a neat and proper pile, he moved them to the side, dropped his feet to the stone floor, and rose slowly.

"Thank you, Ambassador," he said. "I believe we are done."

Del didn't move. He didn't know what he should have expected, but it certainly wasn't this. He had been distinctly commanded by the chancellors to return to the wall every six months with full reports. Surely Shallai did not intend the information he gleaned to be wasted on the likes of Ian Manzig. Where were the chancellors? Where were the dignitaries of the Fist, the makers of treaties and trade agreements? Where were the people who cared? All of these thoughts came and went in an incomprehensible rush. He couldn't move, because if he walked away then it was over. His report was hardly four feet away, a small wealth of information compiled into a handful of pages, which he suspected would find its way to the latrines behind the barracks as soon as he had gone.

The deacon raised an eye at him. "Is there something more you care to say, Ambassador?"

Del looked at him directly. "Have you no questions for me?"

The deacon was silent for a moment, then his eyes narrowed. "Let me tell you something . . . *Ambassador*," he said, putting just enough of a twist on the title to make it derogatory. "I'm not very interested in the Bedu, and I'm not very interested in reading about them, or asking questions about them. In fact, unless you come to me and say that the sand-dogs have suddenly been swallowed by the desert, I'm not very interested in anything about them at all. Do I make myself clear?"

Before that moment, Del had thought he merely disliked the deacon. But just then he began to realize that his dislike had rapidly burgeoned into something far more powerful. Out of respect for something—whether it was the idea of authority or the greater good of Shallai—he kept his tongue under tight rein and his composure intact. There was nothing more he could do.

"You've made your point, Deacon."

"Good. Then we understand one another."

Del marched for the door, eager to be gone.

"Dismissed," the deacon said to his back.

• • •

In the spring of the thirty-fourth year of Goliath Endekin's reign as Fist of Shallai, the Mugh-shin initiated war with the empire. Thrusting across the Geijin strait and into the northwestern provinces, they came on the backs of mammoths, tusks tipped with steel and hooves shod in iron. Despite heavy fortifications and many soldiers, the city of Riddick fell in a battle that lasted only two days. The Mugh-shin occupied the city, and from there staged waves of strikes penetrating the mainland toward Jericho itself. Del had been among the Bedu for two years when the invasion began, but did not learn of it until much later. For more than three years Ian Manzig delighted in his secret, willfully neglecting to share information with the ambassador.

Del's trips to Gideon's Wall had long since become trials of patience and temper. The deacon never gave him audience right away, and because he was at the mercy of the deacon's whims, Del was forced to confine himself in the bare chamber where he had slept when he first came to the wall. It was always colder than he remembered in that high stone room. He would sit on the edge of the sagging cot, with only the spiders to keep him company, until the deacon tired of his game and sent for him. A wait of several days wasn't unusual. When finally summoned, Del would deliver the pages of his report and immediately leave. He never stayed longer than necessary, and rarely was more than a word spoken between them.

On one occasion, the deacon kept him waiting longer than usual. Five days passed before he finally summoned Del, and when the ambassador came to him, he was seated as usual at the only chair at his table, tips of his boots pointed skyward.

Without a word, Del crossed the chamber toward the deacon, and once he came close enough, became aware that the man had been drinking heavily, although it was barely midday. He had the telltale reek of stale wine and sour breath. The deacon's bleary eyes followed his every move, and plastered across his unshaven face was the self-righteous smirk Del had grown to despise so much.

Ian was always so proud of himself for maintaining his charade of importance, and Del could hardly stand to look at him without grinding his teeth. Without a word, he dropped his report on the table, and immediately turned to leave.

"No greetings from you today, Ambassador?"

Del halted. An instinct told him to keep walking, but this he ignored. "Greetings, Deacon," he responded in a bland tone flat with forced formality. "I trust my visit finds you well?"

Del heard the deacon chuckling heavily behind him, thrilled with some secret joke, and he shifted his glance to the side, as though he could twist his eyes around to see behind his back. But he did not turn. He hoped he wouldn't stay long enough to warrant it.

"Come," Ian said. "Talk with me a while, Ambassador."

"But what will we speak of, Deacon?"

"We are both soldiers. We'll find something."

Del mulled over three of four excuses to leave, but discarded them all. With the uncanny impression of stepping into a trap, he turned at last to face the deacon. Ian Manzig held the report in his hands, flipping the pages idly, but reading nothing. The smirk was still on his face, and it broadened when Del turned. Del thought that the deacon looked fatter than on his last visit. On the table was a half-finished goblet of red wine, which the deacon grabbed and emptied with a quick toss over his shoulder. Fatter and drunker. After refilling it, he slid it toward Del. "Drink," he said. "We have much to discuss."

Del's eyes touched on the goblet, but he did not move.

"No? Suit yourself. I've been meaning to ask you for some time now, do you really think the Fist cares what happens here?"

"We are an occupied territory of the empire. Why would the Fist not care?"

The deacon shrugged slowly. "These are troubled times for Shallai. The Fist has a great deal on his mind. There is rebellion among the provinces of the east, and the war with Mugh-shin only makes matters more complex."

A shock ripped through Del. "We're at war with Mugh-shin?"

The deacon acted innocently surprised. "Surely you knew?"

Del tried to keep calm, but it was a supreme effort. "You know that I have no contact with Shallai other than you, Deacon. How am I to know anything unless I am told?"

"Did I not tell you last time you visited?" He squinted his eyes, making a mockery of trying to remember an event he knew had never taken place. "War is no small matter. I can't imagine forgetting to mention something of such importance."

"How long?"

"More than two years now." But then he brushed it away with one hand. "It's of no consequence. What I want you to understand is that with the Mugh-shin war, the unrest in the east, and the constant threat from the Shadrakan empire, there is little time left for the Fist to devote to the comings and goings of the sanddogs, don't you agree?"

"I *don't* agree," Del denied.

The deacon's grin vanished. Ian Manzig was a man who understood the gauntlet through which Del's reports passed. The ambassador's carefully written and lengthy reports were stripped of detail and condensed by the deacon's aides before being sent northward to Jericho. Within the halls of the Keep, the reports passed up a chain of prefects and statesmen, each step of the way suffering from further compression before being presented to the Fist's high chancellor. If the chancellor found time, which was rare, he glanced over what had become of Del's original report. If he deemed it important enough, he summarized for the Fist. What Del did not know, and what Ian Manzig only suspected, was that after four years and eight reports, not one had ever climbed as far as the high chancellor.

Ian Manzig breathed heavily through his nose. "Tell me, Ambassador," he snarled. "What is your purpose among the Bedu?"

"Why don't you tell me, Deacon."

"But what fun would that be? I want you to understand this, Ambassador. I want you to see what I see, and understand what I do. If I give you all the answers, what do you learn?"

"I don't have time to play games."

"We are not playing games, Ambassador. We are finding truths."

"Then get on with it."

The deacon's anger flared. "You've been duped, Ambassador. If you believe the lies Shallai has told you then you are as stupid as the sand-dogs."

"What lies?"

"Pull your head out of the sand! Shallai knew, long before you or I, that war was brewing with the Mugh-shin, and Shallai is well aware of the constant threat from the Shadrakans. Shallai is powerful, but we do not have the resources to fight three wars at once. The Bedu are going to have to wait their turn. Gideon's Wall is a temporary solution to a problem that cannot be addressed just yet; a cork in the neck of a bottle." To illustrate, he made a fist and smacked his palm over top of it. "I am simply the watchman of the cork. And you . . ." He chuckled deeply, pointing a thick finger at Del. "You are something else entirely. I hope you understand that you're not meant to be an ambassador forever. You play the part for now, and you do very well with your reports and those sand-dog rags you call clothes. But these things are for appearances only. 'Ah,' the sand-dogs will say. 'Shallai wants to forge peace with us. Look, they have sent an ambassador.' But they are wrong. Shallai only wants to keep them believing there will be peace until the time comes for war. When that time comes, you'll be given new orders, and do you know what those orders will be? Would you like to guess?" He glared at Del a long moment, then shook his head in disappointment when no guess was ventured.

"You're not an ambassador. You're an *assassin*."

"You're wrong."

"Really?" Ian Manzig snorted. "Then why did Shallai send a hired sword to do the job of a diplomat?"

When Del had no answer to give, Ian shook his head. "You live in a soldier's world, Ambassador. You follow orders without understanding why. You see nothing." He downed the rest of his wine, then slammed the goblet to the table and wiped his dripping

80

mouth with the back of his hand. "Keep writing your reports, Ambassador, if it helps you sleep better at night. But at least open your eyes."

Del's anger was gone. In its place, churning slowly in the pit of his stomach, was fear of the possibility that Ian Manzig might be right. The deacon must have seen the dim light of suspicion in his eyes, because when he leaned forward to peer into Del's face, a cruel smile turned his lips.

"Ah," he said. "The assassin begins to understand."

Del instantly wiped all emotion from his face, shielding his feelings with a cold barrier. He hated to be read. "I don't believe the Fist thinks like you."

"Perhaps not," Ian admitted readily enough. "But I can tell you for certain that he does not think like *you*."

Del was already headed for the door. His thoughts had become a circus. He imagined the battle at Riddick, already three years past. He thought of how possible it might be for the armies of Shallai to turn their attention southward once the war with the Mugh-shin was finished, and he wondered if one day he would wake to find armies surrounding Aba Ajraan, and orders in his hand telling him to put a knife in the kalif's back.

"You're a naive man, Del," the deacon called after him. "Don't make the mistake of thinking the rest of the world shares in your stupidity."

Suddenly, Del stopped and turned. "Why do you hate me?"

"Because you're one of *them*."

"Then why do you hate them?"

The deacon spread his hands in a exasperated gesture of mock helplessness. "Because I am bored, and have nothing else to do, Ambassador."

Ian Manzig, still glowering, followed Del to the door, and slammed it at his heels. From beyond the thick wood, Del heard a muffled "Dismissed!"

Book Three
The Bedu

"The thing that does not die is the honor of a deed done mightily."

—Bedu proverb

One

Harness bells jangled in the dead heat of the wasted lands bordering the Sands. The camels of the Saar caravan were tied head to
tail, and they shuffled in a single file line across the desert at a tired
pace, their cloven hooves beating a thin, endless track across the
shifting sand. With necks bending and stretching in time with their
gait, the bells strung along their harnesses kept steady rhythm, and
the bright purple and gold tassels hanging from their halters
bounced and swayed as though dancing.

Piled upon their humped backs were goods to be traded or sold,
heavy bundles secured with rough rope and leather straps. There
were long, tightly rolled rugs of brilliant colors, and reed baskets
over-stuffed with figs and dates, while others contained the beans

of the queffa bush or the dried and cured leaves of the jaela. All would be traded away among other tribes, and the baskets would be filled again with fresh goods to be traded elsewhere. Trudging beside their laden animals, the Saar tribesmen kept their camels aimed toward the setting sun by tapping them with white sticks crooked at one end.

The caravan had come out of Nadalli territory, bumping for days across stony plains as it followed the western trade route through barren stretches of salt flats and past ranges of low black hills. Curving along the outer fringes of the Sands, the traders kept the high dunes of the desert interior to the south. After many days the route had finally brought them to the string of oases that marked the western border of Haaj territory. Coming out of the wastelands, the palms and long grasses seemed a paradise.

Entering the oasis while the sun was still high, the Saar tended to their camels before themselves. They worked quickly to unload the beasts, laying their loads on the powdery sands, then leading the animals to the shallow watercourse that was the heart of the oasis. Reeds grew thick and long at the water's edge, and the throaty burping of bullfrogs hiding in the mud stopped only when the tribesmen ventured too close. The Saar filled leather buckets with water, and the camels crowded together to eagerly drink their fill. Only after the animals had been cared for did the Saar drink for themselves.

A small fire was built near the edge of the oasis, and wet reeds were piled upon the flames, sending plumes of gray smoke into the dusty sky. The signal fire would inform the Haaj of their presence, and an escort from a nearby encampment would be sent to bring them into the territory. All through the late afternoon and early evening the Saar let their fire smolder.

As evening fell, the sky darkened to a deep blue-black and stars poked through the roof of the heaven. Several of the Saar stayed awake by the fire, their swords close at hand. The deserts between the tribal territories were uninhabited and unforgiving, and as far south as they were, there was need for caution. Sthaak were ever roaming into the territories at odd intervals, and it was not unknown for them to steal sleeping traders from their camps, leaving a tapering trail of gore and screams into a black desert night. Such abductions were frequent enough to make traveling too near the unmarked border of the Sands a dangerous gamble.

But the night passed quietly. The cool air was thick with the sweet smell of figs and sugar from the baskets, and it filled their dreams with riches. All night the frogs spoke across the water one to another, and the little black crickets in the reeds played their music. In the morning the sun rose, and they covered the fire with more soaked reeds. All day the pillar of smoke rose to the sky. But no escort came.

Three days they waited.

On the fourth morning, Al Sadat stood belligerently at the rim of the oasis. He shaded his eyes with a sun-browned hand, fat fingers laden with gold rings and precious gems. He could not remember ever having waited more than a day for an escort into any of the Bedu territories, and his mood was spoiling as quickly as his figs. He glanced at the two Saar tribesmen tending the fire. He would have told them to make it bigger, but they had done so yesterday, and it was already twice as big as it needed to be. Al Sadat scowled. "They're not coming," he said to his son.

"They will come."

"If they were coming they would have done so already."

"Maybe they cannot see our smoke."

"They can see our smoke from Aba Ajraan there is so much of it," Al Sadat snapped. "If we make more smoke we will block the sun." He continued to stare into the desert, as though by the mere act of watching the emptiness he could make the Haaj escort appear out of a mirage. "We will go in without them," he declared.

"It is not customary, Father."

"Is it customary to keep us waiting three days? My dates are spoiling. If the dates spoil who will buy them?" Again there was a long silence. He also had in his many baskets a small chest full of uncut emeralds. These he was not concerned about. The emeralds were for the Jaggi only, and at the outpost they traded the finest steel weapons for them. No, he was hardly concerned about the emeralds, nor the dried *queffa* and packages of salt, which did not spoil. But the chest of emeralds was only very small, and he did not have much *queffa* or salt. Most of his cargo this trip consisted of baskets brimming with figs and dates, which were unhappy being too long under the sun. Spoiled figs were bad for business, and bad business meant less money, and less money meant unhappy wives. Ultimately, unhappy wives could induce ruin.

"We will go without them," Al Sadat declared, then uttered the punctuating grunt of finality that succeeded all decisions of importance. He waved an impatient and heavily ringed hand at his son. "Pack the goods, we leave now. Tell the men to pack everything."

Without giving his son the opportunity to relay his order, he immediately stormed off toward the camels, shouting out orders that went unobeyed as he passed. "I said pack everything! We leave now. Put that fire out. Go! Move!" He could be heard clapping his hands sharply. "The time is now. The figs will not wait."

Ahmad, the eldest son of Al Sadat, watched his father leave. Crouched by the fire, five or six of the Saar tribesmen were looking after Al Sadat with blank stares. They had not moved. When Al Sadat passed out of sight, their eyes swiveled to his son. Ahmad sighed heavily. "Pack up," he told them wearily.

His order was obeyed.

As soon as he was alone, the trader's son crouched on his heels and gazed into Haaj territory. He drew a small Jaggi knife from the hidden sheath at his wrist, and toyed with it. After a moment he set the edge against his palm. The steel of the blade was pure and smooth. It had been able to cut bone when he'd bought it, and had never needed sharpening in three years.

He drew the blade lightly across the soft flesh of his hand, slicing through the pale tangle of scars already there. Blood welled up, and he watched it thoughtfully as it pooled in his palm. He didn't feel pain until a few moments had passed, and even then it came as a cool, dull throb.

Ahmad closed his hand to a fist and squeezed until red trickled to the sand between his feet. The spilled blood carved a pattern in the sand, which he studied with casual expertise.

"Bad luck," he said to himself, shaking his head slowly. He flicked his wrist at the sand, and a spray of blood from his palm splattered across his runes, destroying the meaning he had interpreted in them. He rose, wiping his bloodied palm against the black of his robe. Gripping a piece of cloth from his sash, he held it tightly in his cut hand while wrapping it around his fist, then pulled it snug. He shook his head again. "Very bad luck."

• • •

Haaj territory hugged the borders of the Sands. Towering to the south were the first of the mountainous dunes which dominated the uncharted desert interior. The Saar caravan had stopped in a shallow valley that opened into the place the Haaj encampments had once been.

Side by side, Ahmad and his father stared into a plain littered with torn tents and broken poles. All that remained of the Haaj was a landscape of desolation. There were still bodies, but most of the corpses had been covered with drifts as winds from the desert labored to bury the dead in a shallow grave of sand.

"What has caused this?" Al Sadat wondered in horror.

Grimly, Ahmad shook his head.

"Jaggi?" Al Sadat pressed.

"Maybe. Maybe another tribe."

Al Sadat chewed thoughtfully on the inside of his cheek. "There has not been war among the tribes for many years," he reminded his son.

"There has *never* been war with the Jaggi."

Long moments passed, then finally Ahmad half-turned to the tribesmen behind him, and with one hand signaled them forward. He followed immediately after, proceeding bravely into the waste of the Haaj encampment.

"What are you doing?" his father called anxiously.

"I'm going to find answers."

"It is dangerous!"

"Stay with your figs, Father. I will not be long."

Ahmad explored the sprawling ruin of the Haaj encampment, feeling as though he were treading on freshly laid graves. The other tribesmen had fanned out around him to pick through the ruin, careful to never stray too far or wander out of sight. As he walked, the glint of sun touching something shiny caught Ahmad's eye, and he went to investigate. Whatever it was remained wrapped in a piece of canvas nearly buried by the sand. He sank to his knees beside the torn canvas and gripped it with both hands. Pulling upwards, he dragged most of it from the grip of the desert, then brushed the sand away from the glimmering object that had caught his eye.

It was a bauble the size of a child's fist, and it rested heavily in his palm. Staring at it closely, he found that the murky inside seemed to be shifting subtly. He continued to watch, and became dimly aware of how hot the orb was in his hand. It was difficult to hold, but the smoky heart of it was beautiful, and he continued to stare. It wasn't even a moment later that he began to realize how uncomfortable he had become. The sun seemed ten feet over his shoulder instead of crawling down into the western dunes. There was a scratching sensation deep in his throat. Suddenly dry and painful, his eyes blinked, and a prickling discomfort made him squint painfully, as though sand had burrowed beneath his lids. His vision blurred.

Dropping the orb, Ahmad leaned forward and rubbed his eyes until they watered profusely. The tears eased the pain, and he continued to blink rapidly to restore his vision. Abruptly realizing how dry his throat was, he swallowed roughly, and tasted dirt in his mouth. Running a parched tongue through his cheeks, he discovered bits of sand there, and grit around his teeth. He spit while uncorking his waterskin, raising it to his lips. But instead of the water he was expecting, a rush of fine sand spilled into his mouth. Gagging and choking, he did all he could to rid his mouth of the dry grains, and with a curse he turned the skin over, dumping the sand at his feet. With a rough cough he spit sand. It was as though the golden grains were invading every part of him.

Ahmad's eyes went to the orb lying in the sand. Quickly, he stuffed it into a small sack and looped it through his sash. His father had followed behind him, and now came to look over his shoulder.

"What have you found, Ahmad?"

"Nothing," Ahmad said. He had suddenly grown nervous, and he lifted his eyes to the dunes around them.

"I thought I saw—"

"We should leave now," Ahmad interrupted. "This place is not safe." Before his father could object, Ahmad put two fingers in his mouth and whistled once, quick and sharp. The tribesmen immediately halted their searching and started back toward him. One of them handed him an object he had found in the sand. It was a thick scale, roughly leaf shaped and nearly the size of hand laid flat.

"Sthaak," Ahmad said with some disgust. He turned it over in his hand, then tossed it to the sand. The sthaak had most likely come after the fact to gorge themselves on dead flesh. Few things attracted sthaak like a corpse.

The last of the tribesmen were gathering to him when Ahmad happened to lift his eyes to the great dunes bordering the Sands. There he saw a lone figure watching them from the crest. The distance was too great to make out his features, but he was robed in black, his head and face wrapped tight as though to protect every inch of him from the sun. In his hand he held a thick rod, which seemed equally capable of acting as a staff or a weapon. Ahmad slapped his father's shoulder and pointed. "Jaggi," he said with a troubled frown.

"A hunter?" his father asked nervously.

"I can't tell. But it looks big."

"Look at its hands," Al Sadat said anxiously, squinting at the lone figure as though able to discern such fine detail at such great distance. "You can tell by its hands."

"I said I can't tell," Ahmad snapped.

"What's it doing here?"

"It doesn't matter," Ahmad decided. "Let's go."

"But it *does* matter," Al Sadat insisted, his sudden sense of justice swamping his fear. "What if it saw what happened here? What if it's responsible?"

"All the more reason to leave!" Ahmad hissed. "Don't be a fool, Father. The Jaggi have never interfered with the Bedu, nor we with them. Why would they start now by destroying an entire encampment?" He glanced back to the dune—and his glare hardened instinctively. During their brief but heated exchange, two more of the black robed figures had stepped to the crest.

"Look!" Al Sadat rasped. "There are three!"

"I see them."

"There are three Jaggi now!"

"I see them, Father."

Both men at once decided the time to leave was past due. Having ventured quite a distance into the Haaj encampment, they were a long way from their caravan, and when they turned from the Jaggi on the dune to start back, they were shocked to see two more Jaggi standing by their train of camels. Now Ahmad could tell for certain; these were Jaggi hunters without a doubt. They stood taller than the camels, holding the reigns so the frightened animals could not pull free.

"This is not good," Al Sadat said, then cursed violently once again, more out of anger than fear. "What are they doing here? What do they want from us?"

Calmly, Ahmad turned his eyes back to the crest of the dune. Where there had been three Jaggi, there were now fifty . . . and now a hundred.

Then came the dreadnaught.

Ahmad had seen a Jaggi dreadnaught once before, but it had

been long ago, and the vessel had been so far out in the deep desert that it had seemed part of another world. They had never—*never* come this far north. But now there it was, a monstrous vessel rising ponderously over the sandy mountain, sails fat with hot wind. Its hull was a smooth, dark wood, and it bulged at the bottom as though built for the oceans. The sheer bulk of it drifted at them slowly, and the air swelled with the vibration of a thousand deep voices all intoning the same dreary note. The sound of it resonated deep in his bones, filling his body with trembling.

As though one was not enough, behind it came another. The massive bodies of the airborne dreadnaughts obliterated the sun and cast the ruined Haaj encampment into deepest shadow.

Scant moments ago, Ahmad had not trusted his first feelings, but the arrival of the dreadnaughts had cleared all doubt from his mind. The Jaggi were responsible for the annihilation of the Haaj.

As the dreadnaughts moved into place high above, the hunters started down the dune.

Most of the Bedu tribesmen were scrambling for weapons or places to hide, and some of them had dropped what they carried and fled. Ahmad sighed deeply. Where would they hide that the Jaggi hunters could not find them? It was better to die fighting.

Calmly, he drew his curved sword and stood his ground, watching the advancing hunters. This was not how he had hoped to die, but it was better than many ways he could imagine.

At least the Jaggi kept their blades sharp.

Two

It was three days past the winter solstice when the kalifs from the outer tribes crossed into Ajraan territory. Together, they represented three of the seven Bedu tribes: the Saar, the Nadalii, and the Bayt Kathir. Messengers came ahead of them like leaves blown before a storm, hunched over the powerful necks of stallions bred by the master horsemen of the Saar. They pushed the beasts to their limits, racing across barren plains and beneath cliffs of red stone. The messengers reached Aba Ajraan two full days before the kalifs, and the news of their coming spread like blood spilled into water.

On a frigid desert night the kalifs caught up with the harbingers of their coming. It was late, and the sun had long ago fallen below the western cliffs, dragging with it all the colors of evening, and leaving a bare sky littered with stars. On the southern banks of the Ashkelon, in the shallow dunes just beyond the outskirts of the city, a tent had been erected to receive them. Soft fleece had been spread on the floor of the tent, and water drawn from the river was heating in clay pots over open fires. Finely ground *queffa* beans had been added to create the black and pungent brew favored by the Bedu on cold nights. Although the shelter was closed tight, the desert winds were persistent, and they struggled to encroach on the warmth sealed within the tent. Pushing against the hides from outside, they probed the loose overlaps for torn seams and hidden gaps.

Del sat with the kalif Ibn Khan and his firstborn son, Jiharra. They were quietly awaiting the arrival of the kalifs. They had been alone for some time, and they sat around the small fire, gray smoke from the boiling *queffa* curling toward the slanted ceiling. The three men were comfortable in the silence, having already said much of what needed to be said. When finally the heavy drapes at the mouth of the tent parted, they looked up expectantly together.

"They have come," said a breathless Bedu messenger.

Del watched the drapes fall closed on their last moments of peace and stillness. "They won't want me here," he said to Ibn Khan.

The kalif and his son were already rising to their feet. "They never do."

A moment later the drapes were drawn aside. Del and Jiharra moved to stand slightly behind Ibn Khan, and they studied each of the kalifs as they entered. The Bedu of the desert interior were a stern, uncompromising breed, and their kalifs were no less toughened than the people they governed. Dark of hair and skin, the lines of their lives were etched into hardened faces. He had met with these men before, had seen them many times, and had come to expect their pride and stubbornness. But this night was different. This night they were burdened with grievous woes. He was disquieted by the impression of great age they conveyed, as though gloom and defeat had seeped into the marrow of their bones, stripped them of strength and pride, and left them feeble old men.

Del was noticed immediately.

Ibn Jalawi gestured at the ambassador without deigning to look at him directly. He spoke to Ibn Khan as though Del weren't worthy of attention. "Send the spy away," he said.

"He stays," Khan replied.

Unspoken words passed among the three visiting kalifs. It was Ibn Jalawi who spoke again, his tone offering a warning. "These are matters of grave importance, Khan."

"Then you'd best speak quickly before I lose my patience."

The two kalifs glared. They were gauging wills, deciding without words whose neck would be stiffest.

Del already knew the outcome; it was always the same. He remembered an incident at a gathering less than a year past when Ibn Jalawi had refused to speak unless Khan sent the 'northern spy' away. Ibn Khan had refused, and for three days Ibn Jalawi had maintained his silence, unwilling to budge. Finally Ibn Khan had threatened to cut out his tongue unless he used it.

Now, in the uneasy stillness that had blossomed within the tent, Del kept his eyes pointed at the floor. After serving five years as ambassador he had learned the wisdom of a shut mouth, and had made it his habit to speak little and listen much. Often he could achieve such stillness that his presence was virtually forgotten. Although the kalifs of the outer territories had never managed to completely overlook his existence, they had learned to ignore him very well. Since they could not make him go away, they treated him as though he were empty space.

"We haven't time for this," snapped a new voice. It was Ibn Yussef, the kalif of the Bayt Kathir, and his sharp tone stressed his impatience. Stepping forward, he took hold of Ibn Jalawi's arm and pulled him back, ignoring the sullen glare he received from the offended kalif. He was left facing Ibn Khan alone. "Our people are dying, Khan. The sthaak have risen from the Sands, more than we can fight, and they cannot be stopped."

Ibn Khan's expression was grave. His eyes shifted to each of them in turn, and all nodded, giving solemn affirmation of the dire news.

Each of the three kalifs bore the same dark tidings, and their stories were the same. At the onset of winter, merchant caravans along the trade routes bordering the Sands had begun to disappear. As the days passed, nomad encampments farther north were found in complete ruin. The Bedu occupying them had vanished, leaving behind ripped tents filled with wind. Entire herds of camel were found split wide and left to rot under the sun. It seemed as though the desert itself had acquired a taste for Bedu flesh, and had taken to devouring their people. Ken'dari dispatched to the southern rim of the territories often never returned, and those that did told of deserts teeming with sthaak. The beasts were rising up from the Sands. Trade stopped, and the people of the tribes began to dread with intensity. Each day, packs of roaming sthaak ventured farther into tribal boundaries, no longer restraining themselves to ravaging the trade routes and outer encampments. They had found courage in numbers, and they attacked where they had never dared before. And where the sthaak went, drought followed. Even though there had been rain that year, wells and oases dried as though the water had turned to sand. Some families traveled for leagues across the waste for wells that had supplied water for generations, only to find empty pits dry as bone. The herds that had not been slaughtered by sthaak began to starve, as did the people.

Ibn Khan listened to their grim tales one after another, and when it seemed all had been told, he rose from the gathering and went to stand alone. His mood was dark, and it showed in the simmering pits of his eyes and the tight set of his jaw. When finally he turned, his eyes singled out Ibn Yussef, the kalif of the Bayt Kathir. "Where are your people now?" he asked quietly.

"In the hills and caves beyond the black salt flats. There are many storms there, but the caves are deep. At the time I left, there was still water to be found in the deepest of the wells."

Ibn Khan indicated the second of the three kalifs. "And you?"

"The sthaak have scattered all but the most stubborn of my people. Some have fled to territories farther north, and others to the mines."

Ibn Khan's eyes aimed at the last of them.

"It is worse for me," Ibn Jalawi said grimly. "The sthaak came in great numbers from the south. Over five thousand of my people are dead or missing. The rest have gone to the cliffs, but the wells there are dry."

Ibn Khan closed his eyes. "What of the other tribes?"

The old kalif Ibn Fadlan was the only to answer. His white hair framed a brown face deeply lined with wrinkles. "Of the Dahm and the Rhashid I have no news to give," he said. "But the Haaj are gone."

"Go on."

"Three days ago, a Jaggi dreadnaught came out of the Sands. They brought with them an entire caravan of traders, all of them shaking from fear like fresh colts. When the traders were safely on the ground, the Jaggi rose in their dreadnaught and went back into the Sands. As for the traders, they said they had entered Haaj territory and found nothing but waste, as though a war had taken place there. They found no survivors. It was there that the Jaggi found them, and lifted them out of the territory in their dreadnaught."

"Why would the Jaggi be there?" Ibn Khan asked.

"They were hunting sthaak."

"In a dreadnaught?"

"A great many sthaak," the old kalif said. "The traders claimed to have seen Jaggi hunters on the ground as well as in the ship. Laid out on the decks, beneath the sails, were the fangs, scales and talons of many sthaak. Looking south from the decks of the dreadnaught, the traders claimed that the valleys of the Sands were filled with sthaak, so many they could not be counted. They found this in the ruined camp." He lifted a pack that had rested beside him the entire night, and Ibn Khan watched as the old kalif unbuckled the straps and turned it upside down. Amid a shower of fine gold sand the orb dropped soft and firm to the ground between the gathered kalifs. All eyes were drawn to the bauble, but none moved to touch it.

"The traders were glad to be rid of it," Ibn Fadlan said, gesturing at the thing in clear distaste. "They claim it is cursed."

"What is it?"

"The traders did not know, nor do I."

Ibn Khan reached between the kalifs to pick the orb out of the sand. He held it before his face with one hand, then blinked and shook his head. Almost immediately he handed it back to the old kalif. "Put it away," he said.

Instead of taking the orb, the old kalif handed the pack to Ibn Khan. "You keep it," he said. "I have no use for such things."

Taking the pack, Ibn Khan stuffed the orb away and tossed it aside. Turning his back on the others, he moved to the drapes and yanked them aside so that darkness spilled into the tent. He was a powerfully built man, and as he stared into the desert his shadow pushed out in front of him as though cast by a titan. He kept his silence, waiting for someone to speak. But it seemed as though all had been told, and the kalifs said nothing more. In the darkness outside the tent, their ken'dari escorts crouched in quiet patience, firelight gleaming off their eyes.

"Bring your people here," Ibn Khan said abruptly. "All of them. Leave no one behind."

A look passed among the kalifs. "You don't know what you ask."

Ibn Khan curved a warning glance at the kalif, but was otherwise unaffected by the man's opinion. "I can give none of you orders. You are each responsible for your own people. But if we are to face an army of sthaak, then it is better to face them together than each on his own. I am asking you to bring your people out of the deserts and into Ajraan territory. If all that you say is true, then it would seem the sthaak have united, and that can only mean there is intelligence driving them. We face not only the sthaak, but a thing we do not fully understand. Look at what has been done to us already." He swung an arm at the kalifs seated before him. "Your people, the ones left unslaughtered, have scattered across the desert and taken to cowering in caves. We don't know what the sthaak will do next, and we cannot sit idle to find out. If we are to survive we must act with speed."

"What if they return to the Sands?"

"What if they do not?" Ibn Khan returned.

The kalifs fell silent, hiding behind lowered eyes, each privately weighing the few options open to him. Ibn Khan watched them deliberating, then broke their reverie. "I will send ken'dari to the other tribes, asking them the same. We can fight together, or fight alone, the choice is for each of you to make on your own. As for me, I'll go to the Jaggi."

He was met with disbelieving stares.

"Where will you find Jaggi?"

"At the outpost."

"The outpost is surely abandoned by now."

Ibn Khan shrugged slightly. "It's the only place our people make contact with them. Where else am I to go?"

"What do you hope to gain from the Jaggi? They care nothing for us."

"The Jaggi have lived in the Sands since before our grandfathers. They have weapons we do not have, and knowledge we need if we are to fight the sthaak."

"You're wasting your time," the kalif of the Bayt Kathir broke in. "Even if you chance to find a pack of hunters you'll get nothing from the Jaggi. They'll offer you no pity, and certainly no help."

Ibn Khan disregarded the kalif's remarks, enduring their silence for a time. When it became clear that no one was prepared to dispute him any farther, he gave a firm nod. "I leave tomorrow. The rest of you will do as you see fit."

He left them seated there, but the tension was already stretched thin between them, and the three remaining kalifs had no more words to trade, and no more thoughts to share. They filed out of the sheltering pavilion without speaking, returning to their own tents outside the city to face the sleepless night ahead.

• • •

Del and Jiharra remained after the others had gone. They re-kindled the fire, and crouched over it in silence.

"You'll go with him?" Del said.

The heir of Ajraan shook his head. "He'd never allow it."

Del studied the younger man. Jiharra's skin was dark, but the ken'dari tattoos weaving around his forearms were darker. Although there were no glaring differences in his outward appearance to set him apart from the rest of his people, Del could plainly see the difference in his bearing. He had a lean yet solid build; back straight and shoulders broad. He wasted few movements, and in his eyes was the glow of authority. This warrior son was the pride of his father. And he was, of course, right in believing the kalif would not allow him into the Sands. If father and son were lost at once, both family and clan would be bereft of two generations of leadership.

Jiharra lifted his eyes. "But you . . ."

"I would be a nuisance."

"My father will want you with him."

Del rested his elbows on his knees. He put his forehead in his palms and stared at the fire. Neither of the men knew what could be said. In the silence, they shared their fears.

For a long while they remained, until Del pushed the breath from his lungs and rose. Jiharra rose with him.

"Del."

Del had turned to leave, but stopped to look back.

"Go with him."

"Jiharra—"

"Say you will, Del."

"What good would I be?"

"It is always good to have friends at your side."

Del said nothing.

"You will go in place of me. You will walk with him where I

101

cannot."

There had always been friendship between the ambassador and the heir of Ajraan, but Del had never thought their trust in him could extend so far. He didn't deserve it. His throat was dry, and he swallowed painfully. "I'll go," he said.

"Tell him tonight. And take this." He picked up the sack that had been tossed aside by the old kalif and passed it to Del. "It should not be left here, and I don't want it."

Del hefted the sack, testing its weight. He judged it to be somewhat heavier than a sackful of gravel.

"You know where to find him?" Jiharra asked.

Del smiled wryly. "Always."

With the sack and its strange orb over his shoulder, he left Jiharra alone in the pavilion, and made his way along the rocky path leading down from the ridge toward the lights of Aba Ajraan.

• • •

Del found Ibn Khan roaming the dusty corridors of the palace. Long had the ancient home of the sultans been in disrepair, left abandoned in the days of turmoil after the execution of Ibn Kassad al mar Rhudaj, the last sultan of the Bedu. Since then, time had been steadily scraping away at the palace of Aba Ajraan. Huge sections of the outer wall surrounding the grounds had split and sagged, leaving piles of loose stone and wide gaps. The smell of history was thick within the palace, imposing on all who came there a gloomy sadness. Empty were the bell-shaped towers, the marble chambers, and the garden courtyards. Within the peeling walls, the rooms once lived in by the sultans and their families had become home only to black-winged bats nesting high in the dark corners, and mice that skittered nervously along the walls. Tracks left by the brave ones crisscrossed through the decades-old layer of dust. Magnificent gardens once vibrant with color had been left untended, perishing in the heat, and debris consisting of the mismatched pieces of broken furniture lay scattered about the halls.

When the palace had been abandoned, the thieves had come to plunder. Now all that was left were useless odds and ends, worthless even to scavengers. Caked with dust, they seemed relics.

Tonight, Ibn Khan had chosen the deserted ballroom as his place of contemplation. A spacious chamber, the ballroom might have been mistaken for a cavern had the walls been made of jagged stone instead of polished alabaster stones. These ruins, choked though they were with brambles and memories, had been a playground for him as a child, made all the more intriguing because he had known even then it was a place that should be left undisturbed. The shadows in the chambers of the palace offered boundless opportunity for adventure to a youthful imagination. He had explored every inch of the ruins, even as his children had played there after him, and even now his children's children, exploring the same empty rooms he had explored years ago, making fresh discoveries of old places.

Concealed in the deep shadow of a broken pillar, Del watched the kalif. With each step, dust billowed out from around Ibn Khan's sandaled feet, clogging the light of his torch. His black robe hung nearly to his heels, and every so often he would stop to peel a strip of sagging plaster from the walls. It was clear from the haunted look in his dark eyes that he saw the room not in its current state of collapse, but as it had once been. From the way he gazed with distant longing at the open space, it was as though the palace were a home held just out of reach.

"Out of the shadows, Del," said the kalif.

Stepping out from behind a wide pillar, Del moved down the three shallow steps to the littered floor of the ballroom. "Am I so clumsy that you can hear me at forty paces?"

"You breathe loudly," the kalif informed him.

Hands clasped behind his back, the kalif turned a pensive expression upwards to the torn and faded tapestries that still clung to the walls. "Can you imagine what it must have been like?" he mused softly. "The seven tribes united by a common leader? In those times we were proud of ourselves. In those times we were strong.

Now . . ." He paused, his gaze lingering on a remaining scrap of trash unwanted even by the thieves. With the toe of his sandal he tipped the small stack of rubbish. "Now, because of one man's insanity, there is only this; debris and cracking walls."

"Ah," Del said with understanding. "You brood."

The kalif glanced at him, and smiled without humor. "I brood," he admitted, then lifted his eyes back to the ceiling. He remembered the day Del had first come to Aba Ajraan. He had hated the northern ambassador just as he'd hated all of those before him, those fat and slovenly pigs who looked down on him and his people as though they were little more than apes. When they had first met, Del had told the kalif that he was different, and only after Ibn Khan looked past his distrust did he discover that Del had not lied. There were few men in whom the kalif of Ajraan placed more trust than Del.

"My people are dying, Del. Out there in the deserts they are being slaughtered, and there is nothing I can do to make it end." He exhaled heavily and rubbed a hand through his short hair. He was frustrated and tired. "The future does not appear to be a good one."

"The future will be here soon enough," Del said. "We can judge then."

Ibn Khan appeared to have not heard him. His eyes were empty, as though seeing a place far away. When he blinked out of his thoughts, he looked to Del with sharp eyes. "Why did you come here, Del? Surely it wasn't to talk me out of my brooding."

"Your son sent me to speak with you."

"Did he?"

"Yes. I'm coming with you tomorrow."

"My son's brilliance?"

"Not entirely."

Ibn Khan watched Del a moment, then looked away. It almost seemed as though he had discarded the conversation already, but Del had known the kalif long enough to let him have his thoughts uninterrupted. He would speak his mind in his own time. Soon enough he did.

"The journey will be a long one."

Del did not answer.

Ibn Khan looked at him directly. "We will be traveling very close to the Sands," he said. "The heat is terrible. There are few wells and many sthaak."

Del was silent. He also knew that if Ibn Khan didn't want him to come, he would have simply said no, and there would have been no discussion.

"Tomorrow then," Del said by way of closing the conversation. "I'm going home now. Suri is cold and lonely without me."

"That is the way of wives."

"It is a way I am fond of."

Del thought he would go then, but found himself reluctant to leave. He looked at the floor, and toed a broken piece of wood once part of something larger. He kept his silence for some time, feeling the oppressive weight of the abandoned palace slowly crumbling around him. It seemed a sorrowful thing, the empty halls and the corroding structure. He thought that it must have been a beautiful place once, and he gazed up at the tiled marble roof, where the high windows were dark, and the vines had begun to creep in through the shattered walls and empty places where windows had once been.

"It won't be long before it is gone," he heard Ibn Khan say quietly.

"A new palace can be built."

"What good is a palace," the kalif said. "If there are no people?"

"Your people will survive. They always have."

Ibn Khan hardly heard the ambassador. He looked around the corroding chamber, frozen in its decay. Every time he came, there were more things broken, more scattered stones, and more cracks reaching up the walls and across the floors. It was funny how the corrosion never progressed while he watched, as though his presence alone was enough to hold the palace together. The disarray was as familiar to him as the lines and scars on his hands. It would have been wonderful to rebuild the palace, to bring his people together. Many times he had walked the littered halls, dreaming of the day his nation could be whole again. He smiled, as he always did, at the thought, then remembered the sthaak, and his smile left him entirely. "This time will be different," he said to himself.

When the ambassador failed to answer, Ibn Khan turned, only to find that Del had already left him, and it made him wonder how long he had been lost in his fool's paradise. He stayed in the carcass of the ancient palace most of the night, staring at the empty space around him, and wondering at the fate of his people.

Three

The kalif's estate had been built in the shadow of the palace, a stunted forgery of a structure designed during a mightier day. Although small in comparison, there was space enough for the kalif's extended family, and the tiny palace was home to well over thirty people. Ibn Khan's wife had yielded to him three sons and six daughters, and between the nine couples there were a total of twenty-three grandchildren. Always there was life and laughter in the court-yards and corridors, and never was there lack of children underfoot. Oftentimes, usually just after a near-collision with a pack of children racing around a corner, Ibn Khan would say to Del, "The Father has given me a great many offspring. Sometimes I think He is trying to murder me."

Over the years, Del had become incorporated into the ranks of their extended family. Ibn Khan's sons and daughters, as well as their respective wives and husbands, slowly warmed to him, and eventually became friends. The children had come around much faster, after six weeks regarding him as less of an oddity and more of a family member.

In the eastern wing of the estate was a small suite of three airy chambers reserved solely for the ambassador and his wife. From the balconies of his rooms, Del could look down into the inner courtyard, where the gardens surrounding a deep well flowered year round with the purple and yellow blossoms of the aromatic *jurolai*. In the mornings, above the sound of the breeze and the river, he could hear the distant roaring of camel trains as the traders brought their wares into the bazaar, and in the afternoons there were children playing in the courtyard below. There were palm and date trees filling the yard below, and their wide fronds were a deep green. When the wind blew they filled the chambers with leafy rustling.

Not only could he see the courtyard, but the old palace as well, and also the waters of the Ashkelon and the deserts beyond. Late in the evenings, when the sky turned a blue so dark it was nearly black, he would stand on the balcony and watch starlight glittering in the waves of the river, as though someone far upstream had cast diamonds into the water. But when the sky darkened, his eyes always returned to the palace, and he watched for ghosts in the windows. The ruined palace had always seemed like an old man to Del, quiet and patient, waiting for someone to come and sit with him again.

The hour was late when Del finally entered his chambers. It was a night of roaming winds and untamed breezes. The filmy drapes hanging at the open windows of the balcony swelled fat with crisp air, first blowing the drapes inward, then sucking them back. The wind carried the sweet scent of spice and citrus blossoms from the orchards west of the city. He stood for a long moment, breathing deeply.

Removing his sandals and his shirt, he went to stand at the entrance to the balcony. The floor was cold against his bare feet, and he could almost taste the water of the river, a cool scent mixed with the subtle aroma of mud and grass. Parting the drapes slightly with one hand, he peered out from the shadows of his chamber. Even at this hour there was light from the moon, which had not yet set, and he turned his eyes to the Ashkelon, where the warm waters were breathing steam into the chill air. He had always loved the way the fog rose from the river, roiling over the rocky banks during the night in billows so thick they seemed alive. The palace, along with most of the southern quarter of the city, was swallowed nightly by the heavy fog.

When he had taken his fill of the air, he walked on bare feet into the bedroom, where, next to his bed, a single candle spilled trails of pale wax onto a wooden stand. Suri always lit one for him, and the light of the little flame mixed with moonbeams to fill a corner of their small room.

She was sleeping, turned on her side and curled around a soft pillow. He crouched at the bedside to watch her breathing.

He had been in Aba Ajraan nearly two years before he found her. It had been spring, the night of a festival that celebrated the flooding of the Ashkelon. Pavilions had been set up along the swollen banks, and paper lanterns hung from ropes strung across the river. All up and down the river, and even across the rushing waters, the night was alive with music and laughter. It had been hot that night, he remembered, and the men bared their chests to dance while the women wore loose silk pants of bright colors and strips of cloth wrapped about their breasts. Their bare feet punched divots in the sand of the riverbank as they leapt and danced to the music of pipes, drums, and flutes. Wrists laden with bracelets of silver and gold swayed in the air, fingernails painted brightly. Del had been walking the sands of the riverbank with Ibn Khan, moving among the fire-pits and dances, and they had talked of the Bedu nation, and the common history shared between the tribes.

"Each of the tribes is descended from one of the seven sons of the Prophet," Ibn Khan had told him as they walked. "In that way we are like brothers. And although we are separate now, we share the same lineage, we are all the progeny of the same man."

"Tell me of the Prophet," he'd said.

"The Prophet was sent from the Father," Ibn Khan said simply.

Del had thought back to the stories he'd been told before coming to Aba Ajraan, legends of a dark god and his murderous prophet, of his blasphemy and eventual banishment. In Shallai's eyes, the Prophet had been a dark and tortured soul. To the Bedu, he was the father of their people, a connection to their gods. He had wondered then if perhaps the stories had been remembered the way Shallai wanted to remember them, and not the way they truly happened.

Ibn Khan had pointed to a woman who had swayed near to them. Her eyes were on Del. "She wants you to dance," the kalif had said.

"I don't know how."

Ibn Khan had smiled. "She will show you."

Del had looked to the woman, and all he saw were two sultry eyes beneath dark lashes. She had held out her arms to him, her twisting wrists luring him forward.

Del closed his eyes and breathed deeply. Amazing as it was to him, if he concentrated, he could still summon to memory every detail of that night. Less than three months later, they had married. Some of her family had protested the union so passionately that Del had assumed they would have him murdered. Of all the men in the desert, they said, Suri had to pick the only one who burned in the sun. Only her father, a portly Nadalli spice merchant, had blessed them with his whole heart, and made it clear that anyone who didn't approve of the marriage could leave his home and live in the Sands.

Del opened his eyes and released his breath slowly, allowing the memories to slide away. After undressing quietly, he leaned over her and blew the flickering little flame into oblivion. As gently as he could, he slipped into bed.

110

"You've been a long time gone," she said as soon as he had settled against her.

"I know," he answered.

"It's cold without you."

Del enjoyed a private smile. "I suspected it would be."

"And I've been lonely." Wrapped in his arms, she snuggled deeper into him. He took in the rich scent of her hair and the press of her body against his. He didn't want to, but he began to speak, telling her of the kalifs, and all that had been said among them. Somewhere in the middle of it all she had turned to face him, and they lay with their heads on the same pillow, faces together and breath mingling. Her searching eyes delved straight into him.

"What will you do?"

"Ibn Khan is traveling to the Jaggi outpost. He plans to ask for their help."

She was silent, but beneath the covers her hands slid to touch his arms. "You're going with him, aren't you?"

"I am," he said quietly.

Suri regarded him for a long moment, captivating him with her simple, open stare, and the tips of her fingers, then closed her eyes and moved into his arms. She burrowed her face into his neck, finding a place there as easily as a fox in a den. "When will you leave?"

"Sunrise."

"You'll be careful," she said.

"I will," he whispered into her hair. "I promise."

• • •

Suri woke in the small hours before morning. She did not know what had dragged her from the writhing landscape of her dreams, but as she sat up in bed she heard only silence. Blinking away the confusion of the last threads of her dreaming, she looked to Del—and found that her husband was not beside her. Casting off the thick blankets that covered her, she slid out of bed and padded softly to the door leading to the common room.

Bare-chested, Del sat cross-legged on the hard floor. His back was rod straight, and his hands rested lightly on the length of a scabbarded sword. The weapon was simple in design, long and only very slightly curved at the end. It was a Shadrakan blade, forged by the weapon-smiths across the eastern ocean. Single edged, the blade was plain and smooth. It boasted no etchings on its surface, and no words had been engraved into the steel. The hilt was wrapped in well-worn black leather strips, and appeared to have been made as simple as a weapon could be.

Hearing a sound behind him, Del glanced over his shoulder. The room was empty. After taking a long, slow breath, he stood up and leaned the sword in a corner of the room. Turning away from it, he moved back into his bedroom and found Suri lying where he had left her. He stood by the bedside for a long moment, watching her sleep, then slipped gently into bed and folded her in his arms. "I love you," he whispered softly, hardly a breath behind the words.

And I, you, came the unspoken reply from a wife who was not sleeping.

Four

They came out of the depths of the Sands. A living wave of howling demons, the sthaak boiled out of the frigid cold of the desert night and swarmed into the sprawling encampment of the Bayt Kathir. Killing without bias, they tore into tents of the Bedu, hardly pausing to rip the life from those hiding within. Massive legs carried them swiftly across the terrain, claws digging deep and easy into both sand and flesh, and the Bedu were overrun like children beneath the hooves of stallions. Many of the Bayt Kathir awoke in confusion, surrounded by the din of the slaughter, and ran from their tents only to find death quickly in the form of curved talons and rows of jagged fangs.

The carnage lasted only a short while. The Bayt Kathir were

unprepared for the sudden attack, and in the confusion were divided and scattered. As the massacre wore on, and the sthaak swept through the encampment, the terrorized screams of the living grew fewer and farther between. Bristling with spears and swords, small knots of survivors encircled the last of their families, desperately trying to keep the creatures at bay. None of them lasted long, and the desert drank the blood of the Bayt Kathir.

When their gruesome work was done, the rampaging creatures vanished into the desert. In their wake a terrible silence flooded the desecrated camp of the Bayt Kathir. Torn tents and shredded lives lay scattered about the sand, and the silence rang like a scream.

Five

They met in the windswept courtyard of the ancient palace while dawn was still a hazy band of dark blue lying heavy across the eastern horizon. Ibn Khan had arranged for three ken'dari to accompany them to the Jaggi outpost and back, preferring a small group so they could travel quick and light. For most of their journey they would follow the unmarked trade routes, only straying when they veered toward the eastern or western territories. The border of Ajraan territory lay three days to the south, and from there, it was a five day journey across the wasteland to the perimeter of Saar territory, where they would replenish with fresh water, food, and supplies.

Ibn Khan had just finished tying the last of their supplies onto the back of a camel when he looked to the ambassador. Del was standing next to the mount he was to ride, one of the older grays in Ibn Khan's herd. She stood on bandy legs, and had a scar down her left flank where she had narrowly escaped being dragged down by a pack of desert wolves years ago. His hand stroked the thick hair of her neck. As he spoke to her softly, her ear turned toward him, as though vaguely listening. When Ibn Khan approached, Del stopped speaking, but continued with the rubbing of her neck. Khan thumped the beast's withers fondly, then put his ear to her side to listen to the solid beating of her heart.

"She is old, but she is still strong," he said.

When the last preparations were finished, Ibn Khan led them out of the empty courtyard and into the streets of Aba Ajraan. The clop of hooves rang loudly against the cobblestones, and the grinding creak of leather made strange music with the jangle of harness bells. They left the outer perimeter of the city and crossed the river, where the mist was still thick.

The three Ajraan ken'dari joined them at the outskirts of the city. A stern and reserved trio, they added themselves to the procession with minimal words spoken. Del noticed that they went barefoot, seemingly oblivious to the rock shards and freezing sand beneath their feet. In the dim light and the shadow of their hooded robes he could not see their faces, but he knew each of them bore the winding and curling tattoos of the ken'dari. The intricate runes covered most of the skin on the left sides of their faces, flowed down their necks and often decorated the upper portion of their shoulders and chests. Del once inquired about the meaning of the tattoos, and Ibn Khan had answered him solemnly, "They are blessings and prayers; blessings for themselves and their brothers who fight beside them, prayers for brothers already dead."

"What need is there for ken'dari?" he had asked. "The Bedu have no enemies."

"We have not always had peace, Del. Not with Shallai, not with the Jaggi, and not with ourselves."

"When you were ken'dari, whom did you fight?"

The kalif had not answered for so long that Del thought he had chosen not to answer. When he finally spoke, his voice was laced with regret. "Many years ago there was conflict between the Ajraan and the Saar. There was fighting for years. I lost many brothers, many friends."

"What started the conflict?"

The kalif shook his head. "Another day, Ambassador. Ask me another day."

For the first hour after leaving Aba Ajraan, the air was laced with chill, and the sun seemed a cold red orb sleeping on the brink of the world. Behind them, the horizon swallowed the ground they had covered, and when the sun rose full and hot over the desert, it found five men and seven camels in a single file line bearing southward into the rolling hills and red cliffs of Ajraan.

The traveling was easy those first days. The terrain was gentle, and there was no shortage of grazing for the camels. With reaching lips they pulled leaves and twigs from passing plants, happy only as long as they were chewing on something, be it fresh greenery or cud from a past meal. The desert would turn barren soon enough, and there was no guarantee of finding any grazing at all once they left Ajraan territory.

Three days they traveled before reaching the border. There was a nomad encampment in the dry hills there, a pocket of dingy tents around a sunken well called Kitrum. Some distance away, a herd of camels were grazing on thin grass and acacia bushes, their front legs hobbled to keep them from wandering too far. Beyond them stood a small boy with dark hair and a long staff. He wore a simple white tunic, and he watched Del with a curious stare while his sheep stood stupidly about him, bumping and bleating at one another.

Ibn Khan went in search of a nomad or trader who could sell them a camel to replace one of their own which had gone lame in one leg, and the ken'dari went about refilling the skins at the well and watering the animals.

Shading his eyes against the sun, Del looked south. The wastelands were a stark plain of baking sand, and for the first time since

117

leaving Aba Ajraan, he began to wonder at the sanity of an attempt to cross it. He reminded himself that Saar territory was some-where out there, only five days away. But beyond that was more wasteland, more heat, and more emptiness. Out of the corner of his eye he noticed a group of five old men seated in a circle close to the well. They were barefoot, and while some wore dirty shirts of deep brown and gray, several were clad only in loincloths. Their skin was nearly the color of ebony, and seemed the texture of burnt crust. He looked at them, and saw that they were crouched around an arrangement of bowls and jugs like imps devising mischief. All were staring at him.

One of the nomads waved a bony hand to gesture him over.

Del looked toward the tents, but there was no sign of Ibn Khan. He glanced toward the ken'dari, but they were occupied with the camels. No help there. He looked back at the nomads, and again they summoned him with gestures. Without wanting to, he walked toward them, moving slowly in the hopes of never reaching them at all. But he did reach them, and they bid him to sit, so he joined their circle, crouching in the spot widened for him.

"He is even more absurd up close," one of the old men said, apparently putting the finishing touches on an earlier discussion. It was obvious they were unaware of his fluency in their tongue, but Del saw no reason to tell them otherwise. So he kept his mouth shut and let them scrutinize him out loud.

"Where did the kalif find him?"

"It is the man from the north," one said.

"How do you know?"

"Bin Fatima has been to Aba Ajraan many times. He has spo-ken of the white skinned man from the north. This is he, the am-bassador."

"How can you be certain this is not another?"

"It is he," snapped the old nomad. "How many white skinned men from the north can there be in Ajraan territory?"

"Look at his skin," another said. "So light."

"He is going to die if the kalif does not take him back to Aba

Ajraan soon. Look at him. Already he is peeling."

The others laughed, showing bright teeth behind cracked lips. Their eyes squinted when they smiled, bony cheeks pressing them nearly shut.

Del followed the conversation with his eyes, giving no indication that he understood the slightest scrap of what was being said.

"Give him some *pashii*," the first old man said.

"But I do not want him to cry."

More laughter.

"Just give it to him. See if he likes it."

The nomad next to Del filled a small bowl with liquid from one of the jugs and handed it to him. Del was familiar with *pashii*. It was but one of the wicked products brought about by the distillation of several different kinds of rice, as well as a combination of various other ingredients such as jurolai stems, orange peels, and goat's milk. Most of the *pashii* he'd drank had resembled watery milk, but this particular brew had the cloudy appearance of dirty rainwater. Apparently the nomads did not favor milk. Del held the bowl in his hands and sniffed at the contents. The potent aroma stabbed his nostrils and made his eyes tear. This was not the *pashii* he knew.

The nomads were grinning at him. Thinking he didn't know what to do with the vile liquid, one of them cupped his hands and pretended to drink. The others were lifting their hands, urging the bowl to his lips. Were they so eager to see him choke? "Drink," they were saying. "Drink, drink."

Tilting the bowl to his lips, Del took in a large mouthful of the burning fluid. The second it entered his mouth he knew it was going to be bad, but he tossed it back regardless.

Fire crawled up out of his gut. It spread over his chest and lungs and took root under his tongue. One drop from each corner of his mouth ran down to his chin, and even those felt hot. Scraped raw, his throat clenched, and he felt his chin lowering to his chest. It took everything he had to keep his face from twitching and his shoulders from scrunching up around his neck. He wanted to let his tongue out of his mouth just to keep from retching. It was important to him that he keep still, though, if only to preserve his pride in front of these people.

The worst of the pain subsided soon enough, but he knew the fire in his belly would smolder for hours. He knew that his left eye had been twitching, but otherwise he had held together handsomely. Parting his lips, he exhaled long and slow, and the breath that escaped was like heat spilling from an oven. Wiping the dribbles of stray *pashii* from his chin, Del handed the bowl back to the nomad and forced an appreciative smile.

"Delicious," he told them in their own language.

The nomads were highly impressed with his vocabulary. "Delicious," they affirmed, and all around the circle, back and forth, they agreed that it was indeed delicious. When Del left them some time later, having uttered nothing more than his one-word lie, the nomads sent him off with a blessing they did not think he could understand.

"Do not die in the desert!" they called.

Their laughter, like the cackling of desert jackals, trailed him for hours.

• • •

Kitrum Well marked the beginning of the great emptiness between the territories of the Ajraan and the Saar. Out there, beyond the border, the red cliffs of Ajraan flattened to barren plains of thin sand and vast expanses of sun-baked flats. Heavy salt deposits formed a fissured crust over the land, and boulders, rocks, and gravel were its only adornment. Life was scarce in those wide, waterless tracts between territories, and wells, when they could be found, were few and far between. Often they were merely dirty puddles hidden at the bottom of ancient watercourses, or tiny springs which had to be dug out from beneath layers of sand, some of them producing only a few bucketfuls of bitter water before running dry. Such was the desolation that separated one tribe from another, and there was much of it, for the Bedu territories, were spread far and wide across the desert. The trade routes, winding from one territory to the next, were all that linked them together.

Occasionally Del spotted ranges of low, dry hills in the distance, and often there were strange rock formations, boulders and stones piled high to break the monotony in massive proclamations. In many of these landmarks were deep caves and sometimes even pristine pools of clear water. The ken'dari always knew exactly where the water could be found, where the wells were, and which way to the best grazing. The desert was theirs; they spent their lives in it.

The days passed slowly. Most mornings they broke camp before sunrise, rising from their slumber while the air was still cold. One of the ken'dari would prepare a simple meal consisting mainly of dried meat and dates. If they had water to spare, they made a thick porridge and squeezed into it the juice of dates. Each and every morning, it was someone's duty to boil water over a few sparse flames with which they made hot *queffa*. They shared the dark brew out of a single bowl, each man taking only a few sips before passing it on.

On one particularly cold morning, while Del's eyes were still puffy from sleep, and his bones ached from the previous day's riding, the *queffa* bowl was put into his hands and he drank thankfully. The taste was strangely different, and only after he drank did he look into the bowl and notice its unusually light color.

"What is this?" he asked.

"It is *queffa*," one of the ken'dari told him.

"But what's in it?"

"Milk."

Del looked up at the man. They had brought no goats with them, and Del knew that they had not filled any of the skins with milk. They carried only water, as milk was a luxury while traversing the desert. "Where did you get milk?"

"We are fortunate," the ken'dari said, pointing to the camels couched nearby. "Bin Jalawi's camel, Umbarak, is in milk now."

Del glanced at the camel. The beast was calmly chewing her cud with the others, and watching them with big dark eyes. The ken'dari read his thoughts and smiled at him. "Drink," he said. "The *queffa* will keep you awake and the milk will keep you strong. Drink."

Del did as he was told, then passed the bowl on.

When the *queffa* was gone they loaded the camels and pushed out, every small noise clear in the chill cold of the desert morning. They walked beside their camels for the first few hours, keeping the pace slow and even. As dawn bloomed into daylight the ken'dari mounted one by one. They would tug on their camel's reigns so the animal lowered its head to the ground, then use the long neck or a bent leg as a step to reach the high saddle. Del was typically the last to mount, waiting until the sun became too hot, at which point he climbed to the saddle and rode until he became too sore. Back and forth he went, from the ground to the saddle, fighting discomfort until a halt was called.

In the evenings, the setting sun drenched the desert with hot light. As it sank deeper into the west, the sky blossomed with red, as though the sun were a dagger burying itself slowly into the flesh of the world. After the intensity of the sunset reached its peak the blood began to drain, leaving a bland sky the colors of ash and gray.

Many nights they pressed on long into the darkness, and when Ibn Khan finally allowed them to stop, the darkness was already losing its chill bite, and the sky was beginning to lighten with the coming of dawn. On one such night, Del choked down his small portion of tasteless bread in an exhausted stupor, then washed it down with water so bitter it nearly made him gag. The well they had found earlier that day had been buried under four feet of sand, and they had spent an hour digging to reach the muddy spring below. They mixed the acrid water with small portions of camel's milk, but it did little to disguise the taste. Seated on the sand near the fire, Del had just finished swallowing a mouthful, all he could force himself to drink despite his thirst, when Ibn Khan crouched beside him.

"Are you well, Ambassador?"

Del looked at the sand beneath his feet, concentrating on keeping his food and water where it would do him some good. Despite the coldness of the night, the back of his neck was sweating, and his cheeks felt hot. The previous day he had emptied his stomach after drinking particularly vile water, and although the ken'dari were kind to him, he saw the looks on their faces, and could almost see them wondering why they bothered to feed and water him if he was just going to waste it on the sand.

"The water of the desert doesn't agree with you," Ibn Khan said.

"I'll live," Del muttered quietly. He didn't look at Ibn Khan as he swallowed another mouthful of the milk and water mixture, grimacing as it went down.

"I don't doubt that," the kalif answered.

They made camp that night on the eastern edge of a white plain, and it seemed he had barely shut his eyes when one of the ken'dari shook him awake. Dawn had not yet broken, and the camels were already saddled and prepared for travel. "It is time now, Ambassador," the ken'dari was saying to him. "We still have far to go, and time is short."

Dragging himself to his feet before fully awake, Del tripped to his camel and mounted. His blood and bones were made of lead, and he half-slept in the saddle until the sun crested the horizon. When he woke, it was to a ringing in his ears and a tight pain in his skull. After that, sleep was impossible. He rode in discomfort, his eyes fixed on the swaying back of the ken'dari riding in front of him.

• • •

Ajraan territory was six days behind them when the sandstorm hit. A blind, mindless beast, it dragged itself up out of the southern deserts, a monster intent on devouring everything in its path.

The ken'dari saw it while still far off, a dusty brown smudge lying across the horizon. Forced to seek shelter or brave the storm in the open, they made for a range of red cliffs in the distance, pushing the camels as fast as they dared. Shifting sand gave way to a flat sprawl of hard rock deeply scarred by gullies and shallow ditches. The cliffs rose up some two hundred feet, and the jagged ridge above was knife-sharp against a yellow sky.

For more than an hour they rode in the shadow of the cliffs, and soon the high wall began to dwindle, and the ground rose slowly into a range of low hills. The camels struggled for footing among the loose stones of the slopes, forcing their riders to dismount and walk beside them. Higher they went as the sky slowly turned the color of burnt orange the wind grew stronger at their backs.

Soon after entering the hills they discovered a cave entrance sheltered among a landslide of boulders. They coaxed the reluctant camels into the dark mouth, and led them down a twisting passage, around boulders and rocks, and finally into a wide cave hardly high enough for the camels to walk without bending their heads. After the camels were unloaded and couched, Del made his way back up the crooked tunnel to the mouth of the cave.

The desert outside belonged to another world. The sky had already begun to darken, shedding the yellow glow for a threatening red. All around him, the air was charged with energy. He could taste it in his mouth, feel it pulling at the hair of his arms. Among the steep crags the wind moaned.

Leaving the relative safety of the cave, Del climbed toward the top of the hill, scrambling over loose stones and using dried brush for handholds. Upon reaching the top he stood and turned south, facing into the hot breath of the advancing storm front.

Heaven-high and coming fast, the wall of sand dominated the sky. Del had only a few moments to take in the view. The range of hills within which they had found their cave bumped across the desert like a crooked spine. What caught his eye was a broad plain of salt flats around which the hills curved. The plain was of such size that it would have taken them four days to cross, and the mountains on the far side were dim shadows. Far out in the flat emptiness, so distant he could barely see, was a cluster of ruins. Blocking his eyes against blowing sand, Del could just make out a tangle of broken stone walls and toppled pillars. He watched until the wind began to scrape sand across his face, then made his way back down to the mouth of the cave to take shelter from the storm.

• • •

The sandstorm crashed against the hills. The skies caved in, and a torrent of howling winds flooded the desert, sending sheets of sand and debris ripping through the waste. Lightning arced across the sky while thunder beat the ground in an attempt to crush the life out of the hills. For two days the storm ravaged the desert.

That night, as they sat around a small fire pit dug in the sand of the cave floor and ate strips of salted meat, Del told Ibn Khan of the ruins he had seen in the flatlands, and he learned of the place the Bedu called the *umm'al ghul*. Legend claimed that the Prophet himself was entombed somewhere in the *umm'al ghul*, an ancient city swallowed by the desert. To mark the spot where he lay, the sons of the Prophet had carved his name into the stone face of a pillar, but since then the wind and the sand had wiped away the name. After their deaths, the knowledge of the final resting place of the Prophet was lost.

"Is the Prophet truly buried there?" Del asked, gripping at a particularly tough piece of meat with his teeth.

Ibn Khan could only shrug. "Who can say?"

"You have never been there?"

"I've been inside the *umm'al ghul*. But there is nothing there, only ruins."

Del fell silent for a time, then looked to Ibn Khan, sitting across the fire from him. "What was the name of it?"

"Of what?"

"The city. What was the name of the city before it was ruined?"

Ibn Khan shook his head. "It was not built by the Bedu."

"The Jaggi?"

"It is definitely not Jaggi."

"Who else is there?"

The kalif gave a small smile. "The desert is old, Del. Some nomads believe it is the oldest place in the world." He turned his eyes toward the entrance of their cave. "A place so ancient must keep a thousand secrets. How can we, who live for but a breath compared to the desert, hope to know all her mysteries?"

That night, as he slept beneath his blankets with his head close to the fire and his feet lost in darkness, Del dreamed of a misshapen beast hunched at the dark center of the *umm'al ghul*, a malicious thing reeking of filth and rotting flesh. It prowled the ruined streets of the *umm'al ghul*, pounding on the walls of his dreams with hairy fists as it shuffled through the bones of the dead. He dreamed that it came up one night from the dark caverns to hunch behind a fallen pillar on the salt flats below, and peered up with a cold eye at the dark cave in which he slept.

• • •

After a day and a night the sandstorm abated. Once again, the desert receded into a silent lull filled only with devastating heat and wind. Out from the cave they came, leading the line of camels, blinking and squinting against the brightness. Down the hillside they went, stepping onto a desert floor scoured clean by the storm, and in the growing light of morning aimed themselves toward the Sands and left the range of low hills and the *umm'al ghul* behind them.

• • •

On a night much like the ones before it, they made camp in a sandy hollow rimmed with boulders. The lip of the hollow shielded them from the chilling winds born nightly in the desert, and helped to trap the warmth of their fire. Because there was no grazing, the camels were couched to keep them from wandering, and they sat with their legs folded under them in the darkness. The light of their fire played against the slope of the hollow, and strayed into the darkness to be teased by the wind. It was a moonless night, and the shadows beyond their meager camp seemed dark enough to be solid, sliding around at the edges of their vision, sneaking closer and then melting back when watched too carefully. Del stared wistfully at the heat of the flames, but even they looked cold and lonely in the darkness.

Sitting cross-legged at the fire, Del pulled his sword from the bundle against which he rested. Removing the scabbard, he set it aside and produced a vial of oil and a worn rag. With care, he began to oil the weapon, rubbing a slick shine into the steel starting at the base of the hilt and working his way up the length of the blade. Ibn Khan watched Del working, and for long moments not a word passed between them. Finally, the kalif leaned forward. "A fine weapon," he said with some appreciation. "I've never seen anything like it."

"It's Shadrakan," Del said without diverting concentration from his task.

"What is 'Shadrakan'?"

Del smiled faintly. "It's a place far away, a very great empire across a very deep sea."

"Even greater than your own Shallai?"

Del shrugged. "It might be."

"You have been there?"

Del's eyes touched briefly on the kalif's face. "I was born there."

Ibn Khan's brows leapt to attention. "Now this is something I did not know. You have always had us believe that Shallai is your home."

Del shook his head. "I was born in a city called Graven, in the Shadrakan empire."

"What is it like there?"

"Hot. But not hot like here. The air is so wet in Graven it can hardly be breathed." As he spoke, Del tucked the oiling cloth into the scabbard, and from a small box at his side pulled out a tiny satchel, the contents of which he dumped into his palm. From among several stones he selected a flat, rough whetstone, and he slid it the length of the blade's already sharp edge in one even stroke, producing a raspy hiss. "And it rains in Graven every day."

Several of the ken'dari had wandered close to listen, and exclaimed soft disbelief at this declaration. "What do they do with so much water?"

"They waste it," Del smiled. "And they never have to worry if there will be more."

"Rain every day," the ken'dari mused, shaking his head in wonder.

"And because of it," Del went on, "there are no deserts in the Shadrakan empire. Instead of sand, there are *jungles*." He resorted to Shadrakan because there was no appropriate word in the Bedu tongue for such a verdant and fecund landscape.

The ken'dari demanded to hear more of the Shadrakan jungles, and Del told them about the towering boneskin trees, with bark white as fresh milk, and of the benyouk and their living vines. He described the wet darkness beneath the canopy, the stultifying closeness of the undergrowth, the wide leaves and thorns and thickets.

"How far can you see in the jungle?" a ken'dari asked him.

Del extended an arm and waggled his fingers. The ken'dari warriors looked to the far horizons, suddenly imagining a world where their boundaries were reduced to three feet in any direction.

One of them shook his head in severe disapproval. "I would not like that," he said somberly.

"How can you see your enemies coming?" another asked.

"You can't," Del said. "If you are lucky, you can hear them. But some things in the jungle go very quietly."

"Are there sthaak?"

"No sthaak," Del answered. "But there are things in the jungle worse than sthaak."

"What is worse than sthaak?" the ken'dari challenged.

"The ven men and the wroth," Del said. "And other things."

"Tell us," Khan invited him, eager to hear.

Del declined, shaking his head. "I've never seen any of those things, only heard stories."

"Then tell us, at least, how one born in a place so distant finds himself playing the part of Shallai's ambassador among the Bedu?"

"It's not much of a tale," Del said.

The kalif grinned easily. "You lie, Ambassador," he chided. "There is a story in you."

Seeing that the kalif would have his tale, Del gave it to him without further struggle. "I'm only half Shadrakan," he stated. "I never knew my mother, and my father raised me alone. He never said anything about her; who she might have been, or why she wasn't there. He was quiet almost all the time. When I was twenty he killed some people . . . some boys. So we had to leave." Del's hand worked stone against blade mechanically. The hiss of the whetstone had no company.

"My father wasn't right in the head," Del said. He suddenly halted the sharpening, and tapped the side of his head with the whetstone. "He was sick. Something happened to him, but nobody could tell us what. He'd always spent a lot of time in the jungle, and they say a lot of things can happen to a man in the jungle. A lot of things can go wrong."

Del's voice had tapered off, and his hands fell still. He continued in a quieter voice. "My father had friends who knew people—physicians and surgeons. They came to see us when he started to act strangely. Some of them stayed with us a long time, studying him, asking questions and watching everything he did. They thought maybe it was a disease they'd never seen, a virus from the jungle, or something he'd gotten from the ven men. But if he'd been in contact with the ven the couldn't remember, and so they never knew what it was. They still thought maybe they could help him, but when it got bad they left. He was only violent sometimes, that wasn't as frightening as the other things. He would talk, and his voice was different, his eyes." Del's mouth twisted as he struggled to find words. "Not different in the sense that he *looked* different, but that it seemed there was someone else behind his face, or looking out of his eyes. He was changing, but the changes came and went, so that some days he seemed himself, and others . . . he wasn't. But no matter how bad it got, there was always a part of him that saw the world clearly. And that part of him was always very scared at what was happening."

Ibn Khan leaned forward. "Del. You don't have to—"

"I'm not done."

The kalif hesitated, leaned back.

"After he did what he did I got us out of Graven. I didn't really have a choice. We had to go. I sold what I could and booked passage to Shallai. We spent days before the ship left living under the docks at the waterfront. People were looking for him by then. We boarded the ship at night, dad with his whole body wrapped in a blanket. When we landed I spoke only a few scraps of the local tongue, not hardly enough to get by." Del laughed at himself in the remembering. "I'd never stopped to think that the whole world didn't speak the same language as me. I just didn't know. So I became a soldier."

"And your father?"

"He didn't make it."

Khan looked at his hands, one thumb rubbing slow circles in his palm.

The unease in the moment was lost on Del, and he carried on after only a brief pause. "At first I didn't think Shallai's corps would even consider me because of my Shadrakan blood, but they never even suspected. I looked enough like everyone else to mostly fit in. I pretended to be mute so I wouldn't have to talk, and because I couldn't understand most of what was said to me they thought I was deaf as well. They made me do all the things no one else wanted to do: cook and clean, wash bedding and mend armor. Even after I could speak enough to get by I hardly said a word unless I had to."

Del set aside his stone, then sheathed his blade. "As long as I did whatever they put in front of me to do and kept my mouth shut, nobody bothered me. I did a lot of listening that first year, and a lot of watching. I wasn't treated too badly, and by the time it was required of me to speak at any great length I was good enough at covering my accent to go relatively unnoticed, as long as I spoke slowly. That's when they took me away from pots and pans and sent me off to fight like everyone else. Why waste a perfectly good man polishing steel when you can have him kill men instead?"

Khan was nodding slowly. "You were a soldier for a long time?"

"Twenty years," Del said. He fell still and quiet a moment, thinking about the blur of years between then and now, and how it seemed there should be so many more than twenty. "In that time I must have marched back and forth across Shallai a hundred times. I don't think there's a city north of the Sym territories I haven't seen. Always there was fighting to be done, mostly with the Shadrakans."

"You fought your own people?"

"The Shadrakans were never my people."

Ibn Khan fell silent for a time, watching pensively as Del spilled sand from one hand to the other. "And how does a warrior of twenty years suddenly become an ambassador?" he finally asked.

"Luck."

"A fortunate accident, hm?"

"I didn't say *good* luck."

This coaxed a smile from Ibn Khan, and he cocked his head. "You don't like your life in Aba Ajraan then?"

Del hid his own smile. "I didn't say that, either."

"So it was nothing more than luck that brought you to us?"

"I don't know. I suppose someone thought I'd done enough fighting for one lifetime." He scooped up another handful of white sand, contemplating the dry stream as it drained from the bottom of his fist. Then he brushed his hands together and looked at the kalif. "Maybe they were right."

Khan was still nodding, his eyes fixed on the rivulets of sand running from Del's fist. "I have never seen anything outside of this desert. It has been my whole life, and sometimes it seems so big that it is hard for me to imagine a world large enough to contain anything else. Perhaps someday, when all is well between your people and mine, you will take me to your home, and show me the places you have seen." His eyes lifted to the horizon. "I think that I might like to see the jungle."

Del watched his friend's face soberly. He wondered if there would ever be a day in which all was well between Shallai and the Bedu. He tried to smile despite his doubt, but the effort was only half successful. "I would like that," he said, and although the smile was without life, the hope was sincere.

Six

At the perimeter of the Sands, where the plains of the flatlands met with the red and gold dunes of the desert interior, there stood two enormous pillars of stone and rock. Thrusting heavenward, the twin formations defied the emptiness surrounding them, standing as sentinels between one world and the next.

The outpost itself lay in the rocky saddle between the two formations, dwarfed by the towering architecture of the desert. For fifteen years the outpost had been the only point of contact between the Bedu and the Jaggi. Never did the Bedu venture into the Sands, and rare were the occasions when the Jaggi came out. Only at the outpost could the two races be found mingling, and even then their interactions were kept brief almost to the point of rudeness. The Jaggi wanted gems and stones from the Bedu mines, as much as could be brought to them, and for these they paid high price. Bedu merchants came bearing caskets of the precious stones, and the Jaggi brought blades forged from dark steel. Such weapons were highly coveted by Bedu warriors, so expensive that usually none other than the ken'dari carried them. Other things were known to pass hands at the outpost, trinkets exchanged after a trade; a bracelet of bone for a necklace of wrought silver, an article of clothing for a satchel of spice, or a gold ring for a sash. These things, once owned by a Jaggi, often claimed high price among the Bedu.

Once a hub of activity, the outpost was now void of life.

"Not a soul," Ibn Khan said quietly. They had been watching from the crest of a dune some distance to the north, and between the base of the dune and the outpost was only a bleak salt-flat, cracked and blazing white under the sun. It was not difficult to imagine why the merchants had left the outpost abandoned. At the very edge of the Sands, they must have been the first to become aware of the sthaak horde. Either they had left, taking their wares and fleeing back to tribal territories, or they had stayed and died.

Del gazed beyond the outpost, where the sculpted dunes of the Sands lifted to the sky, their peaks and trenches carved by the wind. It seemed a place of vast loneliness to him, and he wondered what, if anything, lay buried beneath the great dunes of sand. Only the two rock formations rose higher than the dunes, seemingly towers built by gods. "What's out there?" he wondered aloud. "Where does it end?"

"It doesn't."

"It can't go on forever," Del said, but received only a blank look. After a moment, the kalif clicked his tongue, and his camel moved forward, her hooves slipping in the shifting sand. "Let's get this over with."

• • •

It had always been simpler to begin any explanation of the outpost by telling what it was not, rather than what it was. It was not a city, nor had ever aspired to be one. There were none of the things that were to be found in a typical city or settlement: no homes, temples or taverns. These things would have been useless in such a place. Organized was another thing that the outpost was not. There had been no formal plan applied to its layout, for it had grown slowly, in stages and layers. Tight alleys connected narrow streets that wound around and doubled back. Structures were built and torn down and melded together as need called for, daily changing the maze-like layout of the outpost. A route that led from one place to another might cease to exist from one day to the next. There was little of lasting permanence at the outpost, save the outpost itself.

What the outpost was, in simplest terms, was one vast, ever-evolving bazaar. Built around a central well, rounded stone and mud-brick structures had burgeoned over time to become the sole place in all the desert where Jaggi and Bedu came together.

It was utterly empty.

Judging from its outward appearance, it might have been deteriorating under the desert sun for decades. What few wooden structures there were had given up trying to remain upright, and had let their sun-blistered wood sag to the ground. Some of the booths shed bleached shingles, while others slumped like legless beasts dying in the heat.

Moving cautiously, Del and Ibn Khan made their way through the narrow and crooked alleys searching for life. Two of the ken'dari were walking the perimeter of the outpost, while the third had gone to explore from the far end, and they all made their way toward what might have been considered the central hub of the outpost.

If he had not known better, Del would have sworn to any god that the outpost had been abandoned for years. Not only were there no people, but there was hardly any indication that there ever had been. The only life they saw were the reptiles. It seemed an army of lizards had conquered the outpost, and were now gloating in their victory. The smaller ones scattered in jagged streaks when startled, scampering short distances before vanishing beneath the rocks. The larger ones never bothered to move. Baking themselves on blistering rocks, they watched with eyes as black and pebbly as their skin, half-napping and hardly concerned. Only when approached too closely did they aim their heads at him and hiss threateningly. Closer still, and they abandoned their rocky thrones, diving into the narrow crevasses around them.

Stepping out of a shaded alley, Del and Ibn Khan found the central well. Stalls, shacks, and covered pavilions—all empty—surrounded a circular yard at the center of which squat a round stone well. The sand of the yard was trampled with the tracks of camels and men. They approached the well, adding their tracks to the hundreds already there. Halting at the rim, Ibn Khan looked into the dark pit filled with shadows black as oil. Picking a rock off the ground, he dropped it into the well, and moments later, a dull thud echoed up to them.

"Dry," the kalif said.

Reminded of his own thirst, Del lifted his waterskin to his lips, tilted his head back, and—

Froze.

At the far end of the yard, watching them atop a stone booth two floors high, crouched a massive figure garbed in heavy robes the color of pitch. Its head and face were wrapped in thick russet cloth, and only two pale eyes peered out from the shadow of its wrappings. It was too large to be human. Del slowly lowered the skin, his eyes fixed on the figure. "Khan," he said.

The tone of his voice carried urgent warning, and the kalif immediately looked up, following the line of Del's eyes until he saw the figure on the stone booth.

"Jaggi," he said instantly.

As if in response to the word, the figure lifted a massive crossbow, and before either man had the opportunity to react, fired the weapon. The Jaggi missed, and Del flinched visibly as the steel bolt cut through the air just over his right shoulder, trailing a low whistle and a thin steel chain. An enraged shriek severed the dead calm behind them, and both men whirled around to find that the Jaggi had not missed after all. A sthaak had emerged from a dark building hardly thirty feet behind them, and had been stalking them across the yard. The Jaggi's bolt had punched through scale and flesh, shoving the creature to the ground in a clumsy stumble.

"Run!" Ibn Khan shouted.

Ignoring the steel bolt in its abdomen, the beast gave chase, lurching after its fleeing prey on all fours. Sand and gravel churned beneath its talons as it fought to overtake them.

There was a low stone wall seventy paces away. It was too far; Del knew he wasn't going to make it. Even as he ran, his hand scrambled for the long dagger tucked in his sash. He could hear the beast behind him, heavy footfalls punching the sand, and he knew that any moment he would feel its jaws around his neck and its claws digging into his back. One leap and it would be on him.

Jerking the knife from its sheath, he decided he didn't want to die running. Abruptly, he dug his heel into the sand and whirled around, blade coming up.

The creature was in the air, jaws wide, arms reaching.

"Down!" Ibn Khan screamed. Two steps behind, he launched himself at Del.

The ambassador had never dreamed of being hit so hard.

The kalif's full weight crashed into him just as he had braced himself to meet the sthaak, and he felt as though someone had thrown a wall at him. There was a flash of blackness—lost moments.

When full awareness snapped back he found himself on his back, staring at the sky. Everything hurt. Jerking his head up, he came eye to eye with the sthaak. The beast was hardly five feet from where he lay, groping for him. For one stunned moment he did nothing but stare at the creature. He could not understand why it wasn't killing him. And then he saw the chain. It was attached to

137

the bolt in the sthaak's gut, and it ran back to the stone booth upon which the Jaggi now stood. Fixed to a thick metal spike driven into an immovable boulder, the chain was all that kept Del from being devoured. Burning with bloodlust and maddened by frustration, the sthaak bucked and jerked against the chain.

Del had fallen just out of reach.

Before then, Del had never seen a sthaak, and his immediate need was to put distance between himself and it. Scrambling backwards, he bumped into Ibn Khan, who was only now struggling to hands and knees. Del twisted to his feet, then bent to help the kalif rise. Ibn Khan was barely able to carry his own weight, and they staggered a short distance before his legs gave out and both were dragged to the ground. On his knees and still fighting for breath, Del looked behind him.

Past the beast, the Jaggi had leapt from the stone shed. As heavy as the hunter must have been, it landed with heavy grace. Only then did Del notice what had remained hidden by its long robes. The Jaggi had no feet. Instead, it walked on hooves the color of dirty bone. It had left the giant crossbow behind, and taken up a long rod of steel. One end was sharpened to a thornlike point, the other fixed with a blade.

As the sthaak gnawed at the bolt skewering it, the Jaggi gripped the chain in one gloved fist and gave a hard yank. Instantly the hunter became the object of the sthaak's hatred. Rising up on crooked hind legs, it advanced threateningly on the hunter, dragging the chain behind it. The sthaak lurched forward, then dropped to all fours before launching itself at the Jaggi, choking with fury and bristling claws and teeth.

The hunter stood his ground calmly. Only at the last second did it crouch low and brace its pike in the ground. Already in the air, the sthaak impaled itself on the weapon, its weight driving the steel shaft through its scaled body. Blinded by rage, it clawed and snapped at the Jaggi's face, mere inches away. The Jaggi dumped the sthaak to the side, where it writhed against the shaft impaling it. From a leather catch on his back, it removed a second pike and drove the rod through the beast. The sthaak shrieked again, a noise containing as much rage as pain.

After that, the Jaggi made quick work of the beast, drilling the immobilized body with its pike until the struggling was reduced to helpless scraping. At last, even that ceased.

Spellbound by the systematic execution, Del hardly noticed that Ibn Khan had pushed to his feet and staggered several paces away. When he turned and found the kalif gone, he twisted around to see his friend slumped several yards away. Halfway to the shade of the alley through which they had come, his legs had given out on him, and he'd slid to the ground with his back to Del, one leg folded beneath him and the other splayed in front. His chin was bent to his chest, and his arms hung at his side. There was a trail of blood leading to him.

In that instant, the last part of Del still thinking clearly understood what had happened, but withdrew in shock, leaving him to discover on his own what it already knew. Del heard himself call out to the kalif, and when he got no response, fear began to mount. He was on his feet and rushing to the fallen man. Forgotten were the Jaggi hunter, and the sthaak, and everything they had come to do. The ten steps to the kalif seemed an endless journey. Falling to his knees beside Ibn Khan, he looked eagerly into the kalif's face, and found it the color of ash. The kalif's shirt was soaked with red down to his waist.

And then Del found his dagger.

It took him a moment to fully realize what he was seeing, and even then it didn't seem real, didn't seem possible. The sight of the hilt jutting from Ibn Khan's right breast had reached into his mind and erased all comprehension. He stared at the leather wrapped handle in horror, pushed so deep that no blade was left showing. Although the kalif's eyes had been closed, they cracked open to look up at Del.

"It's bad," he said in a hoarse voice.

When the ken'dari rushed onto the sandy grounds of the well, the first thing they saw was the Jaggi hunter standing over his kill,

139

watching them with its empty white eyes. The hunter's rod was pinning the dead sthaak to the ground, and the sand was painted red around them. When they saw the fallen kalif and the ambassador, they rushed to lend aid, their shadows crowding out the sun in long bands. Even after they saw the kalif's grievous wound, their steady calm never cracked.

Del was pushed aside while the three ken'dari crouched over the kalif. He backed away some distance, only then noticing the blood on his hands. He tried to transfer it to his shirt, but the flesh was already stained. Still numbed, the most important thing seemed to be getting his hands clean. He crouched down to scoop a handful of sand from the ground, and scrubbed his hands with the coarse grains. But the stains would not be removed. A moment later he looked up. Near the well, the Jaggi hunter was still standing over the dead sthaak, watching with eyes the color of foggy milk. Its eyes fixed on Del, but it made no move to either come forward, or go away.

Someone called his name, causing him to look up sharply. Crouched by the kalif's side, the ken'dari named Zayid was beckoning to him. "Come, Ambassador. Your hands are needed now."

Numbly, Del rose and went to kneel down by the kalif's side, opposite Zayid. The ken'dari had put his face close to Ibn Khan's, and was speaking gently. "Kalif," he said.

Ibn Khan opened his eyes to look at the ken'dari.

"We must move you now."

The kalif let his eyes slide shut.

Zayid gestured to Del, and together they carefully hefted Ibn Khan to his feet. The kalif coughed once, and blood spattered his lips and chin. Other than that, he kept silent, eyes closed and head drooping. He tried to walk with them, but halfway to the shade his legs began to drag. Del and the ken'dari ended up carrying his weight between the two of them, and his feet scratched furrows in the sand. They set him gently against a low stone wall, next to a small fire one of the ken'dari had kindled. Only then did Ibn Khan open his eyes. He sought out Del, and his hand reached out to take hold of his sleeve. He opened his mouth to speak, but coughed again. Twisting his head, he spat blood to the side, then pulled Del closer. His words came out in bloody whispers.

"Jaggi," he said, and his eyes pointed back to the well.

Del looked over his shoulder. The Jaggi had not moved. It was still watching them quietly.

"Go," Ibn Khan bade him. He let go of Del's shirt, and managed to push his arm away before his hand dropped back to the ground.

Del shook his head.

"Go," Ibn Khan insisted in as strong a voice as he could muster. The effort caused his wound to flare, and his face contorted. "It is what we came for. Do not let it leave. Do not . . ." but his words were interrupted by a spasm of pain, and he let his head roll back. His breathing was wet, fighting through the blood in his throat. He blinked heavily, and he fought to focus his eyes. "Go," he said again.

Cursing inwardly, Del pushed to his feet and left the shade of the alley. The Jaggi watched him approach alone, its strangely pale eyes fixed on him from behind the wrappings wound about its face. As Del drew closer, he saw that hooves were not the Jaggi's only oddity. Its left hand possessed only three massive fingers, each the thickness of two. The hand and forearm were both overly powerful, seemingly capable of crushing stone and wielding thunder. With this overlarge hand it gripped its thick staff.

Del came as close as he dared. The Jaggi made no move to greet him, and they faced one another over the body of the sthaak. Del noticed that it had left its rod impaling the carcass, presumably in case the beast decided to live again.

"I owe you my life," he said.

The Jaggi ripped its rod out of the sthaak with one quick pull. While Del watched, it drove the tip into the ground several times to cleanse it of blood. Raising its arm, the Jaggi pointed its weapon back across the wastelands toward Aba Ajraan, a message not subject to misinterpretation. Go home. Turning away from Del, it began to walk toward the south end of the outpost, its hooves leaving deep tracks in the gravel.

"Wait!" Del cried out after it.

The Jaggi did not stop.

Determined, Del followed after the lumbering figure. "We need your help. We have come from Aba Ajraan to find you—to ask for your help; for the help of your people."

The Jaggi passed through a cluster of ruined shacks, a forest of broken wood beams and half-standing walls. It had to duck to pass through the frames. Entering a wide avenue, it bore left, Del trailing not far behind, feeling like a needy, pestering child begging in the wake of an oblivious parent. He grew sick of it quickly. Stooping as he walked, he scooped up a hail sized stone, skipped forward once for momentum, and cast it at the departing Jaggi with enough strength backing it to nearly tip himself off balance.

The stone found its mark, connecting solidly with the Jaggi's upper back.

It stopped . . . turned.

For better or worse, Del had captured the Jaggi's attention.

It began to advance with a dangerously purposeful stride, but Del stood his ground, refusing to back down. "We didn't come this far to be ignored," he said, breathing heavily from the exertion of keeping up with the Jaggi's longer strides. The Jaggi did not slow its approach, and Del had the sudden, fleeting thought that the throwing of stones had probably not improved the situation. He considered fleeing, and even took a step backwards, but bolstered his courage with anger and planted his feet firmly.

The Jaggi stopped hardly four paces from Del, and it was only then that he appreciated the full stature of the creature. It looked down on him with milky eyes, and he could hear it breathing as one hears the hot snorting of a bull in a pen. Its great three-fingered hand flexed on its thick rod, and Del heard the dry creaking of the leather it wore. They stared at one another for a moment, each seeming to wait for the other to speak.

Del began, but was forced to stop, swallow, and begin again.

"My people need your help. We are being massacred." For the first time, he considered that the Jaggi had no idea what he was saying. He had assumed they would know the Bedu tongue, but apparently he has assumed wrong, and he felt the fool. Standing beneath the white eyes of an angered Jaggi, he felt defeat crush in on him.

Now what, O great ambassador? he mocked himself. Opening his arms in a helpless gesture, he hung his head and—

The orb.

Fumbling at the inner pocked sewn into his robe, he practically tore out the seams to get at the small bundle wrapped in white cloth. He'd carried it all the way from Aba Ajraan, and now he unraveled it as the Jaggi hunter watched. Del let the wind take the white wrapping when it fell away, and the Jaggi's pale eyes shifted to the orb. He couldn't have said what he'd hoped for, but if the Jaggi had knowledge of the sthaak, then they might also have knowledge of the orb, its origins and its part in the events transpiring. Recognition and—was it fear?—lit in the Jaggi's eyes, and for Del, it was enough to inspire excitement and hope.

"You know what this is," Del said. "You've seen it."

The Jaggi half-turned, using his rod to point farther down the desolate avenue. He began to walk again, gesturing for Del to follow.

The Jaggi led him to the outskirts of the outpost, to a place where massive boulders decorated the ground like the bare shoulders of sunken giants. Atop the crest of the largest rock crouched a second Jaggi hunter, and some distance from him, a third. They seemed to be sentries keeping watch over the empty streets. Somewhere within the maze of boulders was a wide clearing of sand. It was a large space, and the boulders surrounding it afforded a view of all the land around. It seemed a fine spot to hide the small army that took shelter there now.

There might have been as many as two hundred of them, but Del was never given the opportunity to count. A few glanced at him with disinterest, while others ignored the new arrival completely. His escort led him through the ranks of the army and brought him finally to a Jaggi hunter crouched in the shade of a heavy cluster of rocks. The escort held out an arm to block Del, then moved forward alone, leaving the ambassador to stand uncomfortably by himself amid the onlooking Jaggi. There were words spoken, gestures, and in due time the crouching hunter rose to approach Del.

To Del's surprise, the Jaggi spoke in a heavily accented Bedu tongue. "You carry a seed?" it asked him. Its voice rumbled, ocean deep.

Del's brow creased. Seed?

The first Jaggi prodded Del's long robe with the butt of his rod, at the place where his inner pocked was concealed. They meant the orb. Hurriedly, Del withdrew the shimmering bauble to display for the waiting Jaggi. The orb attracted attention, and the hunters in close proximity edged closer to catch a glimpse. Its pale eyes fixed on the orb, the Jaggi seemed both awed and frightened. Heated words were exchanged, as though the orb were a source of contention. Finally, reluctantly, the Jaggi hunter again faced Del.

"What do you want?" it asked.

"The Bedu are dying. The sthaak . . . the creatures you hunt, they are killing us."

The Jaggi remained silent, pale eyes never shifting away, never blinking.

"We need your help," Del said bluntly.

The Jaggi shook his head. "We cannot help you."

"The Bedu are prepared to pay. They will give you everything."

"Cannot help," the Jaggi repeated.

"Many Bedu have already died."

"More will die. The *sidii* cannot be stopped."

"*Sidii?*"

From his chest, the Jaggi lifted a necklace decorated with a dozen curved and wicked claws. They were sthaak. He showed them to Del. "*Sidii.*"

"What have they come for? What do they want?"

"The *sidii* want nothing."

"Then why do they kill Bedu?"

"The *sidii* kill because it is all they know," the Jaggi told him. He spoke with hesitation, struggling with the foreign words. "This is the season of *udan*, the time that comes only once a great while. The *sidii* carry the seeds up from the bottom of the *elgaar*—the black mountain."

Del tossed the smooth orb to the ground and toed it toward the Jaggi. "And this is one of their seeds?"

The Jaggi's eyes flitted over the orb.

"This is what they're destroying us with?"

"This is only one. The *sidii* carry many seeds up from the black mountain. Deeply they are planted, in water and in dirt. From these seeds will grow this," and the Jaggi swept its massive arm out to indicate all of the desert surrounding them.

"Tell us how to stop it," Del said abruptly.

"It cannot be stopped."

"Then tell us how to fight the sthaak."

The Jaggi shook its head. "Do not fight."

"You fight them," Del challenged. "You hunt them."

"In the season of *udan* there are too many."

Del stared at him defiantly. "Then all of the Bedu—all of my people, and all of yours—will die?"

"The Jaggi will not die," it said. "The Jaggi have gone. We will return when the *udan* has ended and the *sidii* are again sleeping beneath the Sands."

Del was already shaking his head. "I don't believe you. There's a way to stop them. There has to be. They bleed, they die. They can be stopped."

The Jaggi maintained its silence.

"They can be stopped," Del repeated angrily. "We'll stop them."

"You will not be the first to try."

Del was afraid to ask what that meant. A nubulous menace loomed behind him, unable to inflict terror or become real unless he turned to face it. The Jaggi brought it alive for him.

"In the *udan* before now the *sidii* destroyed the Poloi. They were a great nation, a nation older and stronger than the Bedu, and more fierce. They built tall cities above the Sands, and great caverns beneath. They are gone now, and their cities are gone, because of the *sidii*. They did not listen. They fought the *sidii*, and they died. When the seeds are planted, the Sands destroy all. This cannot be stopped."

Del struggled to wrap his mind around the Jaggi's words, but the implications were too vast. An empire destroyed and deserts grown from seeds out of dark mountains. For a long moment Del simply stood—mind numb, emotions drained.

"Where have your people gone?" he asked.

The Jaggi pointed into the deep Sands.

"Across the Sands?" Del questioned.

It nodded.

A long silence ensued. Del did not want to break away.

"You have gods?" the Jaggi asked without pretext.

It took Del several seconds to understand the question. Eventually, he nodded. "For what they're worth."

The Jaggi nodded his approval. "Pray to them. Pray that you run farther than the *sidii* will follow."

Had Del's heart been able to sink any deeper, it would have drowned him beneath the sand.

"You should go," the Jaggi said. "Leave this place."

Del concentrated on the words, letting them saturate him deeply, and he found that he agreed with his whole being. Leave this place. Leave it all behind: the Sands, the Bedu, everything. Get out. Get out and stay alive. Almost in a daze, he nodded his head slowly. Yes, get out.

He bent to retrieve the orb, but the Jaggi next to him raised an arm, barring him.

Del's mind sharpened with suspicion.

"You should not take this," the Jaggi told him. "Your people have enough trouble; you do not need more."

Del's teeth clenched in resentment. "We'll decide what we

need."

The Jaggi seemed to consider a matter, then gestured to a hunter nearby, who rose and brought a small leather pack with it. The pouch was square and thick, with buckles and straps all around it. He handed it to Del.

"It is a trade in your favor," the Jaggi said.

Still suspecting foul motives, Del opened the pack. Inside was another orb, heavy and alone.

"It is the same," he said.

"No," the Jaggi said. "This is a seed from another place. It will remake the world in different ways."

Del reached into the sack, and brought the orb into the light. Unlike the other, the one that had been brought out of the Sands by the sthaak, this was not the drab color of dust and sand. It was faintly green, and it felt wet to the touch. But when he took his hand away, his palm was dry.

"Take it to your people," the Jaggi said. "But understand it will not help you fight the *sidii*. It will not save you."

"Then what good is it?" Del asked bitterly.

The Jaggi shook its head. It seemed almost disappointed. "Your kind thinks only of this day, and never the next. Take it home with you, Human. Leave it for those who come after. There can be a rebirth. Is that not what you want?" At this, it shook its head again, slow and full of regret. "Another empire of Men. The Sands would be better.

"Go now," it said. "We are done."

The Jaggi retrieved the orb in the sand and turned its back. The one next to Del lowered its arm, and the others moved their attention elsewhere. Almost immediately upon his dismissal, Del was treated as though he were no longer present.

With the sack and its strange new seed in hand, Del felt that something had been left unfinished. "What is it like?" he asked abruptly. "Across the Sands." The question had no precedent, but Del felt strongly that he should know.

The Jaggi stopped and looked back at him. After watching him

147

a brief moment, it turned its gaze south, and for a little while stood motionless, seeing over the dunes and across the endless desert. When it returned its gaze to Del, its pale eyes seemed very human. "Nothing like this place," it said.

It was exactly what Del wanted to hear.

• • •

They removed Del's dagger from the kalif's chest before the sun set that night. When they cauterized the wound, it took all four of them to hold him down, and he screamed brokenly around the stick clamped in his teeth. When it was done, the kalif lapsed into a restless sleep fringed with pain. For some time the ken'dari crouched around him, humming and swaying gently. The sound of their prayers floated upwards with the glowing ashes of the fire, voices melting together into one incomprehensible stream of words.

They made camp that night right there in the narrow alley of the outpost. Their fire was small, and although the ken'dari cooked a simple meal of rice and stew, Del ate nothing. He watched over Ibn Khan as the kalif shifted and moaned in his sleep, wrestling with death, and every breath a struggle. Later, one of the ken'dari returned Del's dagger to him, dropping it at his feet as he crouched near the fire.

"A good blade," the ken'dari told him softly.

Del stared at the dagger between his feet, seven inches of hateful steel resting in the sand like a silver viper. He couldn't bring himself to touch it, and all night he left it where it lay.

Seven

Three days it took Ibn Khan to die.

They had left the outpost despite his condition, judging it better to attempt the long journey back to Aba Ajraan than to sit and wait for him to stop living. Unable to walk, and hardly able to ride, they'd been forced to tie his wrists to the saddle to keep him mounted. He would slump in his saddle, head down and eyes closed, a ken'dari walking to either side of the camel to keep him in place should he try to fall. For days they pressed on, their pace slow, but their marches long.

Somewhere west of the Rhashid flatlands they stopped at a well on the rim of a dusty yellow plain scattered with dying bushes and black boulders. Ibn Khan was brought down from his saddle, and they helped him to sit in the shade of a couched camel. His wound had ripped open, and the bandage they had looped under his shoulder had bloomed with a wet red stain. A steady trickle of blood had painted a streak of red down his arm and across the back of his hand. He was awake and aware, following them with glazed eyes as they watered the camels and refilled the skins. They spent only a short while at the well, and when it was time to press on, the ken'dari prepared to lift him, but he pushed them back with his good arm.

"No more," he said. They were the first words he had spoken in the three days since leaving the outpost, and his voice was cracked and dry.

Zayid crouched in front of him. "It is not far now, Kalif."

Ibn Khan nodded westward, and they followed his eyes to where a chain of low dunes were framed against the sky.

"Take me there," Ibn Khan said.

"But Ajraan is to the north, Kalif."

"I'm not going to Ajraan."

The ken'dari said nothing for a time, then nodded. He glanced at the others, gestured to their new destination, then he and Del hoisted Ibn Khan to his feet.

The dunes the kalif had chosen were somewhere between the outpost and the southern perimeter of Saar territory. Within them, the ken'dari sought out a deep hollow sheltered on three sides by a crescent-shaped dune the color of rust and gold. From the crest could be seen the mountains of Ghanim, a jagged strip of distant peaks receding to the northeast, while to the west storm clouds were piling up like dark towers, promising to bring rain to the desert for the first time that season, and probably the last. If it rained even a little, the desert would bloom in the spring, and there would be good grazing and full wells for years to come.

They laid Ibn Khan in the shade, and built a fire close to keep him warm. Del crouched nearby, watching over the kalif in case he should awake and be in need of anything. As night fell, the ken'dari drifted away one by one to sleep, but Del remained with the kalif, keeping his small fire alive. The kalif looked frail and withered, and there was a dreadful heat rising from him, as though a furnace burned beneath his skin. His consciousness came and went in furtive spells, and he breathed only with great effort. Even in sleep his pain was terrible. Del could see it twisting across the muscles of his face, drawing low groans from behind dry lips. When the moon rose above the crest of their dune, Del turned his face upwards, basking in pale light so brilliant it cast shadows across the sand. He could almost feel it on his skin, glowing light from another world. It was a clean feeling, to be touched by something so distant that it cared nothing for him or any of his pain.

It was not until very late that Ibn Khan spoke. Until then, the only sound had been the popping of sticks in the fire. The kalif's eyes, bright and wet, had opened to find Del seated at his feet. He watched Del as though peering out of an open grave.

"You think this is your fault?" he whispered.

Del said nothing, but it was enough.

"You will tell my family. You do not have to lie."

Del could only nod.

"Tell them I was not afraid to die."

The kalif coughed then, and blood came up. Del dipped a piece of cloth into a bowl of water and touched it to the kalif's cracked lips. Ibn Khan's right arm was drawn to his chest, and his hand was trembling and rigid. Death was concluding the slow process of chewing the life from him. Toward the end, Del could see that the Ibn Khan's suffering was great. He stayed with the kalif all through the night, listening until the breath rattling in his lungs finally, mercifully, fell silent.

• • •

They dug the kalif's grave within sight of the well, and marked it with a small pile of skull-sized rocks. It was a good spot, with the mountains of Ghanim in the distance, and the soft, curving swells of the dunes close by. They worked through the early hours of the morning, while a slow breeze blew across the flatlands from the southwest, carrying sand and grit on its lonely campaign across the desert. The grave was simple, with no adornments or engravings to tell who was buried there, only the little pile of stones and a mound of freshly turned sand. In time, the sand would be flattened by rain and wind, but the rocks would stay, a monument to the unknown dead.

After the final stone had been laid the ken'dari mounted their camels, but Del remained standing over the grave. They looked to him questioningly, but he waved them on. "Go," he said.

Shrugging, the ken'dari turned their camel's northward toward Aba Ajraan. Del watched the line of long-necked beasts shuffling across the plain, and as they shrank farther away the solitude of the desert folded around him. He looked to the grave, and thought of Ibn Khan encased in sand. No words had been said over him, and although the ken'dari had already gone, Del felt as though his business was unfinished. Over the years he had found the Bedu to be a very pragmatic people. Sentimentality had to place among them, and lasting grief was equally unwelcome. The Bedu had no cemeteries in which to visit their dead. There were only these small unmarked graves scattered and forgotten throughout the territories. He remembered what Sumir Attalah had told him of the *Qa'taan* during his sojourn at Gideon's Wall. There was no direct translation for the word, and the little man had been hard pressed to describe it. "The *Qa'taan*," he had explained. "It is the place beyond death."

"What is it like?" Del had asked.

The little man had taken on a pained look, the same scrunched up face he always used when Del began to ask questions he didn't want to answer. But he'd struggled anyway to explain a thing that defied explanation. "It is the *Qa'taan*," he had said, as though the word itself should be sufficient. "It is not like anything here. It is a different kind of life."

"Different how?"

"There is no more pain. No hunger, or thirst. In the *Qa'taan* you need nothing. You have no body, but you still live. You become like the wind."

"There are women in this *Qa'taan*?"

Sumir had scowled and frowned. "Women, no—"

"Women are not allowed, then?"

"Yes. Women go to *Qa'taan* just as men do, but no longer are they women. Nor are the men as they are in this life."

Del had wondered if the Bedu nomad's faith in this mystical place called the *Qa'taan* made the death of a friend or a loved one any easier to understand or accept. He had asked, and Sumir had smiled sadly before answering, "Not for me, Ambassador."

"In Shallai, they believe in a place after death, too," Del had told him. "They call it Paradise. It sounds something like the *Qa'taan*, but in Shallai's Paradise there are women."

The little man had tried to put an end to the conversation by offering him a rapid nod, but he'd been too agitated to fool Del. "Paradise," he had agreed quickly. "The *Qa'taan* is Paradise." But Del had thought that he just didn't want to talk about it anymore.

Now, as he stood over the kalif's grave, Del wondered if the *Qa'taan* was just another fairy tale to ease the pain of death and add meaning to life, or if perhaps there was some truth to it. He did not think on it long though, for the wind had begun to pick up, and the blowing sand had caused his eyes to water profusely. He pulled a fold of his head-cloth down around his face, leaving only enough space for his eyes and the bridge of his nose.

It was time to move on.

"Farewell, Kalif," Del said quietly. "May your gods have a place prepared for you." Before turning away, he stooped down to prop his sheathed dagger against the stones of the grave, the same blade that had cheated the proud kalif of his life. It had been easy for Ibn Khan to absolve him of the responsibility for his death. But such forgiveness was far more difficult to accept than to give. It was his blade that had taken the kalif's life. His blade, and his hand. For that, he did not live long enough to forgive himself.

Eight

Kitrum Well was crawling with Bedu warriors. While still far off Del could see the tiny disjointed shapes moving on the horizon. As they came closer, he could make out camels, horses, and tents. The warriors had seen them coming, and were emerging from their tents to assemble loosely near the well. They were to learn later that the well, and also many other spots all along the border of Ajraan territory, had been turned into outposts. The warriors populating the encampments had been sent to maintain a constant vigil of the flatlands beyond Ajraan borders.

As Del and the ken'dari approached, the warriors raised their arms, and called out wordless greetings that seemed thin in the hot air. Some of them took off their head-cloths and swung them around as they shouted out.

Riding next to Del, one of the ken'dari said, "They are not all men from Ajraan."

Del glanced at him. The warriors were still far enough away that he could hardly make out faces, let alone tribal associations.

"I see warriors from the Saar, and from the Bayt Kathir," the ken'dari continued.

"And the Dahm," added another, who was riding behind Del.

Del twisted in his saddle to look back at him, but the ken'dari's eyes were fixed on the distant encampment, and he only flicked them momentarily at Del.

"How can you tell?" Del asked.

"Look at them," the ken'dari said, as though the reasons were obvious. Del looked, but the men were still too far away for him to tell anything about them at all.

"And the camels," the other ken'dari said. "Over there, some of the camels grazing are darker than the others; those are Dahm breeds. And the Bayt Kathir camels are larger; you can see them there," and he pointed to the west end of the encampment, where a dozen camels were roaming in a loose herd. Del had to take their word for it, as the distance was still too great for him to distinguish one camel from another. He thought instead of what the presence of such a mix of ken'dari boded. If the warriors of the Dahm, the Bayt Kathir, and the Saar had taken to guarding the borders of Ajraan territory together, that meant they must have abandoned their own. His suspicions were later confirmed when he learned that four of the seven tribes had gathered in Ajraan territory, driven from their lands by the sthaak. Their camps now lined the banks of the Ashkelon.

It was not long after they entered the encampment that the dire news of the kalif's death spread among the warriors. Despite being the bearer of such grim tidings, Del was treated with the same customary respect which the Bedu offered any weary traveler. Still caked with the dust and the heartache of his journey, he was led to the well, where they sat him in the cool shade of a lean-to. The water they drew for him from Kitrum Well seemed sweet compared to the foul stuff of the desert, and he drank until he could stomach no more. Removing his overworked sandals, he tossed the now useless strips of leather out of the shelter, then washed from his feet the crust of dust and blood, scrubbing until the skin was pink and the water in the bowl had turned black. Although the soles of his feet had grown callous, the heels were cracked deep enough to bleed, and only after he scraped out the dirt embedded in them did they become almost too tender to walk upon. A plate of dates had been set close at hand to curb his hunger until a meal could be prepared, and he selected one now and crouched in the shade. He chewed slowly while watching the activity taking place out there beneath the sun. Although it was a small encampment of no more than fifty men, he couldn't help comparing it to the solitude of the desert. In doing so, he felt surrounded, and he longed for the emptiness of the wastelands and the freedom he had found there.

That night the warriors slaughtered a goat, and from the meat made a thick stew stocked with chunks of whole onion. Every man's bowl was filled with a mound of rice drowning in butter, and upon this the stew was served. The warriors, like all Bedu, ate without the aid of utensils, fishing for the fatty lumps of meat with fingers and thumbs. When they were done, they drank the broth from their bowls, or soaked it up with hard bread until the last drop was gone. Del had grown accustomed to this method of feeding long ago, and it seemed natural to him now. Having thrown his filthy sandals into the fire, he walked barefoot among them that night, barely noticing the sharp pebbles and cold sand beneath his feet. He spoke not at all, and they respected his silence, never once pressing for the details of Ibn Khan's death. There was no suspicion, no accusations. Halfway through the night, one of the warriors gestured to him as he stood near the fire. "The ambassador looks like a true nomad now," the Bedu said.

Del looked down at himself, at his bare feet, his long shirt stained with his travels through their lands, his head-cloth, and the camel-stick which he had grown so used to carrying at all times that it seemed an extension of his arm. He had begun to fit better among these people that he did among any other. "If your gods saw fit to make me one of you," he said quietly. "It would be a gift I could not repay."

He slept in a small tent that night, and the next morning, long before the break of dawn, the ken'dari raced to Aba Ajraan ahead of him. They had traded their camels for horses, the sleek, long-legged kind bred for racing, and their mounts painting two fading streaks of yellow dust toward the horizon. Although they didn't know it, Del was already up when they left, watching their departure from behind the curtains of his tent.

He left soon after sunrise, not because he craved to be back in Aba Ajraan, but because he wished to be alone again. And so as the pale light of dawn was filling the desert sky he set out on his camel, following the tracks of the ken'dari at a much slower pace.

It was three days ride to the city of black tents, and Del dreaded the hour of his return every step of the way. Despite the hunger, the thirst, the burning days and bitterly cold nights, he gladly would have turned back into the desert to face it all again—if only someone braver than he would stand in his place when the time came to look Ibn Khan's son in the face and tell him that his father was dead. He tried to imagine it was he who was buried in an unmarked grave in the desert. How would Ibn Khan tell Suri? What words would he offer after breaking her heart? What sort of comfort or apology could even begin to ease the wounds inflicted by the news he would bring? And would any of it be worth the breath it was spoken on?

• • •

Jiharra was waiting for Del in the deep ravine just north of Aba Ajraan. Cut by a river from another age, the base of the canyon was covered with pale sand and polished black rock left behind by the rushing waters. Flanked on either side by high, red cliffs, the ancient riverbed seemed a long, deep scar in the desert.

The kalif's heir had come alone. He sat outside a tent pitched in the center of a sandy belt of the ravine. He looked up as Del approached, and rose to his feet. Jiharra was dark in every way. His eyes and hair were the color of pitch, and his skin was a deep brown. He wore a long shirt of pale white, and a simple belt of woven wool. There was a dagger at his waist, and a curved scimitar across his back. He wore nothing on his feet. Judging by these simple garments alone, he might have been any Bedu nomad come to greet Del, and not the kalif of all Ajraan.

Stiff and worn, Del slid from his saddle to face the kalif. Outside of the canyon, the wind from the south had been strong, and he had wrapped his head-cloth round his face to keep the sand from scraping at his skin. Now he pulled the wool down around his neck so the kalif could see his whole face, and not just his eyes. He would not hide from telling the son that his father had died.

"Welcome home," Jiharra said quietly, and he clasped Del's wrist with both his hands. The grip was firm, sincere. "You have been missed." His eyes moved past Del to the vast emptiness behind him.

"My father is not with you," he said softly.

Although he had taken his fill of food and water at Kitrum Well, Del's stomach was a hollow pit. His silence was awkward, and nothing seemed right; not looking at Jiharra, not looking away. He felt crippled, sunk in his own lame silence, yet if he could have found any words to say, they would have been wrong. After a long while, Del managed to meet Jiharra's eyes. "I'm sorry," he said.

"How did he die?" Jiharra asked outright.

Del's mind readily offered up the blunt truth which had already robbed him of sleep; *I killed your father*, he thought. His gaze dropped under the weight of shame, and he found that he couldn't bring himself to say the words with Jiharra looking him in the eye. He wanted them out, but somewhere inside him the words were stuck, and so he went around them. "It was an accident," he said quietly. There was no reply, and when he looked up, he was surprised by the compassion he saw on Jiharra's face. It played on his shame, and he loathed himself for his own cowardice. "It was by my hand," he said bitterly, barely able to fit the words past his shame. "I am responsible."

Jiharra breathed deeply, then looked toward the cliff face as though there were something there to see. He pondered for a long moment, then looked back to Del. "You claim responsibility, yet you ask no forgiveness."

"I don't want forgiveness."

"Why not?"

Del erupted with rage. "I didn't steal from you!" he shouted. "I didn't break a promise to you, or insult your family. I killed your father! You don't forgive that."

"What would you have me do, Del?" Jiharra shot back. "Hate you for the rest of my life and yours? Or should I just kill you here?" Slipping his dagger from its sheath, he stepped to Del and pressed the point against his stomach.

Del made no move to stop him.

"Tell me that my father wanted you dead and I'll do it for him," Jiharra said through clenched teeth. "Tell me that he hated you for what you did. Tell me that he didn't forgive you." Receiving no answer, he shoved Del's chest, and pressed him with the knife. "Tell me!" he snarled. "Lie to me. Say that my father would have killed you himself if he'd been able, and I'll do it. I'll put my knife in your gut and leave you here to die, and I'll never look back. This is what you want? You want the responsibility and the punishment. It's an easy lie. Say the words!"

The kalif gave him long seconds, but Del was silent.

Jiharra removed the knife, shaking his head. "My father forgave you, Del. I won't kill you, and I won't hate you either. We are men, you and I. We are friends. And friends do not treat one another in such ways."

Del closed his eyes. He would have preferred the execution.

Jiharra stepped near and placed his hand firmly on the back of Del's neck, pulling their heads close together as though imparting a secret for the two of them alone. "You are a man of honor, Ambassador," he whispered with passion, eyes burning. The words bit deeply. They made his chest ache, and when he felt the sting of tears he tried to pull away, but Jiharra would not release him. "My father loved you, and he trusted you. And so shall I. No accident will change that."

Jiharra took his hand off the back of Del's neck, but continued to glare at him. Almost angrily, Del wiped two hot tears from his eyes.

"Now come," Jiharra said gently, gesturing toward the tent. "You have had a long journey, and I have water and food waiting in the shade. Come and share them with me, Del. You and I, we have much to discuss."

• • •

They sat for the rest of the day in the shade of the tent, drinking cool water and eating plump dates. When the sun dipped below the cliffs, they left the tent and built a fire in a fissure of the cliff wall, where the wind could not touch them. Feet near the fire, they drank fresh goat's milk and ate ribbons of salted meat while they talked. For a long time Del spoke of Ibn Khan, and of their journey to the outpost. When the tale reached the point of the kalif's death, Del's voice became subdued, and soon after he stopped speaking entirely. He turned his eyes into the shadowy darkness beyond the fire and fell silent, listening to the wind roam up and down through the canyon.

"So there will be no help from the Jaggi," Jiharra said.

Del shook his head. "We found hunters there, but nothing else. They gave me this." He pulled the drawstrings of his pack and pulled open the mouth, revealing the orb. "The Jaggi called it a seed."

Jiharra took the sphere and held it lightly. With his thoughts lost in the misty interior of the orb, he drug from memory an old piece of prophecy. "'From the Sands will rise a demon with a sword

160

of pain and a seed of poison," he recited. "He will rend all breath from the land, and undo all things which have been done. The waters and the hills will turn to sand, and the desert will drink blood.'" He stopped, and rubbed with his thumb the smooth face of the orb. "Or something very similar," he muttered in closing.

Del watched Jiharra closely, until finally the new kalif looked up at him. "Words of the Prophet himself," the kalif explained.

"Not a pretty picture," Del commented.

Jiharra shrugged. "I've yet to hear a prophecy that paints prettily."

Del said nothing for a moment, scrubbing at a pestering itch in his scalp.

Jiharra hefted the orb. "And what do they intend for us to do with this?"

"Nothing," Del answered. "They said it would not help us."

"Then why give it?"

For those who come after, Del thought. But he wouldn't say it, because it was too much like admitting they were already dead. Instead, he held the sack open wordlessly. When Jiharra returned the sphere to its place, Del cinched the sack tight and held it out to Jiharra. "I've carried it long enough. I don't want it near me anymore."

Jiharra took the pack and set it beside him.

"The hunter told us that the rest of the Jaggi had already returned to their homeland across the Sands," Del said, filling the uncomfortable silence. "He said they would not help us."

"Across the Sands," Jiharra mused. "I did not think such a place existed. Most of us still believe the Sands go on forever." Ripping a bite from the meat in his fist, he chewed at it thoughtfully. "So the Jaggi will be no help to us," he concluded suddenly. "This is bad. Hardly unexpected, but bad nonetheless." He brushed his weary gaze past Del before aiming it into the desert toward Aba Ajraan. "You have been gone a long while," he said. "And things have changed in Aba Ajraan."

"What things?"

"It is not good here, Del," Jiharra said. "The sthaak are coming, it is for certain now. They are coming here, to Ajraan, and they are killing everything along the way. We have scouts everywhere in the desert, the best of our ken'dari. Every day the creatures come a little bit closer. In the past days they have been seen ranging as far north as the fringes of Saar territory. Since you have been gone, three tribes have been swallowed, and the rest are deserting their homes and their territories to flee to Aba Ajraan in droves. Camps crowd on top of one another for leagues along both banks of the Ashkelon, and even southward into the plains, and still every day refugees continue to pour into the city." The new kalif shook his head in amazement. "I have never seen anything like this in my life."

They sat in silence together, and as the moon rose into the wide strip of black sky above the canyon, they heard the distant howl of wolves. Both men looked into the darkness surrounding their tiny sphere of light.

"I wonder . . ." Jiharra said softly, but fell into a silent reverie, his thoughts lost elsewhere in his imagination. Del waited patiently, and Jiharra looked at him momentarily. "I wonder what they fear?" he asked out loud.

"Who?"

"The sthaak. What do they fear?"

Del watched the kalif, but said nothing. Eventually, Jiharra was driven by the urge to explain himself. "The Bedu are being herded by the sthaak. They have driven us from our homes, slaughtering as they go, and we scatter before them." He put his hands close to the fire, as near as he could until the heat scratched against his palms like a thousand little claws. "Perhaps then, there is something behind the sthaak, something out of the deepest interior of the Sands, something herding them toward us. And they fear this thing as much as we fear them."

Del looked deep into the fire, remembering the sthaak at the Jaggi outpost, how it had shrieked at him with pure hatred, and how the Jaggi had pierced it again and again with its rod before it finally died. He tried to imagine something terrible enough to inspire fear in such a beast. He thought hard, and for a long time, but his imagination wouldn't produce for him without bending toward the absurd, and finally he gave up.

"Or maybe they want something," Jiharra ventured to guess.

"What would the sthaak want?"

Ibn Jiharra shrugged. "I don't know. But desire would imply intelligence, and I don't know which prospect frightens me more: a thing that puts a desert full of sthaak on the run, or the sthaak possessing more than animal intelligence."

Del didn't like either idea. He tried to eat more, but the ribbon of meat in his hand had become unappetizing to him, and the portion he'd already eaten was a lump of clay in his stomach. He tossed what was left in the fire, and watched the fat melt into tiny wisps of smoke as the edges blackened. Looking back to the desert, he noticed that the wolves had ceased their howling. "Jiharra," he said softly, and the kalif turned to him. Del hesitated, then released the thoughts in his head in one breath. "Take the people to Gideon's Wall. If the sthaak come, we can fight them there."

For a very long moment the two men stared at one another across the fire, but Jiharra offered no expression to betray his thoughts.

"Did you ask this of my father?" he finally said.

"No."

"But if you had, what would he have said?"

Del took a deep breath, noticing suddenly how cold the air had become. He took a long time answering. It would have been easy to lie, to tell Jiharra that his own father had planned to lead the Bedu to Gideon's Wall to seek safety behind that fortress. But it would have been an ugly lie. The alternative was to tell the truth, to say it as Ibn Khan himself would have said it, and in doing so possibly condemn every last Bedu to a terrible end. He made up his mind, but from the time he parted his lips to the time the first words spilled out, his decision turned ten times over. The truth and the lie tangled and tripped over one another just inside his mouth, so that for a moment he sat there with his mouth open, but wordless. Until finally he forced himself to speak.

"Your father never would have agreed to take his people to the wall," he said bluntly. His relief was immense for having finally spoken, but his heart dropped into a pit, and his whole body felt like weeping at the words he had just spoken. Even as he continued, he had to look away from Jiharra, and fight to keep his voice steady. "He would have thought it cowardly and dishonorable. To be driven from the deserts without a fight would be worse than death. Even if he were the last man, he would have stood against the sthaak alone."

Jiharra had dropped his gaze to the fire as Del spoke, and he continued to stare as though the flames had seized all his thoughts. He took a long time to answer, and when he did his voice was soft, and his decision final. "I'm sorry, Del," he said. "But I won't take my people to Gideon's Wall."

Del felt the last of his hope drain from his heart.

"But what will you do, Ambassador?" Jiharra asked directly.

In a puzzled manner, Del cocked his head slightly to the side. "What would you have me do?"

"Do you miss Shallai?"

"Why would I miss Shallai?"

"It is your home," the kalif said.

"Aba Ajraan is my home."

"But have you never missed Shallai?"

After a moments hesitation, Del nodded. "Sometimes."

"Do you miss it now?"

"No. Not now."

"When the sthaak come, we cannot fight them and win."

"They are not here yet," Del said, then quickly continued before the kalif could speak again. "Leave off with this game, Jiharra. If you have something to say to me, say it. Haven't we known one another long enough to speak our minds?"

Invited to speak bluntly, Jiharra did so immediately. "You should go," he said. "Take Suri and leave this place. Take her far away, to your home in Shallai."

Del cocked a brow. "You think Suri would leave?"

"Put Suri in a sack. It is not her choice."

"You believe it is wrong to lead your people to Gideon's Wall," Del countered. "What makes it right for me?"

Mulling this over, Jiharra kneaded his palm with a thumb while watching Del closely. He remembered how his father had once hated him, this soldier turned ambassador sent from Shallai to spy in broad daylight. He had hated him just as he had hated all the others sent before him. His father had lost sleep, so passionately did he abhor Shallai's presence breathing down his neck day and night. But when Del outlasted the others sent by Shallai, Jiharra had observed his father's irrational enmity for the soft-spoken northman first diminish, then vanish entirely.

"Ruthless dedication coming from you will never surprise me, Ambassador," Jiharra said. He paused, eyes still set on Del even though the ambassador had let his gaze drop to his feet. He waited until Del looked up, then caught his eyes and would not let go. "Nor did it surprise my father."

Del's eyes fell again, and he looked aside.

"He loved you, Del. You were a true friend to him."

"Your father deserved better friends than me."

"A better friend than you?" Jiharra mused. "I think such a thing would not be possible."

Del rubbed his eyes, feeling exhaustion taking root there. "I was told once that my duties here were intended to be more than those of an ambassador," he said. "I was told that one day my empire would call on me as an assassin. What sort of friend am I now?"

"You are no assassin, Del."

"I've spent my life obeying orders."

"Killing my father is an order you would not have accepted," Jiharra said forcefully. "We both know you would have taken your own life before willingly harming him. I won't hear this. Your empire, as great as it may be, cannot make a murderer of you."

Del nodded, but it was only an appeasement.

When they decided it was time to return to the city, they drank the last of the milk and kicked out the embers of the fire. It took less than an hour of slow traveling to reach the north bank of the Ashkelon, at which point they stopped to absorb the view.

All around Aba Ajraan the tribes had gathered to defend the last bastion of their besieged nation. The flatlands around the white city were crowded with camps of Bedu refugees, and brightly colored tents sprawled across the plains, giving the impression that the desert had bloomed. By the light of the moon they rode through the camps toward Aba Ajraan, leaving the silence unbroken as they passed tent after tent of sleeping Bedu from each tribe, all come together from the farthest reaches of the desert. How long did they have to live, Del wondered. How long before the sthaak fell upon them? He saw a child with long hair and bare feet standing outside a tent, following them with dark eyes as they passed. The sight made him wish he had lied.

Nine

Nearly four days after Del's return to Aba Ajraan, watchmen from Kitrum Well came thundering out of the desert on swift steeds that had been pushed to their limits. The terrifying news which they brought ripped through Aba Ajraan like chain lightning. The sthaak had at last invaded, and were swarming over the borders of Ajraan. The outposts along the fringes of the territory had been vacated, their watchmen fleeing north to escape the horde and supply their people with warning enough to prepare themselves.

The few tents still clustered on the south side of the Ashkelon were immediately abandoned, as panicked occupants hastily bundled together all they had and retreated across the waters to the overcrowded northern bank. Within the encampments on the north side, warriors took up spear and sword, and added their numbers to the swelling ranks up and down the shoreline.

From their chambers in the kalif's estate, Del and Suri heard the shouts rising up from below. Stepping onto the balcony, they watched the commotion among the camps. It came as no surprise to Del that the sthaak had come. The event was inescapable, something possessing the same certainty with which a condemned man watches the execution of a fellow criminal, and understands that someday it will be him kneeling at the executioner's block. But knowing that death was to come *someday* was very different from knowing that today was the day, and until presently, Del's apprehension had been in a state of hibernation, tucked away behind an illusion of safety cast by the trappings of his own home. And so when the cry of the watchmen reached the ambassador's ears like the call of an executioner, his fear came growling out with a vengeance.

He knew it wouldn't last, it never did. But knowing such things didn't make quelling the present dread any easier. He had always thought fear a funny thing. It was a plague before battle, infesting entire battalions of men, where it corroded the nerves and intensified imaginations, making the bravest of warriors wonder how they could muster the strength to face what was to come. But when the bloodshed began, when the trumpets sounded and the screams of dying men and ringing steel blotted out all else—fear vanished.

Del had heard many soldiers say that in battle there was no time for fear, and he supposed that was partly true. Fear was a little like pain in that respect; both took flight during the frenzied spasms of combat, only to become real again *after*. After the unskilled, unfortunate, and unlucky had been segregated from the living by the bite of steel, after the din of warfare had ebbed into the far-flung moans of the wounded, and after the blood cooled enough to realize that it was over, death successfully held at bay. Both fear and pain had a tendency to creep back somewhat timidly, unsure of how cheerfully they might be received. Pain was easy enough to cope with, it was simple and honest. It was fear that gave trouble.

It was always different after; stranger, more disturbing. The mind obsessed itself with thoughts of what might have happened. Del loathed to think about how many times he had stood on a churned battlefield, looking down on the faces of the fallen and wondering if next time it would be him lying twisted in the mud and staring at the sky. Such thoughts were useless and crippling.

Del turned from the camps below, and Suri followed him from the balcony into the spacious living chamber. She watched from the doorway as he retrieved his sword. Taking it up, he held it firmly, one hand gripping the hilt, the other supporting the sheathed blade. In that simple act was all the comfort of clasping hands with an old friend. Having the weapon in his hands made the life he'd lived before coming to Aba Ajraan seem less the life of a stranger, and more of something that belonged to him. As much as he didn't want that life lost, he didn't want it back, either.

"I don't have a choice," he said in answer to a question that hadn't been asked.

"You're going to fight," Suri said.

Del faced her then, and saw the anguish in her eyes. Looking deeper, he saw too the pride. She would not try to stop him, because she did not feel that he should be stopped. The Bedu were as much his people as hers, and it was his right to die fighting with them. Moving to stand in front of her, he placed one hand against her cheek, and the kiss he pressed into her lips was urgent and sincere. He hoped the passion of it would say all the things he should have said days ago.

Breaking the kiss, he put his cheek against hers, and his lips close to her ear. "I will see you soon," he whispered to her, both of them knowing it was a lie. He left saying nothing more, and when Suri finally opened her eyes, she was alone.

• • •

The sthaak came, but did not cross the Ashkelon. There on the far side of the river they sulked, bunching together at the water's edge—a brooding, seething mass of scaled bodies. There were thousands of them, so close that with a little practice, a man with a strong arm could have arced a stone over the water and hit one. Up and down the rocky banks opposite Aba Ajraan they moved, pacing like jackals behind bars. Some guessed it was the Ashkelon keeping them at bay, that some primal fear prevented them from crossing the waters. Others said it was the sight of the Bedu warriors and ken'dari standing ready with long spears and curved swords. Most believed it was the hand of the Prophet.

All through that first day the Bedu waited with dread. No one dared take their eyes off the beasts just across the river, knowing that any moment could be the one in which the Prophet lifted his hand.

Only the ken'dari stood unaffected by fear, their shiftless black eyes fixed on the enemy. But their numbers were few compared to the Bedu warriors, and their courage could not be measured out to those in greater need. And so they waited, but the sthaak would not cross the rushing waters.

By midafternoon, the apprehension among the Bedu had lost its edge, and by nightfall, nerves had been dulled by the constant suspense. Fear that had once pounded in their hearts with grave urgency, now snuggled into the guts of the men, where it lay in heavy, restless coils.

The sun burned out in the western plains, and the temperature plummeted. As night swept its dark arm across the heavens, mist emerged from the warm waters of the river, climbing upwards like emaciated ghosts rising from watery graves. The air cooled further, and the mist thickened and spilled over the banks. Fires were struck to fend off the clammy touch of the fog, but the sparse flames were only partially effective. The ruddy light reflected in the baleful eyes of the sthaak across the river, setting aflame endless ranks of bobbing and blinking circles. With those endless rows of eyes watching them, most of the warriors could not bring themselves to eat, and while some slept, most didn't bother to try.

• • •

In the dim blue light of early morning, the woman rose from her blankets to look upon her sleeping children. She had not slept well that night, as the ground around the Ashkelon was rife with rocks and pebbles, nothing like the soft sands of Dahm territory. Their tent was small and crowded. They had been forced to leave much behind when the sthaak had driven them from their home, and everything they had not brought with them had been scattered by the sthaak. The herds of camel and goat slaughtered, and the vineyards trampled. Her children were young, and she was alone with them. Her husband, like all the other able-bodied men, had gone to the fringes of the camp, where he waited to fight the sthaak when they crossed the river. As she pulled a shawl about her shoulders, the youngest of her boys awoke, and looked at her with sharp, clear eyes, as though he had never slept at all.

"Is Father back?" he asked.

"Soon," the woman lied to him gently. "Return to your dreams."

Obediently, the boy closed his eyes, and within moments was asleep once more. Slipping outside, the woman took up a coil of rope and a small leather bucket by the mouth of the tent. The sky was a dull black, and the stars shone fretfully. She stood a moment in silence, watching her breath plume in the frigid air. Although the darkness of night had just begun to thin, the surrounding tents of her tribe were nothing but colorless bulks in the darkness, and although she could not see very far, she knew the camps of the Bedu stretched away in every direction, set together so closely that there was hardly room enough to walk between them. She could feel the pressure of people around her, the distinct feeling that not only was she not alone, but that she was in the presence of thousands. She was but one small part of a sleeping giant.

With bucket in hand and rope slung over her shoulder, she wound her way between the close-set tents, making a crooked path toward the wells at the foot of the ancient palace of Ajraan. She had wanted to draw her water early, because she knew that later in the morning there would be crowds coming to draw from the deep wells.

She found the wells abandoned, and thought that the empty courtyard was eerie in the dim light. Crossing the cold sand, she sat at the raised stone lip of one of the deep pits, and slowly lowered the leather bucket into the dark stone mouth. Down and down it went as she fed the rope hand over hand into the well. Long after she should have hit water, her bucket finally stopped. She waited a moment, then began the long pull up. The bucket was heavy, and by the time it emerged from the black eye of the well, her arms were weary and burning. But when she looked down, her eyes widened.

The bucket contained only sand and mud.

• • •

Del had been awake more than two hours before the sun rose to burn away the mist. He had spent his night on the ground, like the rest of the Bedu, with only a blanket to cover himself and his arm for a pillow. Unlike most, he'd slept well.

Rising in the small hours before dawn, he went to scrub his face with water left overnight in a leather bucket, but found it covered by a thin sheet of ice. Tapping through the crust, he dipped his hands and splashed the frigid liquid over his face, then scooped the moisture from his eyes with two fingers.

He remained crouched over the bucket for some time, staring into the fog while the skin of his face burned with cold. Water dripped from his chin and the tip of his nose, and little beads made fast tracks down the slope of his neck. They slid beneath the open collar of his shirt, inducing a shiver as they tracked ice across his skin. In the dreary half-light of early morning, the silence of the Bedu encampment was unsettling. All around him, the ground was strewn with warriors hiding from the cold beneath their heavy blankets. Sheaves of long spears stood among the sleeping bodies like strange and naked trees, each thin branch tipped with a silver bud. The whole bank of the river seemed a landscape littered with black boulders just the size of sleeping men.

He had always imagined time to move sluggishly in the early hours, and he thought it especially so now, weighed down as it was by the oppressive mist. He thought that if the fog had its way, this hour would never pass. Those who slept would remain so forever, while the rest watched over them as they waited for the mist to unfurl and time to begin again. And then he pictured the banks of the Ashkelon as a place where a battle had already been fought, instead of one yet to be visited; that the sleeping Bedu were slain warriors, that the fog was smoke from burning pitch and tar, and that he was the sole survivor of whatever terrible forces had collided there. In the mist and blue-black darkness of morning, the vivid image was a frighteningly uncanny fit.

Unnerved by his own imagination, Del dried his face by dragging the sleeve of his shirt across his nose and forehead, then went back to the place he had slept. There was a large flat rock nearby, and he sat down on it, and drew his knees up. From his position he could hear the constant muttering of the Ashkelon, but could not see the water through the fog. He waited there for some time before the Bedu encampments slowly began to stir with life.

Those camped nearest the water were the first to notice what had begun during the night. The river had thinned. Although the flow was not visibly less, the level had dropped by nearly six inches, leaving a dark watermark on the white stones and soft clay. The news rippled among the ranks of the Bedu in whispers and murmurs. Men began to wonder, some to themselves, and some aloud, whether the Ashkelon would continue to drop. Would it shrivel until nothing but a trickle separated them from the sthaak? The warriors stared across the river at the sthaak pacing up and down the opposite bank, and wondered if it was just their imaginations—if it was just the way their scaled skin pulled back from rows of jagged teeth—or if the beasts were actually grinning.

By the time the sun climbed above the horizon the word was spreading. From his seat on the black rock, Del observed the news rippling past, traveling in whispers from group to group reawakening dread among the Bedu. It made perfect sense to him; a seed had been planted, perhaps on the other side of the river, perhaps upstream, or perhaps at the river's source somewhere in the bare stone mountains to the west. And just as the Jaggi at the outpost had told him, the desert was growing. From the seeds would spring a wasteland as deep and lifeless as the Sands. A great swirling maw would open up and devour not only Ajraan, but the homes, lives, and every last trace of those who defended it. The river was only the beginning.

A messenger sent by Jiharra found him there not long after sunrise. It had not been difficult to locate the ambassador, as he was the only northman among the Bedu, a fact that made obscurity impossible. Del had moved only a little, and still sat facing the river, which could now be seen through the thinning fog. The messenger, a young man with plaited hair and a ripped shirt, came to stand beside him. "Ambassador," he said, keeping a respectful distance. Twice more he had to say it before finally being rewarded with a slow and resigned look from the ambassador.

"What do you want?"

"The kalif has asked for you."

Del turned a deaf ear on him.

"Ambassador?"

"And what does *he* want?"

"He only said that he wishes to speak with you."

Del rolled his head forward, then around, feeling the bones in his neck popping, each one a tiny jolt of pain. He had been sitting too long like this. Why would Jiharra want to see him? What more was there to say?

"Ambassador—"

"I heard you," Del said quickly, holding up his hand to prevent the young Bedu from repeating himself. As much as he wanted to be left alone, he knew he would not be able to ignore the messenger away. Relentless persistence was an inherent trait of all Bedu, and he knew without a doubt that the young messenger would sooner starve than return to the kalif without the quarry he had been sent for. And so Del came down off his rock and stretched, arching his back and kicking feeling into numbed legs. When he was ready, he took up his sword, which he had leaned against the rock, and faced the patiently waiting boy.

"Lead," he said tersely, gesturing with his hand.

Like a hound cut loose from its leash, the young man dashed off toward Aba Ajraan, cutting a crooked path among groups of soldiers and pits dug in the ground for fires. As they came closer to the city, they were swallowed by a mixed sea of tents from nearly every tribe. The black shelters and miserly lean-tos were densely packed together, as though there were not room enough in the world for all of them. The sight reminded him of the filthy shanty-towns he had seen while on the march through war-torn lands. Such places were left in the wake of rampaging armies, and they acted as drainage for husbandless women, fatherless children, and wounded soldiers, all bunched together because fear pressed on them from every angle. The people stayed because no one could tell them where to go next.

The messenger raced ahead, stopping only occasionally to scamper up onto a boulder and look back across the tops of tents and people to verify he'd not lost his northern shadow. In this way, the messenger led Del out of the Bedu encampments and into the congested streets of Aba Ajraan. Upon reaching the kalif's estate, Del freed the messenger to pursue other objectives, and proceeded alone.

The estate had become eerily void of life. Gone were the wives and their daughters, and empty were the places in the courtyards where they had once sat. Gone were the children and grandchildren, their spirits and laughter replaced by a morose silence. It seemed every living member of the kalif's estate had been spirited away, leaving only dark corners and footprints in the cold sand. Del walked the halls alone, peering into lifeless rooms and down abandoned corridors. He crossed the gardens, dappled with shade from the palms, and stopped to crane his neck toward the balcony of his own rooms above.

"Suri," he called, and his voice seemed too loud in the heavy stillness. He waited for an answer, but the balcony remained empty.

In the southern wing of the estate, there was a private room behind a thick and heavy door. At the far end of the room was a wide circular balcony overlooking the river, and against one wall stood a rack of various weapons; a long spear with a barbed hook at one end, several falchions, and a myriad of knives and other blades of strange fashion and design. Spread across the stones of the floor at the center of the chamber was a deep rug of rich colors, and arranged in a circle upon the rug were plush cushions. Other than these things, the room was bare. Del and the kalif had often met there to discuss matters of importance, as it was one of the rare places in the estate in which they could talk undisturbed. It was there that he found Jiharra. The kalif had his side to the door, and did not immediately notice Del watching him from the doorway. He was occupied with bandaging his hands in long white strips of gauze. His right palm was already wrapped, and he was just finishing the left when Del stepped through the door.

"Where is everyone?" Del asked.

The kalif looked up with a slight start. His eyes were sunken, and his face sallow, telltale signs of a sleepless night brought on by a troubled conscious. While Del watched, he finished tying the bandage, then ripped the strip with his teeth and cast the excess aside. "I have sent them to the encampments north of the city," he said. "It will be safer there, at least for a time."

"And Suri?"

Jiharra nodded reassuringly. "Suri is with them." The kalif turned to face Del, and his eyes fixed on the sword strapped over his shoulder. "You plan to fight the sthaak?" he asked.

"That was the decision, was it not?"

Jiharra's eyes slid into the distance, focusing on the memory of their discussion in the canyon. "Yes," he said with a slow nod. "Yes, that was the decision."

"And why shouldn't I? I have a blade, and I use it well."

The kalif looked beyond Del, his eyes lost in thought. Del could see that there was something he wanted to say, but was finding trouble in deciding where to begin. Finally, his eyes lifted. "We cannot win this fight," he said bluntly.

"We knew that before. What has changed?"

"The wells have dried, and the Ashkelon is not far behind."

"What difference does it make?" Del asked, aware of his shriveling patience. He didn't need to be reminded that their situation was without hope, it was something he already understood with perfect clarity.

"One man can't make a difference here."

"What would you have me do, Kalif?" Del snapped in a tone sharper than intended. "Shall I hide with the children and hope the sthaak spare me when they've finished slaughtering the rest of your people?"

Jiharra opened his mouth, but Del didn't give him the chance. "Why did you ask me here?"

Jiharra rubbed his palm while considering his answer. When he looked at Del, his eyes were deeply haunted. "I've made a mistake," he confessed. He would have gone on to explain, but the door behind Del opened, and Jiharra's eyes darted past his shoulder. Del turned to see that two Bedu men had entered the chamber. He recognized them as the leaders of the Dahm and the Saar, the last of the surviving kalifs. Both wore curved scimitars at their sides, and belts of knives across their chests. Ibn Salim, the kalif of the Dahm, halted the moment he stepped through the door and spotted Del. His stern gaze touched on the ambassador for a quick moment, then stabbed at Jiharra.

"What is this?" he asked with angry suspicion.

"Come," Jiharra said tiredly. "We have a matter to discuss."

"Now is not the time for discussions," Ibn Balaan said abruptly. He was the older of the pair, and despite his graying beard, he possessed the sturdy build of a warrior. "The sthaak are on our doorstep, and they will not wait for us to be ready before they attack."

"Why did you bring us here?" Ibn Salim cut in, echoing Del's own question from moments before.

Jiharra turned his back on them and parted the drapes of his balcony with one hand. Looking out into the glaring sunlight, the view showed him the blue-green strip of the Ashkelon to the east of Aba Ajraan, as well as a sea of tents beyond the rim of the city.

"When I watched them come out of the desert yesterday I thought that it was the last day of my life," he said quietly. "I have already said my farewells to my wife and my children, and although I am not yet dead, I still do not know if I will ever see them again." He let the drapes fall back into place, and turned to face the three men he had called to see him. "Like you, I joined the warriors and the ken'dari on the banks of the Ashkelon to fight, and to die."

Despite their earlier impatience, the two kalifs were listening to him now, and he continued in an emotionless voice, his feelings detached from the words. "During the night, I began to think that if given another chance, I would do things differently. I would not be so full of pride. I thought then that it was too late, that surely by morning the sthaak would come to destroy my people. All night I waited, but the sthaak did not come." He opened his arms as if to display the life still in him. "And now here we stand, still alive, and even now the sthaak have not come. Perhaps it is not too late to do things differently."

With this, Jiharra turned his gaze, which up until then had been on the two kalifs, to Del. "Ambassador," he said formally. "Will you lead our people to Gideon's Wall?"

Every nerve in Del's body bristled in response to this infusion of fresh hope. He felt his excitement building, and his heart kicked against his chest. Only the presence of the solemn kalifs kept him from rushing forward to grasp Jiharra by the shoulders and shout out in exultation. He felt how a man condemned to die might feel upon realizing the walls of his prison were made of paper. But before he had the chance to answer, Ibn Salim spit on the ground in a show of disgust. "You do not speak for us," he said to Jiharra. "My people are not leaving Aba Ajraan. We will not retreat to the northman's lands."

"If you stay, your people will die."

"At least we will die fighting."

Dismissing Ibn Salim's prideful declaration, Jiharra swung a solid gaze to Ibn Balaan, who had so far listened to the exchange without saying a word. "And what of you, Balaan. Are your people as willing to die as Salim's?"

The elder kalif scratched thoughtfully at his neck, where a three day growth of gray beard tickled his skin. "We have not yet heard an answer from your ambassador," he pointed out. "What does he have to say?"

At this, Del became the center of attention.

"Del?" Jiharra said, inviting him to speak.

Del's voice was soft and calm, his excitement at the prospect of another day of life showing only in the slight trembling of his hands. "I can take you there," was all he said.

"And what of those who guard it?" Ibn Salim broke in, for the first time in five years speaking directly to Del. "Gideon's Wall was built to keep us out of Shallai. Will your people be willing to open the gates and allow their enemy to pass through at a word from you? Who are you to say that they will not turn us away?"

"The gates will open," Del said firmly.

"And what if they do not, Ambassador?" Ibn Salim pressed relentlessly. "What will happen to us then? We will be trapped between the sthaak and the walls of your fortress, and most likely your people will watch us die with smiles on their faces."

A hot knot of anger curled up in Del's gut, and he was forced to check his wrath. "My people are not monsters," he said.

"Nor are mine," Ibn Salim retorted. "But that did not stop you from building a wall to keep us at bay."

"I told you that Gideon's Wall will open for us," Del said defiantly. "You can believe what you will, and trust who you want, but when I tell you that something will be done—it will be done." His eyes continued to bore into the kalif. "The gates will open for your people," he said again. "They will open if I have to open them

179

myself."

Unconvinced, Ibn Salim shook his head. Del's promise changed nothing for him. He faced Jiharra with folded arms. "My people have already been driven from their homes. We are finished with running. Besides, I do not trust your ambassador. What has he done to deserve it, Jiharra? What has he done to deserve the trust of our people?"

"Where were *you*, Salim, when my father petitioned the Jaggi for help?" Jiharra said angrily. "You were not with him. But Del was at his side. He is not even of our blood, but he went to the edge of the Sands because I asked it of him. He went on behalf of *your* people while you cowered in your tent."

The kalif jerked his head to the side and made a noise of disgust. "It is too late for this."

"It is *not* too late!" Jiharra snapped back furiously.

Ibn Salim's own anger flared in response, and he shoved his face close to Jiharra's, thumping his own forehead with two thick fingers. "Think, Jiharra! If we put our lives in his hands, then we are at the mercy of his people. They built their wall to keep us out of Shallai, and now you think they will throw the gates wide for an entire nation of Bedu? Your ambassador cannot speak for his people. How can he say if the gates will open for us, or what will be waiting for us on the other side? He has been among our people more than five years. He knows no more than we do." Casting a dark look at Del, he shook his head. "I would rather take my chances with the sthaak."

"There will be no chances with the sthaak," Jiharra said sharply. Striding to the balcony, he brought down the thick curtains with one great pull, revealing a sudden and expansive view of the creatures massed on the banks of the Ashkelon. "Look at them!" he said furiously, rounding on the kalifs. "Look at what we face. In all your life have you ever seen such a thing? When they cross the Ashkelon, we will be the first to die, and our people will be left defenseless. They will slaughter our wives and our children. Our families will be devoured!"

Grasping the torn drapery in one fist, he lifted the other to his heart. "I have as much pride as you," he said passionately. "But our people are on the brink of extinction. When the sthaak are finished with us, there will be no one left to remember us; no one left to rebuild. And to think that they will have died because I was too proud to ask for help." He shook his head. "I cannot bear the thought of that. I will take the one small chance that they might live, and may the Father curse my pride if it keeps me from saving my people."

Drawing a deep breath, Jiharra put a hand over his eyes and his face, raising a shield against his tide of escaping emotions. Too much was happening at once, and sleep was fast becoming an unaffordable luxury. Closing his eyes for a moment, he let them burn with fatigue, and had to rub them thoroughly to stop the scratching discomfort. When he took his hand away his vision swam with starbursts, but his composure was intact, and his anger under strict rein. "We haven't time for this," he told the two kalifs plainly. "I did not ask you here to consult with you, nor to argue about the course of action I have already chosen. I'm telling you that I'm taking my people away from this place. Now you must ask yourselves if your pride will keep you here. Or will you come with me to Gideon's Wall?"

The silence lasted but a short time.

"I will go with you," Ibn Balaan said quietly.

Jiharra acknowledged the kalif of the Saar with a nod, then switched his gaze to Ibn Salim. The younger man had turned to the balcony. Long moments passed, and silence piled up around them as he stared across the river. "What good are we if we run?" he asked quietly over his shoulder. "What will our people have if we abandon the desert? Are we to live like outcasts among people who loathe us? If we run to them now, we will be scattered, and we will die."

"Our people are strong," Jiharra said. "We do not die easily."

Still with his back to them, Ibn Salim nodded at this. He gave his answer without turning to face them, ashamed to let them see him speaking the words. "The women and children may go," he conceded in a voice almost too soft to hear. "The men will make their own decisions. But my ken'dari will stay, as will I."

When Ibn Salim had spoken, he at last turned to them, and his face was blank. Something had been torn from his heart, and it made him seem smaller. He started for the door, but stopped just before passing Del. He did not look directly at the ambassador when he spoke, and his voice was low enough that the others could not hear the words that passed between them.

"The wall will open for you?" he asked quietly.

"I swear it."

Nothing more was said, and as he watched Ibn Salim leave, some emotion deep inside Del rejoiced at the kalif's decision to stay. There was a nobility in the man that had remained undefeated under threat of death and all the combined forces of reason. But that same part of him which rejoiced at the kalif's unfailing courage, also lamented his own cowardice. He felt the villain for even attempting to tear down the kalif's resolve. In a moment, Ibn Salim was gone, and Del was left alone with Jiharra and Ibn Balaan.

"Go swiftly to make your preparations," Jiharra said to the old kalif. "We have a nation to move."

• • •

When they were alone once more, Jiharra sat tiredly upon the sill of the window and dropped his gaze to his bandaged hands. He wasn't interested in them particularly, it was just that he was too weary to look at anything else. The white rags were stained with blooms of red blood where they crossed his palms.

"What happened?" Del said.

Jiharra unwound one of the soiled dressings from around his fist until it hung loosely, like the molt of a snake. There were deep slashes in the palm. He had been carving at himself. "It is an old practice," he said, staring dully at the fresh cuts. "Many Bedu no-mads believe that spilling blood in sand has a way of giving us glimpses of our future. You only have to know how to read what is written."

"You've been spilling much blood," Del noted clinically.

Jiharra smiled dimly, without heart, and began to carefully rewind the cloth about his hand. "I am very interested in the future."

"What did you see?"

Jiharra lifted his gaze, and Del clearly saw that he was tormented by whatever dark events he had read in the blood shed from his own hands. "I saw you and I, Ambassador," the kalif said momentarily. "I was trapped in a small space, closed in by walls of stone. I saw my face looking out from between bars . . . as though I were a caged animal. I was afraid."

"And me? Where was I?"

"You were looking for . . . something you had lost."

"What?"

Jiharra averted his eyes. "I don't know," he said. "It is only blood and sand. What I read means nothing."

In the uncomfortable stillness that followed, Del felt helpless. He stood looking down at Jiharra, trying to keep from thinking about anything at all. The chamber was hot and bright, and he could hear the distant din of the encampments surrounding the city. There was a low, rushing wind, and the hoarse roar of a camel somewhere in the streets below the palace. His eyes drifted to the balcony as he listened to the familiar noises, letting them wash his thoughts clean. When he realized Jiharra had said something to him, he broke out of his daze and looked at the seated kalif.

"What?"

"You should find Suri," Jiharra repeated. "There will be much confusion soon, and the two of you should be together. Go to the Ajraan encampments north of the city. You will find her there, with Massara and the rest of the family. They will be glad to see you."

"And what about you?"

"There is still much to do here."

"I'll stay," Del began, but Jiharra held up a hand wearily.

"No, Del. Go to your wife."

Del nodded numbly, but made no move to leave. There was something about the heat and the stillness that cloaked his ability to function with lethargy. Rubbing his forehead with one hand, he felt his every adequacy had been crippled.

Jiharra looked up at him, and there was a muted desperation in his eyes, a sort of plea for justification. "Are we doing what is right?" he asked.

"You're giving your people a chance to live," Del told the kalif lamely, but the words sounded feeble. "You're saving them."

"My father would have stayed," the kalif said.

"You are not your father, Jiharra."

"No," the kalif admitted. "But he is all I have to measure myself by."

Del looked at the kalif closely, and saw a man already conquered. He would have stayed longer, but Jiharra offered him a fragile smile, and it helped to ease his mind, if only a little.

"Go now," the kalif said kindly. "You've done all you can here, and your wife waits for you."

Ten

Jiharra might well have been the last living person to walk the dying streets of Aba Ajraan. Standing in the barren avenue outside the closed gates of the estate, he looked in on the abandoned yards through the black bars, and marveled at the speed at which his nation had crumbled. The whole city, and the estate most especially, seemed a foreign place now, cold and dead, and filled with emptiness. He remained there a long while, never having imagined how difficult it would be to turn his back on the only home he'd ever known. When he finally tore himself away, he did not look back again.

Evening had settled like the slow passing of years, draining color and light from the sky, and stretching shadows taut. Moving through the abandoned streets for the northern quarter, the young kalif felt as though he were a ghost haunting a dead place. He was insubstantial and transparent, and wondered that the slightest of breezes did not carry him away on a slow, hot current.

His path led him to the courtyard of wells, and he paused at the edge of the devastation. At his feet, the stones of the street were dissolving. The plaza had become a small desert. At the edge of that wide space it was easy to see what was happening. Two days past, the plaza had been the hub and the life of Aba Ajraan. The wells were deep, tapping into the parts of the Ashkelon which flowed beneath the city, offering water both sweet and fresh. Now, the short, square-roofed buildings all about the perimeter were crumbling with unnatural decay. Stone walls were falling away in great chunks, their remains jutting out of the golden sand like rotting teeth. The structures farther from the wells were in similar condition, and the buildings beyond those were quickly becoming unstable.

The plaza was the epicenter of the disease.

Jiharra began to cross. Halfway to the far side he stopped among the ruined wells. Like a sickness, the sand choked their throats and spilled into the plaza in thick drifts. The desert was crawling up the wells. He kicked lightly at the stone lip, and a piece broke off easily, releasing a small torrent of sand. He broke free another piece, surprised at how easily it came loose, at how fragile it seemed. Despite his gentle grasp, the clump of stone cracked into smaller chunks, and fell to his feet in a hail of rubble. He took a knee and scooped up a portion of sand, then let the collection of fine grains siphon from his fist. When it was gone, he lifted his head to survey his surroundings. Over the caving roofs at the edge of the plaza he could see the towers of the ancient palace. In another two days the desert growing out of the wells would reach it, devouring the homes of his people as it went. In another four, all of Aba Ajraan would be a memory.

Dusting off his hands, Jiharra rose, and moved quickly across the courtyard of wells. On toward the Bedu encampments farther north he went. In the bare wastes of the northern flatlands, beyond the limits of Aba Ajraan, his people were waiting for him to lead them to safety.

• • •

Night stretched a dark wing over the desert, and as the last vestiges of evening were cleared from the sky, the tribes began to move. To the eyes of whichever gods spied on them from the heavens, the escaping nation must have seemed an ocean of twinkling light as torches and lanterns came alive to carve a glowing saffron dome out of the darkness.

And so began the exodus of the Bedu nation.

All through the night that thick and slow-moving tide poured northward as imperceptibly as the crawling parade of stars across heaven's dark stage. The Bedu walked tirelessly, the boundaries of the tribes flowing together until there was only one tribe, moving with one purpose. Through the false dawn of a hundred thousand torches, men herded their families under watchful eyes while camels shuffled sleepily. Children too young to walk were placed in litters instead of on saddles, while their older siblings tramped along beside them. Those with no beasts of burden were resigned to walking, carrying what little they had deemed important enough to take with them on their flight across bent shoulders.

Yet while the vast majority of the Bedu nation were evacuating their homeland, the warriors and ken'dari of the Saar had stayed behind to await the imminent sthaak invasion. There was some obscure facet of their loyalty that filled Del's heart with heavy sadness. Their lives would be brutally stripped from them unless their gods delivered a miracle, and he had uttered enough prayers throughout his lifetime to know that unless the Bedu deities were vastly different from Shallai's, they would not supply miracles on demand. And so they moved with all possible haste, knowing that the only guardian of their retreat was a small force of Bedu warriors, a shrinking river, and a crumbling city.

The Bedu did not break their arduous trek until the sun tainted the sky to the east with the gentle promise of sunrise. Tents were erected hastily before the sun's light could rob them of their already taxed strength, and within an hour a sprawling city of canvas had blossomed on the flatlands. By the time the sun rose, most had sought shelter and shade to collect what sleep they could in the scant hours before the next march began.

Eleven

For three days the desert swelled within Aba Ajraan. On the dawning of the fourth, the Ashkelon ran dry.

Standing among his ken'dari at the core of the ruined city, the kalif of the Saar felt the ground trembling. With nothing to hold them back, the horde of sthaak came thrusting across the dry riverbed, their screams piercing the dawn. The warriors of the Saar fought savagely, and the sthaak did not pass without paying fair toll. The Bedu were overcome like men lifting feeble arms against a storm. In the end, the sthaak swarmed over them, and claimed the jagged ruins of Aba Ajraan.

Book Four
Gideon's Wall

"Shallai has too long been the supreme dominion in the known world. We are fools to the last, comforting ourselves with presumptions and self-inflicted blindness. In our arrogance we go on trusting our beloved Empire will carry on indefinitely. In this we are mistaken."

—Archaist Shen Abbarrak

"The Empire shall stand forever."

—The thirty-first Fist of Shallai, Endiaro Rage

One

The warm little statue weaves its tale, and I write all that I hear.

Some nights it whispers incomprehensibly, spilling valuable words in the Shadrakan tongue, which I recognize but cannot understand. Other nights it speaks to me not at all. Many times I have found myself lying awake in a darkness split only by a single candle, watching it from across my chamber, waiting to hear the faint beckoning of its dry voice. It tells its story in broken fragments and winding tangents, but my patience is long-suffering, and I am diligent in piecing them together.

• • •

The excavation commences with all haste. This very day we made a discovery of great import.

We found the bones of the seriph not five paces from the south side of Gideon's Wall. At first, I believed we had found another beast of some sort, but now I know better. It is animalistic, to be certain, but too human to be purely animal. This is without a doubt one of the seraphim. His skull is massive, the dome large enough for a normal man to wear as a helmet. The teeth are huge, white and sharp, the upper incisors half as long as my finger. This must have been a great beast of a warrior.

We treat his bones with the greatest of care, lifting them out of the ground like fragile treasures. The skull, although thick, is already fractured. Many of the other bones are cracked or shattered completely. All evidence indicates that he toppled to his death from the heights of the wall. What turn of events laid him here? Did he slip from the wall while battling the enemy? Was he murdered and pitched over the wall during some dark night? Or did he leap of his own accord? I wonder what were the circumstances surrounding this noble creature's death.

What stories these bones could tell if only they could speak!

It has often been asserted that the most regrettable loss brought about by the fall of Shallai's empire was the extinction of the seraphim, and here we have stumbled upon one with the fortune of fools.

Since long before the First Age of Expansion there had existed among the people of the empire a great deal of lore surrounding the origins of Shallai's elite warrior caste. Among the most notable tales was a widespread belief that the seraphim were not fully human.

In certain cities bordering the Kashgar Fens the people believed the seraphim to be the last remnants of a greater race, living relics carried over from another age, while at the opposite end of the empire they were considered to be the progeny of Shallai's deities, part god and part man. Scattered about through the rest of the empire, and even across the seas, were countless other theories ranging everywhere from the nearly believable to the wildly absurd. Such a motley collection of myths, lore, and legend lent the seraphim an air of mystery.

Despite the diversity of belief concerning the seraphim, their role was established at the dawn of the empire, and remained constant ever since. The duty of the seriph was, and always had been, to protect. They were the guardians standing beside the Fist's throne in the Keep of Shallai, grim and watchful. They were the godlike warlords leading Shallai's armies to battle. If but one seriph walked among a legion of soldiers, those soldiers counted themselves blessed, for it was said the weakest of the seraphim was worth a thousand men.

There was no shortage of tales proclaiming their deeds. Some could be discarded as pure fantasy, while others invoked a curious kind of wonder. In the library of Jericho was a sweeping mural painted on the walls of the great auditorium. In it was the depiction of a glorious warrior of impossibly exaggerated proportions. His countenance was emblazoned with pure light, and his eyes were fire. In either hand he gripped a sword of lightning, and his massive arms were thrown wide to the heavens. Stretched out to either side of him, adding to the sheer magnificence of the mural and lending itself to the godly legends of the seraphim, were three pairs of great wings. The feathers were white, but the pinions had been dipped and splattered in blood. All about the unearthly warrior, creeping and slinking toward him, were dark-skinned men bearing jagged knives and hatred in their slanted eyes. It seemed their intention to debase him, to tear him down and break his wings so he would no longer be more magnificent than they.

The warrior was said to be the seriph Aadrikk, who fought and was slain during the second Saracen invasion. The legend attached to the painting, and which was engraved on a bronze plate at the center of the auditorium, claimed that the noble Aadrikk, greatest of the seraphim, had been trapped behind advancing enemy lines when he refused to abandon a decimated legion and their wounded. As the Saracen ranks folded in around them, the seriph and the soldiers he had stayed to defend fought to the last man.

It was said that Aadrikk was the last standing, and dispatched more than two-hundred of the Saracen savages before being overwhelmed. After being slain at last, the Saracen warriors removed his head and tore his wings. Even then, they would not step too near the body.

Or so the story went. There were many more just like it, some far more difficult to believe, and some less.

In reality, the seraphim very nearly lived up to the legends constructed around them. Beyond the reach of rank and title, the stolid warriors answered only to the Fist of Shallai, and their comings and goings were questioned by no one, great or small. The people worshiped them as protectors, soldiers revered them as heroes, and their enemies feared them as demons. To all they were the stuff of legend.

• • •

Alone in my tent I sit at a desk littered with parchment. My hands are still caked with dirt, for I have come directly from unearthing the seriph. The figurine is cupped in my hands, staring up at me with blind eyes. It is silent now, but I know it still has much to say. And I have questions.

"Tell me of the seriph," I ask it.

I listen, and it begins to feed its reedy little whispers into my ear.

Two

The Seriph Matthias had no wings. He did not wield swords of lightning, nor did he possess eyes which burned like fire. He had never killed two hundred men—not at one time—and there were no murals bearing his likeness sprawling across library walls, nor legends which proclaimed his heroic deeds. He was no less mighty for the lack of glory.

It was Matthias who had slain the mighty Shadrakan Warlord Kahimagachi during a thunderous cavalry charge at the battle of Redfield. Holding his ground on foot, he had withstood the attack of a dozen Shadrakan warriors. After they had been cut down he tore the Warlord himself from the high saddle of his charging steed, ripped away his armor as though peeling away the shell of a crustacean, and filled his chest with steel. With their mighty Warlord vanquished, the Shadrakans had retreated Redfield.

It was he who had been sent to quell the uprising at Jerfold, when the infamous traitor Thull Reegan had the people of the conquered nation so riled at the injustices done them that they were prepared to take up arms once more against Shallai. On the night before their march for Jericho, he infiltrated their encampment disguised as a proponent of their cause. Bypassing a disorganized security, he found his way into Reegan's private tent while the leader of the rebellion slept. He broke both the traitor's arms, and hung him by the neck from the central post of his tent. Before departing, he put a dagger in Reegan's heart. Attached to the hilt was a message from the Fist of Shallai which stated in very simple sentences that the uprising was over. Next morning, upon finding the note pinned with a knife to the chest of their hung leader, Reegan's rebellion disbanded.

It was Matthias who had been sent with the Fist's wife and youngest child to safeguard them on a diplomatic mission across the sea to Rathania.

Three days to sea they were boarded by marauding pirates along the Shilling Coast. Had the pirates known what passengers the vessel carried, they would have directed their greed elsewhere. Instead, they boarded. After escorting the Fist's wife and child to the galley and instructing her to bolt the doors behind him, he went above deck to visit the pirates. He had developed a tendency to take affronts to the Fist's family personally, as they had always been kind to him. Displeased with the offenders, he had dealt with them harshly. Twelve of them were dead before they began to understand the severity of their error and attempted to disengage. He followed them back to their own vessel. Cornered, many of the raiders turned on him with bared teeth and wild ferocity. He cut them down like children. Those too cowardly to face him cast themselves into the sea. Some made pathetic attempts to hide. But he did not relent. He dispatched the brigands methodically, busting through bolted doors and tearing up hatches until every last squealing thief had been dragged out of hiding and silenced by his blade. When the slaughter was over, he stood alone on the bloody deck of the pirate vessel.

He sank it out of spite.

Twenty-seven days past he had departed from Jericho. With the great capital of the empire behind him, he had followed the old Gainskill trade route southward across the farmlands and light forests so prevalent in the central territories. Unless in need of rations he avoided the denser areas of civilization, preferring to keep himself well-removed from the public eye. His place was on a battlefield, not in a city, and he was too unusual to go unnoticed for long. Had any of the people of the provinces recognized him for a seriph they would have crowded him as though a sovereign lord, begging his blessing for their child, or his aid in some matter of justice or protection. It was for this reason he kept his deep hood pulled low over his face and his cloak tight about him. His business was of an urgent nature, and he had no time to dedicate to civil injustices and petty revenge.

He passed through Tallen, with its stone-paved streets and crowded markets, and from there continued south, putting the leagues behind him steadily. Toward Warren Knoll he went, where the streets were mud, and the hovels slumped inward as though sleeping on one another's shoulders. South of the Knoll, the pastures and farms gave way to untamed foothills and thick woods. The trade route thinned as the land slowly rose toward the distant mountains. Just on the other side of the white-capped peaks lay the sprawling bulk of Jaggonath.

There were two general classes of citizens in Jaggonath: the vastly rich, and the miserably impoverished. Bundled in the comforts of their prosperity, Jaggonath's wealthy conveniently ignored the plight of the less fortunate, while the poor did their best to live one more day on whatever crumbs they could scavenge or steal. The seriph entered only because he'd not eaten for three days. His food had been pilfered by wolves while he bathed in a narrow tributary of the Polotov River, and the bogs surrounding Jaggonath were nearly void of edible game.

It was after dusk when he passed through the east gate, and the streets were empty. He directed himself toward the lower east quarter, where poverty had taken firm hold, like an endless winter. It stripped the color from everything it touched, leaving only the drab and the cheerless. The streets were a tangle of muddy paths, and the ramshackle buildings to either side leaned over the street. He rode past boarded windows and hanging doors until he came to a darkened courtyard, at the center of which sat a squat stone well. One side of the courtyard was occupied by a shabby inn, its door propped open to the rank air of a Jaggonath night. Light spilled into the street, the only spot of color in the whole quarter. Farther up the street, three barefooted children kicked a ragged head of lettuce between them.

He left his charger by the well and ducked through the doorway of the inn, bowing his head to fit. There were a handful of men in the dingy common room, plotting in tiny groups of two or three as they traded whispers over dirty mugs of wine. Subdued conversations died, and every pair of eyes lifted at his entrance. Their gazes followed him as he crossed the common room toward the keeper, a thick man with a scar across his forehead and a twisted nose standing behind a short bar. The seriph put two burnished coins on the bar in front of him and said, "Food," in a voice so quiet it was scarcely heard.

The keeper felt safe behind his rotting bar, so he cocked a suspicious eye at the coins. Each of them was stamped with the crown of the Fist. They would have purchased a splendid meal at a much finer establishment than his. He wet his lips, eyes still on the coins. "We have apples and cheese. There is some bread, but it's old."

"Bring it."

The keeper tore his eyes from the coins, and looked up into the dark hood. "There are better places to eat in Jaggonath," he said bluntly. "Places where this kind of money will buy you real food."

"I don't like those places," the seriph said quietly.

"Suit yourself," the keeper said. He scooped the coins into an open hand and gestured to a young woman. She had been standing by the door to the kitchen, following every word of the brief exchange with her eyes. At his signal she ducked into the back room to retrieve the food. During her short absence, the keeper peered up into the seriph's dark hood, but in the dim light could see no features. Somewhat nervous, he took up a filthy rag and pretended to wipe at stains so deeply worked into the rough wood of the bar they had become a permanent part of the knotted woodwork.

"You're traveling?" he asked with forced indifference.

The seriph nodded. He was firmly aware that the conversations which had halted at his arrival still had not resumed. He could feel the blatant stares of the patrons on his back. The keeper's eyes flicked to the dark hood, then back to the rag.

"Where from?"

"Jericho."

"What news from Jericho?"

"The Oracle has predicted the end of the age," the seriph said with blunt openness. "The empire will collapse, and the cities be laid to waste."

The keeper stopped rubbing his bar. He stared up into the dark hood, unsure of how he was expected to react to such a joke. He hated not being able to see the stranger's face. He didn't know if he was being watched or not, or if the man even had eyes. He had heard rumors of the D'ni in the Draiden Heights who had no eyes at all, only bare patches of flesh. Such thoughts made him shudder. A moment later the girl came out of the kitchen with a bundle folded up in wax paper. She seemed afraid to come close, and the impatient keeper, angry at his own nervousness, snatched the food from her and dropped it on the bar in front of his guest. The seriph lifted a corner of the paper. There were two bruised apples, a fraction of a block of cheese, and a small chunk of bread. One of the apples had already been bitten, the cheese had mold on it, and the bread looked like a dry sponge, black around the edges.

"It's all we can give you," the keeper mumbled.

Without a word, the seriph put another coin on the counter. He turned away from the bar—and saw every hidden stare leap away from him, back into their red pools of wine. They watched him leave out of the corner of their eyes.

In the darkness of the stone yard just outside the inn, he settled on the half-dry ground with his cloak around him and his back against the well. He ate in silence. He had hardly been there a moment before the children, like feral animals, were attracted by his food. They came slowly, standing a little ways off to spy on him with hungry stares, and watched bits of food vanish into the dark hood of his mantle piece by piece. They were waiting patiently for him to finish, stand up, and cast aside the wax paper so they could scavenge for the crumbs which had tumbled from his lap. He held out an apple in one hand and left his arm extended, allowing them to take his offering at their own pace as he attended to his own hunger.

Eventually the bravest of them, moving slowly and cautiously, came close enough to pluck the bruised fruit from his outstretched hand before jumping back like a fox swifter than the trap. After taking a famished bite, the child passed it to the youngest of them, a little girl with a dirty face and tangled hair. The seriph could see that she was pretty beneath the filth. He offered the second apple in the same manner, and it was taken this time without hesitation.

Engrossed with their food, the children circled to the other side of the well to consume the offering. Only the little girl stayed, her mouth full of apple, and her gaze fixed boldly into his hood. She watched him as she chewed, lost in that daze of intense curiosity through which young children regard a world full of people more powerful than them.

"What is it, child?" he asked, his voice low and deep.

"Is that your pony?"

"It is."

"He's pretty."

The seriph considered his destrier. The horse had been bred to be a killer of men, to crush and stamp the life out of anything foolish enough to remain in its path during a charge. Spiteful and belligerent, the animal was constantly glaring at those who ventured too near, as though wanting to step on them. He never would have thought to describe the scowling war-beast as 'pretty'.

"Are you the seriph?" the child asked abruptly.

Matthias turned his head slightly.

"Daman says the seriph will come and kill Grisham of Kalli. Have you come to kill Grisham of Kalli?"

"No," he answered truthfully. "I have not."

"But you're the seriph."

"One of many."

"Then you will kill him," she declared.

"Perhaps it is another seriph your Daman is thinking of," Matthias suggested.

The girl pondered this while nibbling distractedly on the core of her apple. She contemplated him very seriously, and he returned her blunt stare with the same openness. They went on that way for some time, eating and studying one another without the need for words. Before his food was gone he decided he was finished. There was something about children that had always made him sad, and he found it difficult to eat when so saddened. Besides, the cheese had left a bitter taste on his tongue and in his teeth, which not even a mouthful of the dry bread had been able to scrape clean. Setting the wax paper on the lip of the well, he was careful not to drop what was left of the bread, or spill any of the precious crumbs.

"You're leaving," the girl said as he rose.

"I am."

"But you'll be back."

"I do not think so."

"You'll come to see me again," she stated. "And your pony will come too. And you'll bring more apples. And you'll kill Grisham of Kalli, also."

The seriph left the courtyard without his appetite.

Civilization ended south of Jaggonath. The city rested on the rim of a sheer escarpment overlooking the vast Kabwe Plains, where emptiness and sky reigned, and wind occupied the space with a possessive ferocity. The only road beyond Jaggonath had been laid down during the building of Gideon's Wall, and had been left to deteriorate shortly after the construction of the fortress had reached completion. It was the only link between Gideon's Wall and civilization, but as the decades passed it became nothing more than two crooked ruts pushing through an endless sea of grass and angry wind. The seriph followed the road down the escarpment and into the plains, leaving Jaggonath and the rest of the empire far behind.

He soon learned that although void of human population, the Kabwe Plains were far from uninhabited. Herds of enormous beasts roamed the tundra, their shaggy black coats sweeping the ground as they ate their way across the veldt. Dark and fearless, they lifted heavy heads as he passed. There were predators concealed in the grass, meat-eaters which prowled in packs, and bony jackals which fought one another for the bloody scraps left behind after a kill. Matthias was never attacked, but felt their slanted eyes following him hungrily. During the night he heard their growls and coughs as they circled his camp like sharks, but always they kept their distance. His scent had etched fear in their minds.

There was something in the Kabwe Plains that gave the seriph Matthias a feeling of home, and he spent more days crossing them than truly needed.

The afternoon he saw the Mukkaris looming up to the south, he knew his journey was at an end. The road led him to the northern mouth of the Way, where the carcass of a ruined town baked under the sun. The town, its name forgotten, had been abandoned decades ago, after the builders and slaves who had made the wall returned to the more civilized territories of the empire. It had survived for a time, a place where listless soldiers surrendered their wages to liquor and women. But the architects and their builders had been the livelihood of the town, and after they had gone there was little left to keep it alive. As the number of soldiers stationed at Gideon's Wall gradually lessened, the town withered away until completely drained of life, and all that remained was a dry husk overshadowed by the sharp peaks of the Mukkaris.

The seriph rode slowly down the dusty avenue that cut through the center of the town. He passed the brothel, its doors boarded and its windows shattered, and the dark bulk of the cantina, now empty. In less than three minutes the dead town was behind him, and in the past forever.

Three

The north gate of Gideon's Wall was guarded by three disconsolate soldiers. Two were napping in the shade of the barbican, and one was groggily relieving himself against the outer curtain wall. He was in a foul mood, agitated by the heat of the day and the uncomfortable urgency with which nature's call had aroused him from sleep. He was just concluding his business with the thirsty stones when he happened to glance northward. Shading his eyes, he squinted into the Way, then made a type of whining, growling, self-pitying noise in his throat. Holding up his untied breeches with one hand, he stepping over his sleeping comrades and took up a spear from the rack in the cramped guard room.

Weapon in hand, he stumbled over a pair of outstretched legs.

The soldier who owned the offending appendages jerked awake to snarl at him angrily. "Watch it," he was warned spitefully.

"Keep your legs out of the way," snapped the first.

"I'm comfortable here."

"Then don't blame me for tripping over you," he growled, and delivered a quick kick to the soldier's knee, rousing the other to an agitated fit in which he cast a handful of dirt at his standing comrade.

"Cur!" snarled the kicked soldier with the ferocity of the rudely disturbed. But already he was retracting his legs and grudgingly turning on his side to go back to sleep.

"You deserve it."

"Will you two stop the noise," interrupted a third soldier blandly. Earlier he had peeled off his shirt and laid it over his face to keep out the light, and now it muffled his voice.

"Mind your business," threatened the spear-wielding soldier.

"I'll mind my business when you shut your mouth."

His quick tongue earned him a swift kick. When he sat up to wince and grip his injured leg he couldn't help but notice the spear in the other's hand. "What are you doing?" he asked suspiciously, aiming his chin at the weapon.

The standing soldier pointed into the Way with the blunt side of the spear. Still far away, and approaching slowly, was a single mounted figure, his outline warbled by the rising heat.

"What fool comes out here alone?" the seated soldier wondered.

"Whoever he is," said the first, hefting his spear, "he's just going to have to turn around and go back the way he came." He stepped outside the barbican to wait in the heavy light of the sun for the arrival of the lone traveler.

When the stranger was close enough for the soldiers to see his barrel-chested destrier, obviously a breed intended for war, and his dark cloak, their curiosity turned to concern. And when they saw the heavy sword strapped across his back, with a hilt long enough for four hands, and the pair of double-bladed axes fixed to his saddle, their concern shifted to worry. The spear-wielding soldier hailed the stranger the moment he was close enough to make them un-comfortable.

"Stranger," he called. "What's your business here?"

The man reigned his destrier. The beast snorted and stamped the ground. Glaring spitefully, it seemed to want to trample them, but kept still while the dark-cloaked stranger swung out of the saddle and landed his booted feet heavily on the ground, sending up clouds of dirt. He faced them across the distance, but they could not see into the depths of his cowl.

"I have come to see the deacon," said a voice out of the hood. Extending his hand, the stranger offered a small wooden cylinder containing a rolled letter, and waited patiently for someone to come forward and take it. No one did. Intimidated by his stature, the soldiers were none too eager to approach. So they stood where they were and looked at one another, wondering how they would retrieve the note without risking death or dismemberment.

When it was clear he would be kept waiting forever, the stranger found pity on them, and tossed the cylinder across the distance. It landed at the soldiers' feet in a little puff of red dirt. The closest stooped to take it, and fumbled to unroll the letter while still keeping a cautious eye on the stranger. He quickly read the two terse sentences written in simple script; *Welcome the Seriph Matthias. Extend to him all courtesy.*

It was marked with the Fist's own seal.

"Take me to the deacon," said the seriph.

• • •

Ian Manzig was vastly unprepared to play host for one of the seraphim. Slouched in a chair at the head of the long table in his chambers, his bare feet were propped up and his lap cradled a bowl of boiled beets and mutton. He was busily spooning the sopping gruel, boiled to tastelessness, into his maw when the door was pushed open and he found himself suddenly in the company of a heavily armed giant. The deacon froze with a spoonful of watery mutton halfway to his mouth. His eyes widened, then narrowed.

"What is this?" he demanded.

A frightened soldier jerked forward to supply Ian with the seriph's note, which the deacon ripped out of his hand in an exaggerated show of agitation. Snapping open the letter, his eyes flew over the words, and it took him but a scant moment to digest their meaning. He suddenly felt bare. The words on the paper were a death sentence, and the seriph his executioner. The food in his mouth had taken on all the properties of wood pulp. He wanted to gag, but forced himself to swallow with sickening effort, then slowly wiped his greasy mouth with an already dirty sleeve. He rose to face the hooded stranger, and although he was not outright afraid, he was still glad the table was between them. "Seriph," he said with as much respect as he could muster in his numbed state. "I am . . . it is an honor."

In truth, it was nothing of the sort. Ian Manzig had never met a seriph he trusted. He hated how the mindless citizens of the empire had placed Shallai's hulking butchers upon such lofty pedestals, their adoration stopping just short of worship. He resented the unchallengeable power and authority bestowed upon them by the Fist, and despised the fools who glorified them as champions. If the people knew what he knew, they would not be so quick to exalt their so-called guardians.

There were no histories of the Seraphim Rebellion, and in fact, any knowledge at all of the uprising was a rare thing, as the details had been sunk deep in a mire of lies and half-truths. Even had the full story been revealed, most would have disregarded it as fantasy. After all, who wanted to believe that their precious seraphim could turn on them so easily?

The few sages who knew of the rebellion agreed unanimously it had taken place during the reign of Jeroboam Moagheen, and had been masterminded by the seriph Val Quorak. Quorak had been a breed apart from his fellows, something *more*, both in body and in mind. He was as close to perfection as any had come. But his genius had been twisted in an odd way, or so the sages claimed, and he thirsted madly for unattainable power. He worked his influence on the weaker seraphim, and after years of plotting in dark corners he captured the devotion of a small but savagely loyal following. Quorak and his minions contrived to murder Moagheen and seize the empire for themselves.

In the end, the uprising was crushed by the seraphim whom had remained faithful to the Fist, but not before a small but brutal war had raged in the Keep. Val Quorak's zealots were put to death, and their bodies secretly entombed. Quorak himself had most likely met the same fate, but there were those who preferred to believe Moagheen hadn't the heart to execute his most perfect seriph, and kept the twisted genius chained in a vault deep in the belly of the Keep.

Regardless of the measure of truth in such stories, Ian fully believed the seraphim were not to be trusted. They were not entirely human, though he had never been able to decide less, or more. In his ever-humble opinion they were far too dangerous to employ as anything but assassins. It was like keeping dire wolves for pets. Although he never would have said it aloud, he deemed the Fist of Shallai a fool for giving them free rein.

As it were, Ian knew that the seraphim were utilized for one of two purposes: the first being intimidation, and the last being murder, either mass or individual. The seraphim accomplished both exceptionally well. Because of his limited understanding, Deacon Manzig was frantically working to determine for which of these two reasons the seriph Matthias had been dispatched to the wall.

When the seriph drew back his hood Ian's first conclusion, inspired by fear, was murder. The seriph could best be described as a beast, the kind of man with fists made to crush stones, and teeth for ripping flesh. His head was completely shaven, but his brows were thick, and hung low over thin eyes, lending him a look of extreme displeasure. He had let the hair of his chin grow long, and kept it tightly braided. His riveting stare was disquieting, and his incisors were twice the size of a man's. There was a distinct something in the way he moved that attested to animal blood. Lion, the deacon guessed. He is part lion and part bull. Only a little of this one is human.

"I will be staying for some time," the seriph said. His voice was strangely accented, betraying the fact that his native tongue was something far removed from that of the words he spoke. In response, all the deacon could manage was a nod. He was distantly aware that something should be said, but the presence of the seriph had crushed his voice.

"Sit," the seriph instructed him.

"Have I done something wrong?" Ian blurted clumsily.

"Sit," the seriph repeated.

Ian sat. He had become uncomfortably aware of his slovenly appearance, of the way his gut pushed tight against his unkempt uniform, and of his feet which were bare and dirty. The plate of half-finished food in front of him seemed a pile of cold waste now, and he pushed it aside, wanting it nowhere near him.

"Our lord the Fist is concerned," the seriph said. "For some months now Jericho has been a place of grave and disturbing rumors. The people are uneasy, and the Polhedrin Council has become restless. The Oracle has predicted Shallai will be destroyed."

"Destroyed?!" Ian exclaimed. "Impossible."

The seriph ignored him. "The Oracle prophesies of a terrible disaster sweeping across the empire, laying waste to everything in its path. None will be left alive."

"Then the old prophet has finally gone mad."

The seriph watched Ian blankly from beneath the overhang of his brow. His look, frightening in its dull severity, made Ian wish he had kept his mouth shut. "Possibly," the seriph said slowly. "But it is not the Oracle alone predicting such things. There are many prophets in Jericho, both great and small, and many madmen in the streets. You have heard what is said of madmen? That their minds are wild only because they see what others cannot. They too lament the end of Shallai. So to say that our Oracle has become useless without investigation would not be a wise assumption, do you not agree?"

Thinking it dangerous to do anything but agree, Ian nodded.

"The Fist agrees as well. And that is why I am here."

The deacon knew he had missed something somewhere. Oracles, madmen and prophets wailing about the death of the empire. Then suddenly a seriph coming to Gideon's Wall. There was a vital piece missing. He had only to wait, and the seriph supplied it.

"The threat will come from beyond Gideon's Wall."

Ian's mind staggered. "The Bedu?" he gaped in disbelief. "When?"

"The Oracle speaks cryptically. Dates are never given."

Ian was shaking his head. "The Bedu would be fools to attack the wall. The Oracle *has* gone mad."

For a long moment the seriph said nothing. His thoughts were veiled, the inner workings of his mind tucked away in secret places. "There is an emissary from Shallai among the Bedu," he finally said.

"Del," the deacon grimaced. "That one is disagreeable."

"I will speak with him."

Ian Manzig exhaled heavily. Spreading his hands in a helpless gesture, he assumed the posture of a man being asked a great favor. "The ambassador comes only when his mood suits him. His visits are short and infrequent."

"When was he last here?"

Ian rubbed his neck, trying to remember the last time he'd seen the ambassador. Had it been two months ago? Three? They went so quickly, and he paid so little attention. "Four months," he finally answered, feeling it was a safer answer than three.

"Then we haven't long to wait," the seriph said.

Ian agreed, hoping it were true.

• • •

The seriph's arrival created a kind of nervous energy among the soldiers of Gideon's Wall. In the days following his arrival, the

212

soldiers became uncomfortably conscious of themselves, of the neatness of their barracks, the general cleanliness of the grounds, and the rougher edges of their behavior. They found themselves standing straighter, cursing less frequently, and taking their duties a little more seriously than before. Extra effort was devoted to sharpening and polishing.

For all their efforts, the seriph did not mingle with the soldiers. He kept to himself within the small, plain room of his choosing, having refused the sumptuous chambers offered him by the deacon. His door was never open. In short time, he developed into something of an enigma among the soldiers of the wall. The corridor outside his chamber, once frequently traveled, became a sort of forbidden tract. Even while walking adjoining halls, soldiers lowered their voices while passing, and cautiously watched the heavily banded door as though it were the lair of a fire-breathing beast. Much time was spent discussing what manner of secret arts the seriph busied himself with behind the bolted door. He came out for a short while each day to walk the battlements of the wall, staring expectantly into the desert as he waited patiently for the ambassador's return.

• • •

To have properly guarded the wall during a time of war would have required twelve men conducted by an elaborate scheme of circuits and rotations. Such a scheme had been in place the first two years after the wall's completion, but had been gradually toned down over the long and uneventful years. The soldiers had tired of protecting so ardently from a threat that had ceased to be real. Twelve soldiers had been cut back to eight, and then to six, then to four, until finally, for the past decade or more, only two soldiers were required on the wall at any given time, one on the west end, and one on the east.

Two was as low a number as the deacon could be coerced into permitting, and only because they had to at least maintain the *im-*

age of vigilance. The soldiers accepted this as a matter of course, and took their liberties elsewhere. Once, there had been strict rules regarding sentry routes, passwords, and overall responsibility while on duty; now, no one cared what the two men did on top of the wall, just so long as they were there and that they occasionally devoted some effort into the pretense of watchfulness.

Currently, the two sentries were both at the east end of the wall, pretenses to the wind. They crouched together in the shelter of the battlements to keep from being battered too harshly by the sun, and they gambled away their wages with a carved set of bone dice. During the watch, their combined wealth had migrated back and forth between the two of them at least twice.

"Have you heard?" the first soldier asked, giving the dice a quick flip into the corner.

"Nice roll. Heard what?"

"The seriph's going to send us back to Jericho."

The other soldier, a little bit older and a great deal wiser than his companion, stopped just as he was about to loose the dice. He regarded the other with one bushy brow lifted nearly to the receding line of his hair. "Is that a fact?"

"That's what I hear."

"From who?"

"Hallek."

With a forlorn shake of his head, the older soldier threw the dice into the corner. "You can tell Hallek he's a fool."

"Why is that?" He glanced at the dice. "My game."

"For spreading lies. Nobody's going back to Jericho."

The younger man scooped up the dice with his left hand, transferred them to his right, then passed them to his opponent. "Your throw. And how do you know that?"

"Because I'm not as gullible as you." The dice rattled against the stones. "Damn. Another bum toss. I'm almost emptied."

"You've got some in your boot still," the other reminded him helpfully, then plucked up the dice and gave them a quick throw. For the third time in a row, two crowns aimed skyward, an unbeatable toss. "I win again. What luck this is!" He grabbed the dice quickly and handed them over to his companion, who began to shake them up vigorously. Before throwing them, he leaned toward the younger man.

"Listen, boy," he said. "I've been here for three years now, and every year about springtime the same rumor gets started up by some half-wit. Every year it's the same rumor, probably been the same since the wall was built. They say the deacon's sending everyone home and the wall's shutting down. It's never been true before, and it's not true now. I can see you haven't been here long enough to know any better, but you'd be wise to just ignore anyone who tells you otherwise."

"Then why's the seriph here?"

"The seraphim go wherever they want, boy. If he's here on a sight-seeing tour, that's his business. Don't go making up stories on his account."

"Fine. Will you toss the dice now?"

"No. I'm not done. We're an unlucky lot, us soldiers," he said, still shaking up some luck for his next throw. "We do our bit here, then get sent somewhere else. Nobody likes this place, but it's easier to handle if you just accept it instead of fabricating false lies."

"What's a false lie?"

The soldier's eyes narrowed. "You've a lot to learn, boy."

"Just throw the dice."

The old soldier gave a good toss. The little cubes bounced and rattled, until one of them came to rest with a farmer facing up and the other stopped crooked in the split between two stones. The big soldier laughed triumphantly. "A farmer and a crown. Beat that!"

"I'm sorry, but that's not a crown."

"It is a crown," the soldier said indignantly.

"It is clearly a pig."

The grizzled soldier's face darkened, and his big hands flexed in a threatening manner.

"Why don't you throw it again," the younger soldier suggested hurriedly.

"Why don't I," agreed the other.

He tossed the indecisive die again, and this time, after popping and dancing across the stones, it settled on a crown. Overjoyed, he slapped the stones with the flat of his palm. "A farmer and a crown. My luck has changed," he said happily. "Take your toss, and try not to cry if you lose. I cannot tolerate tears."

The young soldier collected the dice and sighed with practiced despair. "Here goes," he said, and proceeded to lay down his fourth pair of crowns.

"Well, that's all I have time for," the young soldier said hastily, collecting his winnings with greedy hands. He was just reaching for his dice when the older soldier snatched them up.

"Give those here," said the young man a bit nervously.

Slapping away his reaching hands, the old soldier carefully weighed the ivory dice in his palm, then gave them a tentative toss. They turned up a beautiful pair of crowns.

"Good toss!" the young soldier congratulated him. Again he reached for the dice, but was shoved back. Another toss. Another pair of crowns. The elder soldier's eyes widened as understanding dawned on him. His face took on the controlled anger of the swindled.

"Trick dice," he snarled.

"I was going to tell you."

The elder soldier whipped the dice at his opponent. Bouncing off the soldier's head, the little cubes of bone ricocheted into the air. The young man winced, hands slapped to his forehead. "Pain!" he cried.

"Hold in your noise," the grizzled soldier snarled. Seizing the young man by his collar, he dragged him to his feet and shoved him roughly toward the battlements. "I should dump you over the edge, you filthy patsy."

"Don't," pleaded the young man, hands still covering his face.

The grizzled soldier jabbed him in the chest with all four fingers, then slapped him upside the head. After that he generally came at him from all angles, poking, slapping, and flicking at every unshielded piece of skin.

The rebuke abruptly ended.

"Gods . . ." breathed the older soldier in awe.

"I'll give the money back," the young soldier whimpered.

"Shut up."

"I didn't know they were trick dice."

"Listen to me, boy," the elder soldier said, the tone and measure of his voice changed from a moment before. "Go get the deacon."

"Not the deacon," the young man protested. "I'll cheat no more."

"Move your hands! I'm not going to hit you."

Cautiously, the assaulted soldier peeled his hands away from his face, revealing two angry little welts on his forehead where the dice had struck. Upon looking into the desert, his face went slack with an expression of horror and disbelief.

"The deacon," the old soldier reminded him. "Now."

Nearly tripping over himself in his haste, the young soldier raced across the battlements toward the keep as though death were on his heels. The old soldier was left alone on the wall, dice, money, and cheating rogues entirely forgotten. He kept his eyes fixed on the spectacle far out in the desert, for it was something he, nor anyone at the wall, had ever expected to see. Made watery and thin from the heat rising up from the parched floor, came an army of Bedu advancing on the wall.

Four

Del stood with Jiharra on the shattered plains south of Gideon's Wall. It was a dead place, a scabrous crust overlaying a waterless core, all of it split by an endless web of fissures. Northward, the treacherous cliffs of the Mukkaris leaned skyward, ending the nothingness in a barricade of sheer cliffs. The range gave the impression of a stone curtain dragged across the breadth of the continent. Not nearly as high, but just as steep, the bulk of Gideon's Wall dammed up the only passable route through the Mukkaris.

The sole means of entering the fortress was a tunnel blocked at either end by thick iron slabs. The tunnel was just wide enough for ten men to walk side by side, with the ceiling low enough to touch. The slabs, far too heavy to be moved by strength alone, were raised and lowered by shadowy mechanisms in the belly of the wall. Del passed through the tunnel twice on each of his visits to Gideon's Wall, once coming out of the desert, and once going back in, and each time he would stop at the center of the dark passage to look back the way he had come. Standing in the middle of forty paces of solid stone, he was distinctly aware of his complete separation from both worlds. The darkness beneath the wall was a limbo, a cool blackness in which the troubles waiting for him on either side were incapable of penetrating.

Del and Jiharra had approached the wall alone, and without surprise found the iron wall preventing their entrance. Having left the body of the Bedu nation far behind, they halted some fifty paces from the base of the wall. From where they stood, the trunk of the stone behemoth blotted out the greater part of a dusty blue sky.

Their quiet arrival had incited a chaos of activity atop the wall. Crowds of soldiers had gathered to see the two men below, and the threatening stain of the Bedu nation on the horizon. The two emissaries had kept a respectful distance, watching expectantly as the shapes of soldiers rushed back and forth across the battlements high above. All the while, the massive iron slab which closed off the tunnel into the wall gave no sign of opening.

They had been waiting five hours.

During the first hour, Del made excuses on their behalf; the deacon could not be found, there was no protocol for lifting the slab with an army on the horizon, or the ancient machinery which operated the slab itself had finally given in to age, and they were even now devising other means to lift the barrier. There were hundreds of perfectly sound reasons why they should be kept waiting.

Four hours later, Del's excuses were drained, and his patience tapped. His agitation had become maddening. He paced. Angrily, he jerked himself back and forth across the same narrow tract of ground, as though he did not have the whole of the desert to walk in. His fingers flexed, and his eyes were fixed ceaselessly on the soldiers gaping down on them from the lofty security of the battlements. Although he could not see their faces, he felt the weight of their stares. He would have shouted, but he knew by then that even had his voice been powerful enough to reach them, all of the ranting he could muster would do him no good.

They were being ignored.

His imagination flew up the face of the wall, and what he envisioned there rankled him sorely. Somewhere among the soldiers was the deacon, looking down on them with detestation. "They have been waiting very long," said a nameless soldier to the deacon in Del's imagination. "Should we bring them in?"

"No," replied the deacon. "Let them wait."

Such fantasies were not far from the truth.

Del's greatest frustration lay in knowing the world of safety behind the wall was kept from him by a miserable fifty paces of stone and mortar, nothing compared to the distance they had already come. It was hardly more than a stone's throw away, yet he was helpless to do anything but glare darkly at those quietly denying him entrance. What made the deacon's negligence so infuriating was the nation at his back, waiting to be delivered. Such pressure weighed upon him more heavily than he could bear, arousing in him a tortuous wrath. If he'd been granted the sudden power to strike them dead, he would have done so in an instant, with lightning from his eyes, or brimstone tumbling from heaven. His temper was foul.

Jiharra's composure was a direct counterweight to Del's turbulence. Acting as a much-needed anchor, his presence alone restrained the ambassador from storming Gideon's Wall out of sheer rage, casting stones and curses at the high wall until his voice was hoarse and his arms weak. The kalif endured, knowing there was nothing within his power to do but wait. Seated cross-legged on the hard ground, he had resigned himself to watching his friend pace.

It wasn't until a full five hours had passed that the tunnel opened. With the tired groan of rusted gears and grinding metal, ancient machinery wakened, and the slab of iron barring the mouth of the tunnel lifted ponderously. Like the lid of a giant cyclopean eye gradually opening, the slab retracted into its housing, revealing the channel beneath the wall. Del could see sunlight at the opposite end.

Accompanied by five soldiers, Deacon Manzig emerged from the shadows.

Wasting no time, Del started toward the tunnel, intent on dealing rudely with the deacon. Scarcely did he notice that the soldiers were heavily armed and garbed for battle. Before he had gone three steps one of the men at Manzig's side lifted a bow. With lethal speed, a single arrow sliced through the air just to the left of Del's head. He heard the low whistle, and felt the wind.

Startled to the core by the sudden and unexpected brush with death, Del fell back a step in alarm. Dragging Jiharra behind him, he threw out his arm to forbid further attack. "Hold!" he screamed. "Do not fire on us!" The warning shot had rekindled his already inflamed aggression, and he was enraged by how narrowly the bolt had missed its mark. "Are you mad!?" he shouted, ripping back his hood to show his face. "I'm your own ambassador."

"I know who you are," Ian Manzig called across the distance. "You're close enough."

"We came only to talk. We are unarmed!"

"Do you always bring armies to talk?"

"We are not an army! Aba Ajraan has been destroyed. What you see in the desert is all that remains of the Bedu. We came only to find safety."

"Lies," the deacon said mildly.

"We must talk," Del said, starting forward once again.

"You can talk from where you stand." The deacon made a sharp gesture, and the archer beside him, who had already nocked another arrow, drew back threateningly.

Del halted, brimming with wrath.

"Will you refuse an audience with me, Deacon?" he cried out. "I am an emissary of Shallai, appointed by the Fist's own Chancellors. By whose authority do you reject me!?"

"You are nothing anymore!" the deacon bellowed. "You are a liar and a traitor. The Oracle in Jericho has warned us of your coming. You have committed treason by bringing your army of infidels to Shallai's doorstep, and you must think me a fool if you expect me to entertain you. Your service to Shallai is over! Take yourself and your sand-dogs back to the desert, and stay there for good. Return here and I'll have you hanged."

"You can't be serious."

"Come closer then, and test me."

Del seethed where he stood. He dared not tempt the deacon for fear of being shot dead, and he became suddenly and highly conscious of their complete exposure. If the deacon decided on a whim to have them killed, they would be helpless to defend themselves. He had known that making the deacon understand their plight was not going to be an easy task, but this complete rejection he had not foreseen. The situation had turned ugly faster than he'd imagined.

"Go away," the deacon told him in a bored voice, closing the parley once and for all. But as he turned to withdraw into the safety of the tunnel, he smashed his nose flat against the seriph's chest. The man was like a mobile wall of stone, placing himself wherever was most inconvenient for those around him.

Before Ian could back away, Matthias dropped a heavy hand on his shoulder, rooting him to the spot. The thick fingers cupped the slope of muscle between neck and shoulder, and the powerful thumb rested against Ian's collar bone, offering just enough pressure to make the deacon uncomfortably aware. The seriph's grip conveyed two messages to the deacon very clearly: one, that the parley was not finished until he declared so. And two—as if to reinforce the first—that if the seriph so chose he could crush the deacon's neck as easily as squeezing pulp out of rotten fruit.

"I would hear what the ambassador has to say," the seriph commented.

"He is a traitor," the deacon hissed.

"Allow me to be the judge of that."

Ian clenched his teeth. He had no desire to speak with the ambassador for any reason, but neither did he have a choice. Ensnared, he fumed privately, not daring to propose further objection to the seriph's wishes, but still loathe to carry them out. Finally, very aware of the seriph's hand still propped heavily on his neck, and wondering if it had been his imagination or if he had truly felt the fingers flexing in subtle warning, he grudgingly submitted. Mercifully, the hand went away.

"Come forward, Ambassador!" the deacon called with such authority that it might have been his plan from the start.

Although Jiharra had not understood a word that had passed between Del and the deacon, he fully understood that they were hardly being welcomed in the manner they had hoped. The tones and inflections of the two men's voices as they shouted back and forth had made that truth all too clear. At the deacon's unexpected summons, Del started forward once again, but Jiharra held him back momentarily. He was watching the armed men apprehensively.

"We're not wanted here, Del."

"Where else have we to go?"

With a firm jaw, the ambassador pulled out of Jiharra's light grasp and strode toward the men waiting for them at the mouth of the tunnel. Jiharra followed cautiously, and although he relayed no outward signs of it, Del knew the kalif was vastly uncomfortable. He was cut off from his people, soon to be surrounded by armed men who considered him the enemy.

Entering the small crowd of soldiers, they were met with scowls of suspicion and open hostility. They parted nonetheless, and Del passed freely under the iron slab.

It was cool and dark within the tunnel. He could almost feel the weight of Gideon's Wall above him, a palpable sense of crushing oppression suspended just above his head. Behind him, just before Jiharra could enter, Ian Manzig stepped rudely in front of him, barring the way.

"Not you," the deacon said coldly.

Not understanding the words, Jiharra only looked at him.

Del took the deacon's arm. "This is the kalif of the Ajraan Bedu," he protested. "He has come to represent his people."

Without taking his eyes off Jiharra, the deacon stood his ground firmly. "No," he corrected the ambassador as though speaking to a simpleminded child. "This is a sand-dog, and sand-dogs are not permitted here."

"Are you really so shallow?" Del snarled.

The deacon rounded on him, temper flaring. "Do not forget to whom you speak, Ambassador. Count yourself lucky that you've been allowed this far."

Del's anger expanded.

"What does he say, Del?" Jiharra asked quickly. It was an attempt to capture Del's attention and interrupt the exchange of harsh words before it began. With supreme effort, Del kept himself from laying a torrent of insults on the deacon, who always seemed to know exactly how to bring out the worst in him. His eyes shifted to Jiharra, who was looking to him for explanation. "He doesn't want you in the wall," Del explained from between clenched teeth.

Jiharra had already known this, and he studied the deacon at great length, his face calm and his humbled expression carefully void of defiance. He noted with some curiosity the contempt in the deacon's small eyes, and the way in which the once-powerful man stared back at him as though inviting any challenge of his authority.

"You are a very troubled man," Jiharra commented in a soft voice, knowing his words would be understood by no one but Del. "I see that you fear a great many things, and you seem to be very small." He glanced at Del, and said in a quiet voice, "Tell him I will wait here." And with that, he backed away from the deacon with an air of submission.

"What did he say?" the deacon snapped at Del.

"He'll wait," Del told the deacon curtly. "And he thanks you for your hospitality." Before turning once more into the dark passage, Del fixed his eyes on Jiharra. "I'll return soon," he said simply.

Jiharra nodded.

When Del, the deacon, and all the soldiers were behind the iron slab a lever was pulled, and machinery hidden somewhere within the stones of the wall growled and hissed in complaint. Gears gnashed teeth, and stone ground against stone. As the slab began to lower, Jiharra lifted his hand to Del in a simple gesture of farewell. "Go safely," the kalif said under his breath, but the sound of snarling machinery drowned out the words. He was left watching as the impossibly heavy wall of iron settled against the ground with a shudder, severing the final passage to safety.

• • •

There was a conference chamber of sorts just within the tunnel. Sealed off by a banded door of oak which looked to be a thousand years old, it had been built as a kind of guard's closet, but had never been used by anything but spiders and shadows. The door had been poorly fitted, and as a result scraped awfully against the rough stones of the floor. It would not pull open all the way, and the deacon was forced to put his booted foot against the wall for added leverage. Grating violently in protest, the door finally surrendered to his efforts.

Seizing a torch from one of the soldiers, the deacon plunged into the room. Del followed immediately after. Dark and cramped, without windows or decoration of any kind, the chamber had the murky ambiance of a dungeon cell. The torch which the deacon fit into a rusted sconce seemed inadequate against the stubborn darkness. At the center of the chamber was a table of dark wood, but there were no chairs.

The deacon moved to stand at the far end of the table, while the largest of the soldiers stepped in behind them and pulled the door shut. Once the three of them were secured in the room, the imposing soldier took up position to the left of the door, his hands folded calmly in front of him. He looked less mobile than a pillar of solid granite. At the head of the table, the deacon leaned forward to frown menacingly at Del, both hands flat on the rough wood. "The man behind you is the seriph Matthias," he said by way of introduction.

Surprised, Del looked over his shoulder at the massive warrior by the door. For all his years spent in service to Shallai, he had only been privileged enough to see three seraphim. Most memorable had been the siege at Harcourt, when the beast-like seriph known as the Reaper had scaled the curtain wall of the enemy keep under cover of darkness. For the rest of that night the soldiers of Shallai had listened to the screams from the enemy castle. At dawn of the next day, the portcullis had opened and the Reaper, bloodied and silent, emerged from the keep alone. He'd left seventy-three men dead behind him.

"The seriph has been eager to meet you for some time," the deacon said.

"Why? I don't understand."

"Why would you," the deacon said. "It seems the Oracle at Jericho has become aware of whatever plots you and your sand-dogs have been brewing in the desert. Seriph Matthias has been sent to ensure they are not carried out."

Bewildered, Del looked at the deacon. "I'm planning nothing."

"A whole army and no plan? Disappointing, Ambassador."

"We're not an army," Del objected.

The deacon's attitude roughened unexpectedly, and he slapped the table with the flat of his palm. "Then explain to me, Ambassador," he barked, "what they are, if not an army? How has a desert-full of sand-dogs suddenly materialized outside my fortress, and how do you *not* expect me to consider it an act of aggression?! Give us your explanations, Ambassador," he invited with a flourish. "Tell us your tall tales. I expect fascinating stories illustrating the sheer madness which has inspired you to bring such a pack of worthless trash to the doorstep of Shallai."

Del closed his eyes, taking a moment in his private darkness to tightly leash his boiling frustrations. He arranged his words as carefully as he was able. "There has been an attack on Aba Ajraan," he said in a slow, even tone. "The sthaak have destroyed four of the seven tribes, and Aba Ajraan itself has fallen. What you see on the horizon is all that is left of the Bedu."

Ian raised a brow. "Sthaak?" he said with mock interest. "And who are these sthaak?"

"They're not human," Del explained. "They live in the deeper parts of the desert, along the perimeter of the Sands. They're animals, creatures . . ." He struggled to think of something with which they could be compared, but came up short. "They are terrible."

"Terrible monsters," the deacon repeated, obviously unconvinced.

Del breathed deep.

"This army of sthaak," the deacon said, exploring his imagination. "What is it they want?"

"Nothing," Del said wearily. He was bored of the game.

"Nothing?" Ian said incredulously. "I don't believe you."

Del remained silent.

"Come, Ambassador," the deacon goaded him. "Speak. You have come all this way, chased by demons, and now you have nothing to say. What is it you want from me?"

"Only your help."

"The sand-dogs want help?" Ian marveled. "From Shallai?"

"Yes."

"And you expect me to do what?"

"We need to move them behind the wall," Del continued in his firmly controlled calm. "The women and children can continue through to the north side, into the Way where they will be safe. The ken'dari will stay to—"

Ian choked on his disbelief, interrupting Del mid-thought. He came halfway around the table, gaping at the ambassador. "Have you gone mad?" he demanded, beginning to wag his head in wonder. "You want me to allow your people through the wall? You want me to allow *Bedu* into *Shallai*?"

"Deacon, we—"

"What kind of a fool do you take me for, Ambassador? You

expect me to permit this army of yours into Shallai because you are frightened by demons from the desert? What did you expect me to say? 'Yes, by all means, Ambassador. Bring your army into my fortress. Let us all sing songs and hold hands.' What is going on in your head that you think the wall will open at your whim, at your *lies*?"

"This is no lie," Del stressed.

"Then bring me proof," the deacon said, smacking the back of one hand against the palm of the other. "Show me one of your monsters. Bring it here, in front of my face, so that I can look at it with my own eyes and see what has flushed all the sand-dogs out of the desert."

Del opened his hands in abject helplessness.

"You have nothing," the deacon said. "No proof. No monsters."

Nearly pleading, Del stepped forward. "Why won't you listen?"

"Because you insult my intelligence," snapped the deacon in a sudden flare of wrath. "Why am I here, Ambassador?" he asked angrily, spreading his arms to display himself for inspection. "Why!? Why do you think I have been sent to this gods-forsaken place by our Liege, the Fist?" Abandoning his condescending tone, he jabbed an accusing finger at Del, and his voice became scalding. "You may have forgotten why Gideon's Wall was built. But I have not. This is a fortress of Shallai, Ambassador, built to defend the empire against the Bedu. It is not a hostel for infidels. How can you fail to understand that one simple truth?"

Del opened his mouth to resume his plea, but Ian Manzig quickly held up a hand to stem the flow of words before it began. "You are a very imaginative man, Ambassador. But I think you have been too long in the sun. You're not right in the head." He stared at Del a long moment before putting his final decision in words simple enough for any weak-headed fool to understand. "Take your army elsewhere," he said.

"There is nowhere left to go," Del grated.

"Then let them rot where they stand."

One of Del's most noteworthy talents had always been his ability to retain control. No matter how rampant his emotions ran within him, he kept his composure intact: face calm, voice even, hands steady. But now, in the face of such blatant indifference, he found himself rapidly losing grip. For one man's unprovoked hatred to decree the death or survival of an entire nation was unacceptable. With clenched fists, his vision began to shimmer. On the verge of willingly turning loose his temper, his hands itched to throttle the deacon's throat. With a visible effort, he kept himself in line, speaking with as much reserve as he could manage. "Deacon," he said slowly. "Please be reasonable. These people have done you no wrong. They have done Shallai no wrong. They need food and water. They will die if—"

"What did you not understand about the things I've said, Ambassador?" the deacon wondered, jutting his face forward to study Del with an intent look of open detestation. "Have I wasted my breath on you?"

Del fell silent, staring at the deacon with a look void of life and hope. Something in his mind was in the gruesome process of being mangled, like some hapless animal caught up in the merciless thunder of a cavalry charge, churning and tumbling beneath a cascade of hooves. The only outward sign of it showed in the twitch of flesh beneath his left eye. The deacon's senseless loathing had pinched something in him, some deep nerve responsible for gluing together all the aspects of sanity. For a very long moment Del only stared at Ian Manzig, passionately hating everything about him, yet incapable of mustering anything more to say to the self-proclaimed bigot. Everything other than that hatred had shut down inside him, making way for that one black emotion. Sluggishly, the broken thing in his mind tumbled and twisted, and his wrath began to seep out of control. His faith was murdered. He had nothing left.

"Have you nothing more to say to me, Ambassador?" the deacon asked in a voice loaded with as much insolence as one question could be.

"No," Del heard himself say with a dead voice.

In a deliberately slow voice, the deacon, without knowing what he did, placed the last straw on Del's already burdened soul. "This conversation is over," he said abruptly. "Get out of my sight."

The tic beneath Del's eye shuddered.

Ian had straightened himself imperiously, folding his arms across his chest and closing himself to any further pleas. He felt he had done his duty to Shallai, enduring the insanity of the ambassador for as long as was expected of him. He had no sympathy for the man, nor for the castoff race of nomads he had brought to the wall seeking safety from imaginary monsters.

But the ambassador was not yet finished.

"Who do you think you are?" Del asked in a low tone laced with threat. "What can you possibly hope to gain by watching women and children slaughtered in front of your face?"

"You overstep your bounds," the deacon cautioned.

"Go to the battlements and look at them!" Del pleaded, half in anger and half in supplication. "They did not come to make war. They came for help. Are you too blind to see?!"

"I'm warning you, Ambassador," the deacon said ominously.

"And I am warning *you*, Deacon," Del retorted. "Do not think arrogance will protect you from me."

"Are you threatening me?"

"Yes," Del said emphatically.

"Get out of my sight!" Ian exploded.

"Open your eyes!"

The deacon had drawn the line, and the ambassador had crossed it. With all the frenzy of an emperor in his towering rage, the deacon swung a fist with full intention of splitting the ambassador's skull. To his great surprise, Del deflected the blow, and the deacon found himself flailing backwards against the stones of the wall. Before he could fight back, or even protest the treatment, Del's astonishingly strong fingers were gripping the soft flesh of his throat, clamping off air and voice. The deacon's mouth opened, sucking on nothing. Del's twisted face filled his vision. For one brief moment, Ian Manzig truly believed he had finally gone too far.

"You tempt me," Del whispered in a voice strained with rage. Given another moment, he might have murdered the deacon. The urge had climbed up from his gut, filling him with a desperate, bestial hunger. Frustration churned in him like the waters of a maelstrom, and the violence of it made his hands tremble and his chest ache. He was never given the chance.

In the next instant he was torn from his victim and sent reeling across the short length of the chamber. He had forgotten about Matthias.

"Enough," the grim seriph stated in a severe tone. His eyes were fixed on the deacon, but his left hand was firmly against Del's chest, trapping him against the wall.

Summoned by the ruckus of the heated confrontation, the armored soldiers barged threateningly into the room.

Just recovering from the initial shock of the ambassador's sudden blitz, the deacon flew into hysterics. Livid, he shrieked at his soldiers. "Get him out of my sight! Throw him back to the desert! Take him!"

The soldiers began their descent on Del, determined to manhandle him from the room, possibly even dispensing a few well-placed cuffs along the way, as a lesson to sand-dog-lovers. They would have been successful had the seriph not thrown out a single arm to halt them. That one gesture broke their impetus as effectively as if a stone wall had been dropped in front of their faces.

Enraged, Ian Manzig flailed his arms. "Drag him out of here! I want him gone! He is a traitor and a dog!" The soldiers glanced at their deacon, raving and spitting. Then they looked at the seriph, quietly menacing in his silence. It was not a difficult choice. The simple, steady, and wordless command of the seriph to remain where they stood outweighed the deacon's hysterical call for obedience, and the soldiers lagged near the door, looking everywhere but at the deacon.

With his arm still warning the soldiers to keep their distance, the seriph looked down at Del, and his face was as calm as though nothing were out of the ordinary. "I do not think force will be necessary at this time, Deacon. The ambassador will conduct himself professionally, I believe."

From somewhere within the noisy clamor of Del's passions rose a beacon of calm. It sliced through the chaos of rage, reducing the whirlwind to tatters. So sudden was its arrival that it seemed an explosion of serenity, and made the riot of emotion which had possessed him before seem frightening even to himself. The storm had not vanished, only sought out a deeper place to burrow, waiting for an opportune time to return in greater fury. Ian Manzig saw the sudden change in Del, and it reminded him of the stories of the mad Baron of Grenitch, who worked himself into such fits of vehemence that he blindly committed crimes of unspeakable brutality, none of which he could remember afterwards. Such a capacity for destruction seemed well within Del's reach, lurking somewhere beneath his quiet demeanor, waiting to pounce forth unexpectedly to do murder. Despite his own indignant air, Ian was thankful the seriph stood between them.

To Del, the seriph said privately, "I believe it would be in your best interest, Ambassador, if I escorted you away from this place." His tone was not unkind, but neither was it a suggestion.

"Can you do nothing?" Del implored.

Protected by the seriph, Ian Manzig snorted in disgust. "This groveling makes me nauseous. Save your energy, Ambassador, and be grateful I'm letting you leave with what's left of your dignity. You are lucky I am generous enough to—"

"Silence, Deacon," the seriph commanded.

Ian said not a word more.

And then the seriph was leading Del away, gentle enough to allow him his own pace, firm enough to let him know the choice was not his own. At the mouth of the tunnel, where the shadows beneath the wall gave way to the desert, the seriph turned Del loose. Before crossing the threshold, Del looked at the seriph one final time. The warrior's piercing eyes were rife with flecks of gold, his mouth stuffed with overlarge teeth. His were the kind of jaws designed for pulling meat from bones. Del faced him without fear. The seriph seemed docile when compared to a horde of sthaak.

"I will not let these people die," he said. Without waiting for an answer, he gave the seriph his back, and stepped out of Gideon's Wall.

• • •

Moving from the shade of the tunnel to the glaring brilliance of the desert sun struck Del with a momentary yet painful blindness. The light seemed to roar at him, flushing his world with white. Squinting against the onslaught, he stopped until his eyes had somewhat adjusted, then looked up to find Jiharra standing over him, offering his body to block the sun. Over his shoulder, Del watched the iron slab lowering.

"The news is not good," the kalif assumed quietly.

"No," Del confirmed.

"What was said?"

"Many things," was Del's vague answer.

"They will not permit us through?"

"No."

"Not the women? Or the children?"

Softer this time, Del said, "No."

Jiharra nodded slowly. As natural as it might have seemed to resort to bitterness and wrath, or to curse such unjust treatment, he did not become hateful, and he felt no malice toward the northmen or their impassable wall. Narrowing his eyes against the full brightness of the sky, he looked up the sheer face of Shallai's man-made barrier, and his face seemed peaceful, almost content. "I do not know what is beyond here," he said pensively. "But I would have liked to find out. I would have liked to see your home, Del." After a reflective pause, he added, "It seems sad, to come so far, to be so close, and yet to be turned away."

"The fault is mine," Del said bitterly.

Jiharra was startled. "You did all you could."

"It isn't enough."

The kalif kept his peace, watching Del placidly.

"Why aren't you angry?" Del demanded.

"This isn't your fault," Jiharra tried to explain.

"It is!" Del cried fiercely, feeling a powerful resurgence of the rage that had possessed him while contending with the deacon. "They are *my* people behind that wall. My own people and I cannot make them see!"

In a gesture made pitiful in its futility, Del picked a stone off the ground and cast it with all his might. The missile sailed through the air, then bounced from the wall harmlessly, like a gnat deflected from the brow of a giant. As ineffectual as it had been, the assault seemed to appease the sudden flare, and he stood glaring at the wall and all those dwelling in safety behind it.

"Do you know what the deacon calls your people?" Del asked suddenly, putting forth the question as though it were an interesting bit of trivia. But when he looked at Jiharra, the shame of it was in his eyes.

Jiharra shook his head.

"Sand-dogs," Del said. "He calls you sand-dogs. And he doesn't believe that the sthaak exist, but says that even if they do, and if they come to wipe out all your people, it will be a blessing to Shallai." After saying so, he lifted his eyes back to the wall.

"How proud I am," Del said disdainfully.

Jiharra placed a comforting hand on his shoulder. "Come," he said. "Waste no more of your strength on this. We will return to our families and prepare ourselves. We have our backs to the wall, and the sthaak will not take us without a fight."

"But they *will* take us," Del said with surety. Staring back at Gideon's Wall, he wondered how he had allowed events to swing so tragically askew from what he'd planned. He ached for the power to wind time backwards, just far enough for him to try one more time to convince the deacon. Now that his chance was gone, he felt he'd backed down too easily. He felt that surely there was more he could have said, more he could have done. But it was over. It had been over the moment the deacon had stepped to the battlements and seen the Bedu nation crawling out of the desert. Del had never really had a chance at all. Even so, his failure to reason with the deacon lay heavily on his shoulders. Demoralized, he rubbed his forehead, where a deep-seated pain had taken root and begun to throb. He still heard the deacon screaming in his head.

"What's the use?" he asked hopelessly.

"We are not defeated yet," Jiharra reminded him.

Del rubbed. And thought. "Not yet," he said quietly.

As they started back toward the waiting nation, Jiharra looked over his shoulder for one last look at the towering edifice. "Your people have built something magnificent," he said.

"It's not magnificent," Del countered. "It's offensive."

Jiharra glanced at the ambassador. "I pray your people will be safe there."

Del made no reply. He was no longer listening. His thoughts, aggravated by the jagged pain roosting behind his eyes, ran in tight circles, leashed and tangled and feeding off one another like sharks in a frenzy. There was hatred toward the deacon, whose face he could not banish from his mind, as well as all of the man's ugly prejudices against the Bedu. But deeper, and more destructive than his abhorrence of the deacon, was his own self-loathing. The Bedu had placed their trust in him, and he had failed. His failure had doomed them to extinction. It mattered not one bit that it was the deacon who denied them entrance to the wall, or that it was the sthaak who would do the slaughtering. To Del, the fault was his own. None of these thoughts were distinct in themselves, but all aided in fueling the untamed bedlam in his mind, adding to the desperate sense of urgency leading nowhere.

The solution came unexpectedly enough that he halted in his tracks. Jiharra strode four more paces before realizing the ambassador was no longer with him. He turned, and was immediately touched with concern by the strange expression on Del's face. It was apparent the ambassador had come to a sudden revelation.

"Del?"

"The deacon does not trust me," Del announced. "He wants to believe that I came here to lay siege to Gideon's Wall, to take it from him by force." He looked quickly over his shoulder to the distant wall, as if to verify that nothing had changed, that their situation was still as grim as the moment before. When he looked back to Jiharra his eyes were bright, dancing with something like hope, only more sinister.

"And what *will* we do?" Jiharra asked cautiously.

"We give him what he wants."

• • •

Twisting his hands into bumpy knots of flesh and knuckle, Ian Manzig beat the innocent tabletop with balled fists. Plates from three meals past leapt and rattled, and bowls of stiffened gruel bounced. The quaking upset a pitcher of lukewarm milk, which tipped to its side and rolled to the floor, vanishing in a flat explosion of pure white. Hunched over the frightened crockery, dark brows low and eyes storming, the deacon could think of nothing which would give him greater fulfillment than to put a knife in the ambassador's back.

Immediately after dispelling the insubordinate madman, Ian had secluded himself in his chamber within the keep, where he burned with displeasure. The ambassador and his outlandish lies were crawling beneath his skin. For the ambassador to bring an army of infidels out of the desert under the ridiculous pretense of innocence was infuriating. It was more than infuriating. It was madness! Ian had never cared for Del; the imperturbable ambassador was soft-spoken, and far too clever, traits Ian found disquieting. He did not like people who were smarter than he. But his dislike for Del was not clouding his reason. The fact remained, the ambassador had stepped far out of bounds by bringing such a force to the wall, and the deacon was hardly in a mood to be magnanimous. He much preferred to nurture his grievances.

He took to pacing, broken glass crunching beneath his boots.

236

Back and forth across the chamber he went, tracking milky footprints behind him. Stepping out onto the balcony, he breathed deeply of the evening air, just beginning to cool in the shade of the cliffs. His balcony was nothing more than a cramped ledge, but it offered a full view of the grounds, his private make-believe kingdom, from one end of the wall to the next. Looking across his tiny dominion, he couldn't avoid thinking of himself as the resentful overlord of a cast off empire of dirt and sun. And what a pathetic empire it was. With but a handful of incompetent soldiers and one narrow border to protect, his kingdom had always been a wasted effort. Until now.

Enter the ambassador and his Bedu.

Although the balcony afforded him no view of the desert, he easily imagined the dark body of the ambassador's army, like a distant black tide waiting for the slow turn of heaven to drag it back to shore. He gnashed his teeth. It wasn't that he was afraid of a battle, oh no! He'd always felt he had been made to command, to lead soldiers to war, to swing steel and kill men. But this—this was no war. There were no surprises in war. Wars were planned and agreed upon. They were strategical and organized and calculated. This was none of those things. This was a farce. And Ian Manzig would sooner be damned than have it said he was killed in a war that was not a war.

He was still standing stiffly on the balcony when a messenger crept in to inform him that the seriph was waiting outside for audience. That, too, had only been a matter of time.

"Bring him," the deacon said tersely. He remained where he was, planting both hands on the balustrade as though preparing to hold out against a storm.

"A moment of your time, Deacon."

Ian kept his back turned. Making the seriph wait helped him to feel in control. It was a pleasant, if short-lived fantasy, and when he finally turned, his stomach flipped with a gentle kind of fear. He averted his eyes, pretending to take great interest in the view. The truth was, he found it difficult to look the seriph in the eye for much longer than a few moments at a time.

"I haven't long," the deacon muttered.

The seriph paused, watching Ian closely. He took his time beginning. "My purpose here is not to interfere," he said after a few long moments. "But I believe you have misjudged the ambassador."

Ian cast the seriph a distasteful look. "Have I?" he sneered. His anger had clouded his judgment, and he had momentarily forgotten to whom he was speaking.

The seriph's eyes narrowed slightly. "I find you rude," he stated. He began to advance, his gray eyes betraying only a hint of irritation, a clue indicating the depth of anger beneath.

The deacon's stomach turned again, more urgently this time.

"Normally I am a dispassionate man, tolerant of disrespect," the seriph continued. "And I feel I have been lenient of yours so far. But my patience with you is waning."

The deacon swallowed hard. He opened his mouth, but the seriph lifted a finger, only slightly, to silence him. "Do not speak," he said.

Ian shut his mouth.

"I also do not enjoy repeating myself. But for your sake I will say again, I believe you have misjudged the ambassador. If what he says is true, then a new threat to Shallai will soon make itself known, one potentially far greater than the Bedu, do you agree?"

Ian couldn't answer right away. The seriph continued to watch him, and it was not long before his already fragile nerve buckled under the weight of the chiseling stare. Obviously reluctant to speak despite being granted permission, he spoke in a subdued tone, fearful of meeting the seriph's gaze. "I don't care how much the ambassador rants," he said carefully, his eyes searching for a safe place to settle. "He's lying to us both. I don't believe a word he says."

The seriph said nothing.

"He's a maniac," Ian added.

Taking the seriph's silence to mean agreement, or at least something other than total disagreement, the deacon found the courage to forge ahead. "And even if what he says is true—which it is not— I say all the better. If the Bedu are troubled by nightmares and monsters, let them care for themselves. I will not make their problems mine. *We* should not make their problems *ours*. Let the imaginary beasts wipe them out. When it is done we can go back to Shallai where we belong. I care nothing for them."

"You've made that clear," the seriph remarked.

Ian looked at the seriph sharply, unsure if he had heard a slight hint of scorn. He turned back to the balcony. The sun had fallen beneath the Mukkaris, emblazoning the cliffs with silver and red. A slow wind had begun to blow in from the desert. He collected his thoughts, pulling together scraps to make pieces, and putting together pieces to form pictures. What he saw was obvious.

"You believe him," Ian said. It sounded like an accusation.

"If I believed him entirely, this conversation would be different, Deacon. I agree, the ambassador's story seems unlikely, but I can find no reason for him to lie. The situation warrants closer scrutiny."

"What does that mean?"

"I will visit the ambassador tomorrow, on his own ground."

"What can you possibly hope to gain from that?"

"The truth."

"And then what?"

"Then I make my decision."

Ian Manzig began to realize what was happening. "Your decision," he repeated blandly. He felt that the precious little he owned had just been taken from him, and in exchange he was given the understanding that it had never been his at all. "And what if you return believing his lies?" he said, nearly spitting the words out. "Will you command me to open the wall for his army? Will you override my decision?"

"I will urge you to make a new decision, Deacon."

Ian clenched his jaw. He was quickly learning where the true authority lay. The seriph was in charge, permitting him to retain his own parody of control as long as it suited his ends. Control could be taken from him, and easily, at any moment. Casting caution to the wind, he spoke more brashly than his own somewhat frail common sense would have otherwise permitted.

"What is to keep me from denying you entrance to the wall?" he asked. "If I disagree with your decision, and I am in here, and you out there, what stops me from keeping it that way?"

For the first time, and the last, Ian saw the imperturbable seriph smile, and it chilled him to the bone.

"Be wise, Deacon," the seriph said.

Five

The infiltration of Gideon's Wall began with a single man. Concealed by darkness, the lone assailant held fast to the sheer face of the wall by the small joints of his fingers and toes. The northward face of the wall, after being bombarded by more than six decades of sun, wind and storm, had become infected with a web of interlacing cracks and tiny fissures which had opened in the mortar between stones. It was to these rifts which the attacker clung, moving upward inch by cautious inch. High above ground, cheek pressed to the cold stones and fingers clutching the wall to his chest, one hand explored above his head, foraging for leverage. Once found, his fingers wedged between the narrow lips, tight and deep. He pulled, and the ground dropped yet farther away. His toes found

241

purchase on tiny ledges, and the next hand went in search of the next crevasse. He had been climbing for nearly an hour, and was almost to the battlements. Not far above, seventeen soldiers paced back and forth between their posts, oblivious to the fact that they were under siege.

Before undertaking his arduous climb, the ken'dari had chosen his point of entry with careful deliberation. The sentry posts on the battlements were spaced out at thirty yards across the entire length of the wall, and the shadows that grew where the light did not reach were darker than pitch. He had taken into account the slant of the moon, the location of the posts, and the routes of the sentries as they carried their torches back and forth across the wall. Now, at the peak of his ascent, he waited patiently while a pair of patrolling soldiers marched past. Had they stopped for any reason to lean upon the battlements and look down, they would most likely have been shocked to find a Bedu ken'dari staring back at them, and the offensive would have ended in an ugly way. But they did not stop to look. They strolled on unaware, leaving the ken'dari to heave himself up and over the battlements, as silent and unseen as a black cat in a shadow.

A small group of three guards were tossing dice and trading money in a ring of torch light at the west end of the battlements, where a door opened into a well of winding stairs. Like a dark throat, the well dropped clear to the base of the wall, and the narrow stairs, barely wide enough for one man, curled around the inside of it.

Keeping to the shadows and moving swiftly, the ken'dari glided within four feet of the crouching soldiers, yet they never heard a sound. One more shadow among thousands, he slipped by like a wraith. Down the well he went, descending a great deal faster than the way he had been forced to come up. He emerged in the main courtyard of the wall, empty in the still hours of the night. Hastening along the darkness gathered at the base of the wall, he followed the strict route set for him by the ambassador. So fleeting was his passage that he might have been mistaken for the shadow of something crossing the moon. He made for the wide mouth of the tunnel beneath the wall, and crouched there just long enough to ensure he had not been seen.

There was scarcely any light inside. With the fingers of one hand touching the wall, he went in blindness, leaving behind the patch of moonlight through which he had come. Even in the darkness he found the panel of levers exactly where the ambassador had said they would be. The tunnel echoed with the sound of cranking gears and rusted cogs. The noise lasted scarcely a moment, just long enough for the slab to raise two feet from the ground, opening a band of desert moonlight across the floor and filling the tunnel with a pale glow. The others were waiting, and no sooner had the iron weight lifted than they were inside, rolling silently beneath the slab.

There were twenty of them in all, faces masked with dark cloth. When they closed their eyes, they all but vanished. The ambassador was among them, his sword strapped to his back. He was clad like the ken'dari, all in black, with soot rubbed into the white skin of his face and hands. His sweat had caused it to run.

"Were you seen?" the ambassador asked.

The ken'dari shook his head, and Del glanced up the long length of the tunnel, toward the mouth of moonlight at the far end. He actually smiled. They had breached the wall, and although the night was far from over, they were one step closer to claiming their prize. "You climb well," he complemented.

Organized in a loose group, the band of invaders had just started down the passage when there came a deep thump behind them, as of a giant hammer dropped against the sand. The slab had fallen shut, plunging them into utter darkness.

Del heard a dull thud to his right, followed immediately by the sound of a body slumping to the ground. From behind him came a sharp and sudden cry of pain, but the sound was cut short by the ripe smack of a body propelled against the tunnel wall with great force. He whirled around, but it was impossible to tell what was attacking them, or from where. The darkness itself had come alive to snuff out their lives one by one.

A ken'dari standing very close emitted a low gasp of surprise, then nothing, as though he had been swallowed by shadows. Soon after came a muffled grunt to his right, then another thud. There was a whoosh of air and a heavy slap. To his left, another body hit the ground.

The ken'dari were being methodically eliminated.

Incapable of functioning without vision, and unable to focus on the source of the attacks, Del began to back away, one arm in front and one behind. It was only a matter of moments before the chaos gave way to abrupt silence.

Seven ken'dari had fallen in as many seconds.

Del stopped moving, somehow believing that if he held perfectly still, whatever thing they shared the darkness with would overlook him. His heart kicked in his chest, loud enough to give him away, and his breathing was ragged. Wide and staring, his blind eyes searched the eternity of blackness in front of his face while straining to hear anything at all.

"I suspected you might return," said the voice of the seriph.

Del felt sick.

No sooner had the seriph spoken, marking his location, than a tide of soft and rapid footsteps converged on him from various directions. Del shouted out a warning, but it came too late, and went unheeded.

There were three short bursts of noise, followed in rapid succession by three falling bodies, then more silence.

"Stay where you are," Del called out, a warning for whoever might be left. "Do not move." His voice sounded hollow and afraid in the darkness, edged with fear.

"It is good you came," said the conversational voice of the seriph, closer now. "It saves me the trouble of finding you."

There were footsteps near him, and he twisted his head although he could see nothing but empty space. His hand itched to reach for his sword, to swing and slash in front of him to protect himself from the advancing seriph, but he knew such a foolish action would only earn him pain. So he stood trembling with his heart in his throat, knowing that the seriph was nearly on top of him. He could feel the overwhelming presence swelling, as though the darkness had taken on substance.

A large fist twisted itself in the front of his shirt, and another clamped about his throat. He felt himself lifted off the ground and pressed against the rough stones of the wall.

He must have made some small noise of fear, for a final rush of footfalls came bearing down on them. The hand left Del's throat for a but a moment, and he felt the seriph half-twisting where he stood to deal with the assault. Two more bodies dropped, one with a grunt, the other soundlessly.

"Don't kill them," Del pleaded. "Please don't kill any more."

There was a long pause, during which Del felt the seriph was surveying the tiny battlefield of the tunnel.

"I have killed no one," said the seriph. "And nothing has been broken that will not mend." There came another pause. "The wise ones are heeding your advice, and are keeping still now."

Del felt a heat in the darkness, and he knew the seriph's eyes were on him, his face inches away. His nostrils were filled with the musky odor of an animal.

"But leave off worrying for them, Ambassador. It is your life which hangs in the balance at the moment." The hand in his shirt adjusted slightly, securing him more firmly against the wall. "You and I will decide how this is to end. I will ask the questions, and you will supply the answers. The truth is of prime importance, so let us first agree that there will be no lies between you and I."

"No lies," Del consented breathlessly.

"What are your intentions, Ambassador?"

Del swallowed harshly. "To help the deacon see matters my way."

"You bring weapons," the seriph noted. "And Bedu warriors."

"They are to make me more persuasive."

"Do you plan to kill him?"

Del didn't want to answer that, but was in no position to haggle for an alternative question. It was either admit his guilt, or lie to the seriph. Neither choice was appealing. Without knowing what the truth would mean for him, he offered it in a hushed voice, "Only if I first failed to convince him."

"To permit the Bedu into Shallai?"

"Yes."

"To what end?"

"To save lives."

There was a long silence in which Del steeled himself for the strike that would end his life. He resisted the urge to shut his eyes against it, and instead stared straight into the darkness before him, hoping beyond hope that his answers had not displeased the seriph.

If they had, he was not immediately killed for it.

Instead, Del was slowly lowered to the ground.

When his feet touched the sand and the seriph released him, he nearly collapsed. The stifling presence receded, and the darkness lost its threatening edge. He could breathe again. Moments later, a spark cut the darkness with a sharp flash, then another. A tiny flame jumped to life, illuminating the hard lines of the seriph's face. It grew inside the torch within which it had been planted, grasping the head of tar until a ragged circle of expanding light swelled around him, revealing the confines of the tunnel.

Twelve of the twenty ken'dari lay sprawled in various poses of defeat. When the seriph calmly turned from the torch, he came face to face with the remaining eight.

"No!" Del shouted, flinging out his hands to prevent them from throwing themselves at the seriph. The ken'dari looked at him uncertainly, but wisely kept their distance, eyeing the seriph as they might a cornered sthaak.

"He won't try to stop us," Del told them.

"What is he?" Del was asked.

"He is the Seriph Matthias."

"What is a seriph?"

"They are the warlords of Shallai. They are very strong."

"And they fight well in the dark," one added.

"He's going to help us," Del said.

Although the ken'dari relaxed their guard, they kept a wary eye on the seriph, and maintained a respectful distance. The seriph had turned to face Del. "Leave one of your men with me to assist with the wounded," he said. "You may take the others."

Given leave to proceed, Del and his greatly diminished band were starting down the tunnel toward the inner courtyards of Gideon's Wall when the seriph called to him. "Ambassador," the warrior said, causing Del to turn.

"I urge you not to kill the deacon," he said directly. "He may be a fool, but he is a fool in the service of Shallai. I would be deeply disappointed if he were to die at the hand of a fellow citizen of the empire."

"There will be no killing," Del assured him. *Not yet.*

"Go then," the seriph said. "Be you persuasive."

• • •

The keep of Gideon's Wall was a fortress in its own right, the last place of safety behind the wall. The guards posted at the lower portal were unprepared. Rapidly and silently, they were overrun by the ken'dari, who melted out of the blackness from every direction. Shoving the doors open angrily, Del strode into the night darkened hall as though the keep and all in it were his to command. The unconscious soldiers were dragged into the lofty antechamber, where they were trussed and gagged, and the heavy doors, which had been constructed to withstand the axes, fists and battering-rams of sieges, were pushed shut behind them. It took two men to slide the heavy bolts, made from unfinished timber, into their deep housings in the walls.

Del led the ken'dari up a wide flight of stairs, knowing exactly where the deacon was to be found. There were torches guttering in their sconces, but at such an early hour the darkened halls were void of life. Their destination was the deacon's private chambers, two floors up and at the end of a wide hall.

Without reserve, and hardly slowing his pace, the ambassador kicked in the doors, which seemed to explode inward on busted hinges.

The deacon's sleep was rudely interrupted by the sudden intrusion. Before he had fully realized what was happening, the ken'dari were upon him. He opened his mouth to shout in protest, but a gag was stuffed in it. He made a wild grasp for his sword, but his arm was slapped aside. Seized by the neck, he was thrown back to the bed, where a ken'dari kept him still with a knee in his back. All of his struggling was worth nothing. In a few brief moments his arms were twisted and bound behind his back. Hauled from his bed, he was forced to stand before Del like a criminal dragged before the executioner. Fully awake now, he was not at all delighted to see the ambassador.

Del settled his blazing eyes on his hostage.

"Deacon," he said crisply. "You and I have much to discuss."

Whatever curses Ian might have shouted were muffled behind the gag filling his mouth. Rage had colored his face a blotchy red, and he twisted madly against the ken'dari. He kicked out with his bare feet, determined to wrest himself free. Only when Del bared his blade did Ian settle. Properly subdued, he watched the ambassador with enmity. Breathing heavily around the gag, he wondered what the madman would do with his sword.

He found out quickly.

The sword blurred upwards, and the hilt smashed into the side of the deacon's head. Ian's vision exploded between light and darkness. His knees went lax, and he sagged forward into Del, who seized him by the front of his shirt and eased him into a sitting position on the floor. With a yank and a grunt, Del propped the groggy deacon up against the foot of his regal bed. He crouched down in front of him as though preparing to explain the rules of conduct to a misbehaving child. There was blood seeping from the deacon's scalp, and his eyes swam in shallow pools of tears.

"Let us be civil with one another, Deacon," Del proposed in the

248

perfectly rational voice of a madman pretending to be sane. "We disagree with one another on certain matters, but tonight, we will discuss our differences of opinion like men, and do our best to understand one another." Having said so, he jerked the rag out of Ian's mouth and held it bundled in his right fist. "This I will keep handy," he said lightly. "In case our tempers should flare unnecessarily."

The deacon offered the audacious ambassador a look of disdain. Running his tongue around the inside of his mouth, he tasted the vile dryness left behind by the ambassador's rag. He spit to the side, but the flavor of dirt remained. Offering no immediate protest, he took the time to let his eyes rove about the room. The door through which the ambassador and his sand-dogs had barged was now shut and barred from the inside. Several ken'dari crouched near the entrance, while others relaxed at various locations throughout the chamber. For a tiny force that had just infiltrated an enemy fortress, they seemed unnaturally at ease, like the great cats of the jungle lounging unseen in high places. He counted six. Moving his eyes back to Del, he scoffed at the ambassador.

"What do you think you're doing, Ambassador?" Ian asked. He had adopted the tone one might use in admonishing a fool for a bumbling attempt at what was so obviously a hopeless endeavor. It was clear he was not prepared to take the ambassador seriously.

"It's not obvious?" Del asked him.

"No," the deacon retorted. Too weary to play games, he added, "What do you want, Ambassador? And why have you brought your stinking sand-dogs into my keep?"

Del nodded, willing to demonstrate a fair amount of tolerance for the deacon's rude choice of words. "The resolution of our conversation earlier this day was unacceptable," he explained. "I've come to renegotiate."

"Then you're wasting your time."

"Am I?" Del asked with slight concern. "I feel I have been very successful with my time so far, Deacon. I have crossed a desert, found my way through your defenses, and now here I am, sharing pleasant conversation with the very root of my problems. Why should I believe our negotiations will end without rewarding me the same measure of success?"

The deacon spit on the floor accusingly. "I'm not the village idiot, Ambassador. You didn't come here to renegotiate, so you can drop the farce."

"You're right," Del admitted indifferently. "I did not. There will be no negotiations. I am here to tell you how things are going to be from this point forward. You have little choice in the matter."

A worm of fear had begun to thrash around in the deacon's gut, twisting up into his chest and down into his groin. He was only just beginning to understand that he had lost one of the greatest fortresses ever built to a handful of Bedu warriors.

"The situation is simple enough even for you to understand," Del went on to say. "I do not expect I will have to explain it in great detail. Gideon's Wall no longer belongs to you," he said plainly. "It is mine."

At this, the deacon's eyes danced with frantic sparks. He had suddenly become highly uncomfortable. Panic trembled at the edge of his voice. "You're deranged if you think you can take the wall from me," he said, vainly attempting to uphold his crumbling pretense of authority.

"Then label me mad," Del said.

"The seriph won't let you do this."

Del smiled cruelly. "I think you're wrong."

The deacon's eyes narrowed in suspicion. He looked at the ken'dari around him, then back at Del. Slowly he began to understand.

"He helped you," the deacon said. Bitter anger wrenched the muscles of his face, but there was nothing he could do but seethe in it. "You are a madman and he is a coward. And the both of you are traitors! I don't care if the seriph has been fooled by your lies, Ambassador, I have not. Don't believe for a moment that I will stand aside and watch you lead your Bedu army into Shallai without doing everything in my power to stop you. You might as well murder me now, because I—"

Without warning, Del hammered his forehead squarely into the bridge of the deacon's nose. Ian's head snapped back, and a stream of blood gushed over his lips.

"Don't think I won't, Deacon," Del whispered venomously, his own repressed wrath rising to the occasion.

"You are alive strictly as a formality," Del reminded him. "Your life is worthless to me, and you would do well to remember that."

The deacon touched the tip of his tongue to bloodied lip, tasting the coppery red stain with hatred brimming in his eyes. "I'll remember," he assured the ambassador.

"Excellent," Del said flatly.

• • •

Del kept nothing from the seriph.

In a small chamber where just the two of them stood, Del spilled the events of the past week with all possible haste. Under the seriph's intense gaze he did not dissemble, and did not lie. No detail was omitted. He felt that if he misrepresented even the smallest fact, if he made the slightest exaggeration, the seriph would know, and would not be pleased.

Matthias absorbed every detail.

When Del finished, breathless, the seriph brought him back to the outpost. He asked questions. He made Del repeat every word of his conversation with the Jaggi. And then he made him repeat them again. Only when he was sure he had pried every significant detail from Del's memory did he take his eyes off the ambassador. He thought. He considered, and evaluated. Then he put his eyes once more on Del, and asked his final question.

"Do you still have the seed?"

Del said that he did, that it was with Jiharra.

"Bring it to me."

Six

It had been more than eight months since the Oracle had declared his warning to Shallai—eight months since he had told all of Jericho that the empire was to perish. When he had claimed that the agent of destruction was to come from the wastelands beyond Gideon's Wall, a spirit of shocked outrage had overtaken the ranks of chancellors and deacons of Jericho. Not one of the simpering, overconfident aristocrats would believe that their beloved empire could be threatened by a withered and dying nation of nomads. And because they had not wanted to confront the grave possibility of such a calamity, because they could not bring themselves to recognize the horror, they closed their ears, shut their eyes, and turned their faces away.

The ancient prophet was scorned, mocked, and shouted down. He could not make himself heard. Because the chancellors would not listen, the Oracle took his message to the streets, and soon a dread sense of coming disaster began to ripen in Jericho. As a peremptory measure against a plague of fear, the High Chancellor, working outside the auspices of the Fist, ordered the Oracle apprehended and executed. His crime: treason against the empire.

The Oracle was abducted from his home and delivered to the flooded stone quarry north of Jericho. His frail body was weighted with shackles of iron and tipped into the inky waters, there to take up residence in frigid darkness with the moss-covered bones of all the rest of Jericho's prophets and traitors.

With the Oracle and his disturbing message silenced, the illusion of security once again prevailed in Jericho.

All but the seraphim were at ease.

The seraphim host held private council with the Fist. They implored him to heed the Oracle. Unanimously, they desired to pull the corps of the armies back from the Mugh-shin front. With rolling cannons, ironclads and a thousand soldiers they could make for Gideon's Wall and be there within the year. It was not too late. But the Fist would not be persuaded.

His arguments were many: the Oracle has given himself to nightmares and shadows; he has outlived his usefulness.

The seraphim reminded him that the Oracle had never been wrong.

The Fist argued that the way to the desert was secured. Nothing could pass Gideon's Wall.

Gideon's Wall is manned by less than three hundred soldiers, said the seraphim. They have nothing but the most mundane of weapons. The wall is not prepared for war.

We have a war already, said the Fist. After five years of fighting with the Mugh-shin, only now have they begun to show signs of languishing. To withdraw now would give them the time they needed to renew their strength. It would be perceived as a sign of weakness.

To this, the seraphim replied: war does not come when called. The Mugh-shin can wait.

The sand-men mean nothing, the Fist said. They are few, and weak.

Gravely, the seraphim reminded him that not once in all of his prophesying had the Oracle given mention of the Bedu. The threat was as yet unnamed, the danger obscure.

After five months, the doubts planted by the seraphim in the Fist's mind began to bloom. But perhaps they had been planted too shallowly, for when the Fist finally agreed to investigate the situation at Gideon's Wall, he sent only one seriph. He sent only Matthias.

And now, when the strengths of the empire were needed, when the convoys of juggernauts, rolling cannons, and engines of war would have made a difference—it was too late.

Matthias' commission, and his determination to fulfil it, was made no less clear by the knowledge of his coming death. He would not be swayed by fear; it could not penetrate his resolve. Before the arrival of the Bedu, he had intended to convey his intelligence to Jericho through traditional means: with letters and messengers. But there was no time for such things now, and they would be made meaningless when the Sands swallowed the empire. His information required a medium that would outlive the destruction of the wall, something that would hold secure the memory of all the events that had led to this place, at this time. He knew that one day, someone would come looking for the truth.

The seriph intended it to be found.

• • •

There was a table of pitch willow in the deacon's chambers. It was sturdy and solid, burdensome enough that four men had had to wrestle it into position during the furnishing of the tower.

The seriph tore it to pieces. He ruined it with his axe and with his hands. The rough-hewn tabletop had been cut from the center of the tree, and it was the heart which he sought. When he had hacked through the concentric circles marking the tree's life, he was left with a slab of wood containing the black heart; the core of the pitch willow.

• • •

In his small room, the seriph set to work with slow deliberation. He carved the nonessential away from the core, then cut at what was left until it fit easily in his hand, a smooth piece of the blackest tint. It was heavy and hard, more akin to stone than wood. He trimmed and whittled at it, and slowly defined a crude, stubby shape. When he was done, he held an ugly, imprecise rendition of a man.

He etched on the dark wood with his smallest knife, turning the mean little fetish over and over in his hands, filling the whole surface with winding grooves. From deep within his broad chest he made a low, steady humming. The sound did not die away, but crowded around him in continuing layers. As he worked, the air in the room began to quiver.

• • •

Long before the sun rose, four ken'dari runners were dispatched from the base of Gideon's Wall, each bearing news to his individual tribe that the ambassador had successfully negotiated passage into Shallai. Even as they departed with the tidings that would bring the whole of the Bedu nation to the very doorstep of Shallai, Seriph Matthias stood on the battlements above, making the necessary preparations for their arrival to be met without opposition.

The seriph had assembled before him a handful of influential men, among them key members of the deacon's staff, his retainers, and subordinates. Roused from sleep by his summons, they had come to stand at strict attention to have the present situation—which had until that very moment been unknown to them—laid out in blunt detail.

The seriph informed them that Ian Manzig had been divested of his commission as deacon. As a result, the command of Gideon's Wall now belonged to him. Furthermore, despite Manzig's previous ruling that the 'sand-dog' nation should be left to rot in the desert, the Bedu were coming through the wall. He made it clear that he expected Shallai's soldiers to assist the mass Bedu immigration in every way possible, and assured them that he would hold each of them personally responsible for any of their subordinates who dared defy his command by instigating conflict. Punishment would be swift and harsh. He told them these things with all the tact of a blow to the head.

Those who remained dubious of the sudden transition of leadership and direction kept their suspicions to themselves, and wisely so. It was common knowledge that questioning a seriph could be a potentially unhealthy activity.

By early morning the flatlands just south of the wall were filling with the first desert-weary refugees. They were only the beginning of a veritable flood of human bodies soon to back up against the wall of Shallai's remote fortress.

Under the suspicious gaze of the soldiers on the wall, the Bedu refugees were guided through the dark throat of the tunnel and into the sprawling common grounds of the wall, where they were herded northward into the Way.

It was not long before the tunnel under the wall could no longer accommodate the rapidly gathering masses. To remedy this, a force of ken'dari was sent to keep the bulk of the displaced nation several thousand paces distant, preventing a crush of men and women from jamming the passage all at once. The ken'dari acted as the valves of a dam, regulating the flow of people. The tribes collected behind the ken'dari, amassing in size and pressure until they had become a sea of weary, desert-worn bodies. Trickling out of the dam came a dozen lines of Bedu filing toward the wall, living tributaries draining the vast sea one body at a time.

Halfway through the morning, Bedu warriors were sent to sift through the ocean of their people, relieving families of their children, and mothers of their infants. They brought the young ones to the wall, where knotted ropes had been draped from the battlements, and soldiers high above waited with ready arms and strong backs to haul the children to safety in baskets and wooden lifts. Most of the ken'dari, having delegated their duties of holding back the tide to other men, pulled themselves up the ropes to the top of the wall, where their strength was needed.

Del was on the ramparts when Jiharra climbed over, hauling himself up with ease. They clasped hands, and Jiharra took a moment to look northward, his breath only slightly labored.

"So this is Shallai," he said, to which Del nodded. "It looks much like the desert to me."

Hour by hour, the southern nation pressed itself through the single passage into the wall. For those who watched from above, it was like counting grains of sand as they passed one at a time through a god-sized hourglass. The courtyard beyond the tunnel had become crammed with separated Bedu families, some searching for loved ones lost in the chaos, while others waited patiently at the mouth of the tunnel, sifting through the steady flow of incoming refugees. Elsewhere in the crowded yards of packed dirt, Bedu men tore themselves from their families before sending them on into the Way. They themselves stayed behind, adding their strength to the growing number of defenders. For the most part, the flow of Bedu ran steadily northward, out of the wall's northern gates and into the valley beyond.

As the day wore on an irate officer confronted the seriph, demanding that he produce the missing deacon. The officer had collected ten brave souls to make the stand with him, and apparently all ten had reached mutual agreement that they were no longer willing to help the sand-dogs invade Shallai until orders were received directly from Ian Manzig himself, whom no one could seem to locate.

The seriph, laboring over a thick rope from which dangled a plank seating four children, hardly spared the officer a glance. The heat had prompted him to strip to the waist, and the muscles beneath his skin bunched and wrestled as he worked the rope. Over one massive shoulder, he patiently suggested to the officer that he and his men remove themselves from his presence at once.

The plank reached the top, and the seriph began transferring children to the wall one by one, lifting them as easily as if they were puppies. When the plank was empty, the children were led away with a teeming mass of other children. Taking up the rope, he then began lowering the plank back down the face of the wall, his back to the small mob who had failed to take his advice. When the plank reached bottom and was being loaded with the next bunch of children, the seriph found himself with a moment to spare, and turned his attention to the officer, who stood his ground and repeated his demands.

The seriph scowled, and the area immediately around them cleared.

Forced to make a swift and violent example, the seriph lifted the officer off his feet and proceeded to carry him to the inside ledge of the wall. Three of the officer's lackeys were foolish enough to attempt interference, and were rendered broken.

As though casting anchor, the seriph let the flailing officer soar from the heights. Without pausing to watch the crushing end of his flight, the seriph went back to his rope.

It was the last example that needed to be set.

Seven

The seriph saw them first. His vision was sharper than most, and his vigilance far more enduring. Although the day had dragged itself into a long, cruel ordeal, the seriph had not lagged. Even the ever-watchful sun had lost interest in measuring the tedious progress of the Bedu exodus, and had let its burning eye droop. It assumed the Bedu would still be there in the morning, and so it bundled itself into a fiery red ball to sink wearily into the Mukkaris. But not the seriph. While slaving tirelessly over the ropes, he had kept one penetrating eye constantly on the desert.

The sthaak came just as dusk was settling into the valley. It was the time of early evening when the tint of the sky had softened its glare from hazy white to pale blue, and the clouds had stretched themselves into vibrant streaks of red and purple.

Hardly more than two-thirds of the Bedu had entered Shallai.

The seriph paused in his labor when he first caught sight of them. He watched for long moments, callous hands locked on his rope, gaze fixed on the desert. When there was no longer any doubt, he glanced to his right. Del, along with Jiharra and a northern soldier, were working hard to drag a plank of four children up the face of the wall. The ambassador and the kalif had been working the ropes beside him all day.

"Ambassador."

Del glanced up, eyes bloodshot, face dripping sweat.

"They come," the seriph said.

• • •

The first of the sthaak came loping out of the flatlands in disorganized packs of three and four. Neck and neck they raced, covering the distance between themselves and the unprotected Bedu with astonishing speed. The horde swelled behind them.

Like a field doused with oil and given the torch, the Bedu amassed outside the wall were stricken with fear. There was a stirring in the throngs, an ominous shifting as knowledge of the coming horde rippled through the ranks of the nation. Panic set them alight, scattering sparks among men made of straw. The weight of the sea could no longer be contained, and the established order collapsed. As a single body the Bedu surged forward, clamoring frantically to escape the devastation roaring down on them. The living wave crashed into the wall, every member fighting to reach the only passage to safety. Those in the rear thrust forward with renewed urgency, while those in front were crushed by the weight of a nation at their backs.

The sthaak fell on the Bedu like demons.

Plunging headlong into their prey, the first wave of beasts swarmed over the Bedu. Unable to tear his horrified gaze from the gruesome display, Del watched the full weight of the horde crash into the masses.

The slaughter was terrible.

In an attempt to reach safety, some began to climb the ropes. Most either fell due to their haste, or were dragged back into the chaos to be slain with those they had sought to leave behind. Those who could not reach the ropes strove in vain to claw their way up the sheer face of the wall while the beasts busied themselves with their gruesome work. Tearing through the unprotected ranks of the Bedu, they left a tangle of flesh behind them in their rampage toward the mouth of the passage. In a terribly short time, the sands were littered with bodies numbering in the thousands, and crawling with a sickening carpet of beasts.

A sudden, horrifying thought stabbed through Del's shock. At that very moment he felt a heavy hand on his shoulder. The seriph was there to tell him what he already knew.

"They're killing their way through the tunnel," the warrior said. "It must be sealed."

"Sealed?" Del repeated dully.

The seriph had already moved on, and Del was forced to run after him or be left behind. Into a deserted stairwell directly above the tunnel the warrior led them. From somewhere down below could be heard the faint whispers of screaming, and as they forged downward, the terrible noise heightened in volume. When it seemed they had nearly reached the ground they came to a heavy door set deeply in the wall. The seriph kicked it in without hardly pausing. Pushing through the remains of the ruined frame, they entered a long, narrow hall. The screams of the Bedu had become deafening. Only after he noticed the wide, round holes in the stones along one wall did Del realize where the seriph had brought him.

The wall to Del's left was a divider, separating the narrow passage in which they stood from the rest of the tunnel. On the other side, through two feet of stone, the passage beneath Gideon's Wall was filled with Bedu. The masses were pressing forward in a desperate but useless attempt to escape the sthaak that were steadily slaughtering their way through the ranks behind them. He could vaguely see shadowy figures through the holes in the wall, which had been designed with the idea that a line of archers could stand safely behind this barrier and let fly volleys of arrows at attackers coming through the tunnel. The screams of the masses were so loud that Del was unable to hear the seriph shouting at him until his arm was seized in a rough grip.

"We have to flood the tunnel!" the seriph boomed.

Bewildered, Del could only stare back at him. He made no move to act until the warrior pushed him forward. Numbness had begun to enshroud him. It was the only way his mind knew how to fight against the realization of what he was being called on to do. His legs carried him forward of their own accord. At the far end of the hall he found himself face to face with a massive iron wheel set in the stone. It was half as large as what might be found on a horse-drawn cart, but fashioned from thick steel. Del decided he had gone far enough, and stopped in his tracks, unwilling to take another step toward the rusted wheel. He knew full well what would happen if it were turned, and he was abruptly aware of his own exhaustion. He would have given everything to be taken somewhere else.

"No," he said, but the word had no breath behind it. He took a step back, as though a viper were coiled about the steel, and had risen to face him with dead-black eyes. He didn't want to turn the wheel. He didn't want to murder the Bedu trapped in the tunnel. He didn't want anything to do with it.

Sudden thoughts of Suri filled his mind.

Overcome with the desire to find his wife, he was about to turn away, to flee the tunnel, but the seriph filled the narrow passage behind him, barring his retreat. Shoved suddenly backwards, Del had to twist around and grab the giant wheel with both hands. Even so, he fell to his knees. Gripping the wheel tightly, he felt the cold bite of rust on slick palms. By the time he pulled himself upright, Matthias was by his side. The seriph's fists wrapped around the steel.

"Turn on my word," the warrior instructed him.

"We can't do this," Del heard himself say. He would have backed away, but the seriph quickly clamped one of his own great fists over Del's, locking his hand to the wheel.

"We have no choice," the seriph said in his face.

Del stared into the warrior's penetrating eyes, and knew it was the truth.

"On my word," the seriph repeated, and the command in his voice allowed for no disobedience. Bending his legs, he secured his footing. His hands flexed around the wheel, and his arms bulged. "Now!" he thundered.

Del obeyed blindly. Sealing his eyes and his mind, he summoned every last scrap of his strength and threw it all against the wheel, knowing that if his body gave out before the wheel, he would never bring himself to make a second attempt. Something in him decided that he would not stop until either he or the wheel broke.

For a long moment they remained frozen in their static pose, pitting their combined might against the stubborn device. Cords stood out on Del's neck, and veins lifted across his forehead and arms. The roaring of the crowds just on the other side of the wall had risen to a deafening crescendo, white noise matching the rush of blood in his ears, one rising against the other until he could not tell which of them filled his head. Some part of him still able to think clearly wondered if Suri was trapped in the tunnel, if her voice was among those crying out in terror.

When something deep in the wall snapped, it was a sound more felt than heard. It was the crack of ancient layers of rust breaking away, of machinery freed to act as it had been designed. The wheel jerked, and Del's grip slipped. His hands dragged along the rust, scraping deep gashes in his palms. Falling against the wall, he clutched his hands as blood seeped from between his fingers and trailed down his wrists. The seriph had not let go of the wheel, and his strength alone carried to completion the turn they had begun together. Just out of sight, something clicked into place with the irreversible finality of a headsman's axe striking the block.

At that moment, Del wished he were dead.

There came a distant rumble at the very core of things, a vibration of great cogs rotating, of massive pieces of machinery shifting about, moving into and out of place. Del forgot about his pain. He looked up as a shower of fine dust was shaken loose from the ceiling. A terrible grinding resonated through the walls around them.

You've killed them, said a voice in Del's mind.

The screams grew louder.

• • •

The tunnel beneath the wall was jammed with Bedu. The deafening roar of terrified voices filled the tight confines as the mob crushed forward in its attempt to escape the slaying claws and shredding teeth of the sthaak. At the mouth of the tunnel, where the long passage of darkness opened into the sunlit courtyards of Gideon's Wall, a harsh boom punctuated the confusion. The turning of the wheel had caused twelve steel rods as thick as a man's arm to slide out from their oiled housings in the ceiling. With the rods retracted, the iron slabs at both ends of the tunnel dropped. The Bedu were cast into blackness. Fifteen men and five women were killed instantly by the falling slabs, crushed beneath the weight. Twelve more were fatally injured, legs or arms mangled or severed, and would die later. But the tunnel was sealed. There was no moving forward, and there was no moving back.

A great many sthaak were trapped with the Bedu, but the darkness made little difference to them. Caught in the throes of their frenzy, they continued to kill, flaying about them with a demoniac hatred, murdering all they could reach.

Their spree was as savage as it was short-lived.

In the stone housing above the tunnel, hundreds of iron seals fell away, releasing a flood of sand into the low passage. The downpour washed down over the heads of the Bedu like heavy torrents of golden water. Desperation heightened. Del tried to block out the screams, but the pleas for mercy pierced his hands, which he had lifted to cover his ears. Groping arms reached through the holes in the wall, clawing for escape. Faces pressed against the arrow slots, gasping for the air that was being crushed out of them.

Del backed away until he came flush against the stones of the opposite wall. Hundreds of men and women were dying less than ten paces away, dying because of his actions. For a long moment, the horrible screams intensified as sand drained into the tunnel, rushing up around knees, thighs and chests. All too suddenly the noise ended, cut off abruptly as tons of sand rose to cover necks and spill into mouths. The Bedu were swallowed alive. The narrow hall was plunged into a roaring silence that, in its own haunting way, was far more disturbing than the noise of terror it had replaced.

Del stared at the arms that protruded from the holes of the wall, frozen into stiff claws. Turning his head as though in a dream, he looked to the seriph, who was watching him with an empty gaze, almost as though expecting him to crack into a thousand pieces. The horrible silence pounded on Del's ears, louder than the screams of the Bedu. He looked at his hands. The gashes in his palms were deep, and blood coated his skin. He was trembling, rattling violently against an onslaught of sickness. His knees buckled under him, and he slid to the floor with his back against the wall. He could not tear his eyes from the hands reaching out to him, clutching for the life he had stolen from them.

• • •

Bound hand and foot, Ian Manzig had been placed in such a position that the only two options available to him were to sleep, or not to sleep. The ambassador's sand-dogs had packed him away to an abandoned storeroom in a remote section of the keep, then lashed him tightly to an uncomfortable chair. There they had left him, trussed and humiliated, not even important enough to place under the watchful eye of a guard. No, he had simply been tucked away with the rats, forgotten like a common thief.

For the first hours of his captivity he had called for help until his throat was scraped raw by the effort. But in such a secluded prison there was little chance of a wandering soldier or servant to hear his shouts. His struggles had produced only sweat, and even with all of his thrashing he had managed only to tip himself over and bang his head. All his efforts had earned him was a bloody scalp and a new perspective of the room. Soon after overturning himself, his struggles had been reduced to pathetic squirming, and his cries for help to the muttering of curses under his breath. He had dozed irregularly after that, coming fully awake only when the bravest of the rats had sidled up to nibble on his boots, wondering if he were good to eat. He shouted at them, and kicked as best he could, and they scattered in a chorus of angry squeaks at his sudden show of life. Off they scurried to scowl at him vengefully.

He was just beginning to fall back into a disturbed sleep when the door to his makeshift prison burst open. Del strode into his presence bearing the dead expression of a murderer. It would have taken a blind man not to notice the crazed glimmer in the ambassador's dark eyes, and it struck a deep chord of alarm in the ousted deacon. As Del strode purposefully toward him, Ian took fearful note of the ugly knife in his hand.

"Get away from me!" the deacon shouted, twisting futilely against his bindings. Screwing his eyes shut at the last moment, the deacon tried to turn his face away from the attack. The ambassador's first blow cracked something in his jaw. The second bounced his head off the stone floor, and the third sent him into oblivion for a few short moments. When he next opened his eyes, feeling as though someone had been slamming bricks into his face, he was being dragged to his feet. The ropes binding his hands and feet had been cut away.

Too bleary to offer resistance, he was hauled across the length of the room and slammed against the wall hard enough to force the breath from him lungs. The ambassador took a single step back, facing the deacon with fierce challenge in his posture. The rage in his eyes burned holes through Ian, and he held his knife in a tense fist, every muscle in his body wound tight. He looked prepared to speak, but wrath had washed him of sufficient composure to create words.

Ian could do nothing but cower.

Suddenly, as though he could contain himself no more, Del took a single, quick step forward and buried his fist deep in the deacon's gut. He was rewarded with wide eyes and a lengthy gasp. He struck again, then twice more in rapid succession, doubling Ian over his fist. Holding the sagging deacon on his feet, Del shoved him back into the wall and held him there with a stiff forearm. He leaned forward, his lips coming close enough to tickle the deacon's skin. "There is something I want you to see," Del whispered with contempt. Every word seemed a vast effort.

Before Ian could recover his breath, Del sprang into sudden movement. Leaning backwards, he used his full weight to swing the deacon around and propel him toward the door. Ian lurched several steps, struggling to stay afoot, and just when he was about to regain his balance, Del shoved him again, this time into the hall, where he crashed heavily against the far wall. The ambassador was upon him before he could regain his bearings, seizing him by the arm and pushing him roughly down the corridor.

"Where are you taking me?" Ian demanded.

Del answered with another shove.

The ambassador marched his abused prisoner out of the keep and onto the battlements, where the deacon was granted with his first view of the sthaak horde. His eyes widened, and he stopped in shock. Impatient, Del gripped Ian's tunic and yanked him swiftly toward the ramparts, dragging him when he stumbled. With one final push, the deacon found himself looking down the face of the wall. He gasped at the vulgar display. He would have backed away, but Del was immediately behind him, blocking his retreat.

Locking his fingers in the deacon's hair, Del used his free hand to clamp the man's jaw, forcing him to keep his face aimed at the massacre. The deacon struggled, but Del held him tightly.

"Look at them," Del snarled. His grip on the deacon tightened,

267

squeezing his jaw and his hair in painful fists. "Do you see them? Do you see with your eyes what I see with mine?" Beyond the landscape of slaughtered Bedu was a sight even more deeply shocking. The sthaak horde seethed on the desert floor, feeding on the scattered remains of the Bedu nation.

"Tell me you see them, Deacon."

"I see them," Ian choked.

"Now look," Del said, pushing the deacon's head downward, to the base of the wall. When the deacon resisted, Del slammed a knee into his midsection, bending him forcefully over the parapet. "What do you see now, Deacon?"

Humiliated and hurting, Ian struggled, but the ambassador's grip was relentless.

"Tell me what you see!"

There was no telling how many had been slaughtered.

"They're dead," Ian surrendered. "They're all dead."

Del yanked Ian's head back, baring a long stretch of his neck. "Yes," Del repeated. "They are all dead. Murdered."

Ian could feel the ambassador's breath hot on the side of his face. With his face aimed at the sky, it took him a moment to realize there was a knife at his throat. The blade was pressed tight to the rigid pipe beneath the skin, cold and sharp—one long, slow pull away from ending his life.

"What is fair penalty for such a crime, Deacon?"

Ian Manzig fought the urge to swallow. The ambassador's blade did not allow for that luxury. His stomach lurched, and panic took root. Where was the seriph? Why wasn't anyone stopping this? Were his own soldiers going to stand by and watch as the ambassador executed him? His eyes grew wild. "You have no right—"

"I have every right!" Del screamed into the deacon's ear. He was shaking with fury, and his eyes were pouring tears. "They were my people!" As suddenly as it had come, the explosion of anger withdrew. It was not gone, only curled up snarling in some fiery dungeon. Its breath was hot, and its leash short. At last, the ambassador dragged Ian away from the wall and cast him backwards with enough force to send him sprawling. The deacon ended on his back, propped on his elbows as he looked up with eyes of fear at the seething ambassador. He immediately put a hand to his throat to find if he had been opened.

"Now do you believe?" Del asked him.

Numbed by the visions below and his brush with death, Ian forced his eyes shut and turned his head to the side, ashamed. Had he looked up, he would have seen Del's hands shaking violently. He would have seen the tears streaming down his face, cutting clear tracks through the dirt.

Del's shoulders sagged in exhaustion, as though his rage had been the very life in his bones, and in letting go of it he had surrendered his strength. In an act inspired by disgust, he tossed his knife at the deacon's splayed legs.

"You can have Gideon's Wall back," He said wearily. "I don't want it anymore."

Eight

Del did not know where he was going, though he walked purposefully. He had left the deacon and the scene of the slaughter behind. He felt eyes following him, tagging along as though tacked to the rage he still emanated. Del wanted to scream at them, shout them away. He wanted to curse, red-faced and spitting, until they cowered. Let them feel shame, he thought, though he could not fathom why. He did not try to understand.

He was in the keep, storming down the halls, racing up the stairs—rushing to be somewhere, he did not know. Everything he saw he wanted to destroy. Men moved aside for him. A dark knowledge followed him close, tethered like a beast on a chain, waiting for him to turn and become aware. It was waiting for him to stop, to think. And when he did, when the anger diminished and the turmoil slowed to stillness, he would understand. Without knowing it, he dreaded that moment.

His path ended abruptly at a narrow door high in the tower. Rather than risk stopping—risk losing ground—he threw his shoulder into the door and slapped at the latch until something gave and he spilled into the small room.

It was familiar. It was his. Here was the place he had stayed when he'd first come to the wall. This was his tiny home, unchanged, replete with uncomfortable cot and fuzzy spiders. Breathing hard, he stopped. There was nowhere else to go.

On padded talons, awareness skulked into the room behind him.

A thousand bodies in the sand.

Don't think, Del told himself. Keep moving. Shut down. Close off. Disappear. Just don't *think*.

A thousand bodies, and one of them . . .

"Ambassador."

Del spun, hating the intrusion—grateful for it. The seriph stood behind him, filling the doorframe.

"Get out," Del commanded, raising a trembling finger. "You get away from me."

The seriph came into the room, shutting the door behind him. "I need your help, Ambassador," he said in his deep, calm voice. "You have something I need."

• • •

It was impossible to think of anything else while the seriph spoke. He filled the room with his presence, dominating Del's mind. This was a blessing, and something of a sanctuary.

Del's anger was fading, unable to maintain its weight under the seriph's stare. "I don't have anything," Del said.

"You do," the seriph answered. "I need your umbra."

The seriph's meaning was not immediately clear. Del's thoughts were still threatening, cowed in the presence of the seriph. They

271

lurked in the corners and in the shadows, content to bide their time until they could be alone with Del. He shook his head in agitated confusion.

"I need you to pass a message for me," the seriph told him.

"What message? To who?"

"To whom is not important. It is the message that matters."

Meaningless. Again, Del shook his head angrily.

"Do you think any of us will leave here alive, Ambassador? We have seen the sthaak. We know what we face. None of us will leave Gideon's Wall. But we possess information that is vital, Ambassador. There is this," and he held up the buckled rucksack in which Del knew the seed from the Jaggi was bundled. "What it is, and what it does, is knowledge that must be passed on."

Del had stopped trying to understand. He was afraid to think.

"There is only one way to do this, Ambassador. We preserve an umbra."

Nearly frantic with confusion and the effort of keeping his thoughts battened, Del shouted back at the seriph. "I don't know what that means!"

The seriph remained serene, his voice and temper unmoved. "The umbra is your ghost. The seraphim call it the breath of life. It is what makes men what they are. It is the only part of you that is not mortal. I need yours."

"I don't understand," Del declared in a flustered rush.

"After this battle has been fought, seekers of knowledge will come to this place. They will search to know what happened here. They will find this—" He lifted a rugged little statue of coal-black wood. "They will find your umbra, and you will tell them."

Del's lip curled at the grotesque figure. "Find someone else."

"There *is* no one else, Ambassador. No one knows the things you know. No one has seen what you have seen."

"You know," Del countered. "I told you everything. You do it."

The corners of the seriph's mouth turned upwards into something of a smile. Or it might have been a snarl. "I can't," he said. "I've no umbra. The seraphim are composed of different substances

272

than men, both corporeal and divine. What I lack, you possess."

Del was moving listlessly, hands moist and clenching. He stared at the misshapen idol in the seriph's palm, needing to ask questions, but unwilling to begin the search for words.

"You will feel nothing," the seriph said, his eyes following Del as he thrashed within himself. There was some pity in his voice, but Del did not detect it. "When I've taken what I need you will go back to the battlements; you will fight with the others. Your umbra will be kept safe. In a sense, you will live."

Adamant, Del shook his head. "I don't want that."

"What do you believe?" the seriph asked abruptly. The pity in his voice had dissipated, dripping back into whatever tiny reservoir such emotions were stored in the seraphim. "Does your faith lie with the pantheon of Shallai's gods? With the Bedu's? What wondrous thing waits for you after death, Ambassador?"

"I don't know."

"Then what is your risk? Why are you so loathe to give up what you cannot name?"

Del's jaw tightened. "I don't trust you."

"Your trust is irrelevant, Ambassador. The decision has been made, and you must not confuse formality with choice. You can give freely to me what I ask, or I can take it from you."

Del's sense of self-preservation boiled in panic. The seriph watched patiently as the ambassador's eyes clawed at the walls in search of a way out, some escape he had not seen before. He saw a score of possibilities flash through Del's eyes: to fight, beg, or flee. All of them were false hopes—all discarded as futile. In the end, resignation possessed him. When Del spoke, it was without hope.

"Will I know?" he asked.

The seriph's eyes softened. "There is awareness."

Despair tightened on Del. "How long before they come?"

"I do not know."

Del breathed deeply. What he never knew he had, now seemed precious to him. He looked at the stones of the wall, blank and gray. The color, the emptiness of them, was soothing, like balm on a wound. When he looked back to the seriph, his mind was quiet, an echo of the wall. "Do it quick," he said. And he closed his eyes.

The seriph's hand closed over Del's face, suffocating—

And then he was breathing hard, his heart jerking in his chest, his bile rising. His face was clear, the seriph's hand gone. There was a pain in his chest, a dreadful sick feeling that his heart—or some place far deeper—had been hollowed. The core of him was missing, and everything else seemed to be spilling into the empti-ness left by its extraction. He was sitting on the cot, and the loss of time disturbed him. He opened his eyes and saw the seriph stand-ing back, something cupped in his palm, an eldritch glow on his face and a vague light reflected in his eyes.

It's mine, Del thought. He lowered his face, ashamed.

A moment, maybe more.

"It is done," the seriph said.

Blankly, Del looked up, mind numb, eyes uncomprehending. He barely remembered what had happened. Every moment seemed only loosely attached to the last. Everything had melted away, and he was glad of it. He didn't want to know why he felt so *diminished*.

"I'm cold," said Del. His voice sounded very small.

"It will pass."

Del closed his eyes. When he opened them again, the seriph was gone, and daylight had followed him. Night had pressed through the window and into the stone-walled room. He knew he had been awake for hours, was aware that he had never slept. He recalled the path of the sun as it had tracked across the floor, but there had never been a thought. Nothing had registered in his va-cant stare. As consciousness returned, Del's guard was down, and a single thought crept from the shadows and slipped thickly through his defenses. He blinked dazedly, and thought: "Where is Suri?"

• • •

274

The moon was swollen, rising despite its pregnant weight. Frozen beams of her light dissected the darkness of the chamber in thick, clean bars. Seeping in from the windows, they sliced the emptiness like silver razors.

Del sat on his cot and stared blankly at his open hands, lying like two dead things in his lap. He had wrapped the wounds on his palms with rags, but he could not remember when. The pain huddled beneath the dirty cloth, throbbing in time with his heart. If he looked out the window, he could see most of Gideon's Wall spread out below him, washed colorless by the ghost light of the moon. The grounds of the wall, as well as much of the valley northward, had become one vast Bedu encampment. Their torches and fires burned brightly, and he could hear their distant voices. Chilled air from the desert washed over him, but if he recognized the cold, he made no outward indication. Somewhere in the darkness of a corner a rat scratched listlessly at the floor. He thought he heard a soft voice beyond the closed door.

He stood. His feet were bare, and the stones were warm and sandy. On his way to the door he passed in front of a full-length mirror and stopped to judge his reflection. The stranger that stared back at him was a haggard wreck. He had the haunted eyes, stooped shoulders, and slow moving way of the vagabond. Del studied this man clinically, noting the air of loss about him. He seemed very much alone. A tragedy had struck, some unlucky string of events or curses from above, and had laid him low. The pain of it had hollowed him. This tragedy might have happened yesterday, or twenty years ago; there was no way to tell. Like a hand scraping the soft guts from a melon, it had scooped the life right out of him and left a hollow rind. This man was empty, and he wore his sorrow as though it had been with him for ages.

"Where is your family?" he asked the stranger. "Where is your home?"

Where is your soul?

But the sad, lonely man did not answer.

Despite whatever tragedies had contributed to this broken man's state, there was an equilibrium about him. There was a hopeful grace in the way he stood poised on the edge of despair. Here was a man who moved slowly, who spoke softly, and thought of nothing, praying that he will not tip his precious balance and fall into the pit yawning at his feet. As long as he stood still he would live, or at least survive. He had crumbled inside, but the shell of him still stood strong.

They continued to stare one at another, neither saying a thing, until finally Del turned away from the mirror and the stranger within it. He crossed the length of the room and opened the door wide. The darkened hall was empty save for Jiharra, who was seated at the far end, where the winding stairs dropped away into darkness. The young kalif was already looking up when Del stepped from the room.

"She is not here yet?" Del asked hoarsely.

Jiharra shook his head. "No, Del."

Del turned his bleary eyes to the stairs immersed in shadows. Had he heard footsteps? Voices? He knew she would come. She had to come. His eyes shifted back to Jiharra. "Why are you here?"

"We are friends, Del. Should friends not watch over one another?"

"Do you never sleep?"

Jiharra shook his head. "Not this day, Ambassador."

For a long moment Del did not move. At last, slowly, he stepped from the room and pulled the door shut behind him. In response, Jiharra rose to his feet.

"Where is your family?" Del asked.

"They are with the rest of the Ajraan, north of the wall."

Del nodded. The muscles that spanned his shoulders and neck felt like sheets of lead beneath his skin. Moving sluggishly, he brushed past Jiharra and headed down the stairs. Immediately, the kalif fell into step behind him, but Del stopped and held out his hand. "Alone," he said. "Let me be alone."

Jiharra stopped, but said nothing. His face was blank.

"Please?" Del added softly. "This once."

The kalif paused, then nodded his consent.

Letting his arm drop, Del continued down the stairs, leaving Jiharra alone in the narrow hall. The kalif waited there a short time, watching the now empty stairwell. He let the silence fold around him. In a few moments he slipped down into the shadows to follow the ambassador.

• • •

Del roamed the sprawling camps of the Bedu like a ghost. The darkness of night was a comfort. It wrapped him in a soft cage of velvet and let him wander with a feeling that the world was larger than it was, that there was more of it than he could possibly search. And because of that there was hope. As long as there was a place he had not looked, there was a chance she lived. He turned at every female voice, searching the faces gathered around the fires for the familiar face. Each time he called for her was followed by a terrible moment of waiting. People followed him with their eyes, but he did not see the pity in the looks that trailed after him. He was just another man looking for the lost.

He found what was left of Jiharra's family without meaning to. A fire burned in a small pit outside, and three ken'dari were crouched before it, warming themselves at the blaze. They stood respectfully as he approached.

"Is Suri here?" Del said.

"No, Ambassador," they answered. "Your Suri has not come."

Del nodded in return, but did not leave. He was wondering where he would go next. The ken'dari watched him patiently. There was a movement inside the tent, and Massara emerged.

Ibn Khan's widow had never looked so fragile. The lines of her face were deep, and her eyes were windows looking into sorrow and tears. It was as though the terrible events of a single day had piled ten years of suffering onto her shoulders. She smiled sorrowfully at Del. "Hello, gentle ambassador."

Del could not look at her beyond that first moment. He could not help imagining Ibn Khan, the proud kalif of the Ajraan, standing beside her. He turned his head aside, ashamed to look her in the eye, and his gaze floundered for a place to rest. "I am sorry for coming," he stammered. "I did not mean to disturb you."

Massara held out her hand when she saw he was about to turn away. "Come, Del," she said. "Your presence is a comfort to me, as it was to my husband. There is always a place for you among this family, you know that."

Del paused, suddenly unsure.

"Come," she beckoned again, but had already gone to him. Moving slowly, like a woman crippled with age, she lifted her arms to cup his face in her hands, then curled her arms about his neck to embrace him. She was stronger than Del would have given her credit for, and she held him a long time. Into his ear she whispered, "There has never been a day of sorrow such as this." When she released him and stepped back, Del saw that the sadness in her eyes was brimming, and her tears had begun again. He felt their wetness on his shoulder.

She spoke again, lowly to sneak the words around the catch in her throat. "As much as I miss him, part of my heart is glad that my husband did not live to see this day." She somehow managed a smile, and as she backed away he noticed a limp in her step.

"You're hurt," Del said.

"Not as badly as some."

Del let his eyes fall to the ground, and his voice weakened. "I cannot find Suri," he said. "I think maybe . . . maybe she is lost. I thought she would be here. With you."

Massara's eyes filled with pity, and she placed her hand gently over his. "She has not come here," she said softly. "I am sorry, Del."

He began to speak, but the words died before passing his lips. He was struggling with confusion. It bound him, tangling his thoughts. Lifting a hand to his forehead, he held it there, forcing himself to think, to form words and create speech. "When she comes, tell her . . . I'm looking for her. I won't stop looking. Keep her with you, and tell her I'll be back."

Massara said nothing, but her moist eyes did not leave him. Looking at her, he thought there was something he should understand, but didn't know how to grasp it. When he left the tent he called Suri's name no more, and he did not stop to search for her face among the crowds. Almost too tired to walk, he wandered with his feet dragging and his head hung. His feet took him where they willed, and when he finally looked up he found himself alone at the bottom of a dark stairwell. His senses were scrambled, as though he had stumbled out of a dream. He remembered walking there, but only vaguely, as if it were a memory belonging to someone else. Confused, he placed his hands against the wall to steady himself. On the far side of thirty-six paces of solid stones was the desert. He felt the heat of it seeping through the veins of the wall.

He knew where he was. He had been in this place before.

"Suri?" he said helplessly.

A thread of understanding drained him of hope. Loss and fear crashed in on him, and he began to tremble. He backed against the cold stones, away from the groping hands of the dead, and it was there that his waning strength finally failed him. Sliding to the floor, he drew his legs up, he let his head drop between his knees. The tears came then, a slow release of sorrow dragged upwards from his gut and out his throat. The wrenching in his heart was amazingly real for an agony that was not physical. He curled upon himself in the dark silence of the shadowed hall, and he wept until he was dry.

• • •

It was nearly midnight when the ambassador climbed the wide stone steps to the upper battlements of Gideon's Wall. All along the wall fires had been lit to ward against the chill of the desert night, and Shallai's soldiers, ken'dari, and Bedu warriors crouched together in small knots around the little spots of warmth. The flames glowed on their somber faces and were mirrored in their eyes, as though every man wore his soul in his gaze. He walked slowly among the blooms of fire around which the men crowded. Shallai's soldiers looked at him without recognition, they did not know the face of this man. He was not one of theirs, but neither was he Bedu. But he carried a blade, and he seemed to belong, so their looks were only glances.

The ambassador walked to the center of the wall, and stood by the ledge to stare at the desert below. It seemed a bottomless chasm, and the darkness and emptiness of it were familiar to him. He knew there was something out there that belonged to him, but the darkness swallowed everything, sucking away color, warmth, and life, and grinding them down to a common, meaningless black. For a long time he stood at the ledge, eyes boring into the darkness. When the stars blurred he didn't understand what was happening until he felt the wetness on his cheeks, and touched it with his fingers.

Am I crying? he thought. Strange. I don't feel a thing.

There was a hand on his shoulder, and he turned to find a ken'dari standing behind him. The Bedu warrior nodded respectfully, and gestured to where a group of ken'dari were crouched around a fire. All were watching him. The red and orange light of the fires made the painted runes on their faces and necks seem alive.

"Will you sit with us, Ambassador? The night is cold."

Del let himself be led to the fire, and he took the ken'dari's place close to the flames. He held out his palms, but barely felt the warmth. The fire captured his gaze, and he looked up because someone had spoken. All eyes were turned patiently to him, and he realized that someone had asked him a question, but he did not know which of them.

"When the sthaak come, you will fight with us?" one of the ken'dari asked, and whether it was a new question, or a repeat of the one he hadn't heard, Del didn't know. He looked at the ken'dari, and for a moment wondered what his answer would be. Is that

280

why he had come to the wall? Or was it simply to find a place where he would not have to die alone?

"Yes," he said, but he didn't know which question he was answering.

"Are you not afraid?" one of them asked.

Del looked at his hands. They were not shaking, and so he told them that he was not. There was a quietness during which the ken'dari continued to watch him. The Bedu had no reservations about staring. Their eyes gained them more information than his words could have supplied.

"You have done much for our people," one of them said.

Del pictured a thousand bodies in the sand.

Closing his eyes against the image, he tried to breath deep. The smoke of the fire stung his nostrils and clung to the back of his throat. He knew that in the morning, if morning came, he would still be able to taste it thick in his mouth.

The ken'dari to his right had pulled a small piece of wood from the fire. He scraped the burnt end with his smallest finger, collecting dark soot on the nail. Leaning toward Del, he ran his nail lightly along the ambassador's cheek, tracing a pattern only another ken'dari would understand. When he was done, the ken'dari moved back and looked at the makeshift tattoo painted on Del's face. "There," he said. "You are ken'dari now, and will always be so. Nothing can take that away. Not even death can undo this."

Del looked at the faces watching him, feeling nothing.

"It will be an honor to die with you, Ambassador," the ken'dari told him.

Although he had not heard the words, Del nodded vaguely. He kept his hands to the flames, but the warmth of it refused to touch him.

Nine

The seriph found Ian Manzig in the deacon's spacious chambers. He was angrily cramming provisions into a worn rucksack, moving with hasty purpose. He started upon seeing the seriph standing silent at the door. Spasms of fear and guilt twisted his mottled face. He was drunk.

"I've done nothing wrong," he declared warily, eager to defend himself against an accusation that had not been made. He positioned himself in front of his sack, hiding the evidence of his guilt.

"I am not here to judge you, Deacon."

"Then what do you want?" Ian snapped, sick from fear and angry at his own craven display.

"Only the key to the vault."

The deacon regarded the seriph with a suspicion that came easy to him. He fished beneath his shirt and tore the key and chain from around his neck. He threw it across the room, eager to be rid of the thing if it meant the seriph would go away. Although he was sweating heavily, and still afraid, he managed to sneer contemptuously. "There is nothing in the vault but soldiers' wages and paper," he said. "Hardly bounty worthy of a seriph."

Matthias, key in hand, regarded Ian solemnly. His silence discomfited the deacon, whose snide manner wilted under the dull pressure of the seriph's stare. Fear crawled back into his eyes, as well as drunken uncertainty.

The seriph turned to go.

"You're no better than me!" the deacon threw after him, his bravado rejuvenated.

The seriph, having nothing more to say, was already gone.

• • •

The vault of Gideon's Wall stood at the end of a narrow corridor somewhere below the tower. There was no light, and the air was thick with dust, and smelled of dry stone.

The seriph emptied the vault completely. He stacked the sacks of stamped coins in the hall, ignoring those that tore open to spill their gold and silver guts to the floor. He wanted nothing to distract those who found the vault—nothing to take away from the message. When everything had been removed, the seriph laid the rucksack in the far corner. It looked small and meaningless in the emptied vault, but in it was the seed of a new empire, and the little statue with its captive soul. A tool and a message; instructions to revive what would soon be destroyed.

The seriph looked at the slumping leather rucksack for what seemed a long time before backing out of the vault. He pushed the heavy iron door shut, and there came the heavy clacking of bolts locking into place.

• • •

The desertions began immediately following nightfall and continued until dawn. Under cover of darkness, soldiers that had been charged with the defense of Gideon's Wall shed their duties in the face of fear. Like the slow leak of water from a dam, they passed largely unnoticed from the gates of the wall, shame riding their shoulders and fear nipping at their heels. During their flight they kept their faces covered, heads low, and eyes on the ground. Even in the darkness they were ashamed of their defection. If they happened to see another truant in the darkness, they made certain to look the other away, and altered their course so no paths would cross.

Those who chose to stay suffered a sleepless night. From the heights of the wall they looked down on the beasts in the desert, feeling like condemned men forced to watch the executioner swinging his axe and splitting melons upon the block. The sthaak paced and prowled in agitation, casting sinister gazes at the meat on top of the wall. There was no organization among the creatures: no ranks, command or discipline. Yet through some unseen force they maintained their unity. Occasionally one of the beasts charged the wall on its own, driven by a hatred or a hunger that had grown more pressing than whatever force controlled them. These were filled with arrows from the defenders, and their bodies marked the invisible line in the sand that was not to be crossed.

At some point during the night the beasts began to drag the slaughtered bodies of the Bedu back into the desert. They fought over their own dead as well as the Bedu, sometimes ripping into one another over the prize of a corpse. It was meat, and they roared and clawed at one another to own it. The sounds they made while feeding or quarreling were sharp and piercing, and they echoed off the wall and back into the wasteland, so that one cry turned to many.

Atop the wall, fear spread. It collected in hot bundles in throats and chests. It hollowed guts, emptied souls, and made hands and legs tremble. This fear that soaked into the soldiers was a far distant cousin of terror. It was a slow, sure thing, a weakening force that bent their imaginations against them and picked at the edges of hope with prying fingers. By the end of the night nearly a quarter of the wall's forces had deserted. The deacon himself was nowhere to be found. Ian Manzig had cast his lot with the faceless men that had, at some point during the night, decided it was better to die running than fighting. And after a night that seemed to drag on for days, when dawn crept down from the mountains to peel back layer after layer of darkness until finally uncovering the soldiers huddled beneath—the sthaak came.

• • •

The beasts lifted their heads to stare full into the face of the rising sun. Day broke suddenly, spilling golden light over the mountains and out of the valley. The harsh baying of the horde, which had sounded throughout the night, dropped off in a spreading wave of silence as the creatures were bathed in light. When the attention of the entire horde had been so completely captured by the new sun, every death yet to come seemed but a breath away. The silence before the storm had fallen upon them. And when it ended, the cry that rose up from the desert bore the sound of a thousand deaths.

As one body the sthaak surged forward.

A hot storm of fear and activity swirled along the battlements. Archers bellied up to the parapet in long lines as horns began to shout stridently back and forth to one another along the wall, conveying words without speech. At a certain signal, bows were raised and arrows drawn to cheeks. After a pause no greater than the length of a heartbeat, hundreds of shafts leapt heavenward, released in a chorus of malicious hissing. They seemed to float against the blue backdrop of the sky for but a moment before arcing downwards to bite into the horde. Many of the arrows found their marks, and sthaak crashed to the sand with bolts protruding from chests and throats. Many more continued on despite their wounds. The horns sounded the signal to release twice more before giving permission to fire at will. The creak of ash, the twang of strings pulled tight, and the whistle of shafts racing to deliver mortal injury filled the air atop the battlements.

The sthaak crashed into the wall in a seething black wave. Instead of being driven back by the barrier, they pushed upwards. In an act that inspired terror among the soldiers and Bedu watching from the heights, the huge beasts began to claw their way up the sheer face of the wall, talons digging into stone. Sheets of arrows poured down in torrents, and sthaak dropped off Gideon's Wall by the score, wooden shafts puncturing scale and flesh. Despite the deadly rain, the beasts continued their ascent with slow surety, pulling themselves up the face of the wall with claws that dug into cracks and ledges. Those that came too near the apex drew an urgent concentration of fire from the archers, piercing them with innumerable shafts. Sometimes, even after they had fallen to the sand far below, they could be seen struggling to rise, as though not yet ready to admit their own deaths. But when one fell, another was there to take its place, and ten more beside and beneath it.

It was not long before a clump of beasts too great for the archers to break apart had come dangerously close to breaching the wall. A horn blasted forth an urgent warning, and rushing forward to heed the call came a team of boilers.

The team of three rushed forward with all haste, dragging between them a squat black cauldron filled to the brim with pitch. After muscling the massive pot to the very edge of the battlements, the pitch within was ignited by the flaming head of a torch. Soldiers flinched back as tar and oil belched into flame. A round black cloud roiled from the mouth of the cast iron cauldron. Blazing with intense heat, the fire singed the hair on the arms and chests of the boilers. With a coordinated heave, the men shouldered the cauldron on its swiveled base, dumping a cascade of burning pitch over the ascending sthaak. The viscous waterfall of flame coated the beasts with sticky fire and peeled them off the wall like skin blistering from flesh. The cauldron was rolled back to be filled again.

When finally the archers began to fall back, their supply of arrows exhausted and their bows useless, the rest of the boiler teams moved forward to fill the gaps. They tipped their searing fare on the heads of the sthaak, emptying cauldron after cauldron of black death over the battlements and into the face of the enemy as fast as it could be boiled. When there was no more pitch, the cauldrons themselves became weapons. It took five men to lift each of the great black kettles and send it toppling over the wall. The iron fists spun and bounced on their way down, crushing sthaak against the wall and dragging mangled bodies along behind them. Down they fell, killing as they went until finally lodging themselves in the desert floor.

Long before the fare of the boilers had been spent, men were dispatched to collect anything that could be used to fling down upon their attackers. Working under the pounding weight of the sun, they had rendered three barracks to piles of rubble, and were already attacking the fourth and final when the boilers depleted their supply of pitch. With ropes and pulleys the debris from the barracks was hoisted to the top of the wall, and by the time the last empty cauldron had been tipped over the battlements nine tall piles of jagged stone and brick were waiting to be used.

Laying aside swords, pikes, spears and shields, every man bent his energy to the murderous task of stoning the sthaak. Chunks of shattered rock the size of large children were dropped over the edge. The effect of these was similar to the cauldrons, though significantly less devastating. By early evening all that remained of the four barracks were pebbles and dust. And still the sthaak came.

Undaunted by the vast numbers of their own kind that had already been skewered, crushed and burned from the wall to fall to their deaths, they ascended with insatiable hatred. Sthaak bodies littered the sand at the base of the wall, but the beasts were oblivious. They pushed upwards with hungry urgency, almost as if they knew the defenders atop the wall had reached the end of their limited resources.

• • •

Alkesh Sah had served in Shallai's army for the better part of sixteen years. Prior to his enlistment, there had been a period in his life now so distant that he often entertained the thought that it was the memories of another man's experiences tumbling around in his head. In that time—or in those memories—he had farmed a humble plot of land in one of Shallai's far western provinces. He had been married. He'd had children. Life was straight and simple, exactly the way he liked it.

When the Shadrakans invaded, the call to arms rose from Jericho, and when the news reached his farm he responded as dutifully as any patriot; he packed a woolen blanket, a hunting knife, and set out for Jericho to serve his empire. Upon enlisting, he was provided with a sword, a brand over his heart, and a new purpose for his life—the killing of Shadrakans.

Alkesh had never been a brutal or violent man, but while fighting the easterners he discovered in himself a hidden aptitude for killing men.

Years later, when the Shadrakans had been expelled back across the sea and his duty to Shallai was complete, he set his sights for home—only to find it occupied by strangers.

The years had been long, and his wife was now someone else's wife, his children another man's brood.

Instead of murdering the impostor—as he could have easily done—and reclaiming by force what was rightfully his, Alkesh turned around and went straight back to Jericho. He never thought too hard about that day, nor did he ever regret his decision. It was good enough for him to suppose that he enjoyed his new life better than the old.

Now, amid the swarm of soldiers in their mad dash for readiness, Alkesh Sah stepped cautiously to the ledge and peered down. The desert was teeming with monsters. They could be heard clearly, howls rising up out of a pit of demons. He shook his head in wonder. Never had he seen anything like this. When Shallai had sent her armies to invade the northern reaches of Nemrud Dagh he had fought and killed men who painted their faces like skulls and ate the skin and tongues of captured soldiers, and in the swamps of the Dolahracki he had killed men with eyes red as blood. In the Draiden Heights he had battled the D'ni, who wrapped their faces in black cloth, yet fought with far deadlier precision than men who could see. He still remembered his revulsion when they first captured a D'ni warrior and unwound the cloth from his head, only to discover that he had no eyes at all. All those things had inspired in him a sense of dreadful wonder. But never anything like this.

With a calculating eye, Alkesh watched the beasts from the desert scaling the wall. They were near enough now that he could see their eyes fastening on him. Although his hands were raw and bleeding from handling the rubble, he wished for something more to throw. Over his shoulder, he called to his comrades, "The lizards are coming to die now." Before turning away, he cleared his throat noisily and sent a wad of phlegm down at the climbing creatures. "Curse the lot of you," he said. The life he had adopted in exchange for his wife and his children was about to be cut short in a brutal way, and he couldn't help but feel cheated. He stepped back to take his place among the front lines.

Hands trembling and faces pale, warriors all around him were making their final preparations: tightening straps of shields, and fastening helmets beneath their chins. They tore the sweat from their eyes while stomachs churned and flipped in anxious fear. Blades were bared, spears hefted, and last prayers offered to whatever gods or angels might be watching from the cliffs above.

Alkesh had no time to bother with prayers. He wedged the butt of his pike tightly into the crack between two stones and braced it there with one thick boot. After loosening his sword in its sheath, he gripped the shaft of the pike in both hands and leveled the heavy blade toward the battlements. In less than a moment it would be all that stood between his life and the sthaak.

In the last ominous moments before battle time seemed to stumble forward in irregular, uncertain spurts, as though tripping over itself in its haste to reach an end to the waiting. It was then that a giant voice broke the oppressive air.

The seriph had leapt to the ledge at the center of the wall, putting himself in plain view of the northern soldiers and Bedu alike, and the power of his voice raised the hair of every man within reach. In each hand he held a massive, short-hafted axe, the kind of blade a normal man would have struggled to swing once with both hands.

"Let them hear you!" the seriph cried out, hoisting his weapons to the sky. Stretching wide his cavernous jaws, he bellowed for all to hear, and the raw noise that issued from his maw was not the sound of a mighty man proclaiming his rage and defiance, but the explosive roar from the throat of something purely animal. The detonation of the seriph's thunderous baying blasted over the soldiers, and its effect was far more profound than a thousand eloquent speeches meant to kindle passion and inspire courage in those about to die.

The response to the seriph's savage call was riotous.

A staggering swell of noise to match the warrior's powerful voice rose from the soldiers and Bedu atop Gideon's Wall; the clash of sword against shield, boots stomping upon stones, and the enraged sounds of condemned men screaming their defiance against death. All of the wordless cries they offered up were but weak echoes of the seriph's mighty call, but together they made a sound that shook the foundations of the wall.

Alkesh threw in his voice with the rest, screaming at the sky until his lungs ached and the air around him seemed to quiver and tremble with the sheer volume of the clamor. The shouting of the army aroused in Alkesh some reticent part of his spirit, a part that had always existed, but whose rough and sharpened edges had been smoothed over by humanity and culture. That lower chamber that had been stirred at the seriph's bestial howl now awakened fully. Instincts blunted over centuries were sharpened, and a wild energy coursed over his skin. He felt his blood rise and his nostrils flare. The accumulation of voices drowned out the creeping whisper of fear and doubt in a deafening surge. These things were washed away like gale-torn wreckage.

Scarcely able to think through the storm of sound, Alkesh marveled at the uproar, and thought that if only they could be as strong as the noise they had created, then surely there was no force, human or otherwise, that could tear them down. He was suddenly struck with an overwhelming loyalty, an almost childlike adoration, for this beast of a man who stood on the wall to induce rage against the sthaak. Laying down his life for this seriph would be counted as the highest honor.

After the vibrant commotion of the soldiers had reached its culmination, but before descending to silence once again, the sthaak boiled over the wall.

Alkesh was among the first to die.

The beast that catapulted over the ramparts came for him as though it had crossed the desert lusting for his flesh. Sweeping aside the thrust of his pike with one great arm, it ripped through him like a bull through a paper wall. The pain lasted only a short while, and the shock of dying was more terrifying by far. In the end, he felt nothing as his body flexed and bucked against the hand of death. Before the beast was done destroying him, it was slain. It shrieked in agony when its scaled body was pierced with sword and spear by the men who had stood beside him, and those who had taken shelter behind him.

• • •

Yanking his blade from the thrashing body of the dying sthaak, Del had but a brief moment to glimpse at the slaughtered soldier, alive less than a moment before. The corpse was twisted and broken, its gut torn open where the sthaak had burrowed with its gnawing jaws to reach soft viscera. Its head had broken when the sthaak had slammed the body to the floor, and blood flowed to fill the cracks in the stones.

There was no time to think. Beasts were crawling over the wall, their baleful black gazes hungering for something to kill. Once over the wall, they charged mindlessly. The soldiers let the animals come to them, and the beasts often spitted themselves on spears, pikes and swords in their urgency to reach the meat. At other times smashing through the defenses to inflict ruin before being overborne and cut down. They came in waves, each fresh attack inciting short and brutal battles all along the length of the wall. There were times when the beasts stayed alive long enough—or breached the wall in sufficient numbers—to do a great deal of damage to the defenders, but more often than not they crested the wall alone, then threw themselves upon the soldiers without heed to life or limb. When the fighting fell into a lull, it was only just enough time to roll the dead over the edges of the battlements to make space for fresh bodies.

During one of these frequent lulls, Del looked down at himself. The leather cords wrapping the hilt of his sword were slick with blood. He tightened his grip, and the hot redness squelched between his fingers. The stickiness clung to his skin as though a viscous oil had been poured into his hand. He afforded a quick survey of himself, and saw that his arms and chest were spattered with blood. He wondered distantly how much of it was his.

He looked at the men on the wall. Shallai's warriors fought side by side with Bedu, sometimes back to back. Interspersed among them were ken'dari, who knew how helpless their situation had become. The strength of the defenders was slipping. The weak and the tired were allowing themselves to make careless mistakes which cost them their lives, and often the lives of those who fought alongside them. With each wave of sthaak that came over the wall more men died.

Del's battle ended during an attack not unlike all the others before it. Three sthaak pulled themselves over the wall at once, a snarling wave of teeth and claws. Fighting in a group of eight that had been fifteen before the last fray, Del worked his weapon without grace. The beasts were cut down, but not before dragging half their small group into death. The next wave came without pause, and the four survivors were forced to cast aside their exhaustion. That frantic skirmish that followed was reaching a close when the ambassador's blade lodged in bone. The creature straightened to its full height, jerking the sword from his hand. Black eyes blazing with hatred and pain, its head tossed back and its jaws peeled wide, letting loose a shriek of agony. Weaponless, Del tried to back away, but lost his footing on the blood-slick stones and sprawled backwards. The beast dove to claim its kill.

Del's arms flew up, and he half-turned his body against the assault. He was caught in a vice as the sthaak's jaws clamped down over his arm and shoulder, engulfing him in hot wetness. He felt as though half of him was in the creature's mouth. The jaws tightened and pain burst through him, only to quickly subside to a throbbing, wet numbness. He vividly felt each jagged tooth sinking through his skin, shredding his flesh.

The beast wrenched its head to the side, as though trying to tear his arm from his body. There was a ripping in his shoulder and along the length of his back. Bones cracked. His right arm was free to flail about the stones in a blind and frantic search for his weapon while the beast began to chew the life out of him.

Del's own clarity of thought surprised him. He understood very plainly what was happening to him; he had witnessed this exact scene from other angles countless times throughout the day. First came the disastrous event: a brief moment of distraction or exhaustion induced apathy, invariably followed by that fatal misstep. The sthaak were quick to fall upon a floundering soldier, and the results were always gruesome. Del couldn't recall any single instance—when it was all over—that they had ever rescued a living body after such an attack. The beasts made quick work of a fallen man.

By all accounts, Del was dead already.

Above him, men had converged on the beast, but the thing seemed scarcely aware of them. It was more attentive to the meat in its grip, gnawing and scraping at him with animalistic fervor. Pinned beneath its weight, Del could do nothing but curl inward against the assault. The fiery agony had subdued, and he couldn't even feel the thing killing him anymore. The sthaak had become a banging, grinding weight pushing the air out of his lungs, jerking him first one way, then another.

He thought it would have been more painful than this.

The soldiers and Bedu that had come to rescue him dug into the scaled creature with spears and blades. He caught flashes of movement above him, and the noise of men shouting frantically. Del knew it wasn't that they were trying to save him; it was just that the sthaak were most vulnerable while feeding. He had become a useful distraction.

A Bedu warrior pushed a barbed spear deep into the sthaak's side and leaned into it. The barb punctured a center of pain in the animal, causing it to rear back with a shriek of agony, momentarily forgetting its victim. Del saw red speckling its face and pouring from its fangs. Something in the back of his mind registered that it was his blood. The thing was eating him alive. He could feel life coursing from his shredded arm. One heavy claw came down on Del's chest, holding him in place while it fended off the swarm of men assailing it. Its wide tail furiously lashed the air.

Still groping, Del's one good hand finally found the hilt of his sword. It had fallen from the beast's side, and was lying on the slickened stones. The beast had lashed out at the men to its right, giving those on the left opportunity to move in, filling it with more steel. In a final fit of rage, the dying creature decided to finish what it had started, and forgot everything but Del. The great jaws spread wide and the head surged for his throat.

Del lifted his sword.

Pushed by its own weight and driven by greedy bloodlust, the sthaak never saw the sword standing between it and its prey. The blade slipped neatly up through the soft bulge of its lower jaw, breached the void of the mouth, and punched through the top of the maw to penetrate the soft gray matter of its brain. The tip lodged in the upper dome of the skull.

The beast jerked back as though struck by lightning. The sword was once again ripped from Del's hand as the sthaak flung its neck back, trying desperately to shake free the intruding shaft of steel. It chewed air while the snakelike head thrashed. Its limbs convulsed and jerked in a fit of seizures. The pitch of its vindictive growls rose to an agonized frustration until finally, with a crippling shudder, its struggling ceased and it crumpled to the flagstones. Even in death its eyes remained open and aware, fixed on Del as though hungering still to devour him. Its tail scraped weakly on the stones.

Del had managed to push himself away from the beast, and now he struggled frantically to gain his feet. Slipping twice in blood, he finally succeeded in rising, only to be assaulted by nausea. Dizziness scrambled his vision and twisted his stomach into a violent knot. Blinking rapidly, he realized he had collapsed again. He could not stand. Squinting his eyes against the disorientation, he found himself staring into the eyes of the beast that had killed him. The sthaak's black marble eyes returned his stare, and Del could see the blood-slick blade of his sword running through the cavity of its jaws. There was still consciousness in it, enough life with which to hate him. As Del watched, its eyes shifted. It tried to reach for him, but its claws scratched uselessly against the stones, no longer obeying the command to kill.

Del tried to back away, fearing against reason that the creature would rise up again, but a wash of noise and blackness rushed against him from every side, as though he were a tiny island of light adrift in the rising tides of a black ocean. The glassy black gaze of the sthaak dulled, then finally drained of life—hating him all the while.

• • •

Jiharra saw Del go down beneath the sthaak from less than twenty paces away. By the time he reached the fallen ambassador the struggle to extract him from the sthaak's jaws was over. Del was still conscious, flailing vainly to gain his feet. His mind had not accepted the damage done to his body.

The young kalif caught Del just as he was falling back to the stones. Del looked him full in the face, but there was no recognition at all in his wild eyes.

A soldier of Shallai began to lift Del's legs, thinking that he and Jiharra would dump the body over the side, out of the way.

"Leave him!" Jiharra shouted.

The soldier balked at the sudden eruption, but he didn't understand a word, and stared. Jiharra bared his teeth, struck the soldier's hands away and snarled, "He is not dead yet. Tend to the dead."

Indifferently, the soldier moved away.

Del's hand clutched Jiharra's arm, amazingly strong. He spoke, but the words were in his native tongue, and Jiharra understood nothing. Del pointed to the beast, lying just out of reach. "Give me my sword," he said clearly.

Jiharra cast about for someone to retrieve the weapon, but any soldier not clearing bodies from the wall had already taken position for the next wave of attacks. Jiharra shouted out until he captured the attention of a Bedu warrior in a nearby group.

"The blade," he said urgently, gesturing to the weapon still embedded in the sthaak.

The Bedu man placed his foot against the sthaak's head and drew the weapon free. When Jiharra had it, he looked back to Del, who had fallen into a pale shade. Nearby, the shouts of men and the shriek of beasts heralded the beginning of a fresh attack. Lurching to his feet, Jiharra hefted Del's broken body in his arms, cradling both him and the sword. Leaving the heightening din of battle behind, he made for the tower.

• • •

The seriph waged war against the sthaak with supreme determination. Within the churning and tangled knots of battle he had found his element. Possessing complete command of his weapons and of himself, his force of execution was as elegant as it was brutal. For those who shared the ramparts with him that day it was hardly difficult to believe him the progeny of a god.

Throughout the course of the day, there were countless breaches among the first line of defenses. These lapses of order and communication caused pandemonium, and threatened to flood the battlements with sthaak. Each time the creatures broke through, casting men aside like broken dolls—always the seriph was there to cut their lives short. He came to where the threat was most dire, the peril thickest. With gore-encrusted blades cleaving scale and slinging blood, he held his ground. Though the sthaak beat against him, they could not tear him down. And while man and beast died at every turn, the seriph remained an untouchable bastion of hope.

In spite of the seriph's bolstering presence, the defenders of the wall were still only men. The sight of the dread warrior among them gave rise to courage, but no amount of bravery could dispel their own mortality.

In the space of a momentary lull, the seriph swept his blazing gaze across the surviving defenders. All along the battlements the Bedu of the deserts and the soldiers of Gideon's Wall pitched themselves against the sthaak with wild ferocity. The knowledge of their imminent deaths had served to heighten their passions, yet for all their valiance there were simply not enough of them to hold the wall. Too many men had been lost, and their ranks were thinning dangerously.

If the knowledge of his own approaching death stirred any emotions in the seriph's heart, his face kept them well concealed. He had been created to wage war, and he had done so for the full extent of his life. He had understood from the first days of his existence—days which he could remember now only with fading clarity—that his end would come in violence. But even after the full certainty of defeat became clear; when he understood that he, and all those around him, would die this day, he continued to strive as though victory were attainable.

When the defenders finally broke, there was no mending the tear. A wave of sthaak crested the wall and tore into a detachment of warriors no more than a hundred paces from the seriph. Half the men were dead before anyone could come to their aid, and the short and brutal slaughter opened a gap that was never closed.

Twisted faces wet with blood, the sthaak threw themselves on the men while more gained the wall behind them. By the time the first of the beasts were slain, a dozen more had risen to take their places. In a matter of moments the warriors who had first rushed to help contain the sudden outbreak were now struggling to hold their ground against a relentless onslaught.

Shortening his grip on the haft of his axe, the seriph plunged into the growing knot of sthaak. They received him with tooth and clay, flaying at him desperately. Leaning away from a wild lunge, he lashed out in return, his blade splitting scale and bone. He did not pause to watch the fallen die in his wake. His axe carried him from foe to foe, and he sheared a path through the beasts. It seemed he would carve a place for himself among legends, and almost it seemed he would win; almost it seemed his frenzy alone would be enough to turn the tide of battle once more in the favor of Shallai's defenders.

But the sthaak were too many. The fragile balance maintained by the defenders of Gideon's Wall, once tipped, could not be regained. Ranks of men were divided and scattered while smaller groups were completely overwhelmed. As the sthaak swarmed across the battlements, the defenders buckled under the weight of the sudden surge. Their ranks split, then disintegrated into separate pockets of survivors fighting desperately for their lives. The battle at Gideon's Wall had rapidly disintegrated into a massacre.

In the end, the seriph stood alone.

He had cleared a wide area around him into which no sthaak could trespass. It was a small zone in which the lethal arc of his blade overruled tooth and claw. At his feet sprawled his victims, and around him massed the enemy. Had he spared a moment to lift his eyes from his gruesome work, he would have noticed how the din of battle had faded and died. No more were the battlements alive with the clash of steel and the tramp of boots. Gone were the chortling screams of the dying. The air was filled only with the baying of monsters. All along the battlements the sthaak swelled over the wall.

Burying his blade deep in the skull of a rushing beast, the seriph sidestepped the body as it crashed into a heap beyond him. He jerked the blade free, and spun to face his next victim with a double-fisted grip on the murderous axe. The sthaak received the broad head of the blade across the upper part of its chest and neck. Before it had fallen, two more were upon him. He met the first of them with a open handed blow that would have shocked a tree to splinters, and turned his left shoulder to the other. The beast's fangs sank into his arm, and its claws scraped searing furrows across his back. His axe was wrenched from his grip.

With a surge and a heave the seriph cast the creature from his back and into the throng surrounding him. Bloodied and wounded, he crouched low, spreading his arms and baring his own claws to welcome the beasts. He bellowed in the face of his enemy, and his grinding roar echoed from the lofty heights of Gideon's Wall. The wild beast in him had crowded out the man. The part of him that was human, that had always remained in place as a facade, had at last been stripped away.

The creatures bearing down on him hesitated. They faced a foe as animal as themselves.

Matthias used their hesitation. Barreling forward, he grappled the nearest beast with nothing but hands and teeth to serve as weapons. The creature buckled beneath his rage, and others fell over him as though he were meat for the taking. But he rose up from the crushed sthaak, blood boiling in his mouth and on the skin of his face. His hands crushed scale, and his fangs tore flesh. Releasing an inhuman cry, he charged the outer ledge of the battlements, an armored juggernaut boring through the encircling ring of sthaak.

He reached the ramparts despite three beasts dragging him down. Casting his full weight forward, the seriph seized a fourth in a crushing embrace and drove them into clear blue emptiness. Plummeting from the heights of the wall to the parched desert floor far below, the seriph's howl echoed through the desert long after his body crashed to the sands.

With its last defender conquered, the sthaak were left unopposed, and they massed over the battlements and into Gideon's Wall by the hundreds, and finally the thousands.

Shallai was theirs.

• • •

The pain in Del's chest was alive. It writhed as though seeking comfort in a place deeper inside him. After a time, his nerves deadened. The hurt became distant and only half-real. He felt a desperate kind of loneliness, a terrible heartache that had leaked outside its bounds. He wanted to give himself over to that silent agony.

With an effort that seemed too great for such an inconsequential thing, the ambassador opened his eyes. He was no longer on the battlements of Gideon's Wall. Above him, stones and brick had replaced sky and sun. His own labored breathing filled his ears. Fighting to keep his gaze focused, he let his head roll to the side. He was in the great hall of the tower, and in it there were crowds of men. It seemed he did not hear them until he saw them, for only then did their screaming voices bombard him with confusion as though some invisible hand had thrown back a curtain.

When he saw the men, he remembered the war. Immediately, one sole need rose up through the mire that his consciousness had been reduced to; he must return to the battle. That single, compelling desire filled him, washing away all else. He tried to rise, but men had gathered around him, and would not let him up. They held him down with hands that seemed too strong, and their faces crowded over him. What was wrong with them? Why was he being restrained? A desperate, meaningless panic washed through

300

him, and he felt as helpless as a clod of brambles caught in a flood. Again he tried to rise, but his desires, his panic, his *purpose*, meant nothing to them.

Be still, voices told him. *Do not move.*

His anger surged. He fought them as best he could, twisting against their grasps and kicking at their legs. Why wouldn't they let him rise? Why wouldn't they let him fight? He shouted, but he did not know what words he said, yet still they would not release him. It continued until strong, capable hands grasped his face and held him steady.

"Be still, Ambassador," he was told urgently. He saw the blurred figure of a black clad ken'dari kneeling beside him, leaning over him. Forced to squint through the clouds in his eyes to see the face, Del bent all his wavering focus on the eyes.

"Jiharra," he said, and his voice, hardly a parched whisper, cracked with the vast relief of familiarity. The sound of it surprised him. Jiharra would bring sense back. Jiharra would fight with him. Once again, he attempted to rise, but the kalif held him down.

"Where are we?" Del managed to ask. It seemed very important to know. A bare moment ago he *had* known, but somehow had lost the knowledge. Lucidity touched and went like a breeze. "Where are we?" he said again, his frantic eyes roving for explanation.

"The battle is over, Ambassador."

"No," Del denied. "Who is holding the wall?"

"The seriph is there. Soon he will be dead."

"No," he declared in a clear voice. "We have to fight." Again he remembered the battle, cursing himself for forgetting. He tried to reach for his friend, but his grip failed him. The kalif's strong hands kept him from rising, and dark eyes stared earnestly into his face. "You will fight no more, Ambassador."

"What happened?" Del heard himself ask. "Am I hurt? I don't feel it." He tried to bend his neck down to look at himself, but Jiharra held his face firmly. "Is it bad?" he wondered out loud, an edge of panic creeping into his voice.

"Be still, Ambassador."

"Am I dying?" The words were hard to form, and his own voice sounded slow and wet, hampered by a throat full of blood.

"Be still."

With a violent twist of his neck, Del tore his head out of Jiharra's grasp and looked at himself. At first he didn't understand. His left arm was gone. There was only a chewed stump where his elbow had been. His breath suddenly hitched, coming in quick jerks. His eyes jumped from his arm to his side. Blood coated his chest, and the cloth of his tunic clung like a second skin. Through the tattered pieces he saw the sharp white glare of bone. And then Jiharra had his head in his arms, blocking the sight from him, but not erasing it from his memory.

"It's not me," Del said, pushing weakly against Jiharra. "It isn't me." A thick fog had filled his vision, blurring the world around him, and he blinked heavily in a futile attempt to clear it. Coughing thickly, his head rolled back, then jerked, as though suddenly waking. It took all of his strength to lift his head.

"Where's my sword?" Del pleaded. Too weak to uphold his head, he slumped back. His eyes slid more than half-closed, and his thoughts were embedded in a deep cushion of exhaustion. His hand scrabbled on Jiharra's chest in an attempt to pull his friend toward him, but his fingers refused to curl into a fist. "I can fight," he begged. "Please let me fight."

Jiharra gripped Del's hair in one fist and hugged his friend tightly, with their bloody cheeks together, and his lips close to Del's ear. He did not want the fallen warrior to see him weeping. "We fought bravely, did we not, Ambassador?" he whispered fiercely into Del's ear. "Did we not make war like gods today?"

Del wasn't listening. His vision had darkened. There came a weightless pressure on his chest and throat. It had become impossible to breathe, and the unbearable urge to cry finally overcame him.

"I can fight," he wept. "I can fight if you help me." The tears were carving tracks through the grime on his face.

"We will fight again, Ambassador," Jiharra told him. His hands tightened in Del's hair. "You and I will fight together again, I swear it to you."

"Am I dying?" Del asked.

Jiharra clenched his teeth, clamping his eyes shut against the burning tears. He grasped the ambassador to his chest. "No," he lied. "You will never die." He was still clinging tightly when Del's life fluttered madly and at last broke free, slipping loose from its mold of clay and draining into the air like the last precious sip of water from a torn skin.

Ten

The tower had become the last bastion of Gideon's Wall.

Lifting his eyes, Jiharra swept the crowded tomb with blurred vision. The last surviving defenders of Gideon's Wall had corralled themselves into the wide stone chamber and sealed themselves within. There was no escape, and they knew that the fragile refuge they had found in the tower was a transient thing. It would extend their lives only a short while. The men wore masks of grime and blood, detailed with sweat, loss and pain. Those nearest to Jiharra stared indifferently at Del's corpse. The Bedu knew him well as the ambassador who had led them out of the desert, and the northern soldiers might have thought his face familiar had they chanced to see him during one of his previous visits with the deacon. But there were men both dead and dying elsewhere, and he was no different than they.

The morose silence following the ambassador's death was shattered by a series of resounding blows upon the outside of the great iron doors. The hollow chamber filled with booming, as though the creatures were throwing their scaled bodies against the barrier with a fury that would not be obstructed by mere slabs of iron. They were maddened by the blood they had already spilled, and their frenzied throes had peaked at being kept at bay from the final living prey.

The doors shuddered ominously, and the rasping screech of claws dragging over steel infected the men barricaded inside the tower with shivers and fear. Unconsciously, the crowd receded from the doors, which did not seem enough to protect them from the savage turbulence behind it. All eyes fixed on the iron barrier—Death's final, insignificant hindrance—and all minds turned to thoughts of their executioners amassing on the other side, growing in numbers and strength until it seemed the doors must explode inward with the pressure. Every man could picture the inhuman army crashing through the doors to fall upon them. Already they knew that below them the army was swarming through the courtyards, hallways, and barracks of the wall. They could almost feel that tide of scaled bodies flowing around and through every hollow of the conquered fortress, seeking out every living thing to destroy it in hatred. The ocean of monsters had cut them off from the rest of the world, made them a tiny, sinking island of life.

"The doors won't hold," someone warned.

As though shaking off a trance, the survivors burst into action. Soldiers and Bedu began dragging the wounded and the dying to the rear of the chamber, away from what was soon to be the front lines of a fresh battle. Those still conscious and aware, but incapable of standing, were fitted with shields and weapons and propped up against the stone walls and against one another so they would not have to face their deaths lying down. Those still capable of engaging in battle joined ranks in forming a living barrier around the huge iron doors. Packed tight, shoulder to shoulder and row upon row, their dense ranks bristled with sword and spear, an impenetrable wall of thorns. Expecting the doors to peel inward at any moment, the grim-faced warriors fixed the iron slabs with the full intensity of their concentration, as if they could shore up the doors with their minds alone.

Kneeling at Del's side as the men flowed around him in a final rush of chaos and noise in preparation for the final battle, Jiharra was filled with sudden purpose. Moving swiftly, the young kalif removed his shirt, then hefted Del's body off the floor and slung him over his left shoulder. Using his own torn shirt as protection for his hand, he took Del's sword by the blade. Without turning back, he rushed the limp body of his friend toward the rear of the chamber. A flight of wide stone stairs led him into the upper chambers of the tower, and burdened as he was by Del, he took them three at a time. Behind him, the sound of steady pounding on the doors chased him upwards.

Reaching a landing, he climbed still further, striving for the highest floors of the tower. The resounding booms behind him became hollow and distant as he ran. He was leaving the noise and confusion behind, and it felt as though he were rushing himself upwards into heaven. But then the illusion faded, shattered by the sound of the iron doors of the tower's inner chamber bursting open.

He stopped, heart pounding, to listen. The sounds of battle rushed over him from below, washing up the flight of stairs to fill every room of the tower, then echoing back down in a cascade of noise. The roar of the sthaak and the clash of sword on scale was laced with screams. Urged to greater speed, Jiharra climbed the stairs frantically, Del's weight pressing on his shoulders.

After what seemed an eternity of ascending, he reached the highest floor of the tower. The stone hallway was bare, and the sweltering air was heavy with dust and heat.

His breath coming in deep gasps, Jiharra turned left down the corridor and kicked open the last door in the hall. Storming into the room, his eyes fell on a narrow staircase winding upwards into the darkness of a secluded attic. The way was steep and the steps were narrow, but he bound up them quickly. The door at the top had been locked long ago, but both lock and hinges splintered at the first blow.

It was a storeroom. The dusty stone chamber was half-full of slumping sacks and empty crates. A single wall wrapped the room in a stony embrace, and wide windows let in fat, slanting columns of sunlight. His feet kicked up dust, and tiny motes floated in the sun, spinning lazy circles and obscure patterns in the still air. Above him, the conical roof slanted upwards to a point, his view into the heights blocked only by wooden beams slung with cobwebs.

Jiharra's harsh breathing was the only sound in the dimly illuminated and dusty stillness of the chamber. He could not be sure whether the sounds of battle were unheard because the battle was over, or if he was just too distant to hear.

Trying not to picture what was taking place below, Jiharra moved to the far end of the room and gently laid Del down in the concealing darkness of a deep shadow. Next to the body, he placed the bare sword.

Leaving Del where he lay, he pushed a solid looking crate against the wall and stepped upon it to press his face against the barred window. The small slot within the cut stone afforded him a narrow view, but he could see the base of the wall and much of the inner yards. He could see the Way stabbing northward, a flat path cutting through the jagged mountains, and although they were not immediately within his view, he knew that the tattered remnants of his people were somewhere down that path. They had become a nation huddling in fear, trapped in a foreign land between two enemies.

The sight below caused his heart to sink.

The sthaak were swarming through the wall. They did not stop to burn or pillage, and they gave no thought to plunder or gain. It was as though they came only to wipe out all life, and gave no care to anything else. The tide of monsters rushed ceaselessly northward, and he watched as they flooded out of the northern end of the wall and into the Way.

When he could watch no more, he averted his eyes, and stepped down from the window. Taking up his own sword, he moved to the door of the small storage room and crouched down just outside of it, taking up his last watch as the sentry of a dead friend.

When the beasts came, Jiharra would be waiting for them.

Epilogue

The whispering has fallen silent; the tale has come to conclusion. My time at Gideon's Wall is finished.

• • •

He has spoken to me again, for the final time. He has given me instruction—whispering in my ear exactly what I must do. Two requests he has laid at my feet: one a petition for his empire, the other a plea for himself.

I will not deny him this.

• • •

It is done.

There is a sense of sadness, but also of completion. I am vibrantly aware that this once, instead of merely recording history, I have been allowed to participate. This thing I have done will bring change—when and how much I cannot say, but a difference will be made.

In the blue-black darkness of dawn, I took the rucksack containing the few supplies I had prepared during the night, and walked the short distance from the camp to the excavation site. The ground there is pulled up in a neat grid of shallow pits, and I could just make out the outlines of the wall's ruined foundations. All was eerily quiet in the cold air of a new morning.

Desolation has always been difficult for me to describe. There is silence, and there is sorrow, but at Gideon's Wall these things are only parts of something that weighs more heavily on the heart. It would be an injustice to allow a few words, however well chosen, to describe this place on this particular morning. Already the remains of our presence seem evidence of another age: the tilled ground, the footprints and the broken tools. It is our having been here that amplifies the emptiness. It is our presence that worries at old scabs.

Choosing a clear spot near a section of excavated wall, I dug a narrow pit as deep as I was able. It was no well, but it was deep enough to bury the seed. Before covering it, I watched for some time, waiting for some great miracle to happen before my eyes. It seemed such a small thing, quiet and still at the bottom of its grave. When no miracle came, I filled the hole with dirt and sand, then roamed towards the wall gathering heavy stones with which to build a cairn. I stacked the stones knee-high atop the seed's resting place. I fitted them together with care, so they would not come easily apart. Unless disturbed, the cairn should stand for a great while. It is a crude substitute for a monument, but it is something at least to leave for those who come after me. It was my hope then—and even now—that it will remain forever, although I know such romantic hopes are foolish at best. But if not forever, then at least long enough for others to see. This seems important to me. I stood there for some time, listening to the wind moaning through the ditches and rolling pebbles across the ground. I felt as though a great many eyes were watching with me.

That act—the seed—is for Shallai.

The fire was for Del.

It was a small blaze I made. I fed it blocky sawdust bricks soaked in oil. When the fire was sufficiently stoked, I took the little statue from the rucksack. I handled it gently, my own sentiments imploring me to treat it as a living thing. What he had asked of me was difficult, but it was not my right to deny him. I laid the statue in the flames. The black wood burned strangely; the smoke guttered thick and black. The flames emitted were many colors. It was a long time before the misshapen little figure broke apart and crumbled. I stayed even until the fire was dead, then I scattered the ash.

I would have wanted the same.

• • •

It has been many days since we left Gideon's Wall. Our caravan is laden with bones and artifacts. In a few days more we will have come to Jericho, she of the overgrown streets and whispering dead. From there it is not terribly far to the coast, where our ship waits to carry us back to the Isles. It will be good to see the water again.

We spent a total of sixty-seven days excavating Gideon's Wall. In that time we laid open the collapsed foundations of three buildings, the tower and twelve-hundred feet of the wall itself. More significantly, we unearthed the bones of three hundred and forty six unburied men, three hundred and forty seven if we are to count the seriph. I harbor no doubts this tally is but a fraction of the number that still remain to be found.

Even more intriguing than the bones of the men are the bones of the sthaak. We discovered such a great host of beasts that it would have taken more years than I have to exhume the last of them. We found the greatest concentration just south of the wall, less than two fingers' depth beneath the cracked ground. Digging in one focused area, we laid bare a cross-section view, as though cutting a wedge from a fruit to see what secrets rest inside. Hidden within, we found a profuse number of inhuman skeletons, most of them fully intact. They were stacked layers deep, so thick that it seemed the walls of our ditch had been shored up with bones.

It is dangerous, I know, to take the whispering of ghosts as truth. But all this evidence: the bones of the men, of the beasts, and of the seriph all confirm Del's story. What else am I to believe?

And then there is the matter of the seed. On the day of our departure, two days after burying the seed and destroying the wooden figure, I visited the cairn. What I saw there still fills me with wonder. It is a final validation of the tale that was whispered to me by a captured soul out of the mouth of a wooden artifact. More than that, it is hope. Even now the remembrance of what I saw makes my heart pound and my hand tremble so that I am barely able to write. Green vines had coiled up from between the rocks of the cairn, vibrant and alive. An area twenty paces all around the cairn was no longer a wasteland. Thick green shoots were pushing skyward. There was grass and foliage, all of it new—all of it thriving. Saplings had sprung as though from nowhere.

Saplings—after *two days*.

I did not tread on the ground. I did not dare. Constantly, I wonder what that valley will become in a year—in ten. I find myself always staring back towards the ruin of Gideon's Wall, as though I will see the verdant green of the valley overtaking us, filling this dead land with new life, bringing Shallai back.

I would have stayed longer, though I am certain if I'd chosen to dedicate a single hour more to the task of digging up Gideon's Wall, I would have been faced with mutiny. The men care little for the promise of future mysteries. They have made it clear that they are through with the wind and the sand, and want nothing more to do with this haunted place. Better to have left of my own accord, than trussed and gagged.

In time, others will come to dig upon the surface I have scratched, drawn to this place of broken swords and bloodstained stones just as I was. They will go farther than I. They will bring more men, and they will dig deeper. They will have my maps and my charts to guide them, and a foundation of knowledge from which to build. Perhaps they will find the stories I did not. Perhaps even someday a man braver than all those who came before him will go into the vast emptiness beyond the Way to find the Jaggi, or to search for whatever distant, nightmarish landscape gave birth to the beasts that brought down Gideon's Wall, and the power that laid waste to an empire. I wish, upon that day, that I could be with that man.

I tell myself that I will return someday. I would very much like to see how the planted seed rebuilds the land. I want to know what is learned by those who come after me. But it is not only the promise of healing, renewal and discovery; I would like to hear the whispering of ghosts again, to listen for the stories I have passed over this time. This is impossible, but I am sentimental, and yearn for things impossible. If ever I do return, it will be a long time from now. This world is a larger place than we know, and there is still much to see. I will travel to other places, perhaps to faraway Rathania, where the land is covered in ice, and spring never comes. I am told there is a place there, on a frozen lake in the shadow of jagged peaks, where a keep of black stone was built by a people long dead. It is said that Winter was born there, and lives deep in the bowels of that citadel, forever cold and full of vengeance. It broods in its icy lair beneath the frozen water, waiting for the day it will be released upon the world to sweep down from the frozen land with blizzard and storm.

Yes, I would very much like to return. But for now, the time has come to leave Gideon's Wall to the ghosts that haunt it.

May they find the peace they seek.

About the Author

Greg Kurzawa is the pen-name of author Gage Kurricke. As a founding member of the Anthropological Society of Greater Jericho (ASGJ), Gage has dedicated the greater part of fifty years to the study of various developing subcultures particular to the darker boroughs of the city.

For many years before its renovation, Gage lectured on history and philosophy at Jericho's University of Arts and Sciences. When the university committee approved a charter to tear down the ancient and revered Bringer's Hall to make room for a loofre field, Gage protested vehemently. Bringer's Hall came down despite his objections, whereupon Gage immediately resigned his prestigious position with the university, claiming that loofre was 'the most ludicrous foolery ever to call itself sport.' Immediately following his resignation, Gage retired to the borough of Cog Munge, from which he pursues his study of culture funded by the ASGJ.

Regarding Gideon's Wall, Gage asserts that although the book is a work of pure fiction, it represents a future that is 'at least somewhat plausible.' He takes pleasure in reminding his audience that the deserts beyond Gideon's Wall have yet to be fully explored.